ROAD TRIP Z

M.P. NORMAN

SEVERED PRESS
HOBART TASMANIA

ROAD TRIP Z

WWW.SEVEREDPRESS.COM

ISBN: 978-1-925840-93-3

PROLOGUE

When the end of the world happened: the second coming of Jesus, the war of Armageddon, the arrival on earth of *Lucifer*—the Antichrist with his tribulation and wild raptures ways or some horrible natural disaster never materialized. Predictions about an actual meteorite hitting the earth in the early 2000s that would cause fireballs of debris, rivers of acid and oceans filled with sulfur. Or mega dust clouds engulfing entire countries never occurred.

Skynet—the artificial intelligence that will be given control of the United States' nuclear missiles and initiate a nuclear holocaust called 'Judgment Day' never arrived. Neither did an intergalactic parasite hitching a ride on the new Chinese XI-YING Space Shuttle 3 returning from Mars wipe out humanity.

Was it a defense department weaponized virus that escaped a lab? How about genetic engineering? Not even 'Dolly' the cute, cloned sheep offspring was the beginning of the world's downfall. How about the 'zombie' deer epidemic in the wilderness of Canada? Infected monkeys?

Maybe one of those secret government experiments went haywire, like in the X-Files. You know, the ones where Mulder spends hours combing through government archives searching for 'the truth' as he calls it, while a reluctant Scully just rolls her eyes and wonders what she could have possibly done to deserve a partner that was a complete conspiracy theorist.

It wasn't even consumers worried about radiation from their smart-phones affecting fertility and birthing mutants for the future, which willed the end of the world into existence. (*Never, and I stress, the last explanation never happened.*)

The Black Death killed about 60 percent of the European population in a few years in the middle of the 14th century. Fast forward a century and a half later the native people of the Americas were hit by half a dozen plagues as bad as that catastrophic event: measles, diphtheria, influenza and smallpox and 95 percent of them died.

Even in an age of advanced medical technology and innovation, we can hardly imagine a time where the flu could be deadly. Where HIV had grown to pandemic proportions in the 1980s, and Ebola swept across Africa like an unflattering rash in the 2000s.

But by the time the Z-infection was reported in sixty different countries, across four continents, the truth was nobody knew exactly the reason why or how the devastating global epidemic the modern world had ever known had come into existence.

There are all kinds of emergencies out there that we could have prepared for. But only the true survivalists and zombie enthusiasts were adequately prepared and knew how to handle humanity's worst nightmare. You know that zombie apocalypse survival kit you were planning to put together? (*It may not have been such a far-fetched idea, after all.*)

Take a zombie apocalypse, for example.

That's right, I said z-o-m-b-i-e a-p-o-c-a-l-y-p-s-e twice already. Our culture, especially our pop-culture, is full of tales of the undead walking the Earth. From our religious scripts to slave zombies working the plantations in the Caribbean through to our beloved comic books and fan-boy driven TV-productions.

But, some sort of zombie apocalypse isn't possible, right?

Right?

Guys?

Well, it happened, and it happened fast. The Z apocalypse had wiped out 70% of Earth's human population in just over 200 days, eventually toppling governments and countries like an endless game of Dominoes. With the dinosaurs 65 million years ago, humankind extinction had finally arrived and came with a bitchin' bite. (*Yeah, if you're reading this extract, that's correct!*)

Even with a standard zombie kit at your disposal: such as a firearm, food supplies, and medical know-how, the potential outcomes of a zombie apocalypse show chances of survival are relatively slim. (*You may laugh now, but when it happens you'll be happy you read this, and hey, maybe you'll even learn a thing or two about how to prepare for an undead emergency.*)

1
TRANSMISSION

A long stretch of Arizona highway—highway 89, Coconino County—where the scorching sun melts the black asphalt like sticky pudding. And the yellow dotted lines blend into one another within a blink of an eye. The occupants of a dirty green 4x4 listen eagerly to the radio as they pass through derelict streets full of nostalgia and small-town ideals. The once thriving, friendly community named after the surrounding landscape: Bitter Springs.

The words echo.

Eventually, a female voice glides across the jeep's radio like a knife slicing through butter: "Broadcasting from Hope Radio, folks with your everyday survival bulletins. I have news for all survivors out in the 'Wastelands of 'Merica. If you are traveling somewhere in the Pacific Northwest, Oregon to be precise, then head to Portland. The giveaway prize for those lucky winners able to reach the former city will be an all expense paid vacation to a secured haven."

Static over the airwaves—

A moment of dead air and a cheery laugh follows. "As I said, 'If you are a survivor out in the badlands of our former civilized nation,' then you are in for one helluva treat. Yes. The whispers of a small pocket of resistance are really true. An outpost offering food, water, shelter, and most importantly, safety. So, if you're drifting around in that expansive graveyard of a world, then follow my coordinates and get your ass to Portland straight away. This is DJ Candice signing off with *Nat King Cole's* 'It's a Beautiful Day.' You guys have a safe, wonderful day. More importantly… stay alive."

A crackle of static—

The voice fades away—

The youngest of the jeep's occupants tunes the radio's knob. Tries to entice that voice back. Just a few more words guiding them onwards across the dry Arizona sands. Nada. Zero. No such luck. Just crackles of white noise lost in the annoying static of nothingness.

PART ONE

STRANGERS

2
DESERTS OF UTAH

The jeep cannons from the dusty track onto the crumbling asphalt of the highway, hitting 100mph in several seconds. A black mass of cloud billows behind, filling the horizon with a predatory haze of heat and chemicals, as the silo explodes for a third and final time.

Looks of shitty frustration fill the mud-splattered rear-window; the occupants of the vehicle are tired, in a constant state-of-shock—

Swearing and frustration went hand-in-hand these days just like guns and ammo in a Redneck Community in Hicksville, Virginia, and there's only enough of both to share around the—Thanksgiving table—before the shit finally hits the fan.

"Oh my God! Oh my God!" a girl's trembling voice spills from the backseat of the jeep like milk from a carton and she clutches the fabric of the headrest again. *"Oh my God! Oh, my God!"*

Another voice from her side. "Stay *calm!* Stop *freaking* out." It's a boy of a similar age. (A third figure—an Asian girl—lays between them covered in blood. A bullet-hole wedged in her upper arm.) "What can you find to stem Naomi's bleeding, Mary?" His words are assured, tranquil, even with what had just happened.

"I-I… don't know—*I'm looking*," answers the small, short blond-haired girl. She has a fresh gash across her cheek; spots of blood pooling the slender cut, while she urgently searches the first aid kit by her feet.

"Mary? *Mary!*"

The girl breathes in deeply through her nose. Seconds later, she connects with the boy. "Not a lot, Carl. Tape, cotton balls, alcohol wipes and a little aspirin—"

The boy glances at the girl opposite holding the small medical kit with trembling hands and looks at the girl between them. *Naomi's in bad shape,* he thinks, stroking the injured girls' hair. He sighs in disbelief, is about to answer—

When a cocky voice interjects from behind the wheel. "Whole lotta good that's going do, Mary!" The driver seems determined to put the jeep's suspension through its paces, and the wide-eyed face casts a look at the passenger seat where a spotty teen sits nervously twitching a knee upfront. The driver's wisecracks continue to flow like a badly-timed comedian at a seedy club—where the capital 'C' was underlined. And the jokes weren't at all funny. "You might as well use Jed's dental floss to suture Naomi's wound up."

"Huh?" The teen questions the driver at the mention of his name, raising two thin eyebrows above his youthful stare.

"Shut up!" the blond-haired girl thunders from the back of the jeep. "Quit being a dick, Carlos, I've had enough of your sarcastic comments."

"Eat a dick, Mary," the driver retorts, throwing the insult and a dismissive gaze over his broad shoulders like a drunk who's politely been asked to leave a bar. His eyes shaded by a pair of sunglasses. He's wearing a woolen hoodie; a gun belt is strapped across his chest like an extra in a Western. "We barely survived from that place in one piece, and your hesitation cost us those goddamn supplies we urgently needed!"

Mary had panicked when she was cornered by a mob of Creeps at the silo, and it had cost the rest of the group their supplies they had gathered from the compound (mainly snacks from vending machines, but canned goods from a half stocked canteen too).

The driver shifts gears into third, takes-a-peek in the mirror above his head. He's relishing taking them all on a rollercoaster ride through the desert roads. "She can deal with a little bullet wound, can't you, Naomi?" He casts a half-glance at the injured girl lying between the others but doesn't hide the smug grin widening his lips.

Curled up on her seat, the wounded Asian girl gazes alternately at her friends in a semi-conscious daze and continues to moan in pain. Her cheeks are as red as roses. Blood spills from her hunting arm like water in a creek.

"What's a hole between friends, heh?" the driver adds, unashamedly, the comment sticking like jizz on a hot sidewalk. His grin widening—his comical-timing annoying the others like an irritating rash.

Mary grits her teeth. "Your remarks are crude, Carlos. How can you be so callous? Naomi's hurt—*badly!*"

Carlos purses his lips, forming the first syllables of an apology. "I'm sorry—" smiles, thinks better of it. "How can't you aim straight?" he jests instead.

Mary nonchalantly holds her look at the driver in the hanging mirror; fixed upon his steely eyes were hers. "You *sonofabitch!*" the word pushes from her mouth like squeezy cheese from a tube. "You weren't there with us. You couldn't comprehend how many risks we took. You didn't *see* jack-shit!" She snorts back the fury, face full-of-hate, sweat trickling down her temples. Hatred oozing from her pores.

"Gotcha!" he replies. "Who's twisted your nipples this morning, Little Miss Kansas?" At his own comment, the driver roars in laughter.

Her mouth opens to deliver thunder—

"*Hey!* Cut it," Carl interjects, so commandingly. "Enough, both of you!" The boy in the back looks through the rear window as the plume of smoke swirls above the silo and changes direction and was now following them like a winged beast straight from the pages of a *George R. R. Martin* novel. "Carlos, just drive and shut ya mouth!" he snaps. (Using his 'coercive diplomacy,' to get his two friends to accede to his wishes was always a daunting task), but Carl needed to restore order from chaos in the small movable space they called home while they were on the road. He waits for the driver to comprehend how literal his words were.

"*Oh*, come on!" Carlos chuckles. "After all I—*What* I had to put up—" He falls quiet and brings a thumb and forefinger to his mouth and mimes a locking action, finally nods to his Commander-in-Chief. The President of their Fucking Salvation. The Leader of this Shitty Road Trip through the Wastelands of Zombieland. But questions the former Constitution (Article II, section 2), of the once great land they called 'home,' that gives power to the country's fearsome leader in a time of unrest.

He gets it: his friend is the Big Fucking Cheese in these parts.

Carl turns back around. He's unhappy with the driver's shitty attitude, but doesn't want to provoke Carlos' motor mouth any further (he knows the guy is a loose cannon, *sometimes*, well, *more times* than he'd like to admit. But they are on this trip across the former States together, and together means with all the baggage of each other's bullshit stowed away for the long haul).

A swish of black, unwashed hair covers Carl's forehead. A three-day-old lime tee seriously needs changing. "Mary?" He pushes her name through his gritted teeth while his pale blue eyes find the girl. "Just concentrate on Naomi. Make her comfy. Stem her bleeding with whatever supplies we have at our disposal."

Mary blows her blond locks from her forehead—they'd come loose from her yellow headband—and she smiles back; assured by Carl's words and his tranquil blue eyes. *That's why Carl's in charge, because of his no-nonsense attitude and his willingness to get the job done. Not like Carlos*, she knew—throwing the idiot driver an annoyed glare. (Conveniently for their trip, the Midwesterner thought he was a suave, sophisticated-ladies-man-and-the-leader-in-charge-of-the-whole-damn group but was, in fact, just a shitty-opinionated-dickhead-in-this-fucked-up-world-of-nightmarish monsters.) "At least the bullet went clean through, Carl," she adds, inspecting her friend's injury. "That's one positive outcome."

"Good," he says, "just look—"

As if in a dream, Carl was momentarily frozen. The words are trapped in the bottom of his throat, unable to squirm upwards to form those important syllables. He feels as though he has an out-of-body experience—drifting above his own body while looking down on his friends from above. The blond girl, the Asian girl, the driver, the teen, and himself—desperately driving away from a scene of a crime. It was a curious sensation to behold. A certain moment he'll never forget. But then he plummets straight back down again and enters his own body as the jeep cannons over a dip in the asphalt.

He gulps hard. "Do your best, Mary. Look after her, okay?" And that's when he becomes assertive again. "Don't let Naomi drift asleep."

"Until we've stopped the bleeding?"

He locks eyes with the blond girl. Nods.

"Yeah," she replies, eyes connecting with his. "No problem."

Carl takes the Asian girl's spare hand—fingertips interlocking, breath holding, squeezes gently and gazes at her lying between them.

He had a soft spot for the dark-haired girl ever since they'd first met a year back. He hadn't told her (but everyone knew—*except* Naomi of course), she was still trying to get over the loss of her fiance. That was a while ago now, just as the end of the world knocked on everyone's front door like a twinkly-eyed salesman straight from Hell preaching the Gospel's Word of Righteous and Salvation. (It was a time for praying to the Gods you believed in and the Deities you shouldn't follow, and also, running for your goddamn lives from the hungry undead masses.)

Naomi *moans* again as her best friend tends her injury. Her eyes drifting close. Her olive skin stained by her own blood. Mary does the best she can in a shitty situation, cleans the wound, and talks. "Hey, girl. Keep in there, okay? I'm right here for you, Naomi!" (If there's one thing Mary's good at, it is talking), and her words of support has a calming effect on the injured girl.

***

Meantime, Carl sits back deep in thought.

The plan was simple enough; go to the deserted silo, scout the building, scavenge for supplies and carry on to Portland. Not get separated from one another, panic like dumb teens in a shitty slasher movie (where all the kids are unaware of the immediate danger they are in. And the audience knowing that one teenager is about to be disemboweled by the serial killer, and at the same time, screaming at the TV screen: "Don't go *THERE!* You're all *DOOMED!*"), when all carnage breaks loose.

And it wasn't in the sidenotes: for no one in the group to succumb to injury, either.

Carl glances over and sees Naomi wriggling in agony. Dirt fills her chocolate colored hair. Her skin and clothes too. He gazes back around one final time—sees the black plume of smoke finally drifting away. But, he knows that anyone within a hundred-mile radius would be able to see the mushroom-shaped cloud (*alive or dead!* he thinks), and Carl wants to be as far away from that silo as humanly possible.

He laughs at that word: humanly. What does—human—even mean *nowadays?* Splits the word like he's dissecting a frog in a biology class. *Suck it up*, he tells himself. *None of this is new. This is the world we live in right now. Satan sits on his Blood Throne with his nuts in his taloned hands. The Big Red Dude now resides in the Mortal World with a 'thank you very much' and a filthy smirk plastered across his bearded jaw.*

Carl leans forward, gazes at the gasometer; the jeep's thundering away at a steady pace. He looks to the driver. Oily black hair clings to a solid forehead. A red Rambo-styled bandana adorns his forehead. He has a cocky 'I don't give a fuck attitude' too. Carlos was a dick (possibly the biggest prick on the whole planet right now), and he knows it, everyone in the vehicle knows it. But Carl knew Carlos was an expert driver and was able to handle the vehicle at excessive speeds across the tough terrain. That's why he tolerated Carlos and let the Midwesterner run his mouth off sometimes; it was the only way to shut the guy up.

Carl was uneasy too. Not so much about the destination as the journey itself. The destination was Portland, but their journey so far was becoming unbearable and downright dangerous. It didn't help at every corner they turned, undead Creeps would appear from every crevice and hole like unkillable cockroaches and shit on their parade. (Hell, a parade would even be great around now!) He knew this car trip was never going to be full of fun and balloons, but still, he thought the trip would be safe.

Carl looks down at the girl sandwiched between himself and Mary, and a smile ripens his face. *I'll get you the help you need, Naomi,* he thinks concernedly. *Don't you worry!* The bitter memories of her wound, and the last twenty minutes of sheer-scary-comical-farce beginning to fade away.

3
BOILING POINT

Sometime later, there's a crackle on the airways. A sound.

A familiar voice awakens from the turn of the dials:

"Welcome listeners, freaks, and survivalist geeks; this is Candice, your groundbreaking DJ 'alive and freaking well,' broadcasting to you from my sunny penthouse HQ on frequency 107.6…"

Static transmission over the airwaves continues, and the voice fades into white noise—

The young teen turns the dial—

A few seconds later—

"Are. You. Listening. Somewhere. Out. There. In. The. Wilderness. Of. The. Former. United. States. Of. Bulging. Waistlines. Of. 'Merica?" (She pronounces every new word with a capital letter. "You free loving survivors of the apocalypse. Can anybody read me on 'Hope Radio?'…"

The voice fades again.

Jed keeps playing with the knobs with shaky hands. (The DJ's voice on the airwaves has been their leading light like the Southern Star across the sky; the groups' path through the Wastelands of Undead America for the past week.)

More static. Equal silence.

Nothing. Nada and the teen felt his head sink sickeningly back into the tattered fabric of the headrest as he gives the driver a disheartened look of annoyance. Carlos returns the dismayed stare at the acne-freckled teen and puts his foot down; fourth gear and the jeep picks up speed, accelerating past the desolate landscape of barren, burnt grass and mounds of sand.

Seconds later—

"Jed, can you pick the voice up? Can you? *Jed!*" Mary had bandaged Naomi's wound with a clean rag and given her some aspirin for the continuing pain. But the hole in the Texan's arm is the size of a coin, and Mary knows her friend needs something stronger than the aspirin. Mary anxiously looks at the teen. Her eyes brimming for an answer.

Any response.

Jed likes to tune the radio every hour or so since they first heard the delicate female's voice a week ago. It had been such a long time since they had any communications on the airways that they had forgotten the rest of the world existed. That's when they had decided to leave their encampment (their home for the past year), and branch out in search of the DJ's voice: in search of a—safe haven—in the Pacific Northwest.

Jed disappointedly answers in a choir-like voice, "Nope. Nothing." Scratches his forehead underneath his faded, San Jose Earthquakes cap (it was the hat from the football club's only championship). He turns around. "How's Naomi? Is she going to make it?" His words are almost silent.

"You're fucking with me. Is that a serious question, Einstein?" The driver stares at the teen. "I can never tell when you're fucking with me. How about I give you a 'rampant-rabbit,' then you can fuck with me properly." He was chuckling as he spoke.

"I don't *err*—" the teen awkwardly stammers. (Has no idea what a 'rampant-rabbit' is used for. But considering Carlos brings the—new term—to the teen's attention, and it's used in the same sentence as 'fuck' multiple times, Jed knows it's a nasty word.) "Naomi got shot, man!" the teen sheepishly answers and drops the cap over his eyes—falling quiet. He fiddles with the small, round radio knobs again in a desperate attempt to keep under the Midwesterner's unpleasant radar.

But Jed wishes he has a CB radio—considering the Internet was no more—so he could communicate with the outside world, especially the attractive voice on the radio. He dreams of that voice sometimes, imagines it's the girl of his dreams; long hair, green eyes like Chinese jade. The same dream; they meet while on the road, and he saves her from the walking nightmares that now plague the earth. They leave, together on the back of a Harley (of course, he needs to learn to drive first, and foremost), and after, they'll live happily ever after. (Well, as happily as you can get, nowadays.)

"Huh, figures," Carlos smirks, hands at ten and two. "Go back playing with the knobs, Jed. It'll be the only fun you'll have on this *goddamn* trip."

The insult sticks.

***

In the back, Mary ignores the Midwesterner's continually shitty attitude towards the teen and everyone else who utters the wrong choice words in front of him. *Fucking moron*, she thinks. Instead, she looks across at her best friend hazily drifting away into sleep and brushes the girl's forehead. Naomi had a bullet hole in her shoulder. Mary had put it there. "I'm sorry, Naomi. I am."

"Mmm-Mary... Kay!" the Asian girl mumbles, her words are not cohesive enough to form a proper reply.

"Relax," Mary says, laying a calming hand on her friends' cheek. "I'll take care of you." The Asian girl doesn't protest, just closed her eyes. Eventually, Mary says to the group: "I've stopped the bleeding the best I can. But… we need medical supplies. Morphine for the pain. Sutures to close the wound."

Carlos quips: "Well spotted Captain Clueless of the Girl Scouts Brigade. What are our options, Kansas?"

Hold it together, girl, don't fall into the dipshit's taunt, Mary thinks. She breathes a Yoda-ish deep-ass yawn. Channels the wizened Jedi master's Zen. "We need to turn around. Go back home! Or stop someplace…" It was a stupid comeback, and she knows it before she has even finished speaking.

"That's the million-dollar-stupid-ass-answer-question-combo-of-the-entire-century, sweetcheeks."

"Hey, Carl!" Mary urges. "Can you tell him to stop?"

"Can you tell *'him'* to stop?" Carlos mimics her voice. It's uncalled for, but it satisfies the Midwesterner, nevertheless.

Carl leans forward, addresses the car like the President declaring 'A State of Emergency.' "We made a decision together guys; we can't go back home. We left. That's it. We've gone too far to turn around. No going back now." He turns to Mary, hand signalling their plight. "The base isn't an option…" He thinks a second longer. "We'll find somewhere, though. A pharmacy. A store. Something…" He begins to search the horizon for a building with bountiful optimism. Looks right. Nothing. Left? Nothing. Knows they've just passed a crossroads of a small intersection. A small rabbit-hole of a town. A cluster of houses along the long stretch of asphalt. But no shops. "Will find someplace where we will be able to patch Naomi's wounds. Find painkillers for her injury. She'll recover. She always recovers." And his eyes drift over the injured girl once again.

***

Ever since they had ventured into the 'Crossroads of the West,' the mood inside the jeep had begun to mimic the dusty and gray landscape along the interstate: bitter and unrepairable. Their rare exchanges of genuine excitement were swapped aside like the dwindling food wrappers building up around their feet. Carl had tried to mitigate the anger between friends when they'd first started on the voyage with jokes. Stories of when he was younger. Attending art college (*of all things*), only to realize that once on the journey, everyone up to a certain point couldn't bear being cooped up together for long periods like sardines in a can, chickens in a hen-house (especially with Carlos and his shitty pessimism).

As if on cue, the Midwesterner shares his views hoping to cut the others on those pessimistic thorns of doubt.

"Shit-on-a-stick! Where?" He's annoyed by their supposed leader's constantly, chirpy—*Julia Andrews*—optimism in the wake of the neverending amount of crap that kept coming their way. "Where are we going to find supplies on the Highway to Hell? We're in the middle of Nowhere—*wherever* that is? Or haven't you noticed, Maria?" (He refers to the actress's portrayal of the energetic Maria, the governess assigned to the Von Trapp children, in the classic 1965 movie.) Even with the world ended, Carlos was still a film-buff at heart. "Any way we look at it, there's no goddamn '*Sound of Music*' awaiting us at the end of the trip, either! No Nazis. Jeez, what I'd give to see a whole platoon of the 'Third Reich' rock up from nowhere and lighten the mood. Instead of—fucking *zombies*, everywhere, intent on eating our brains and asses."

Above the jeep, crows fly through the clear sky. Carlos peeks at the birds for a split second, then his eyes re-focus back on the road.

"We'll find medical supplies for Naomi," Carl assertively answers, ignoring the Midwesterner's endless interruptions. And he unfolds a small plastic map from his jacket side-pocket, spreads it out on his knees like a napkin at a fancy restaurant. Jerks his head, navigating with a solitary finger across black lines and less black lines. Seconds later, he finally says, "I know we will, Mary."

She nods.

Carlos continues to banter from behind the wheel. "Where? At the local convenience store? Or a Big Boy's drive-thru? Shit-on-a-stick, we shouldn't have listened to that drifter in the first place. And we sure shouldn't have gone into that silo without knowing the entire picture. We should've recon first, guys. Scoped the place out like a fuckin' Private Eye. It was probably a trap all along—*just* to get us all in one location so whoever 'he' was working with, could skull fuck our corp—"

Carl can't help it.

He's had enough—

"*Goddamnit*, Carlos! What's with the barrage of constant criticism? You're like a leaky pipe spouting crap, man!" He takes a deep breath, leans through the little space that separates the driver and the passenger seat. *Shit. This is a bad idea*, he thinks. *Should've pushed back from engaging with the jerk.* His guts roll, but at the same time, blood rises across his vision.

Meanwhile, Jed cowers in the passenger seat—hiding behind his footy cap—the teen doesn't dare speak. Whereas Mary sees Carl's composure break for the first time in a long time. (*First time on the trip!* she thinks. *Gotta give him credit!*), even with all the hiccups they'd encountered. As ever, she told herself that Carl had gotten them this far in the first place, had looked after their best interests while they were on the road, but as Mary looks at her friend, she can see that Carl is at breaking point.

"I have doubts."

Carl wanted to give people the benefit of the doubt. Yet, deep down, hopelessly knew it was a naïve idea to begin with (and that a smarter, less awful person would have realized this from the very beginning). "You would!" He frowns at the driver. "Try to be positive?"

Carlos' eyes fill with doubt. "I'm already one week into our little adventure, dawg. And it's a shitty fucking start. And don't you dare tell me to give 'optimism' a shot, either! It sucks." Carlos doesn't punch the brake. He eases his foot off the brake slowly, so their fearless—trailblazer of a leader—doesn't go flying through the windscreen. (*Shame,* the Midwesterner ponders, *could have taken control of our happy cartel and been a proper leader*), and the jeep slows to 40mph. An eyebrow lifts magically on its own behind the sunnies. Frowns appear beneath the red headband. "Don't you know the answer yet, dawg?"

Carl is tired of the driver. He tries to maintain calm and clarity in his voice. "The answer?" He is poised and ready, waiting for Carlos to continue his one-man quest for world domination, to be an Emperor, King-of-the-fucking-hill and it begins with taking charge of the group. "You must believe me when I say, I haven't got a fuckin' clue!"

"Don't play fuckin' dumb with me, Carl! You think you're always the badass-on-the-box set in charge. You're not! Ever since we came along on your little adventure, we've gone from one glitch to another. Not finding enough supplies. Placing your goddamn trust in people, especially that drifter on the promise of some extra provisions, and us… wandering into that fucking silo of a slaughterhouse." A devious smirk with a silver-edge blade cuts across the

Midwesterner's face. "Fuck—you's my *problem*, dawg. You luckless leader of men."

As Carl tries to keep clarity to his voice, he realizes as he speaks, each word has sharp teeth: "No one twisted your arm, Carlos. You could have stayed behind! At the camp."

"You're right, dawg. No one twisted my arm. But I couldn't have stayed any longer at that place. I was sick of living like a cockroach in that compound. For what? The rest of my life—dwindling away my days playing chess with old Mr. Kinky and his liver-speckled hands. I'm not ending my days like a belligerent old fart." And the Midwesterner hums the jeep into another gear.

Jed lifts his cap. "Why do you refer to Mr. Klinksy as 'Mr. Kinky' Carlos?"

The Midwesterner shoots the nervous adolescent a disbelieving smirk. "*C'mon*, Jed. You're a smart kid, ain't ya?" His voice is testing, the question is ready for an answer. (Jed blushes red. His education would have taken him to MIT if the world hadn't ended. But the female species were on another level to him; he always felt anxious around the opposite sex.) Carlos continues. "You know how that old man acts with the girls?" He sticks his tongue out, wiggles it about like a slippery, disturbing sex slug. "All hands and tongue. Touchy, touchy."

The youngest of the five blushes continually and slides further beneath his cap.

Jed had seen how Mr. Klinksy's hands wandered inappropriately sometimes when he chatted to a female (sometimes he'd see those girls go off with the old man to his house. The teen never asked questions when he saw the girls return the next morning, always crying, but with something in return). Jed wasn't dumb and knew what had happened: 'services for goods,' he'd overheard the old man saying on more than one occasion to pals.

Jed quietly nods back.

Carlos shrugs. "Plus, I wanted to see if the 'chick' on the airwaves is smoking hot. She sure sounds smoking hot. It's been a while since I saw a decent stunner." And he gives a cheeky wink in the overhead mirror towards the two girls.

Mary catches Carlos' dark eyes staring at her through his tinted sunnies, and the Midwesterner's words struck a nauseating cord within the pit of her stomach. "You're as bad as Mr. Kinky—" she says, shakes her head in dismay, "I mean… *Mr. Klinksy!*"

Carlos releases a short, sharp snort in her direction, "Sure, Kansas. Sure, you did." He couldn't hide the delight in his voice.

The two share an aura of hatred.

A burning bridge of mistrust.

"C'mon, leave it be, guys!" Carl urges them to cease. "Us arguing all the time will not get us any further towards Portland. We need to pull together for the sake of Naomi. She's injured, and we need to find medical supplies and quick."

"We had supplies, or are you forgetting that small detail, Carl?" the driver shoots back. They had also scavenged medical supplies from the silo's infirmary. "If it weren't for Little Miss Kansas over there…" Carlos throws Mary another decisive glare, "…we would be home and dry from that silo, and with enough supplies to last a few weeks."

"What would you have done, Carlos?" Mary hollers, pulling herself towards him. "You were not in my predicament back—"

"*This* again," Carlos says, voice carrying. "For starters—*aimed* straight. Secondly, I'd take every last one of those meat-hungry suckers out." He frowns, looking for weak points, buttons to press. "Instead of shooting your friend in the damn shoulder like a *goddamn* moronic 'Yooper' from Upper Peninsula—"

Mary's eyes are filled with hatred. "Stop the *car!*"

"What? Why? You need to pee? Well, goddamn hold it, Kansas. No ways—"

Her chest is puffed out—the humid air around her warped and feisty. "*Seriously, stop the jeep!*" It's a hoarse scream. She doesn't mean it to be, but that's how it escapes her lips. She's had enough from the Midwesterner constantly talking shit (and especially when his insults ruin the good name of her beloved state). "I've had it up to here"—and she signals the insult by raising her hand to head level—"with your constant, babbling bullshit of negative energy! It is sucking the life out of all of us…" Her words trail. "You're like a nugget of spoiled food, you effing moron…"

"I've had enough. I'm not going to sit here and drive you guys like I'm driving 'Miss Daisy.' I ain't rolling that way. You get me?" he says, indicating the backseat with a dismissive jerk of his thumb. "I'm done arguing. Don't be a bitch, Mary."

Mary reaches over. A straight slap to the back of his head. *Clap.* Carlos' teeth rattle in his mouth. His Ray-Bans toddle forwards on the bridge of his nose. He's surprised, equally pissed off. The jeep veers to the side of the road as he loses control of the vehicle; his temple throbs from another feisty blow.

He yells, *"Damn it!"* Spins towards her, ready to unleash Hell on the Yooper. "What the *fuck*—" Before he can finish his sentence, the jeep buckles, jolts wildly over a small dune and is now flying through the air 'Blue's Brothers style' before the front tires touch dirt followed by the rear, and the suspension buckles, the jeep veering onto the dusty scrubland *screeching* with a violent jolt.

Thonk. Thonk. Thonk thundered from beneath the hood.

"No, no, no. *C'mon,* Baby, just a little further. *C'mon!*" Carlos purrs, smacking his lips together. "*C'mon,* Baby. Don't do this!" It's no good; the hydraulics whine and the jeep pulls to a stop by the side of the road and dies.

4
COYOTE FROWN

They're on a small piece of greenish grass, as yellow scrubland hunkers nearby. Resilient plant-life clashes with wild scrubs full of tiny purple flowers. And old tracks in the ground—car tracks. Two sets. Three sets. And small wonderous eyes, that of coyotes, stare from afar.

Carlos releases his seatbelt; it *swooshes* back with a rush. He spins on the blond girl, thunders like a Norse God: "Great. Nice one. *Goddamnit!* You've killed our transport. *Whatcha* playin' at, Kansas?"

"You're the one who wouldn't shut your trap, Carlos," Mary murmurs, seriously irked by his shitty attitude. She moves close—stares at him with innocent, blue eyes. "You just keep goin' no matter what happens. Just, push and push like you're—"

A whisper comes from the front passenger seat. *"Guys—!"*

Both ignore the small voice.

"What the shit!" he says, cutting her off. His finger stern and straight like a Headmaster at the front of a class. "You wanted 'us' to stop. Now we're completely fucked and stuck in the middle of nowhere. *Christ,* if only you could harness your anger in a fucking bottle like a Genie, Little Miss Sunshine. We wouldn't even be in this damn mess."

She wants to say something, anything.

Rage rising—

Red haze, red rage—

Her voice is a squeak. "Go fuck yourself!"

"I really doubt that's possible." He glances at the girl as if she was nothing more than a piece of trash. "Girl, you're trippin'!"

"I'll freak out if I *want!*"

"Why are you yelling at me?"

"'Cause you're a fucking moron!" Mary replies, with equal confidence.

It's enough—

That mouse whisper becomes a full-on booming roar of frustration.

Jed yells from the sideline: *"Hey! Enough is enough, guys!"* It's the first time the teen has ever raised his voice, and the car falls eerily quiet. "Carl's right! You two at each other's throats at every minute of the day isn't making this situation any easier for any of us! You know, right?" He says all of this without even turning around—just *stares* dead ahead, eyes beneath his cap.

Carlos stiffens. "You're shitting me?" Is all he can say.

"This is one for the record books," Mary states, putting a hand on the teen's shoulder. She squeezes. "*Jed—*"

The teen wilts beneath their glares. Mary's touch. But his voice remains assured. "I'm sick of it, guys. All this hatred."

Carlos and Mary glare at one another like reprimanded children behaving badly. Both utter an apology of some kind to the red-haired teen, but refuse to apologize to one another.

Jed clutches his cap; soothing anger vanishes.

It had to do.

5
REST STOP

While Carlos and Mary continued their awkward unapologetic stairy-standoff, Carl checks on Naomi. The makeshift bandages around the Asian's wound oozing red like someone popping a small packet of ketchup beneath. She has a hole in her forearm, pilled, and sleeping, but is okay. Alive. Relieved, Carl staggers from the vehicle and into the sweltering afternoon sun and hears the sound of the engine turning to no avail.

The jeep's toast. A plume of volcanic smoke rises from beneath the metallic black hood like one of Hawaii's active volcanoes.

Carlos joins Carl underneath the pulsating sun moments later. He ventures towards the bonnet; knows it's too hot to lift. He strolls away cursing and a moment later returns with his hand wrapped in a rag. "Shit. The hood's smoking like a hot plate," his words gesturing to a former life.

Steam rises—

The others gather around the Midwesterner as he checks the engine—

A combined group effort of *So—?*

Was met by—

"The jeep's dead! Dead as us if we can't get it running soon!" he retorts.

Carl leans closer. "Can you fix it?"

As soon as Carl has asked that question, Carlos steps back from the exposed engine and gazes at his friend for a second contemplating an answer. "Sure thing, dawg. Just park it in my garage over beyond, and I'll book it in for an appointment." Immediately, he checks his invisible wristwatch. He adds in an even more sarcastic tone, "How does 5 pm sound?"

Carl resists the urge to punch him. Knows he has to say something quickly before Mary starts a full-throttle beach assault on the Midwesterner which would never end the war between the two hostile frenemies. "Stop being a total dick, Carlos. Can you fix our ride or not?" he demands, his authority shining through as any—a natural leader—does and waits for the D-Day announcement.

He wasn't sure about the answer he would receive.

After a moment, Carlos pulls his hand back from the engine; eyes the metallic interior. Rolls his tongue along his bottom teeth. "Give me some time, guys. I think the radiator's blown." He adds, more of a statement than a question. "Hopefully…" He hesitates a little longer, looking at the steaming gaskets and engine-things (he knows how to fix the basics. Knows a few car-shooting problems, but is no mechanic). He finally shrugs. "*Mm*, we're going to need spare parts. My baby won't run on sheer willingness and a shit load of luck alone." He arches upwards, hand over forehead, like a military salute he looks around the deserted landscape.

The silence of the morning continues.

Carl, Mary, and Jed start to circumnavigate the surrounding area as if they're standing on a ship's deck with weary eyes looking for land (but in this case, a garage would be helpful).

***

The sun is set high and bright; the heat intense.

That coyote vanishes.

Finally, the group settles on a pair of derelict structures across the road. The first building is an old bar, like the kind you would find in an old Western. The films starring *John Wayne* or *Clint Eastwood* on lazy, Sunday afternoons. It has a saloon-styled door too. Built with sturdy timber in its heyday, and surprisingly still standing as the world crumbles around it. Next door, an old converted barn that was now a vandalized general store stood in worse shape. A few beat-up vehicles sit abandoned either side of the buildings. A bluish soccer mum's minivan, a rusted pick-up truck, and two SUVs, both the color of burnt tangerine. An eighteen-wheeled truck sits neatly tucked behind overgrowing bushes to the far side of the bar.

Carlos cranes his neck. "Exposed out here?" he offers, shattering the silence. His hand nervously dances across his side-arm. "I feel like bait. I don't wanna be bait for the fucking indigenous wildlife."

"We better get to work," Carl offers, feeling suddenly hopeful. "I'll take Mary and check out the buildings. Jed can look after Naomi, and you—" he nods at Carlos, "can check out those vehicles for spare parts."

The Midwesterner's reply is instant. "Already on it, dawg!" He marches back around the jeep carrying a brown tool bag in one hand, while the other hand hovers over his sidearm. A moment later, he strolls towards the nearest vehicle. "Time to go to work. Meet back in twenty. Hopefully, no one's stripped out these beauties already!"

Before the group gives a cohesive reply, Carlos is in the compartment of the nearest SUV popping the hood.

There was only one thing to do—

"Mary," Carl says, "grab the shotgun and come with me." She does as she's told and fetches the gun from the jeep. Carl turns to the nervous teen (Jed is fidgeting with his cap). "Look after Naomi until I..." He wants to say *until I get back* but settles on, "I—I mean until we return. Understand?"

"Uh-ha."

"Where's your gun?"

Jed nervously drops his eyes in shame—his baseball cap slants downwards to the floor. He scuffs the dirt with the sole of his trainers. "Sorry, Carl, I lost it back at the silo. But I have my hunting knife." The teen pats his leg, referring to the blade in a leather sheath attached to his shin, a *Bowie*, that he carries around with him for good luck and the occasional killing of the undead.

Carl stares back silently, twiddles his fingers hesitantly; honestly, he didn't want the convo now. He's heard it all before, same old story as the last time.

***

A while back, the teen found himself face-to-face with a monster from a horror movie, cornered within a narrow galley of a plush house. Teeth bared, the Creep came at the teen, wanting nothing more than to devour his young flesh and wear the teen's body as a literal dinner-jacket. But Jed, nervous-as-a-quivering jelly, had already lost his sidearm. With no way out, he turned, dived between the monster's legs and fled through the house.

What followed was a game of Mouse and Predator Zombie.

Every time Jed thought he'd taken advantage and lost the Creep's unwanted attention, the Z was there and behold—sharp-teeth bared like a rabid-infested hound. That was until Jed staggered into a room-of-sorts. A hunting room which belonged to the former owner: a dentist or a doctor who liked nothing better than to go on Big Game hunting trips around the world. On the walls were literally trophy heads: lions, elephants, giraffes and in one corner behind a 17th century armchair, a mounted and stuffed bear. It's when the teen sees it—*a goddamn Bowie* blade sticking out of the bear's mid-section. Jed runs over to the scary-looking great brown bear and pulls the solid-hardwood handle back just as the Creep catapulted its body over a Persian rug. Jed spun in time, and the blade entered the forehead of the creature; a direct blow that finished the Nasty off.

It was how the blade became his lucky charm.

***

Mary mumbles from behind the back passenger door. "You lost the gun?"

Jed nods and swallows hard. Doesn't want to let her down. "It fell from my hands."

"It's the second time you've lost a handgun in the last month. Guns don't just grow on trees, Jed," she says flatly. "It's becoming an issue!"

The teen scuffs his trainers again.

Carl ignores Mary's comments and diffuses the situation. "It's okay," he says, hand on the young teens shoulder. "Hey, take my gun." Carl hands the compact Glock 42 over with his spare hand, But didn't show the teen how annoyed he was. (Firearms were hot commodities nowadays.) Jed nods and takes the black Glock from Carl's grip, opens the rear door and sits with Naomi. "If you need anything—*shout.*"

Jed raises a hand in reply. The young teen perches on the seat—Glock between nervous knees with his legs dangling out over the side.

Mary stares back—wants to add something to the convo; her small eyes appraising Carl.

Carl stares back. "It's fine, Mary." *It's not.* "We'll just make do with the shotgun this time. C'mon. Let's be super quick. We sweep the buildings thoroughly and cleanly. We need sutures. Bandages, and antibacterials, anything. No mistakes. No freaking out this time!"

Mary gazes at Carl; she knows what had happened at the silo was her mistake, and she is determined not to let the same blunders happen again. She nods affirmatively. “Okay, Carl.” Moments later, Mary grabs her small yellow backpack from the back of the jeep, shoulders the Browning Auto-5 semi-automatic shotgun, smiles at Naomi sleeping in the backseat just like Sleeping Beauty in the fairytale; smiles at the teen too. “Be safe, Jed,” she says, wishing they weren’t in this predicament in the first place, but she can’t dwindle on the past. “We’ll be back in no time.”

The young teen hunches his shoulders from the jeep’s doorway like an old man seated at a park bench on a cold, windy day. He sighs, finally raises a hand. “Sure, Mary.”

With that, Mary smiles at Jed one final time, takes a look at Naomi on the backseat and yanks the straps of her backpack and hurriedly catches up to Carl.

6
AT THE BAR, (15 MINUTES PRIOR)

"Hey, bud! Another drink?" the stranger asks. His drinking companion doesn't answer. The figure sits slumped on the barstool, his head resting upon the bar's dark, dusty, oak counter. Forgotten empty pitchers with mummified bugs rest to one side of the bar. The lacquer is grimy, grubby at best. He adds in a weary voice, "The whole wide world's gone to shit, don't ya think?"

No reply.

The stranger pours himself another round of Scotch—*Glen Scotia* 25-Year-Old—from a dusty bottle, tips his mustard fedora as if he's saluting a superior officer before shooting his drinking companion a grim smile of self-satisfaction. "Yeah. I know the feeling," he answers, speaking for his silent buddy. "Sometimes the quiet times are the best," and he lifts the dirty glass to his lips and empties the contents in one hot gulp: tastes of pudding fruit. "It won't remind anyone of childhood, exactly, unless you had rather an alcoholic upbringing, but it has a touch of apple tart in there, a touch of ginger too. It's beautifully balanced," (one to drink down and repeat, except, there's just the one bottle remaining). "Wonderful stuff, buddy."

His companion still silent.

The stranger sits drinking like an isolated man stewing in existential dread.

All around the bar, tables and upturned stools are covered in a thick layer of dust, while an old-style jukebox rests in a far corner: the glass façade has two bloody handprints; dried a long time ago. The last song played, *Michael Jackson's* 'Thriller', shows through the grimy, glass porthole. (In his mind, the track which defines the 80s and a fitting tune to resemble the world now.)

Ironic… really.

Since the man had arrived at the run-down bar, his drinking buddy had remained silent—*like* the dead. No. That wasn't right. *The dead… goddamn moans, right? Like one of MJ's dance extras!* He gazes at the motionless figure again. *More like a corpse. Bingo!*

The whole atmosphere had been stale, not a single customer since late yesterday evening, and even they were sitting quietly in a soft, leather booth by the entrance: void of chit-chat.

The stranger gazes into the spider-webbed mirror that hangs high behind the bar. Three weeks of gray grizzle stares back. "I would tell you straight up," he says with a raising of eyebrows. "I'm a social orphan nowadays."

The two customers in the booth remain unapologetically silent; he made sure of that when they'd tried to jump him the previous evening. Their weapons still in their dead-set hands as their bodies slouched back into the leather upholstery—eyes wide open, staring up at the cob-webbed wood-rafted ceiling—while the stranger's revolver lay beside his drinking buddy on the bar.

The man takes a deep breath, straightens his tanned fedora and flexes his hands, yawns before swinging around on the barstool imagining that the drinking joint had all the character you could ask for in a previous lifetime: sociable bartenders, spacious booths, and saucy regulars. It was the local's bar, their home away from home. But now it was his shelter away from—home—until he'd finished the last of the good liquor and then he'd move on to pastures new. A free-spirit wandering the backroads of America. Crossing a sea of the Undead to get to where?

The Stranger goes over and over his travels in his head. *Weeks on the goddamn road without any sign of life. Shit. It really is the end of the world!* He finally says to his pal on the stool, "It's been a while since I've had time to think, buddy. I remember the world before it turned to shit. It was shit then… and shit now. Come to think about it; not much has changed. Bottom's up!" He sips the whiskey from the glass, savors the taste and adds: "Play it again, Sam. Play it *goddamn* again."

He downs the last of the good stuff while his drinking buddy stays motionless. He was a modern-day Robinson Crusoe with the world as his desert island and his empty bottle of Whisky as his vessel. And the whiskey was superb.

Then a loud noise originates from outside the bar—

Rattle and *clank.*

Sounds like a wood-chipper clonking out on a farm.

He doesn't move; whatever's outside can wait.

Another sound—

The voices jolt him from his happy place, and he shoulders a glance towards the saloon-styled door, expecting trouble to show its 'ugly face,' at any moment.

He wasn't wrong.

7
PESKY KIDS

The saloon door swings open. In fact, it falls off its hinges and crashes to the goddamn, dusty floor in a flourish of woodchip, splinters, and dust motes.

A moment of silence follows—

And Carl and Mary stand by the entrance expecting the bar to be empty of patrons just like the convenience store. It was a silly premise to have. In the blackness of the saloon by the wrap-around bar, two figures sit motionlessly on bar stools.

"Hold the gun on em', Mary!"

"I don't think I can."

"You have to, Mary," Carl commands, his tone grave. "Naomi's life is at stake if we don't get back to the others soon. Trust me; it's easy. Just point and pull the trigger if they move." And he mimics a pulling action with his finger.

Mary nods at the figures sitting at the bar. "They're not dead, though!" Fear restricted to the back of her throat. "They're alive. They're human, Carl."

"I know they're not—the dead. But…" Carl hood-winks a look at the two motionless figures at the bar. One happily sits straight as if he's a strippers' pole while the other slouches across the bar like a drunk. Then he pivots—sees the two *dead* bodies nearby, unease spreading through his body. He refocuses on the two men by the bar. "It means they're just as dangerous!"

"Ok," she answers, the single word comes out hollow of emotion, yet her hands tremble. The shotgun wasn't her favorite weapon by a long shot. It was cumbersome and robust and packed a punch like a heavyweight boxer. Mary could handle a small handgun, but Jed and Carlos had the only two remaining Glocks available, and she knew Jed needed one to look after Naomi, and she sure wasn't going to ask Carlos to swaparoo.

As Mary stands in silence, her hands shake as she sees the two bodies slouching in one of the leather booths. Both males. Bullet holes in each forehead. Fresh blood pooled across the table covering the tattered cloth. Above the corpses—animal skulls cover the walls like a tribute act to all things *Satanic*. Eventually, she steadies the shotgun on the two men sitting at the bar—the pool of sunlight drenching the men with warmth from a nearby window.

Beneath his dusty fedora, the Stranger sees the girl's hands shaking in the shattered mirror behind the bar. He doesn't move; bides his time like a chess player.

"Cover me, okay? If they move…" Carl stops himself mid-sentence and looks at the two figures again. He sees the slim barrel of a revolver lying on the bar just in reach by the guy with the fedora. It looks like a lizard lazing on a cool wall in the afternoon sun. "Shoot em', Mary!" he finally declares, moving forward with his arms outstretched and his palms facing towards the outsiders like a Police negotiator trying to coax a jumper down from atop a building.

The Stranger allows a respectful silence; it gives him time to suss out the situation.

Carl takes another two steps.

"Why would I move, kid? Can't a guy just drink in peace?" he titters, fingertips gently tapping the top of the bar. *Tap. Tap. Tap.* "Anyway, this place is full of..." He pauses for a moment allowing some all-important time to pass between tribes... "dead company."

"You'll be in pieces if you make a move I don't like!" Carl answers assertively, aware of the threat.

The Stranger silently muses. "I really doubt that."

Carl looks sceptical. "I think you're clever enough not to make a move."

"Maybe true, kid."

Carl stiffens. "I'm going to come over, search you first. Your friend second. That's all. When and if I'm happy enough you're not a threat... you both can leave. But the revolver and any other weapons you have stashed away... stays with me! You can come back and collect them after we've left this place. You have my word."

The Stranger doesn't say anything.

Carl's happy enough the man understands the options allocated and takes another step forward. He can't see what the guy has hidden underneath his long black jacket. All that was showing was a pair of authentic cowboy boots—minus spurs-and a military survival pack that sat on the concrete floor next to the barstool. The Stranger's companion was dressed in hunting clothes—a red and black patterned jacket and slacks.

Carl begins to say: "Okay. I'm coming—"

That's when a growl instantly silences him.

Mary takes that as a bad sign. She stiffens.

The Stranger shakes his head. "I heard you the first darn time, kid." And he lifts a hand, tilts the fedora and scratches his stubbly chin. The thick growth itches his weathered face. Immediately, he spins around, facing Carl. Carl staggers back a step and watches as the guy shoves his pal off the stool. The body hits the floor with a loud *clank*, and a few bones snap. A skeleton's head goes rolling across the dirty floor like a bowling ball along a lane. "There you go, kid..." He says with a flourish of hands. "We mean you no harm. So leave!"

From behind, Mary feels a bead of cold sweat materializing on her under-arm and trickle down to her elbow. It reaches the dry joint and falls to the ground. Then she stifles a *yelp*.

Carl steps back a fraction, so he's adjacent to Mary. (His task made easier as now there is only one individual to worry over.) The headless corpse lays on the floor; the skeleton's head beneath a pool table. He shoulders a look towards Mary for a second.

Both are quiet.

Nervousness rattles their bones. But Mary's nervousness shines through to her exterior, and the shotgun begins to shake her hands again like a train thundering along a railroad.

***

The Stranger eyes Mary first; sizes her up like she's a greyhound at the tracks. Blond. 5'6. Pretty. Athletic. Track team in her junior. Possible state championships. Wears denim dungarees, a yellow rucksack slung over her shoulder. Her hair is done up the 'Martha Stewart way,' with a yellow ribbon, and unlike the former American celebrity who could wield anything like a pro, the girl wields a shotgun like an amateur.

Then he stares at Carl: Taller by four inches. The kid's harder to read though: Crystal blue eyes. Looks like a frat boy, but isn't. Slim, slick black hair, reminds him of 'John Connor' from The Terminator franchise (*not the godforsaken TV series*), but the *Arnold Schwarzenegger* movies, and more precisely, T3. He loved that film, loves the franchise.

The two friends, not much older than twenty-something. *Generation Z,* he assumes. Have used the Internet since a young age and are comfortable with technology and social media, but wonders if they're comfortable with firearms. The kid is empty-handed, but boy, the Stranger is sure the kid's in charge the way he's giving orders to the girl.

Orphan. Maybe?

The Stranger looks across the dim bar at the two Gen Z. *I like the odds.* "There are monsters aplenty in this world right now, and there are men who are willing to kill you where you stand just for the shoes you're wearing!" he says. "Steal your belongings. Rip the clothes off your luckless back. And have a go at your pretty friend standing next to you, kid..." The last words leave his lips slowly; the implication hoping for a lasting impression.

Mary quivers. Wishes she'd awaken from this nightmare. She understands what the guy means, and the stranger's words bring about a flash of memory.

Mary had seen a girl, not much older than she is now being dragged from a car by two heavy-set men when the plague of all plagues had first begun. She followed the screams, saw the unimaginable sight unfolding before her eyes, and shot the two men; blown their brains out the back of their heads. Went to the girl's rescue, but it was already too late, the girl was half dead from the attack. She remembers stroking the girls forehead, whispering 'It'll be okay' to the injured girl, and finally putting the girl out of her nightmare. What was clear from that day, however, was that evil still persisted in a world of new horrors. Mary takes a deep, cleansing breath, and let the anger subside, focusing on the guy that had triggered that awful memory.

Carl gulps hard. "Which one are you?"

"Neither the first or the second."

Carl doesn't move but can feel Mary shaking beside. It is uncontrollable, and he reaches out to grab the barrel of the shotgun, steadies the steel. Mary breathes a sigh of relief and relaxes—slightly, but her hands continue to tremble. Deep inside, her emotions wept for that poor girl. A moment passes, and the tension fills the old bar like an odious fart fills an enclosed space.

"Don't worry, kid. I'm the third choice. Just a patron of—*our*—former, great Nation *looking* for a place to drink quietly. Rest my weary head. That's all."

He continues in a flatter tone. “You’ve already disturbed my drinking companion.” He kicks a foot out and knocks the skeleton’s leg; the leg bones shatter. Blunter this time. “And the quiet mood in this fine establishment, too. Just be on your way, and let me drink in peace.”

“Sorry. Can’t do that!”

“’Course you can.”

“No. I can’t.”

“Why?”

Carl can’t risk letting the guy leave the bar without being frisked. He can’t risk his friends outside being compromised, and like best buds, courage and Carl begin to edge towards the bar again, ready to take the man’s weapon.

The Stranger massages his temples beneath his hat. *Shit is about to get real*, he thinks. Can’t let that happen. “Hold up, kid. Don’t be a fool,” he commands like a Drill Sergent in a parade.

Carl stops dead in his tracks. The man radiates confidence. Chin up. Broad shoulders. Back straighter than that strippers’ pole.

“Why should I?” he says foolishly and looks at the man in the eyes. “I’d rather continue.”

The Stranger tilts his fedora, cocks his head. “Goddamnit, kid, what the hell ya playing at?”

Carl lingers on that question for a moment. “I’m taking charge of this operation!”

“You’re taking charge of nowt, kid.”

“Carl!” Mary says, feeling a sickening certainty rise in her stomach that Carl is making a huge mistake. She knows this encounter is wasting time. “You have a plan?”

“Yes.”

The Stranger doesn’t break Carl’s glare. “No,” he rasps, “you seem to be struggling with something!” He turns to Mary. “Your friend doesn’t know shit, girl.”

Carl retorts: “Depends on which perspective.”

The Stranger groans. “First, you hand your gun over to your unqualified friend, who seems to be unable even to hold that bazooka in a straight, darn line! Let alone shoot a bound, and gagged turtle plumped down in front of her face. Then you swan over and try to frisk me like an LAPD cop looking for an extra fun time. Straight away, two blatant mistakes.”

Carl looks over at the guy and knows he’s right. He hasn’t thought properly about this plan. If Naomi or Carlos were here, instead of injured or scavenging for parts, then Mary wouldn’t have been his backup.

“Well—*how* about ya put that elephant gun down for starters?”

“I can. I won’t.” Carl replies. Thinks for a moment longer, *it’ll leave us vulnerable*, wonders if he should add some smart ass comment. Knows Carlos would, if the Midwesterner was here in his place but doesn’t.

“Jesus Christ. I know how this goes. You two stumble upon this building looking for supplies, I take it? You’re in a rush for some reason. I don’t give a *shit,* why? You don’t give a *shit* why, either! But you’re right out of luck. The bar's empty. The general store next door might have some supplies hidden away. Why don't you go check there? I know good people when I see them. You know what, though? I see kindness in your faces. Fear too. And you both should leave. Plus… I just don't have the time for these games. I'm tired. Let me finish my darn drink in peace."

***

Some grueling minutes later, Mary has been aiming the shotgun at the man in the bar for what feels like a millennium now, and her arms are getting tired, those beads of cold sweat keep coming, and she wonders why this isn't easier. "Maybe he can help us, Carl?" she asks, and her grip on the shotgun loosens slightly, and the barrel slacks downwards like a guy's cock after ejaculation. (The Stranger sees this, and waits), Mary and Carl don't.

"You know our rules, Mary!"

She nods. "I do. But—"

"This guy is armed, Mary. He's unwilling to give up his pistol. He can't help us."

"I can't, can't I!" the man quizzically says; his gaze leaving the barrel of the girl's shotgun and finding the boy's eyes. "Why can't I help, kid?"

"Unless you're a part-time mechanic or medic, then… no… you can't."

"Huh, that's quite a job criteria you're throwing my way."

"Enough with the wise-cracks, Mr!"

Mary stands aside. "Carl! Carl?" she says her friend's name as though it's a song stuck on repeat.

The Stranger folds his arms and stares at Carl with jet-black eyes. "For someone claiming to be in charge… you're doing quite well so far. Besides," he says, "your friend requires your attention, kid."

Carl's voice explodes: "What, Mary!" His tone isn't friendly. He doesn't mean to snap at her, but the mysterious guy is beginning to get on his nerves. A laugh comes from behind, and Carl turns back around. *"Shut it!"*

The Stranger pauses. He looks down to the floor, hiding his grin and black eyes beneath his fedora. *Time's ticking, kid. And the bomb is ready to go off in your hands!*

"We need to get these supplies back to Naomi, Carl. She's injured. We need to help Carlos with the jeep, too!" Mary says everything she shouldn't say in front of the man sitting by the bar, as dreadful images of her friend's injury are beginning to weigh her down with guilt.

They had only found a few supplies in the abandoned store, but it's enough to take care of Naomi's wound before it becomes infected.

"Whatever this guy says… whatever he's trying to do to unsettle us, Mary… we can't allow him to drive a wedge between us!"

With that, the shotgun loosens from Mary's grip; the barrel dropping towards the floor.

***

Just as Carl turns to face Mary, the man stands abruptly—lunges forward and swipes the shotgun from her grip. A sudden push and Carl feels himself falling into Mary. Bodies collide. Butt bones smack the floor. Seconds later, they both land on their backsides, looking up as the man hovers above; the barrel of the shotgun rather close to their noses.

"As with any drama, the characters evolve," he sarcastically states. "And I might ask what the hell is your plan now, kiddies?"

Mary's heart pounds like a war-drum. She looks up at the man, hands shielding her eyes from the barrel (hoping that her hand-shield will protect her delicate features from a close-range bullet to the head). Carl, on the other hand, can hear her heart *thud, thud, thud*, it's so loud it would wake the dead if they weren't already alive. Doubt and stupidity shroud his body like an early morning fog drifting across a lake. He should have seen it coming.

Carl and Mary sit as powerless as Victorian ladies in 19th century London.

"Stay still. Be quiet!" the Stranger says before lowering the weapon. "I don't appreciate having a shotgun aimed at me. How does it feel having a loaded barrel shoved in your face?" He pauses, lets the question hover over Carl and Mary for a second.

They don't respond.

"I'm not going to hurt you. Just passing through, minding my own business, like I already stated. But, it seems you require help, and I need a ride. Let me take a look at your vehicle or friend, and if I can't assist, then we'll both go our separate ways. Deal?" He leans closer, standing over the two millennials with a hand outstretched. Eyes as wide as rabbits in headlights glare back. He likes the girl's yellow headband—it suits her delicate face, while the boy wears slacks, a cool black jacket, and a faded lime 'Kinks' t-shirt. He admits, the kid's got a good taste in music.

8
CHOICES

Carl and Mary desperately look at one another from the dirty floor. Carl tries to think of a comeback, a reason why they shouldn't take the deal offered to them by the guy standing above with their—*own*—shotgun pointed at them, but can't. Instead, he senses an opportunity and makes a lunge for the Browning Auto-5 and by trying to become a hero provokes the Stranger, and what follows is the cold, hard truth in their dire situation. The man is too quick, and he pulls back the gun from Carl's clutches and slams a boot into his ribcage which throws the boy backward.

A yelp of pain later—

"Hold on. You don't want to do this, kid. I got you by about 80 pounds."

"Carl?" Mary says, her frantic heart slows.

Carl's gaze flicks to the right. Mary stares, her lips closed. He understands her unspoken words telepathically, *don't be a fool, he's offering us a deal.* His chest hurts. Finally, he catches a breath. "How do we know we can trust you?"

The man nods—his fedora rising from his forehead—to the two corpses occupying the corner booth of the bar. "Point of fact; you'd be as quiet as those two morons over yonder! Equally as dead."

Mary cocks another look to the two stiffs, swallows. "Oh!" she says. Right now, however, her fear has returned, but she wasn't going to let herself tumble in that torrent of panic and doubt. *We're goin' to have to trust this guy!*

Hesitation set aside, Carl reluctantly sticks out a hand and is hoisted like a bag by the guy's firm grip; Mary follows her friend's impression of luggage.

The Stranger's voice perks up. "Now, then, where were we?"

Mary pauses, letting her heart slow. "Starting with a proper introduction will be nice?"

"Darn straight, Miss," he begins. "I'll go first. Hi. I'm Deckard. Pleased to meet you both."

"Mary Johnson," Mary replies and pushes the blond bangs out of her eyes, straightens her headband.

"Mary, that's a beautiful name," he says, pulling a line from every 'John Hughes' movie ever. "That your boyfriend?" His eyes find Carl again.

Carl puffs. "Oh, no. I'm no boyfriend. Just a friend." He looks nervously at the man-with-a-name-now-holding-the shotgun. "I'm Carl. Carl Roberts." Sticks out a hand. "Pleased to meet you."

The man shakes it, eventually finds Carl's eyes scanning the elephant-killer. "I guess you'll be wanting your firepower back, hey, Carl Roberts?" (Carl silently nods.) To Mary, he says, "Here, take it. I trust you know how to handle one of these?" He flips the shotgun in the air, grabs it by the barrel, and hands it properly to her. "But don't be making me into swiss cheese, you hear!"

Carl can feel Mary's giddy fingers quivering as she takes the Browning by its stock from the corner of his eye. She looks at him for a comforting, reassurance glance. He gives it.

Mary grabs the stock and lowers the weapon to her side. She has a hunch, deep down, knows the guy is no danger to them both. There was no need to debate any further what was about to happen, and Mary and Carl exchange a nervous look before her eyes find the man once again. "Now what happens?" she asks, a small smile forming at the corner of her lips.

Deckard laughs. Relief settles; he sure didn't want to kill the kids, but left with no other choice, he would have added their faces to his growing list-of-kills—*never* to regret the little interaction. He scans both their faces, watches the two millennials with interest. "I like, ya," he says, "both of ya. I'm a good judge of character. Here, my CV's outstanding. You need a mechanic or a medic?"

9
THE REST OF THE GANG

Four minutes later—

A scream emits from outside the bar followed by a *tap, tap tap* of gunshots.

Everyone turns and stares at the door—

A cry of 'Help!' resonates closely—

Carl is the first to act. He pivots, turns, his shoulder hitting the remaining saloon door like a quarterback proceeding to block as part of a play—knocks it open. The outside sun hits him square in the eyes, along with a terrifying sight. It's almost a dizzying Dreamscape of 'I Told You So's' thumping his head with big fucking hammers.

The Stranger turns, grabs his sleeping revolver from the top of the bar, and follows the kid to the open wilderness of the morning. Ready to take on the whole, darn world of monsters that roam the wastelands of the Utah desert while royally tipsy from the half-bottle of 25-year-old Scotch he's just drunk by himself.

Mary's fast on their heels too; the small, yellow backpack slides off her shoulder—she catches it just before it hits the floorboards. She follows with the trailing shotgun by her side and reaches the door just as the sun penetrates her vision.

***

By the time they are all outside of the saloon, Carlos is face-to-face with a Creep by the faded orange SUVs. His gun lies two feet away in the dirt. "Jesus Christ. *Fuck.* Help, ya guys!" he hollers, as he dances a nervous dance with a nightmarish monster.

Carl's vision clears, and he says something—*inaudible*—by the saloon's entrance, the hot wind takes away his words with a mean swipe.

Mary gasps; words also lost.

In the near distance, Jed is inside the jeep with the Glock 45 pressed against the glass—

The door locked—

Twenty feet away, the Z had its mouth open, moving around the edges of the nearest SUV. Thin streams of saliva drip from the Creep's sharp teeth as a greeting. Then its teeth completely disappeared when it shut its mouth again: fusing the two separate pieces of flesh together to form a continuous, sealed sheet. The Z opened its mouth again, tearing itself—the fleshy lips—apart. Carlos had the nauseating thought to throw up but resists the temptation at seeing the contents of his stomach splashed across the floor like a Jackson Pollock's masterpiece. But before Carlos' muscles can twitch into action, more movement comes from his left, and another Creep is running full pelt towards his face. Sunken, skeletal shoulders; scabs falling off the flesh flung outwards like octopus tentacles—ready to attack. This Creep's mouth is wider than the diameter of its own body, allowing it to swallow prey far larger than itself. A hideous noise ensues.

Sounds of wailing banshees—

The sounds grow to a wild shriek—

Carl wants nothing more than to fill the monster with lead, hand instantly hovering over an empty holster. But the way it moves is primeval—*fast*. Instead, he yells: "Move, Carlos! Move your fat ass, outta its path!"

But the warning comes too late.

His reaction time is far too slow, and as Carlos thinks to throw up an arm to shield his face, instead of moving out of the way like any sane person in the face-of-danger, there is a loud *Bang* followed by a second *Blast*. Carlos feels the dirt floor hit him in the back—his Ray-bans go flying. A moment later he's gaping at the Z's half-exploded head flying through the air like a punctured football. The rest of its body held itself above Carlos for a few seconds—spasm like a figurine made from jelly—then slumps across 'its' prey with a dead weight that knocks the Midwesterner for six. Bone, brains and red mush makes his woolen hoodie look like it has gone through a blender.

***

Seconds later, Carlos rolls around, eventually looks up, over the headless corpse; he can hear his friends yelling questions at him. Hands appear on the Creep's squishy shoulders, and together, Carl and Mary roll the headless corpse off their companion.

"You hurt? *Carlos!* Carlos, did it bite you?" comes a voice.

Wheeling in slow motion, Carlos catches Mary's tentative gaze once before he clocks the first Creep's head (the one who'd knocked his gun from his hands), spread like a messy turd in the dusty ground. Next, his hearing returns, and like a conveyor belt, more questions come his way.

"I—I'm good," he finally answers the first question. "No. No. It didn't bite me!" he says to the second question and takes a gulp of fresh air. "The *fucker* just came outta nowhere—it was *fast*. So goddamn fast." He looks around and sees the 'Usain Bolt' of all zombies' exploded head in the dirt; sharp-pointy teeth glaring back as his sidearm lays in the dirt like a limp dick in the heat of a drunken one-night-stand. "Jesus! Fuck man. I very nearly pissed my pants. I think I'm gonna puke!" He lunges over, hands in the dirt, but his stomach is empty.

"You alright, there?"

"Uh, yeah. Thanks, Carl!" he utters, but doesn't mention Mary in his I-am-alive-thank-you-very-much-acceptance-speech-for-the-worse-possible-interaction-with-the dead.

Mary's face stretches into an unhappy frown from the blatant snub.

Carl sees the look on her face (she's thoroughly annoyed by the lack of gratitude from the Midwesterner, and she spins away with the shotgun in hand and a deep *F-you* Carlos growl). "It wasn't my doing!" Carl states.

The Midwesterner has already stopped listening—

Carlos strains his eyes; the heat from above is intense. Wipes grit from them. Then he sees a figure standing in front of the shaded doorway with a 1930s vintage Enfield revolver. Carlos swears he can see little puffs of clouds emerging from the end of the barrel. He looks back at Carl. "Who the fuck is that?" he says in the politest tone he can muster.

Carl stammers for a response—it comes far too late.

"Haven't you two ever heard of stranger danger?"

Mary and Carl exchange a look.

"He's the guy that just saved your life, man," Carl replies.

Carlos sits hard back against the SUV, scuffs his trainers through the dirt, before staggering to his feet, swaying a little and grabs his sunnies. He's unhurt otherwise and starts dusting himself down like nothing ever happened. He turns, inspects both bodies. Both Z's are still wearing clothes, well, rags. No shoes though. The body of the infected is bubbled and scarred and reminds him of a wild pig skewered over an open flame: a tasty bucket of human flesh kinda reminds him of a KFC chicken basket. *Finger-licking good!* At that moment his own threads look like their tattered clothes, with other people's blood splatter.

Carl says: "You sure you didn't get bitten?"

"Do I fucking look infected?" he says, flicking a chunk of brain matter off his t-shirt and onto the ground. He starts to lift his sleeves. "No. Fucking. Bite. Marks. Dawg!" One pissed-off word at a time. He goes to undo his trousers. "Wanna have a closer look?"

Carl stares at the Midwesterner for untold seconds—doesn't want to see his junk—finally shrugs. "Calm down man…" he says, hands raised in front of his chest. "Just asking!"

"Seriously, I'm not a fucking-all-you-can-eat-buffet for these suckers. Right?"

Carl pauses, looks at Carlos and then knows the Midwesterner was (*oh, so gratefully fine*).

***

That's when—

Carlos begins making his way toward the Stranger by the saloon's entrance.

He wants to greet the man who's just saved his life personally. Shake his hand. Show his gratitude. Enlarge the guy's cock and inflate his ego all at the same time. As Carlos approaches the outsider, he notices a hardened weariness that strengthens the man's features, and it doesn't help that the guy is wearing a tanned fedora and long leather jacket either. He reminds Carlos of a character from a *Stephen King* novel or an old Spaghetti Western.

"Thanks for the save, dawg!" he gestures with an outstretched hand.

The Stranger stashes the vintage revolver, straightens his military frame. "No worries. Looked like you needed a helping hand," he replies, gripping Carlos' hand firmly and stares at the red bandana decorating his forehead, (reminds him of the fictional character 'John Rambo' played by *Sylvester Stallone* in the Rambo films). He continues to shake. "But I'm not the only one you should be 'thanking' bud." He nods toward Mary. "You did extremely well, lass. You know how to handle your firepower after all," he adds with a distinctive smirk.

The words are greatly received.

"Oh, uh—*thanks*," she answers, throwing the shotgun up and over her shoulder like a G.I. Jane on frontline duty. "I'm normally a terrible shot with this thing!" A smile pits her lips.

It takes a few seconds for the info to sink in, but when it does—

Alarmed, Carlos hollers: "Excuse me? *Jesus!* You nearly took my fucking head off, Mary. Thank God you were a better shot than you were back at the silo. I didn't want to be spending the rest of this damn road trip as bed buddies with Naomi!"

Mary doesn't answer straight away. In the quiet patch, she grows aware that Carlos has outgrown how-to-become-a-bigger-ass-than-he-could-possibly-be award

She cries out some combination of "Fuck you" and "You asshole" (she's not really sure which) but is annoyed by the Midwesterner's attitude and blatant refusal to acknowledge her saving his life. Mary finally gives him the finger and storms away towards Jed.

The teen is sitting on the bonnet of the jeep—*Carl's* Glock in hand. Wind fluttering beneath his cap. He opens his mouth to say something to Mary but decides against it. Her stern footsteps were doing the talking.

***

Carl calls after Mary to no avail. She carries on walking towards the jeep, muttering obscenities under her breath like confetti at a wedding and doesn't look back at any of them. He regrets another lost chance to align himself with Mary over the Midwesterner.

"Women, hey? Maybe it's her time of the month," Carlos jokes. "Jam doughnut time? The Strawberry Parade!"

Carl folds his arms tight to his chest. "Why?" he asks, wants to pull himself from this foul mood. He doesn't find the comment funny or helpful in any way.

"I don't know," Carlos shrugs—pulls his sunglasses back to his eyes. "Damn funny, is all, dawg." He chuckles at his own response.

Carl stares at him, wants to add more—

Doesn't get the chance—

The Stranger cuts in—

"I just met you, bud, and I'm already sick of yah!"

"He has that effect on you. Don't worry; it'll pass in time," Carl assures Deckard, raising his sun-kissed eyebrows.

"I hope so," he swiftly replies. "Otherwise, it'll be a *helluva* long journey all cooped up." He starts to count with each finger. "I, yourself and Mary. The teen on the bonnet. The funny guy, too! That's five. I'm guessing your injured friend, also? We will be like baked beans in a can. And no one wants to be down-wind when the shitter finally blows," and he grins broadly. Carl smirks too. "Anyone else you got stashed—" he looks at the jeep parked beyond—"in your cozy home?"

The question stays unanswered.

Carlos intervenes. "Am I missing something?" He looks at Carl then the gun-toting stranger secondly, then back towards Carl again. "Excuse me; you don't even know the dude's name… and you're already inviting the guy along with us? Whatever happened to first name introductions, dawg? A bite of lunch. You go straight into foreplay, you're bound to get your dick bitten off! Or come away with a severe infection."

Carl shakes his head, says to Carlos: "It's all fine. We've come to an arrangement." A pause. (Carlos snorts at the statement, considering the basis of the group's decisions was supposed to be a democracy.) Carl continues, regardless. "Oh, yeah. Carlos, this is Deckard. Deckard, this is Carlos Haseltine."

"Driver Extraordinaire," Carlos adds. (*Asshole*, Deckard thinks). And the two continuously gaze at one another; sizing each other up like two raunchy bears rising on hind legs. Two lions about to claw the shit from one another for the right to lead the Pride.

The exchange continues—

Both stand their ground playing who's got the Biggest Dick in the Yard Routine. Sure, Carlos was not-as-fit as he'd like to be (not a Baywatch extra), but had athletic muscle compared to the Newbie's bulk muscle.

It was a Shindig at Highnoon. An Alpha Male Rodeo Fuckfest.

Carl notices the testosterone coming from the two men like morning moisture rising on a humid day, and adds with a flick of a hand; "Naomi is in the back of the jeep; she's er—the *wounded* member of our group."

"Is her injury serious?"

Carl lingers on the question. *Hope not!* He finally answers Deckard's question. "No. Well… erm—" fumbling for words; eyes go wide. "Just a bullet wound."

"Sounds serious to me."

He quickly adds: "The slug was in her shoulder. It went clean through. The pain's what's hurting her the most."

"I'm pretty good at dealing with bullet wounds. Patched up a few friends in my life. Pass me a suture kit, and I'll be your personal Florence Nightingale."

"It's fine. Mary is more than able to attend to our friend's wound now we've got some medical supplies," Carl answers, throwing a look to where Mary was—now—attending to Naomi from the jeep's open door. He continues: "And that's—*Jed* back there!" (Deckard peers behind Carl towards the youngest of the group standing by the jeep), before Carl addresses Carlos. "Deckard is going to help us fix the jeep for a ride."

Carlos scowls at the unceremonious declaration of help.

The fuck he is! he thinks, but says to Carl: “You sure about that, dawg?” Turns back to the Newbie. “What kinda name is Deckard? It sounds like the name of a character that has been looted from a Ridley Scott film. Just Deckard? Or you got another name to go with?”

“Marion,” he answers. “Marion Deckard.”

Carlos scoffs. “Why, Marilyn? That’s a damn girl’s name!”

“Not Marilyn. Marion. My old man was a John Wayne fan. Couldn’t get enough of the ‘Duke’; thought the guy was nothing short of a legend.” Deckard considers his father’s hero for a second longer. Films he watched with his Pa on Sunday afternoons when he was just a sprog. “In fact, the guy was a great man. A bona-fida American Institution.”

“Uh—*no* kidding. I guess it could have been worse!” Carlos utters mischievously. Before Deckard can come back with a suitable reply, Carlos turns back towards Carl. “Are we seriously taking in every stray we find? We barely got enough room as it is in the jeep!”

That finally convinces Carl.

“Yeah. We are. Problem?” Eyebrows raised, waiting for a comeback. None came. “Unless you’ve managed to sort our ride out?”

“I was in the middle of it, dawg. Until I got rudely interrupted by the fucking undead intent on making me into a culinary dish of human meat.”

“Hey…” Carl bends down and picks up Carlos’ gun, hands it to him. “Don’t drop your protection next time, it might just save your life!” Carlos takes the small firearm from Carl’s hand. His jaw flexes, his mouth working to form silent words. Carlos searches for an opportunity for a comeback.

A minute of silence is cut short by—

“Mind if I take a gander at your vehicle?” Deckard asks, breaking the uneasy standoff between the two friends, he assumes. “Best if I’ll make myself handy if you’re going to give me a lift.”

“Sure, be my guest, Marilyn,” Carlos snidely answers and stows his sidearm, removes his eyes from Carl’s and starts to walk towards the jeep, silently. He sticks up a hand, middle finger extended, “This way, cowboy!” and signals for Deckard to follow.

As Deckard passes by, Carl says in a flat tone, “You will get used to the guy.”

“Sure, kid. Whatever you say,” he answers and a few moments later joins Carlos by the engine. Meanwhile, Carl goes back to the derelict bar and continues his search for extra supplies.

10
MECHANICAL WOES

Carlos is under the bonnet, poking at random engine parts. Seconds later, "I've found these in the way of spare parts from the abandoned SUV," he declares and points towards the ground by his feet. Car parts are spread out across the ground in no particular order—just mechanical chaos strewn in Utah sand.

Deckard gazes down, rubs his chin silently; isn't sure if he should be happy or irritated by the Midwesterner's lack of car knowledge. "Hell…" he says in a throat-churning way, studying the useless parts on the ground. "Wow! You stripped all these parts out good and proper. For what reason? You some kind of hoarder?" He remembers several hoarding-related television shows where individuals collected a mishmash of clutter. Nowadays though, everyone seemed to be a hoarder, except instead of collecting collectables, everyone collected firepower, food and water.

Carlos still has his head under the hood of the jeep. "Thought it was the radiator at first," he says. "With the engine spilling a copious amount of smoke into the atmosphere like it was 4th of July. Gasket, secondly. Or this!" He points at something long and metallic in the pit of the engine, finally turns back to the guy. "Now that I think about it, I guess maybe that didn't really answer your questions."

"It didn't answer any of them, bud. And now, I've got about ten more."

Deckard lifts his fedora a little; it offers his face shade from the hot sun. "Move over, bud," he grumbles, "let's take a gander of the mechanical chaos you've created beneath," and gently shoves the Midwesterner out the way.

"Hey, be careful, cowboy!" Carlos quips.

He's about to return the unwelcome shove with an added curse. But sees Mary standing by the rear door shaking her head; her slim lips part: silently she mouths, *Don't be a fool, Carlos!* The warning is clear as day. That's when Carlos sees the vintage revolver straddling the man's thigh and remembers the splattered Z's cranium lying in the sand. He thinks better of it.

A moment later—

Deckard's voice filters from beneath the hood: "Found the problem. Just needs a new fan belt, bud." He points to the fabricated belt. "See the cracks across the ribs." He draws a line across each of the cracks.

Carlos leans beneath the hood, closer, and into the now cooled engine and gazes at the serpentine belt; each rupture reminds him of a crusty, dry desert floor.

Deckard shoulders a glance. "It's the most common indication of a belt simply at the end of its lifespan. Nothing more to it." He points to one of the wrecks by the bar. Carlos follows suit. "Take the belt from the older SUV's engine you haven't gotten around to butchering yet. It might not be an identical match to the one you have, but… with some innovation, the belt should fit nicely into place if we're lucky enough. Think you can manage the job, bud?"

Carlos shrugs. He's annoyed by the stranger's—superior mechanical knowledge—and more than pissed at being bossed around by the 'John Wayne' impersonator. Finally, he mutters, "No sweat, Marilyn." A toothy grin. A snide comment for the cowboy to chew on. "Be back shortly, *pardner*." He walks away, beckons Jed to come along with a whistle like a pet dog being summoned by its master.

The teenager had been quiet since the incident with the two Creeps, hadn't spoken to the stranger, either, and kept by Mary's side as she attended Naomi's wound. Jed finally nods, climbs down from atop the jeep and joins Carlos—heading towards the abandoned vehicles, leaving behind Deckard to disassemble the engine from the patched-up toolkit that lay beside his feet with all the other mechanical bits and bobs.

11
DECISIONS, DECISIONS

An hour goes by.

While Deckard and Carlos steadily work on the engine, Jed stands on lookout duties (on top of the jeep with Carl's binoculars, surveying the area for danger). It was quiet, just a few large black birds gathered nearby, eagerly waiting for the humans to depart so they could feast at the dead fleshy parts which were splattered in the dirt.

In the meantime, Carl finds a camping stove and gas canister hidden away in the back of the soccer mum's minivan. Good enough to sterilize a pair of pliers or a knife blade to cauterize the bullet-hole in Naomi's arm.

Sometime later, Mary gives Naomi some morphine tablets she and Carl had scavenged from the general store hidden beneath an overturned shelving unit behind the checkout, then broke out an array of medical supplies they'd found from the stores untouched first aid box which she'd found in a small side-room. Naomi winced as Mary cleaned out the wound but otherwise didn't complain. The bullet had entered and exited the shoulder, and as Mary looks at her friend's wound, she realizes the bullet hadn't damaged as much flesh as she originally thought. Which was good, because what was about to happen to the Asian girl was going to be incredibly painful.

Now, it's time for the hard part—

While Mary attended her friend, Carl starts a fire on the camping stove. Once it had been going for a while, he finds a valid implement to do the dirty work—wound cauterization. Using Jed's Bowie knife with the ornate leather handle. After cleaning the metal, he puts it in the flames and heats it to the point just before it begins to glow red, pulling it from the fire and letting it cool.

Next, they got a stick for Naomi to bite down on. Gave her some alcohol for Dutch courage. And then comes the moment everyone had been dreading. As Carl held her down, Mary gently presses the hot blade onto the wound, holding it long enough to seal it, but not so long that she burns into her friends healthy body tissue. The Asian girl struggles in pain; eyes watering and teeth clenching on that stick. Then Mary does the same on the back of the girls wound, applying it in short bursts so she doesn't overdo it, checking the bleeding as she went.

After the seventh scream, Naomi feels numb and begins to slip in and out of consciousness from the pain.When she didn't see blood flowing, Mary knew she'd done a bang up job.

Mary knew infection was a real danger with cauterization, making sure to clean the wound afterward as best as she can, dousing the closed wound with alcohol.

The process was tough for the others to endure, but at the same time, it catapulted Mary beyond her normal boundaries of survivalist and straight into

Rambo-like mode, and she had to do whatever it took to continue Naomi's journey towards adulthood.

After ten more minutes—

Silence.

Mary blinks away the start of some tears as she gazes at her friend slumped on the back seat. She finishes stitching the wound. *Hold em' in, girl!* She won't let them come.

Carl touches Mary on her shoulder. "You did brilliantly." He grips tighter. "You did Naomi proud." Adding assertively just in case she needed those extra words of encouragement.

Mary lingered on that compliment for a moment. Finally, she grits her teeth. "Thanks. I'm no nurse, though," she replies while she covers Naomi's wound in a clean gauze pad and wraps it with a bandage.

"But you're the best field-doctor we have!"

The speed of her guilt hits her hard and she wipes a solemn tear away. "Look, I think I maybe messed up back at the silo. I let fear get in the way of our job. I shot Naomi in panic. I… I didn't mean—"

Carl squeezes her shoulder again, cutting her apology off. Knows she feels redemption for her mistake, which led to Naomi's injury. "No worries, Mary. Naomi's fine. She'll be back on her feet soon enough. You did well to pull her out of there. She's still alive, and that's the main outcome. Hopefully the car too! We'll be on our way soon. Okay?"

She catches his gaze. *He's bullshitting*, she thinks, *but he's too kind to me. I hate him for that.* She didn't. "The car… I nearly fucked that up as well!"

"No. No," he says. Whether he liked it or not, a shudder runs up his arms with spindly little feet. In the back of his mind, he knows Mary nearly screwed their ride over. Their entire trip would have ended right now, smack, bang, in the middle of Utah. Instead of the 'safe zone' in Portland. Like any good leader, Carl doesn't dwell on the girl's mistake, he reassures her. "Look at me, Mary." She does. "You keep saying you fucked up—"

"So far, I keep being right."

Carl considered her words then pushes her doubts out of shot. "We all go through hiccups, Mary. But it's the way we deal with those problems that make us all the better. It'll be fine. Trust me. Let's deal with one problem at a time."

It takes a few moments for his words to take effect.

A flimsy smile at the corner of Mary's mouth. "Okay." She turns towards Naomi again and strokes the girls forehead, checks her pulse. Heartbeat. Naomi's vitals was looking good. The Yooper doesn't take her eyes off her friend, just tapes the bandage into place. "There," she says, grimacing. "All done. Wound cleaned and bandaged."

Carl handed Mary a water bottle, knew she'd done a fab job, and finally left both girls in the back of the jeep to be together.

***

Forty minutes later, the hood came down over the engine, and Deckard begins to wipe his hands with an old rag. "Finished!" he calls and picks up his fedora that sits on the wing-mirror and places it onto his fading, dark hair and flicks the rim. "Luckily the jeep was a compatible model with the older-model SUV," he announces as he is surrounded by the group of Gen Z. "It had only one serpentine belt and not multiple belts to remove and replace."

It made his job a lot easier.

Everyone is thoroughly impressed by the man's handiwork and congratulates Deckard one-by-one; even Naomi has managed to drag herself up and out of the back of the jeep slightly tipsy from the alcohol to meet the Newbie—arm in a makeshift sling.

Soon, Marion Deckard was pacing back to the bar where he'd sprung from; he'd earned his Golden Ticket out of the middle of nowhere (he assumes!)

***

Carlos watches as Deckard ducks back into the entrance of the abandoned bar. "I know we're about to have a group discussion!" he says. "What is the plan? What about the Good, the Bad and Marilyn! We seriously giving lifts to strays?" He wears a new clean, black t-shirt that says in big white letters *'What do you Miss Before the End of Days?'*

Carl pauses and thinks for a moment. He turns back immediately to address the fears of the group as they huddle around him. "He helped fixed our ride, guys. We can't just take off and leave the poor guy behind," he states—reasoning why they should welcome him aboard.

"*W-we* know… nothing… about him!" Jed stammers, he's still unsure too.

"About time one of you guys ruled with me," Carlos states, giving the teen a rare smile. He stares at the group and slaps the teen on the back. "That's what I've been saying all along." Another serious look. (Carlos had been saying 'they shouldn't trust the guy' and 'we should leave him behind the first chance we get!' while dismantling the SUV earlier with Jed.) He gives the teen another slap on the back for the support.

What a cheap, prick, Mary thinks, but says, "He saved your life. Or did you forget that major incident already?" She looks at the Midwesterner through a sullen grin. (His face scowled like a bulldog chewing a bumblebee.) And Mary knew Carlos remembers how close he was to death. "I guess we'll find out in due time if we can trust him. Heck, a promise is a promise."

Carl nods.

Startled, Carlos glances at their leader. "You can't be serious, dawg?"

Naomi speaks: "I'm with Mary, y'all," she says in a thick, Texan accent (but her looks resemble that of a Native Osaka Girl); it was due to her mixed heritage. Her mom's Japanese and her father was born and bred in the 'Lone Star State' of Texas.

Carl looks at Naomi, smiles. He's happy he's got her approval. "Is this gonna be a problem?" he states affirmatively, snatching a glare at the Midwesterner.

Carlos crumbles from Carl's gaze. "Shit, dawg, why ya'll lookin' at me? I just wanna know if we can trust the gunslinger. Uh-huh. How we know he ain't got a history of naughty business? Skeletons hanging in the back of a dusty closet? Underneath a garden patio or a garage floor? Crimes committed against other 'Alive' people compared to the Z's who wanna chow down on your skull-candy? We could end up with the same circumstances as before with that drifter giving us directions to that shit-hole-infested-silo-of-a slaughterhouse."

A breeze carrying the distant stink of the recently deceased corpses of the dead drifted through the hot air reaching their nostrils in turn like a hot beef pie left out on a window ledge to cool.

Carl, Mary, and Naomi stare; the Midwesterner's reasoning why Deckard couldn't—shouldn't—be allowed to join them on the trip were out in the open for all of them to consider. Dissect.

"Listen, it's not gonna be like before. Its gonna be different. This time we are in control of the situation," Carl promises.

"So you keep saying," Carlos interrupts.

Carl nods, or his head wobbles. When he speaks again, his words are plain and simple. "Okay, Carlos. We put it to a vote. Deckard to stay? Raise your hands." Both girls nod in agreement—hands straight up. Jed bites his fingernail nervously, shuffles away from Carlos (his hand goes up: it's a unanimous victory).

Carlos looks at the teen.

"I thought you had my back, Judas!" (Jed falls quiet), and so does Carlos.

"So it's settled. We take Deckard along on the trip. We don't need to take him as far as we're going. He can get off whenever or wherever he likes. Any funny business and he's gone too. Agreed?"

There's another universal show of nods.

Carl lingers a little while longer, expecting a comeback, a peep from the Midwesterner: nothing came.

12
WELCOME ABOARD

Marion Deckard eventually reappears through the only remaining saloon-style door of the former, beloved bar on the outskirts of a rundown town in the middle of nowhere. He carries a military survival bag over his shoulders. He'd half expected a plume of dirt from a jeep frantically speeding away in the distance but was pleasantly surprised to find the group of kids still waiting around for him, and a smile ripens his grizzled face.

"We're all happy to have you along on our travels," Carl welcomes the newest member of the group with an outstretched hand and a smile.

(He considers the proposal for a second, knows a lie when he hears one.) Eventually, Deckard takes the young lads hand. "All right, kid. That does it." He shakes. A grin forms. "I appreciate the hospitality."

In front of him, the two girls, Mary and Naomi, sit on the car's hood. Each smiles a warm welcome. While the youngest by far, Jed begins to rearrange the luggage on the roof rack, the teen making for extra room inside the vehicle for another body. Meantime, Carlos *(the asshat,* Deckard thinks*)* sits behind the wheel—eyes shaded by sunglasses—and frankly not giving a shit about the whole damn deal.

"The car drives better than it looks!" Naomi adds, as she hops down off the bonnet, her injured arm in a sling, and approaches the new guy.

"Well, we'll just have to find out, Miss—"

"Naomi." She gestures with her other hand. "Naomi will do."

"Sure will, Miss—*I mean*, Naomi," he says.

Naomi glances inside the jeep. She finds the Midwesterner casually glaring through the tinted window as they chat away. He hides behind his expensive glasses, sulking like a whimpering dog in a kennel who's been disciplined by its master. "Don't mind the dickhead, he's just not a fan of strangers," she says. From within the car, Carlos knows all eyes are on him, and he pretends not to notice.

Deckard arches towards her. Whispers back: *"I know the feeling. Thanks."* It brings a laugh from her. "Where can I store my bag?"

Carl comes around. "Up top!" he answers and holds out a hand for the one-piece luggage. Deckard hands the duffel bag over to the kid who takes the weight with both hands (the bag is actually a lot heavier than he'd imagined it would be). "Heavy!" Carl adds but doesn't ask what's inside. He knows never to ask a stranger what he's carrying until they'd chatted a bit.

Deckard helps to lift the bag to its new resting place above the jeep, glimpses of his old life poking through the top. Jed takes it, places it on the roof-rack and starts to tie a line around the fabricated bag, and passes the other end to Carl, who starts pulling on the line, knots it into place.

"So… where to?"

"Portland."
"Pacific Northwest, huh?"
"Yeah, Oregon."
"Be nice this time of year."
Carl looks at him. "Yeah. Hope so. Never been before."

PART TWO

ROAD TRIP

13
ROAD BUDDIES

With their ride fixed, Naomi's wound treated and any extra supplies and gas they'd scavenged safely stored on the roof and the back of the jeep, the derelict bar on the edge of some, long forgotten town breezed away into the hazy distant background. A few miles west, and they were absolutely alone on the road in the middle of Mormon country, not meeting a single car coming in either direction.

The chances were slim (they were always slim). But once or twice they thought they saw a vehicle, Carlos decreasing the jeep cautiously, just in case of other survivors. But every time they approached the vehicles, they were either abandoned by the sides of the road out of gas or just another wreck long abandoned by their former owners.

Carlos floored the gas, sending a plume of dirt and fumes into the hot air. The Midwesterner made a point of shifting again really loudly, engine revving in an unequivocal statement. He was impressed by how the jeep drove, how fast and quiet the new fan belt blended in with its new surroundings. Deckard had done a brilliant job at fixing the engine, and the same could be said about the guy mingling with the group.

"*Purrs* like a kitten, Marilyn!" Carlos hoots, hands on the wheel, ten and two. He feels the need to call the guy after 'Marilyn Monroe' the famous American actress, instead of his proper name, 'Marion', even though everyone else was calling their new driving companion by his last name. "You a mechanic in a former life, Marilyn?" he says, overjoyed at being behind the wheel once again, and away from the two decapitated Creeps.

The newest member of the group had taken the front passenger seat, relegating the youngest member—Jed, to the boot. (It was a tight squeeze, but it was what it was. Plus the teenager was the thinnest out of all of them, so it made it easier for him to squeeze in with the rest of the supplies.)

"Not quite, Carlos," he answers. "Marine, actually. Captain."

Carlos thinks for a moment, then says: "*Woohoo!* I guess we should be saluting you? Or calling you, Captain?"

"No," he replies, his voice an empty echo of a gun chamber. "Why, Captain? You weren't in my unit!" And shrugs his shoulders looking across at the Midwesterner behind the wheel. "Besides, I thought you got a kick from calling me Marilyn! Besides, I ain't no darn dame."

In the back, Mary lets out a snigger of amusement.

Carlos smirks, his lips forming into a smile. He'd been found out. "How'd you guess?"

"You were emphasizing the 'Blond Bombshell' part much more than you should have been."

Carlos lifts a hand—drops it hard onto the wheel. "Fair do's, dawg! I'll stop." He whistles softly to himself before continuing in a lighter tone. "I guess you saw a lot of action when the world ended, huh? And I bet those skills still come in handy now? Hey, Marion!" (He correctly uses Deckard's birth-certificate name for the very first time.)

"You could say that."

From behind the passenger seat, the voice of Mary: "Huh, you should know! The guy saved your hide within a minute of seeing your withering face rolling around in the dirt, Carlos!" Her quip hits home hard like a punch in World Heavyweight fight decider. Carlos glares hard-out at Mary in the overhead mirror, tries to think of a comeback and desists after a few seconds, carries on driving, ten and two.

So annoying.

That unsettles him, it seems, and Mary suppresses a smug grin, making sure to capture the moment for a later time.

"Where were you when civilization crumbled? What's your story?" Carl asks taking the lead in the questioning, and also diffusing the tension between his friends at the same time.

Carl sits behind the driver's seat next to Naomi. The Texan girl had dozed off from the combo of liquor and morphine and was now snuggled in a deep dream underneath Carl's arm. The awakened group of friends are eager to find out any info regarding their new road-buddy.

"It's not really worth telling."

"Why don't you let us be the judge of that?"

"My own X-Factor committee?"

Mary laughs. "Something of that nature. Yeah." She watches him with intensity. All around the jeep the others wait eagerly too.

Deckard doesn't hold back.

"Up in Canada. St. John's, Newfoundland to be precise. Training camp. New recruits and general exercises for a year or so. It was eerily calm up there for a while. And then, all of a sudden, the radio and television and internet were exploding with news, and everything was all zombies this and undead that, and every goddamn airplane back home was grounded for quarantine." He leans back in the seat as if he's unloading a heavy burden. "Stupid idea, if you ask me. But I guess the ol' U.S government had to do it to stop the spread of infection to the rest of the world. Plus the Federal Government shutdown played a major part in operations. Republicans. Democrats. I guess no one won in the end, even when the undead was knocking down the front door to the House of Representatives."

Carlos interjects: "Too fucking right, they did!"

"Jeez, just let the man speak!" Mary says from the back.

Carlos isn't to bothered by this as she is. He laughs it off. "'Kay, no need to get your panties in a twist, Kansas!"

A full minute goes by, and Deckard ignores the conversation between the two frenemies and flicks his fedora with a middle finger. They finally stop.

"You see, the airlines were the initial carriers. And then everybody with any kinda medals was yelling at my unit to clean our weapons and gear up and board a bus. We headed to the border and held that position for a while. We ended up as a secondary security measure, a backup to the (CBSA) Canada Border Services

Agency and the (RCMP) the Mounties, screening the fleeing civilians who were trying to cross into Canada from Vermont and New York."

"Jesus. Yeah. I remember," Carl says. "Everyone got the same friggin' idea once the airports and private airfields shut their doors to the general public. Let's all just escape into our neighbor's backyard! Sure! It sounded like a great idea, huh?"

Deckard nods. "Our orders were to process all evacuees and check for 'Infection' bites, scratches, high-temperatures, etc. We screened every citizen that wanted to cross onto Canadian soil. In those first few weeks, the Canadian government only received three suspected cases of infection. Yeah, the protocols set by the top brass, actually held for a while, and daily life seemed just to go along as normal."

"But..." Carlos chipped in. "There's always a but?"

The invisible hands clutching Deckard's memory kick into gear. "Sure. You're right. We weren't processing the lines quickly enough. Jesus, all everyone wanted to do was to escape from the walking dead of their former loved ones. Not patiently wait in an orderly line getting screened for the epidemic contagion of the century!" He seethes at his own words. "Eventually, fights broke out, and acts of violence occurred in the long lines that stretched hundreds of miles. One of my squad got stabbed, another shot. Five more died in similar incidents. Multiple civilians."

"Jesus!" Mary says, her words filled with genuine sorrow for those fleeing families. But that was a long time ago, and she hoped enough of those people did pass Canada's borders unharmed.

"I remember, everyone still had access to the radio and online devices with live images or recorded footage around the globe," Carl states.

"Yeah, kid. People became *loco-crazy*, and the rumors flowing through the stuck six million plus fleeing US citizens were that any day now, Canada was about to shut her once 'All Welcoming' borders on them and give everyone a two-fingered All-American Salute."

Jed nervously asks, "*T-that* can't be right?" propping himself up on the backseat like a Doberman going on a trip with its master.

"Is that true? Did that actually happen?" Mary asks, edging towards the front of the car. She starts to curl a dangling lock of hair that's come loose beneath her headband around a solemn finger; her blond locks claiming identity from her Finnish ancestry.

Mary remembers how close her home town was from Canada's border: a stone's throw. Her old school friends, even some of her remaining family: five cousins and two remaining aunts were all still living in and nearby Marquette, a major port town that nestles on Lake Superior. Hoped some of her family just took their rowing boat over to the safe lands of Canada when the outbreak hit.

Carlos says, "Do the math, you two. It's the real deal."

The image of Canada shutting her borders on its closest neighbor—and American citizens stirs an unwelcome silence in the jeep (and the memories of seeing all those thousands of people stuck at the border captured by the rolling cameras of every U.S broadcaster pulled at their heartstrings).

"I'm not sure. I was on the front line in the thick of the action trying to stop the infection from spreading outta the US and into its damn neighbor's backyard," Deckard answers Mary's question. "Maybe some 'Big Old Politician' figured out on Parliament Hill, first and foremost, there was no way to save everyone, and secondly, the outbreak was too far widespread." Turning from his seat, he asks the kids in the back: "But what would your government do if you had six million-plus uninvited refugees rock up to your front door and ask to be let in? How would your social welfare handle all those hungry mouths? Shelter all those sleepy heads? How the hell do you patrol the International Boundry? The Canada–United States border is the longest international border in the world between two countries. Fact. We had limited resources."

Everyone contemplates the questions coming from the ex-Marine.

Deckard takes a deep breath before continuing. "Yeah, before we knew what was happening, the tension and unrest had already started, and those lines of impatient refugees had bubbled to the surface. Before my unit and others alike could take control of the situation, the borders were breached, and—"

"Jesus! Couldn't you have stopped them?"

Deckard looks at the young lad poking his head over the backseat, hands gripping the upholstery. "My unit was a hundred strong. The frontline CBSA staff which patrolled along the 8,000 or so kilometers of the International Boundary another six hundred. Remember the film, Zulu?"

The mention of the 1964 British war film depicting the Battle of Rorke's Drift between the small British outpost and the 4,000 strong Zulus in January 1879 was met by a barrage of confused stares, mainly from Jed and Mary.

On the other hand, Carl nodded, he remembered the film starring the legendary English actor Michael Caine, he'd liked to watch that film when he was younger with his pop too.

"It was a catastrophic failure on our part in underwhelming the entire situation. Before we knew what was happening, we had lost control of our positions and the border, and then…"

Mary finishes: "Canada fell?"

"Yes. She. Did." Each word flutters from Deckard's patriotic mouth. *The whole damn country collapsed!* He recalls the memory as if it had only happened yesterday before his voice becomes stronger. "What could we do? Hundreds of thousands of people crossed the border between our two countries when we lost control, and any of those perhaps thousands were infected!"

"What did you and your unit do?"

Deckard peers back at the youngster. "We didn't open fire on the crowds of refugees if that's what you meant!" (The teen sits uncomfortably in the boot of the jeep and breathes a sigh of relief.) "Half my unit had family in the States. We had no choice but to let those fleeing civilians through our checkpoints. In the end, when the stampede of the crowds had dwindled, my unit fell back and regrouped at a nearby base. We waited for orders. None came."

"At least you didn't open fire, like our Mexican compatriots on the other border," Carl says in an uneven tone. "How many uninfected did they kill? In the thousands, maybe tens of thousands if I remember rightly!"

"I guess so," Deckard agrees. "Last I heard, Mexico had it easy, what with them having that huge wall protecting them and all!"

The thought brings a barrage of amused looks to the entire group.

Mary grimaces. "Yeah. Thank God for our former-tanned-businessman-turned President and his bright ideas, huh! He diverted millions of Federal funds from Emergency services and other federal programs to finance the construction of barriers along the U.S.-Mexico border."

"And adding fucking machine gun towers all the way across those walls like some kind of homage to John Carpenter's Escape from L.A." Carlos sarcastically adds. "Made it even easier for the Mexicans to keep on plowing American lives into the ground."

"I remember the acting defense secretary at the time told reporters that he had set in motion a process to identify candidates, where the President could drain more money from. The armed forces were one of them." The hairs on Deckard's neck stand as he mimics the line he'd never forgotten. "I just want to make a point of this," he says in the former, defense secretary's voice. "We are following the law, using the rules, and we're not bending the rules, O.K.?"

***

Since the last administration, the US government had achieved funding for the President's boldest and prominent campaign pledges: 'I will build a great wall on our southern border, and I'll have Mexico pay for that wall,' the President said during his campaign speech. And after continuous Government shutdowns, and the Democrats in Congress unwilling to vote for a bill providing that money, for the President—the wall was finally built across the Mexican-American frontline with significant private investments, funded from U.S. taxpayers, and through a renegotiated trade deal that eventually cleared U.S. Congress.

It was built to keep out illegal immigrants entering America, but effectively it had enclosed the land off from the rest of North America, and in the early days had sealed the fate of millions of Americans trying to escape the Z-pandemic. Some hardline US politicians said that the hostile act of war—*from* the Mexican president, on the American people trying to flee the epidemic was retribution for the wall being built in the first place, and the illegal deportation of millions of illegal Mexicans. And to make the wall a deterrent for the smugglers—on both sides of the border—every hundred yards a heavy fortified gun placement was constructed.

But eventually the infected spilled over—or under—thanks to the constant 'smuggling' tunnels. And the great wall and the early survivors who were granted asylum under the New Mexican Reserve Treaty between Mexico and America were quickly on the run again as the disease rapidly spread through Central America then South America like wildfire.

***

"So—what happened with your unit?" Mary asks, nervous of the answer she'll receive from the man. "Why did you leave your position?"

Deckard looks at her for a moment, before his war-torn eyes slip closed, remembering those troubled times of hopelessness. "We waited patiently for our orders from the high branch for a couple of weeks. Guessed they… they forgot about us," he quips, opens them again. "We had a solid Command Center an hour from the border: high walls, a formidable defense. It was suitable at first, almost comfortable. We kept the Infected at bay for a while. But half of my unit wanted to head back to the States to see if they could find their family. You know, blood is thicker than water and all that jazz. The NCOs and I couldn't force anyone to stay. We had to make our own choices. We knew this. That's why many chose to leave the compound. But once they had gone, it left the compound defenses weakened, and one night in the middle of a torrential storm the walls were breached by a massive horde. Hell, all hell broke loose, and within an hour or two, the base became overrun with the infected and fell."

The car fell eerily quiet, waiting for the ex-Marine to continue with the grim tale.

"We had to cut our losses. If we stayed in the compound, we were dead anyway. A few of us made it out alive, took what we needed to survive, and decided to venture back onto US soil. I split with my group back in Oklahoma City and been on the move ever since. Occasionally I'd find settlements, mostly small band of survivors dotted here and there. Sometimes, solo survivalists who'd 'bugged out' before the outbreak, but otherwise, I'd try to keep away from settlements and people. I only make contact if I have a sense that everything will be okay."

"Just like us!" Carl says, more of a statement than a question.

He nods.

"More so, we just bumped into one another." He forms a smile. "But, yeah. You're right."

Her heart twists in her chest like a fish in a net. "You got a family?" Mary asks.

"Car collision killed my parents when I was seventeen. Had a brother, once, but lost contact with him the year after. Family squabble, you know how it is sometimes. No other siblings to speak of. That's why I headed back to good old Oklahoma. Fond memories of the place, but there's nothing left to speak of the Cherokee Nation anymore. Shame really, she was a glorious city full of lovely people. Friendly. Lively. Great bars too."

"Shit, dawg!" Carlos curses and throws a look at the ex-Marine. "You know… we're all orphans these days. Right?" and he keeps on the gas, the jeep a steady pace.

"I guess in a way, we are!"

By the time Deckard is done with his story the jeep falls quiet once again.

14
MARY AND NAOMI'S STORY

They drove quietly for a while without undue excitement or panic across expanses of desert and saw no other cars on the road. They avoided any large towns or population centers if they saw signs of the infected and took the back roads if possible. But sooner or later, they had to drive through a few towns, always aware of their surroundings. The smallish sounds from Zs and ghostly ghouls could be heard. Creaks of gates and wooden shutters. Blinds flapping loosely in broken lounge windows.

They passed isolated and dry gas stations with rows of rusting abandoned vehicles jamming the lanes. The concrete forecourts had handwritten signs that said: NO MORE GAS. Occasionally they saw rows of abandoned and boarded up houses, some on a hillside overlooking Utah Lake. In the far distance, on the other shoreline, Provo Peak rising above the thin cloud-line.

It was subtle at first, subtle enough that no one noticed the uneasy tension building in the jeep with no one talking to one another until the deadlock was finally broken.

"You kid's sparse on chit chat?" Deckard asks. "I don't know anything about you all. Mind telling me what you did prior—"

"—*you mean* before the world turned to shit!" Carlos finishes the sentence, not bothering to look at the ex-Marine, his hands on the wheels, his eyes fully focused on the road ahead.

"Sounds correct," he replies, turns to Mary. "If you don't mind me asking, where did a pretty girl like you originate from?"

Mary found herself blushing at the small compliment but nevertheless gave an answer: "I worked for a vegan deli in New York, nestled in Manhattan's lovely Lower East Side. The shop was happily named 'Vegan Delicatessen.' It was a very niche market, and it suited me down to the ground. The pay packet was okay, the hours were reasonable, and I enjoyed meeting new people. I loved New York in the winter months, especially looking out for snow moons. But I originally call Michigan home! *Go Michigan Wolverines. Go! Go!*" she chants fondly as if she's a cheerleader inspiring her home basketball team from the sidelines.

Looking at the girl a smile ripens the ex-Marine's face. "Never been to the Big Apple, always wanted to go, though but never had a chance once I started training. New York, New York, what a city hey!" he says, posing in his best Frank Sinatra voice.

"You would have loved the city. The parks, the people—it was all so great before the outbreak tore it apart." A tear runs down Mary's cheek as she remembers how the city used to be. The people she met. The friends she made while living in the great City of Hope. She wipes her eye quickly before anyone notices.

Deckard sees the Michiganian's tear and quickly changes the subject. Next up, he nods at Naomi. The Asian girl was still sleeping on Carl's chest, her arm in a sling. "What about Sleeping Beauty?"

Mary looks around. "Naomi! She's a Texas native, lived her whole life back in Dallas. Homegirl at heart, Lone Star State all the way. She was a wedding planner, really passionate at her job. Her mother was from Japan, and was the one who took her on as her understudy in the family business." She lets out a little laugh. "And a gun enthusiast too."

"You don't say!" Deckard chuckles. He's amused how the Asian's job and hobby went so hand-in-hand. The Marine catches Carl gazing at Sleeping Beauty in the rear-view mirror. "Are you two an item?" he asks, hoping to be right for the second time of asking.

***

Carl had known Naomi for several months now since he'd first met her and her—now—deceased fiance on a supply run. He'd been in a scavenger group of five others when they'd stumbled on a half-a-dozen trapped survivors fighting for their lives in a derelict convenience store. Naomi and her group were surrounded and out of ammo, and the store was being overrun fast by a mob of infected Zs: *too many* when Carl thought back. It was then when he'd come to the group's rescue, blowing dead-after-dead away in a desperate attempt to help the survivors, that Carl saw Naomi for the very first time. Her black hair drenched in sweat. Eyes wide with terror, but fear never held her back. She shielded the rest of her group from the advancing infected with only the butt of her hunting rifle.

Carl could still see clearly Naomi's last moments. The decomposing 'dead' advancing at her. The girl's realization that this was how practically all living things born on Earth have died—with teeth tearing through their muscle and bones.

The rest you'd say was history, but unfortunately, on that day Naomi's fiance was bitten (and you never recover from a bite), and the girl never recovered from losing her childhood sweetheart and never truly understood how Carl felt about her.

Carl had fallen madly in love with Naomi Osaka Jefferson, and he was sure she was the one. He knew it in his heart, felt happier and more content than he'd ever felt in his life when he was around her. He was wilfully drowning in the girl's black hair; her hair unwashed for the past week, but still had the slightest hint of strawberries. He looked back at the Marine; the question still burning brightly in his mind.

"No," he finally answers. "We're not an item. Just friends."

15
CARL AND CARLOS' BACKSTORY

Deckard didn't press with the conversation. He could see it in the kid's eyes that he wasn't ready to explore his—*inner feelings*—with the rest of the group, and especially with a stranger he'd recently met. Instead, he asks: "What's your story, kid?"

Carl clears his throat and carries on with the fakest-of-fake smiles ever to produce a smile on a conveyer-belt-of-fake smile. "I was born at Fort Lawton Army Hospital in Seattle, Washington. Mum and dad both served, office jobs mostly. Never combat. Both were duty-driven, though."

Deckard knows the story. "It's a lonely place to be."

"Uh-ha. Mismatched family schedules... long work trips… financial stress and crazy work hours. Sounds like modern American family life, right?" Carl replies, fondly remembering his crazy upbringing.

"Throw in the risk of injury or death in the workplace. A strict culture of conformity and you've got the life of a family in the armed forces, kid."

Carl felt angst-ridden as the memories of his childhood flooded back. "Yip. I was always on the move from one place or the other. When I was old enough to make my own decisions, I moved away and took a two-year course at Art College, eventually settling in New York," he hooks a wink over to the front of the jeep, "where I met Carlos."

"We were escaping across the Hudson River to the New Jersey side."

"Remember, you had that large white chef's hat on! Your whites weren't exactly white no more, and you had two meat cleavers in your hands."

"Yeah. I remember, dawg!" Carlos grins, the memory fresh in his mind. "I always wanted one of those chef's hats."

Deckard scratches his chin; the bristle was thick. "You two been on the move ever since?"

The Midwesterner takes the lead: "Yeah. We knew the city was lost when the living dead were coming right up Third Avenue. I was working in the kitchens at one of those fancy-dancy restaurants where all those rich folks went to eat their healthy lunches filled with lettuce and whatever crap rabbits ate. Back then, everyone wanted to be healthier. Gluten-free. Vegan free, no-calories-proper-food free, etc." Carlos gazes out of the window, recalling his former life as a kitchen hand. "God—*the markup* on those meals was so hideously high. Just five of those skinny-ass lunches added up to more than I earnt for the entire week!"

As Carlos speaks, his distaste for the extreme wealthy is obvious. At the same time, the others sit tentatively engrossed with the tale.

"For me, the most surreal moment was standing in the kitchen with some of the lower-paid staff looking out of the cubby hole and into the restaurant. All of us watching the undead tear those rich, healthy folks apart. I'd never seen panic like that in my whole life!"

"Oh my God," Mary mouths, shocked by his words. "You never told me this before."

"You never asked!"

"Holy shit!" Jed adds, his voice rising from behind them all.

Carlos continues. "I know, right! I couldn't focus on anything over all those terrifying screams. I just knew I had to escape. Take a holiday that would last forever. I took those meat cleavers and stole that fucking white hat from a shitty chef who always looked down upon the lower workers. Funny thing; that cowardly bastard was trying to hide behind the ones who he'd always stood upon. So, I drove a path straight through those zombie bastards like Lewis and Clark crossing the western portion of the United States, and a few of us managed to escape."

"*Jesus!* Was everybody this messed up when the world ended?" Mary wonders aloud.

"Times like that, you just gotta disconnect from the world and do whatever it takes to survive. I did, and here I am now driving your lame asses around like Miss Daisy."

"Sounds like you threw down some *ghouls* back in the day, Carlos!" Deckard says in a measured voice, thoroughly impressed by the Midwesterner's backstory.

"Sure did, dawg," he answers. "Best decision I ever made was to get out of Dodge before the celebrity elected Mayor, and his Fucking Retarded Bureaucrats tried to close the city off."

"Absolutely. I'm behind you a 100percent," Carl agrees. He remembers how quickly the unstoppable mass of infected had spread through the boroughs of New York and how the Mayor had ordered the entire city to be separated from the rest of the States—all through his social media feeds. (Predictably, not a lot of residents paid attention to the warning.)

It was a completely botched job of a fuck-fest.

***

Within a week of hitting New York City, the dead had spread throughout the East Coast, overrunning Philadelphia, Boston, and Washington DC. Likewise, Seattle, Vancouver, San Francisco, and Los Angeles fell on the Western Coast.

And the infected hordes kept growing… and growing… until… 35 days later, much of the US was conquered (though, surprisingly, not all of it). The undead hadn't yet made it to New Orleans or Florida. Maybe if they had been faster, it would have all been different. Maybe the summer's unconventional high heatwave did its part in slowing the dead down? Perhaps, even if the airlines had imposed that 'no-fly' ban sooner rather than later or the (CDC) Centers for Disease Control and Prevention had acted quicker when a man in Tallahassee was infected from a visiting relative escaping from Washington.

Shortly after the first outbreaks, the world's governments started suggesting that maybe the U.S. should ban its citizens or foreign nationals on their U.S.

holidays from leaving the country, and the pandemic wouldn't have spread to every corner of the globe.

It took three months for the dead to overrun the entire United States. Cities fell astonishingly quickly. But zombies were much slower to spread into rural areas (and areas like the northern Rockies and the Appalachian Mountains at the highest point in Mount Mitchell in North Carolina remained zombie-free for a long time).

***

"It was a shitstorm in a teacup waiting to happen," Carl says, laying a hand on his compatriot's shoulder. A gut-clenching moment passes between the two, and for a fleeting moment, their friendship comes thundering back like a locomotive along a track.

Suddenly, Carlos says, "It's going to be bumpy for a moment or two, guys!"

He shifts gears and steers carefully around a mud-filled sinkhole that has opened up in the middle of the road; brown mud spat from the tires covering the bonnet and windows as the jeep bucked a small trench at the side of the road. Deep within the hole, covered with years of sloppy green swampy water, a glimpse of rusted metal glitters back like a dime dropped in the mud. (The sight is a miserable-fear-intoxicated-moment-of-despair for the group, but they eventually pass the hole, and the sunken contents, and drive onward.)

Minutes later, Carlos looks over to the ex-Marine. "I'm from a small town. Corydon, originally!" he says, while the window-wipers clear his field-of-vision.

Deckard shrugs his shoulders.

"Sorry. Don't know the place!"

"Wouldn't expect you to.

"It's in the Harrison Township, Harrison County, Indiana. Located north of the Ohio River in the extreme southern part of the U.S. state of Indiana, and I mean the extreme southern part!" The Midwesterner smirks as he remembers his birth place.

Jed gazes back with raised eyebrows, as did Mary.

Carlos stares at them, notices their blank expressions. Finally, gazing at the ex-Marine's equally blank face, he laughs. "See, Marion; no one knows that place even existed. Hell… I don't even think the people who lived in Corydon knew the town existed."

"Sounds pretty grim to me."

"*Aaggghhh*, no biggie. Like I said," Carlos explains, "it's just another hole-of-a-town that has been sucked dry of life since this country ceased to be the Land of the Free and Living. It's fine. I'm not offended. The whole place is gone now."

Deckard frowns at the Midwesterner's reply, understands all across the States that similar towns were all gone.

And Carlos continues driving.

16
JED'S STORY

Deckard tilts his fedora, taking in everything that the kids had to say. It seemed like all of them had been through the meat grinder—literally—and had a story or two to tell. Then the ex-Marine gazed back towards the youngest of the group. Jed reminded him of a young Ron Howard—*portraying* Happy Days' Richie Cunningham with his ginger hair and a wry smile.

"What about you, kiddo?"

Jed gawps back from the back of the jeep, tweaks his MSL cap and stammers nervously. "*M-my* whole family's from *S-san F-fran.* I have three sisters, Nicole, Eli, who are—" he stops himself mid-sentence from the undeniable truth that his sisters were gone, "were younger than me, and Audrey who ran her own PR firm with her husband, Matt. They had a daughter, Quinn. I used to do crazy stuff with her when I was younger, like painting her mom's bedroom a pumpkin color when Audrey was away on a business trip one weekend. One side of their dog turned orange as it decided to sleep next to the freshly painted wall." Jed lets out a little laugh at the fond memories. "I had an older brother too; John, he worked for MLS.Fan.com (Major League Soccer). It was the online forum for all the fans to talk about footy."

"Is that who gave you your cap, your brother?"

Jed tweaks his blue and white cap once again before answering. "Yes. John got me hooked on soccer when I was younger. My brother used to take me to the home games at Avaya Stadium whenever he could." He hesitates for a second. "Do you—I mean, *did* you follow soccer?"

"No. Wasn't much a fan, to be honest, kiddo," Deckard says. "Basketball was more of my game. Oklahoma City Thunder with that exciting Kiwi export—*Steven Adams.* A talented fella with some slick moves. Big and grizzly too. He quickly grew into one of the NBA's best centers. Came away with a career-high 30 rebounds and averaging a career-high in points. A constant starter for the All-Star games in five consecutive seasons. Oh. Hell. Adams was a great—" That's when Deckard knows he's been swept away in his passion for the game and stops himself from saying too much more.

The teen makes eye-contact with the man, doesn't understand half the sports jargon but smiles anyway. He buries his memories and continues. "My Mom and Dad were both accountants, and I was a computer whiz graduating early into Academy before San Francisco got hit. I also had a pet dog named 'Wilson the Wonder Dog'; it was a German Shephard…"

"*Jeez,* Jed," Carlos mutters from behind the wheel. "I don't think Captain Marion wants to know your entire life story."

The words seem to incense Deckard even further, but he ignores the Midwesterner's subtly shitty standards of sympathy for the teenager. Instead, flashes the youth a smile. "Sounds like a lovely family you have there, kiddo."

"I know," Jed nods to the question and counters, "I mean… I did."

“I’m sure they’re at peace now,” Deckard adds kindly.

Jed flashes a thoughtful smile back towards the ex-Marine before looking through the passenger window; his past temporarily lost. His memories fading. He stares at the trees zipping by, imagining Mario, the Italian plumber trying to keep up with the jeep, jumping over obstacles and avoiding enemies. But instead of Goombas and Hammer Bro’s—the original baddies of the popular Nintendo game—they were replaced by flesh-hungry zombies. (Funny thing was, you could kill all those baddies with a bump to the head.)

Seconds later, he leaves the imaginary game and the new visible hostile world behind. “Yeah, you’re right!” he nods. “They probably are. But that was a long time ago. I’ve got an adopted family now,” and he gestures to the others with a firm smile. Mary nestles a hand onto the teen’s shoulder and grips tightly like a supportive parent. Jed appreciates the small gesture and frowns at her.

As the outside world passes, a couple of isolated houses, and shops, here and there. Some of them run-down, others boarded up by barricades later, the ex-Marine thinks about the youngest member of the group’s shitty backstory.

And then fades back to nothing again.

“How’d you end up with these knuckleheads, kiddo?”

“I was on a school excursion to New York when San Fran became overrun with Zs. I tried to make my way back home to my family with a few classmates after the teachers had ditched us.”

Carl mutters: “Talk about responsibility!”

“I hoped the dead dragged those damn bastards to the depths of hell, for leaving you to fend for yourself, Jed,” Carlos adds unashamedly as he drives around three slow-moving-flesh eaters shambling across the deserted road. One was tall and thin; ribcage exposed through a maroon-colored shirt. The other two were short, clumps of hair missing from their heads and skinny also; bulging ribcages hidden beneath torn discolored t-shirts.

Mary says: “Carlos, that’s so cruel!” She steals a look at the three dead corpses shuffling together like friends on a walk, wondering how long they’d been crossing the countryside side-by-side.

“What you getting jacked-up about? Did I hit a sweet-spot!” Carlos retorts, throwing a dismissive glance over his shoulder. “Teachers, *huh!* Educated my ass. The bastards needed to be taught a lesson for leaving Jed all alone in New York. *Christ*, Mary! Marvel’s Street Level Heroes weren’t going to come to his rescue.”

She shakes her head, not understanding half of the lingo coming from his mouth. “Look, there are a billion things which could have made those teachers give up their responsibilities. But… I can tell you, the undead was one of them. Probably top of their agenda!”

“Tell that to Jed and his fucking dead classmates,” he unashamedly scoffs.

Mary looks back, she wants to say more, opens her mouth too—

“He’s right. Maybe that’s what they deserved,” Jed hesitantly replies, breaking the heated exchange between his two friends.

Jed had never forgiven those teachers for abandoning him and his classmates when the outbreak happened. But was too young to realize those people must have had other responsibilities besides him and his classmates: other lives, spouses, children, etc. But still, he'd lost three best friends on that School Field Trip of Death, and there was no forgiveness for that abandonment in his heart.

Mary grips harder.

The teen gulps back the doubts.

"But no good people were willing to give a lift to a bunch of 13 year-olds fleeing New York during a zombie apocalypse. In the end, I ended up alone and ran into Carl and Carlos along the way," he says from the back of the jeep. "Never made it back to my home in San Fran, to my family."

Mary thinks but does not say: *I feel for him, I truly do.*

Seconds pass.

Jed carries on. "Been with these guys for a long time now. Met Mary a month after we left New York and Naomi back at base when Carl brought her in. We had a camp a week away before we ran into you. It was a sweet deal; I liked the people there, I got to bunk with a few friends I made over the years."

Deckard nods approvingly as the youngster categorizes the events of how he'd met each of the others in a handy A to Z pamphlet. Also understands that everyone in the car meant a great deal to the youngest of the group.

"Then we decided to follow…" and Jed stops short.

Deckard notices there was a growing pause—sees both Mary and Carl staring at the youngster. *What were these kids following?* He thinks, wanting to no more.

Jed was just now becoming aware of his slip. He finally realizes Mary and Carl are glaring at him, mouthing at him to *stop talking, you're telling him too much!*

He does.

And they continue down the road in quietness.

17
UNDENIABLE TRUTHS

The former Marine noticed the way the teen had just stopped talking and knew something wasn't right. Taking control of the conversation, he asks, "So why aren't we heading back to your camp? What drove you kids out this far? What were—or are you looking for all the way in Portland?"

Reaction. Carl nervously looks at Mary. Mary, in turn, looks at Jed. The teenager at both of his road-buddies. Meanwhile, up front, Carlos is strangely quiet like a thief had stolen his voice. One false word and the real reason they're on the road will bubble to the surface. Carl suddenly feels the weight of the man's stare and Naomi's subtle frame upon his ribs; her body feels like a 100 lb weights, while Deckard's questions feel heavier, as evident by his thousand-yard stare.

Carl has to shift his body to get comfy, finally clears his throat. "Just exploring the land. Get some idea of what's out this way."

Deckard's eyes dart around the interior of the jeep. *Something's not right.* He thinks. Knows it and thumbs his tanned fedora. "Don't try and bullshit a bullshitter, kid!"

A solid, monolithic silence sat in the vehicle as the friends eyed each other, mutely.

A tense moment follows—

"Seriously! Tell me the truth. You're not out here for the sights and scenery of the Utah desert. Nor for the vibrant wildlife. You sure don't look like Attenborough's enthusiasts," he says, referring to the English natural historian. "It seems you had a pretty 'sweet deal' back at your camp the way young Jed was explaining before he suddenly became a timbering mouse?"

"Eh, we did…" Carl starts to say, self-consciously. "I mean—"

"Look, Captain Marion…" Carlos takes point in the convo. "You helped us; we're helping you. It doesn't mean you have the right to invade our personal lives. We won't just roll over for you, while you scratch our underbellies, saying, 'Who's a good boy!' and we'll tell you anything you wanna know just because you asked nicely."

Deckard raises both hands gently in front of his heavy-set chest—just above the glove compartment. "Hey, I didn't mean no offense, bud. The whole world is a shitty place at the moment, and I just wanted to know why you kids left your 'silver lining' home behind?"

Carlos looks impatiently at the ex-Marine; he still doesn't trust the guy. Mutters, "A change of scenery."

Deckard gets it, understands the driver doesn't want to divulge certain, privileged info, because revealing that tidbit of information will probably leave them all exposed to uncertainty.

Carl cuts in: "We were following a signal—"

Carlos spins around, hollers, "What the shit, dawg!"

In the back, Carl glances at the driver; he has a look in his eyes that says *for God's sake, keep your trap shut and be quiet for once on this goddamn road trip!*

Caution prevails.

Carlos knows that look and knows what it means: but he can't help himself, and keeps on going like a talkative parrot. "We already giving Marion a ride. You wanna give every secret away to every goddamn stranger we meet on the road? What the fuck, *Carl—*" but stops short, an eyebrow triggered to stand alert as he hears Mary's voice now—louder, and real. Not in his head. But all around.

"Enough, Carlos," she intervenes, silencing the Midwesterner in one swift go like a parent disciplining their child, "focus on the damn road," and the Midwesterner frustratedly returns to driving, hands on the steering wheel. To Carl, she says: "You're right. We should tell him. Go ahead."

***

Deliberation answered: Carl nods, a firm reply to the Yooper. Turns towards Deckard and spills. "Like I said, we are heading to Portland. But we're following the instructions of a voice over the airwaves directing us there. A DJ Candice. A survivor—"

Carlos can't help himself, and interjects in a juvenile voice, "She has a sexy voice. Probably goes with her robust body, too!" (Mary rolls her eyes in annoyance at the sexist statement.) "I'm just stating the facts, Mary!" he adds with a filthy wink which Mary can't see because of his sunnies. But a dirty smirk closely follows.

"Er—*yeah,*" Carl says, ignoring the Midwesterner's constant interruptions. "She's been broadcasting over the channels once every day for the last month. Sometimes her frequency is hard to pick up—like her signals being jammed. Other days… it's easy to listen to her broadcasts."

Mary says off the cuff, "Not only does she offer practical survival skills, but she also circulates news about other survival communities."

Deckard raises an amused brow. "It must have been something valuable she was peddling to entice a bunch of kids to leave a secured base. This voice—the DJ! She from Portland? You've managed to speak to her?"

"Don't think so."

"Lemme ask you something?"

Carl glances at the ex-Marine.

"Go on!"

"This trip you're taking. Is it you running away from something? Or running toward it?"

The gang falls quiet; contemplating the question.

"If I had money riding on it, I'd say both," Carl answers for all of them. "One-day last week, she said, 'There is a safe haven and a working Government on the Western Seaboard.' A place where we can live without fear. A secure outpost. And we thought why not, let's go and find this place…"

"We had enough of living where we were," Mary cuts in, very sharply. "We had to go and see what she was saying was true! See if there was an American dream left. Well… in what remains of the country."

"Or she could be some crazy woman broadcasting out of a radio tower in the middle of nowhere."

Mary: eyes like daggers, "It is real," her words drive home with force.

"You sure?"

Carl: "We are!"

"Hmm," Deckard raises that quizzical eyebrow again; his face is far from convinced by their words full of hope. "It sounds like you're all chasing a McGruffin?" (Everyone looks at one another, wondering what a McGuffin is?) "*Aarrgh* by the look on your bleedin' faces, you ain't got a darn clue?"

Mary: "A what?"

Jed: "No. Nope. Zilch."

"It's one of those odd 'movie terms' that have an equally odd purpose for its nomenclature," Carlos says as easily as riding a unicycle while juggling batons-of-fire (his passion for anything-film related shining through to the surface), and he clocks everyone's faces in the back of the jeep staring at him in the over-hanging mirror.

Deckard nods. "Spot on." He's impressed by the Midwesterner's movie knowledge, and equally surprised they shared the same passion. "Loosely defined, a 'McGuffin' is an object, person or goal that gets characters in a movie trying to find that central purpose, control it, hide it or destroy it. In some cases, you never find out what the McGuffin is! Just that it's important to move characters in a plot from point A to Point B and so forth. And in your case, that 'McGuffin' is this mysterious voice over the airwaves beckoning you to come and find a better life in this already shit world."

"You don't say?" Mary retorts.

"Sorry to spoil your illusions, kids," he takes a deep breath. "But I've heard all kinds of rumors since the U.S. devolved itself into a zombie-infested wasteland. Right from the beginning, all those politicians said, 'the flailing, hungry, murderous undead would not be welcome amongst the living,' and every last one of those pencil-pushers were wrong and are now looking up at us from the grave." Deckard draws a heavy breath and explains: "Along with my travels on the Eastern coasts, I found a small band of survivors sheltering on a bridge. People were going about their everyday life. They seemed to be doing well. They too talked about a safe zone which offered salvation and sanctuary. They too, sent out an expedition. None came back. Then there was a small community of survivalists on an island in the middle of a lake. A few houses lined the rocky shore. They traded with me. They were nice people, and they too told me about radio transmissions broadcasting about a safe zone, somewhere near Florida. Again. Same thing! They sent a scavenging party out into the wilderness. None returned."

Deckard now knew he'd gained the group's full attention.

"What's your point?" Carl asks pointedly.

"Back East, people think there's a safe haven in the West. The same goes for the West. People think there's a sanctuary in the East. I believe there are still some functioning military units somewhere in the States. But they're keeping themselves on the down-low. You don't want every stray coming to your front door, looking for shelter, asking for handouts… using your already stretched resources. But a proper working government—*not a fat chance* in Sin Set Boulevard!" He breathes in a significant and steady lungful of air. "You really think there's still a world out there? Free from all of this chaos and madness? Gonna come to rescue you like the goddamn U.S cavalry rescuing Custer?"

"That doesn't mean that there isn't such a place! We need to know we are not alone in this world. That there are scientists in some secure underground lab out there working on a cure…" her voice trailing off, Mary immediately presses her hands to her knees.

The jeep falls silent.

"Fine." *I'll go along with the assumption that there is hope if it'll keep the peace!* Deckard feels the plucky courage of the blond girl shining through her exterior; he doesn't want to break her hard-shell-of-confidence like a spoon on an egg. "If you're willing to take a risk on what you believe, then you should go and grab that sucker with both hands," he says. "Or in your case—to find hope waiting for you all in Portland. But all I'm saying is sometimes… those risks… just aren't real."

18
SUNSHINE SPLINTERS

Saratoga Springs 'the belly button' of Utah, just west of Utah Lake and part of the *Provo–Orem*, Utah Metropolitan Area. Twenty-so years ago, the southwesterly drift of Utah residents made the town with its subdivisions and golf courses with the Lake Mountains as a backdrop of perfection, continuing to diversify and change as it grew with a new, younger, vibrant and hungrier generation. (It was not your grandmother's Utah County anymore but a hive of new-era activity and one of the fastest-growing U.S. cities to date.)

The town absorbs them as they pass-through like a shit gently being pushed through a clogged colon.

Carlos eventually pulls the jeep up, cuts the engine, and they stop outside an old antique store: windows boarded up. A sign on the filthy glass says: CLOSED. Further down the street, more shops, the windows, and doors are all boarded up on each abandoned property. Another street up, they see a sign that says: Salt Lake City. Graffitied over the official letters in bright red is a warning: 'DEAD AHEAD, TURN AROUND.'

Carl ignores the warning, *the sign's probably been tagged a long time ago.* He checks the surrounding area first; satisfied it's all cleared he leaves the jeep.

He is followed one at a time by the others, all except Naomi (the Texan still sleeps; still dreams of good old-times with friends and family and loving hugs from her dead fiance). The asphalt hot beneath their feet. Deckard's the last out of the jeep, he descends easily to the ground and surveys the area, hand on gun-trigger; his army training showing through, as does, Carl. Both men—wits—are alive and kicking. The road is a mix of boarded-up shops and rubbish, a far cry from the hustle and bustle of what the town once was.

Nothing stirs. Nothing moves.

Carl proceeds to remove the plastic maps from an elastic band. His map of Utah is a series of interconnected red and blue lines—the Beehive state had abundances of federal highways and interstates. Finds the one he's searching for. Rolls it across the hot bonnet with both forearms, outstretched like a rolling pin flattening flour on a kitchen top (two corners turn back on themselves). He runs a finger across a great lake. Salt Lake City International Airport. A mountain range. "Here!" he says, stabbing the map with an incisive finger. "Salt Lake isn't far. Just a short drive away."

Deckard peers at the map. "Last I heard," he says, "the city's CBD was a heavily-infected epicenter of dead civilians running amok. A Black Area. The main highways were barricaded by the National Guard when the city fell a long time ago."

"If there's no chance of going through the damn city streets, we should bypass this whole shitfest!" Carlos quips.

"We could do it!" Jed gestures from the rear. "If we keep to the side-streets, through the outer neighborhoods… we'll be able to avoid the main CBD while scooting around the edges!" The teen's voice like his input was always quiet and surprisingly precise.

Both ideas don't matter—

"It's a nice idea, Jed. But it'll be dangerous. The best course of action, we should make a detour and head around this group of mountain ranges. See!" (The group follows their fearless leader's trailing finger on the map which showed a drivable route around five peaks which ended with them coming up on Interstate 80, west of Salt Lake City.) "We go this way, and we'll remain on course to Portland and at the same time bypass the entire CBD and what lays in wait for us." Carl feels optimistic, and sure his plan is the better plan. "It'll take us a little out of the way… but be worth it in the end."

Carlos states: "Gas will be a problem." Thumbs his chin. "Jed's idea could work."

"Shouldn't be, Carlos. From what we managed to scavenge from the bar, we'll have enough for the next couple hundred miles or so. Chances are, we can pick more up on the way."

"Chances are, we may not!"

"Okay, okay, I see your point," Carl replies. His voice was accommodating to the pessimistic comment coming from the Midwesterner's trap. He asks the remaining members. "Okay. We have to make a call, guys. Show of hands. The first option; keep going through the city, keeping to the outskirts. Second option… go around the ranges and come out on the other side?"

"Very civilized," Deckard comments.

"Have to be," Carl answers. "It's gotten us this far."

"If only the darn Senate was this organized before it fell."

And the ex-Marine flashes a gritty smile at the fact.

"Life is a series of choices, and we'll make 'em together," Carl replies. Sometimes, though, he was not sure. He thought what he was doing was the right thing, though.

Deckard stares at Carl. *He knows what he's doing, even if he doubts himself.*

Finally, the group makes their choice: four for the detour (Deckard raises his hand too). One to go through the outskirts of the city. (The one hand up in the air against the detour was from Carlos. The Midwesterner was always the opposing force in the group of road-buddies.)

"Good job, guys," Carl agrees before inspecting the street map carefully for a final time. He continues: "We'll keep going and take the second left we come upon. It should lead us straight out of town."

Everyone nods to his suggestion.

Seconds later, they are back in the vehicle.

Cautiously, Carlos sticks the jeep into gear, leaving the antique shop behind, along with all the other businesses, and they venture over a brow of a hill and take the second left that leads away from Saratoga Springs along Cedar Fort Road past a fancy Golf club north of the Lake Mountains.

19
DETOUR

The curling drive through the geographical continuum of Utah desert along long stretches of dark curving asphalt which led from Saratoga Springs to Cedar Fort, a small, derelict town, shows the gang that given time, nature will flourish without the interference of man.

Everyone just stares through the windows at an empty gray post office covered in creeping vines. A blacksmith which dated back to the American Civil War, and which served the needs of the troops stationed at nearby Camp Floyd stood on the verge of collapse, and abandoned brick houses, front lawns overrun with foliage littered the quiet streets of the once proud rural community. Soon, behind them, the town is swallowed up by the fir trees—*the large evergreens* growing stronger and fuller as they drive-through not stopping, just observing.

They pass another, similar township. Everyone was on guard; ready and waiting for signs of the undead. But the towns were just other ghost towns on the 'Road to Nowhere', except for a few, slow shambling Zs wandering through shacks of former homes.

The population now: zero.

Nothing stirred. Nothing attacked.

They continued driving along the winding roads and past derelict houses and then through a canyon covered in Bigtooth Maple trees that gave the Utah foothills and mountains their outstanding fall color. Vast, flat scrublands ventured endlessly onwards to the west with a group of mountain ranges sitting to their east.

***

Further afield, the road lost many of the features that defined it as a road: road signs, then asphalt, and the gutters, and in some places, the surface was just pot-holes of broken and cracked asphalt like dried-out-skin. Three, slow hours later, and traveling past a few more dilapidated towns, they finally reached Interstate 80 (that ran from downtown San Francisco, California, to Teaneck, New Jersey, in the New York City Metropolitan Area).

Coming up on the main highway, no more than a quarter mile to the east of them, they could see pockets of abandoned military vehicles scattered like toys across the tarmacked surface of the Interstate. Large concrete barriers made the road unpassable in either direction. Behind the barriers: Cars. Cars and cars and cars, stopped dead on Interstate 80. And beyond, in the distance lay the Great Salt Lake, the largest natural lake west of the Mississippi River where ancient terraces were etched into the landscape along the everlasting shorelines.

"So…, here we are!" Carlos states, gazing off in the distance at the barrage of armored vehicles across the road that resembles a band-aid across a split thumb. *A Marine's wet dream*, he wants to say but holds his tongue. Instead, says,

"Must give you a right military hard-on to see all this mighty fire-power, Marion?"

Deckard laughs at the Midwesterner's choice words. "Sure does," he says, mockingly. "I'm amazed the hardware is still here!" And he takes out a pair of binoculars, scans the distance for signs of life: nothing stirs. Re-focuses the lens and sees the Grade-A arsenal (the M240G/B machine gun) on top of the High Mobility Humvees, each high-grade gunbarrel flops downwards like a limp dick, void of ammunition, void of operators, void of resistance; all, long gone. *Or, all military personnel dead by the fleeing population of the city?* Questions he knew he never wanted answers to.

"That's one helluva long tailback!" Carl suggests, more of a statement than a question.

"It doesn't look that bad," Jed says as he pushes himself forward over the backseat.

"Retrospect, no, kid," Deckard agrees with the youngster. "But I'm guessing the line of vehicles stretches all the way to Salt Lake CBD."

Carlos just said "Hmmm," and drove the jeep at a steady 10mph up onto the highway ramp.

Meanwhile, Mary's not interested in the boys' conversation. Instead, she studies the landscape with a keen biologist's eye. A flight of birds captures her attention. Mary is not a keen-birder but did detect the colorful formation of feathered friends as a variation of ducks. Soon, the birds redirect their flight path and land on the surface of the water one-after-the-other. She couldn't count how many there were nesting on the exposed mudflat but guessed it was a faraway, safer place to 'touchdown' rather than on land. (Much of the lake is ringed by extensive wetlands making the lake one of the most important resources for migrating and nesting birds.) The sight was truly beautiful, and rightly so was 'one of the great views on the American Continent' even with all the military vehicles and endless lanes of rotting cars which sat like discarded, empty cans tossed aside, close by.

That's when she hears Carlos' voice filter over the compartment of the jeep like an attendant's voice over a plane's PA system: "Running low on gas. Time to stop and fill 'Priscilla' up guys." (The Midwesterner had named the jeep after an Australian film he'd once seen. Honestly, Mary had never heard of the comedy film '*The Adventures of Priscilla, Queen of the Desert*' before. But Carlos had insisted it was a genuine film, and their vehicle and mobile home were named a year ago.) Carlos pulls the jeep over to a rolling stop by the side of the road and cuts the engine.

Carl looks over the Midwesterner's shoulder at the gasometer and says, "Jeez, that drive sure took a toll on the gas."

The driver nods in agreement. "Well?" he mutters, turning to the back. "Go, fill 'Priscilla' up, Jed. 'She' and 'we' ain't stopping here for the rest of eternity twiddling our damn fingers."

It was Jed's job to fill the tank up (and to make sure the spare jerry cans were filled if they'd managed to find additional gas that wasn't contaminated), his only jobs on the trip.

"You coming to help me?" the teen asks.

"Do I look like the hired help!" Carlos retorts. "No. So. Go. Do. It. Yourself. Jed." Each word punctuated like a fist to the adolescent's chest.

(The engine turns over one last time and stops.)

The teen was hoping for help pouring the gas from the jerry can into the petrol tank for a change. No such luck. He gently hollers: "Okay," and pulls himself up, climbs over the back seat—rolls over Mary like a poor stuntman in a shitty straight to DVD film, apologizes to her at once—opens the door and falls out. A second later, he dusts himself down, stretches to the heaven's above, and goes around to the jerry cans attached to the back of the jeep.

***

"Carl! Where are we?" Naomi suddenly asks, sitting up straight.

"Hey, you're finally awake," Carl says, leaning in close to her. He touches her brow, checking for a temperature. "You feeling okay?"

The morphine or whatever Mary had found back at the bar, and which was now pumping through Naomi's system (and it was deliciously good), was working overtime.

She answers, "A bit sore in the arm. But I'm fine, I think!" and gazes at her bandaged shoulder before looking around the compartment. She saw Carlos sitting up front with the Marine. While Mary sat to her left; they both flashed a nervous smile at one another.

"You're injured?" Naomi croaks and touches her friend's cheek.

"Oh, this!" she says, almost forgetting she'd cut her face back at the silo. "It's truly nothing. Minor. It's all."

Mary felt her careless mistakes coming back to her; how she'd shot her friend in the arm. "I'm sorry for shooting you back at the silo, Naomi," she apologizes for the countless amount of times. "I didn't mean—I *panicked* when we got cornered. There were so many of them coming from everywhere. I…I—"

Naomi didn't care about anything. Didn't care that Mary had shot her in the shoulder also. The Texan sees her friend's eyes filled with grief, and at the same time, frantically searching for forgiveness. (The Native Texan had always been brought up to forgive for genuine mistakes. We all hate screwing up. Of course—*she did.* Naomi did it quite a lot when she was younger. Shagging her best friend's boyfriend when they were on a break was her biggest and literal fuck-up. And there's nothing worse than that sinking feeling that you've made a miscalculation, offended someone when you didn't mean to or shot someone by accident.)

Eventually, she says, "Stop beating yourself up, girl, because of a silly miscalculation. It's 'kay! You managed to pull me away from harm's way in time. You saved my life, Mary."

"I did. But I shot you, though!"

"I know. Luckily you're a terrible shot, Mary. The bullet went clean through my arm, there's no damage…"

As Naomi continues talking, Mary loses focus of the words coming from the Texan's mouth. Outside, she sees Jed through the open window about three feet away from the car, on his feet but bent over at the waist, gripping his pants at the knees. He is breathing hard out as if he had just run a marathon and was on the verge of throwing up a winner's medal. By his side sits two red jerrycans.

She pushes the door open. "Jed? You all right?"

He didn't say anything and continued to breathe heavily—still looking at the ground, still holding his pants, still breathing uncomfortably in deep rasping breaths.

"This doesn't look good!" Deckard judges.

An unsure group reply of "Yeah, it doesn't, does it!!" quickly follows suit, and everyone gets out to see if the teen is okay.

20
FUCK YOU, JED

Two minutes later—

"You're fucking joking, Jed?" Carl says, a couple of decibels too loud. "Tell me, you're fucking joking? C'mon, Jed!"

"I *mean—*" He tries to search for a grown-up answer to dispel his incompetence. "I…I…"

All around the teen; it seemed as though the whole world had fallen silent, even the wind had stopped blowing. The girls stared silently back. Meanwhile, Carlos held his breath; feeling the almighty warning-of-a-shit-fest-fast approaching, and for once, he wasn't on the receiving end of a judicial pummelling.

They wait for the teen's stuttering to turn into actual words, a complete sentence spoken in the English language: and an apology for his monumental mistake.

Carl was about to explode. He didn't get mad often, and it took a lot, especially riding all day cooped up with Carlos like sardines in a can. But once the pin on that grenade had been pulled, there was no containing it, and unfortunately, Jed felt the aftermath.

Explosion: Fists tensing, Carl lunges towards the teen, grabbing hold of his t-shirt and throws him hard against the window of their mobile home. "This isn't some geeky little fantasy quests on one of your game consoles you get to roleplay in, you little shit. *Christ!* It's your job making sure the jerry cans are filled whenever we manage to find extra gas." Jed tries to scramble away, slip from Carl's grasp, trying to explain why he failed to fill the fuel cans, except, angry Carl has a tight grip on his threads. "What kind of moron are you to forget to fill 'em up?"

Jed continues to stammer. "I, but I—"

"You're *what?*" Carl yells. "Don't you dare say 'Sorry' to me, Jed! We're past that point of sorriness. Understand?"

The teen couldn't answer. His mouth forms an O, but no words follow. He nervously fiddles with his cords, and at the same time has a 'look' on his face that has pulled Carl's pin; a feigned expression of a doe staring nonchalantly into car headlights about to be roadkill. It took—years and years—of practice to come up with that look, and Carl wants to slap it off Jed's face as soon as possible.

Naomi scrambles to the teen's rescue. "Carl, so help me, I will slap the shit outta you! Let him go!" she demands, doing her best to step between them—one armed. "It was a genuine mistake!" She pushes back on Carl's chest with her free hand.

But it was already too late.

Pulling his cap over his eyes, Jed doesn't want to make eye contact. Instead, he starts rambling at a steady pace. "I totally understand you're *upset—*"

Carl sidesteps Naomi's intervention. *"Aaarrrggghhhh!"* he screams and throws the teen to the ground with both hands. Stomps forward; a dark billowing cloud of anger thundering towards a target.

Everyone else stands back by the sight of Carl exploding in a ball-of-uncontrollable rage.

Carl didn't know what else to do. If it were the Midwesterner who'd fucked up, he would have pummeled him already. But it wasn't, it was the youngest of the group who'd royally screwed up.

"Yeah, a mistake that will most probably get us all killed!" Carlos jests while shaking both empty jerry cans in the air. He couldn't help but intervene. "Fuckin' hell, Jed!"

"Shut your trap, Carlos!" Mary retorts as she goes to Jed's side; a comforting arm around the boy's shoulders. "You're not helping in any possible way!"

"It's my plan not to!"

"It was a genuine mistake—"

"Fuck off," he answers, unapologetically, drops both cans and steps into the circle thumb-pointing the teen, and then Mary. "How is she even calling the shots?" The rest of the group had fallen quiet. "Carl? Don't pretend you can't hear me. I'm standing right in fucking front of you. How are we gonna solve this mess if—"

Mary hisses. "We're not going to solve it by continuing arguing about it, are we? Y-you effing moron!"

The Midwesterner pauses. He was pissed or irritated, or both (it was hard to tell sometimes, considering he looked that way most of the time). He looks at the rest of the group, and the quietness stretches into a sullen smirk.

"It's all gonna be okay," she whispers into Jed's ear—her maternal instincts taking over—as the boy sits with his cap pulled over his face; eyes cast down to the ground in terror, but mainly, shame. "We can get over this hiccup."

"Carlos is right, Mary."

She looks up; the words come from Carl. *He's sticking up for the Midwesterner, what the holy crap!*

Carl looks down at the pair on the floor, then at Naomi who stands by her friend's side. "It was the biggest fuck up that shouldn't have ever happened!" (The girls know he's correct.) Then Carl shoots a death-stare at the teen. Jed is desperately backing into Mary's bosom, his cap still shielding eye-contact. "We have our jobs for a reason, Jed! All of us. Understand?"

Mouth opens. The teen nods.

"I don't know what the hell you were thinking back at that bar, but how could you have been so stupid as to forget to fill up those cans?"

"*Y—you* know, with all that has happened; Naomi getting shot back at the silo. *M-meeting…* Deckard at that bar and Carlos getting jumped. I—I kinda just *forgot!*"

Carl tries to be calm, find his hidden Zen deep within. His Happy Place. It doesn't work. He loses his cool again and stomps closer. And then it is on. Carl reacts. "What a lame fucking excuse!" He grabs the teen by the collar—fist balling—pulls him from Mary's protective grasp.

Mary: "Carl, nobody sanctioned this problem—"

His hand jerks towards her. "You're right, Mary. No one did!"

And Mary realizes she can't change Carl's mind; what is about to happen, will happen.

But it never comes—

"You have to calm down, Carl. Beating up Jed isn't going to help the situation any further," Naomi says, her voice commanding, nurturing. She squeezes Carl's shoulder. It makes him stop. "It could have happened to any of us!"

Deep breath. "I am fucking calm, Naomi," he yells, releases the teen. Turns to her—face like thunder. "I'm perfectly fucking civil towards him."

Everybody stands around the frighten teen in a tight unit of loathing.

***

Finally—

Carl concedes defeat. He needs a moment away from the teenager, from the girls too and storms away from the group to a cluster of 60ft native oaks. (Naomi calls after him, *"Carl! Come back!"*) He ignores her voice. Beneath his feet, dark green and yellow leaves go *crunch* like he's walking across a mound of dead beetles. As he walks, he tries to suss away around the 'big problem' of Jed's huge fucking mistake that will probably get them all killed.

Leaving the goddamn gas behind! He muses behind deep breaths. *Jesus, at this moment, only gas is keeping us alive along on our trip to Portland.* It was as valuable as food and water, more so. And the gasoline market was soon to be closed on them forever, if not so, already. *Goddamnit, how come he's such a tool!* Carl tries to force a cry of bitter frustration back down his dry throat. "Shit! Fuck! God! Piece of shit!" The profanities come in waves, as he kicks the dried leaves in a blizzard of hopelessness. Kicks the gray-brown peeling bark of the trunk—just one at the moment (the others can wait their turn).

Get it together, a voice says deep from within. *You need a plan! There's always a plan.*

He turns to look at the group, sees Mary and Naomi helping Jed up off the ground. Sees Carlos having a go at the teen, *castrating the little prick,* he figures, and this time, rightly so. And off by the side, Deckard just sits in the passenger seat of the jeep, drinking from a silver hip-flask, wondering what the hell he's gotten himself in for. *Contemplating life,* he figures.

Behind the ex-Marine and their empty ride, the convoy of vehicles waits idly on both lanes of the highway stretching all the way to Salt Lake's CBD.

It's got to be done.

Carl makes his choice, and he finally walks back to the gang.

21
BEST LAID PLANS

As soon as Carl gets back in touching distance, he finds himself between Mary and Naomi, both with their arms crossed, expecting leadership from him.

Mary hesitantly asks, "What happens now?"

His teeth chatter together. "Our only choice now is to venture past the blockade and search all those vacant cars beyond. I'm hoping one of the close vehicles will have gas in a tank. Hoping we will not have to go further than we'll need to." (But he knows deep down, the further the cars are away from the central hub of civilization, the less likely they will have a full tank of gas. Knows over the years, high ambient air temps can promote evaporation in the tanks too.)

"It's a long way to go on foot in hostile territory, kid!"

Carl gazes at the former Marine; he is still sitting down, sipping slowly from the flask. "I know. But it's our best chance. Hopefully, one of those vehicles still has some gas left in the tank."

"It's a big hope," Deckard replies. "And if they're dry?"

"Then we're screwed," he answers before looking at a nervous Jed standing in between Naomi and Mary. He was trying to stay calm. The teen gazes back with those roadkill eyes once again.

"Oh, shit. Who goes?" Carlos interjects, stealing the lead. "I'm all for volunteering and such, but when the shit's not my fault, I don't see why I have to go risk my ass for the group."

Mary looks at Naomi. Naomi looks back at her friend. She turns to Carl. Carl knows that Texan look. It's the look that says *I'm Gonna Go Full Steam Ahead Mode and You Can't Stop Me, Y'all.*

Eventually, Carl intervenes. "You don't need to, Naomi. I'll go. Hopefully, it won't take long, and when—"

"Why not?"

The question lingers for a second longer than it should have—

Carl looks at Naomi and her bandaged shoulder. "You know exactly why! You're injured, so you can't go, and that means we have to leave someone here to take care of you. Carlos can stay behind with the jeep and look after you as—"

"I can shoot. I can handle myself!"

"I know you can, Naomi," he answers. "You're a better shot than all of us put together. But your arm!"

Naomi blows some dangling hair out of her eyes; knowing she'd be no good with an injured arm if ever they got cornered, but still, Carl's compliment was well received. She turns to Carl. "Okay, you decide who goes."

"I decide? No, I don't. I told you, I'm not the leader. We all vote to decide," his words are filled with leadership (even if Carl didn't believe he was the leader, everyone listened when he spoke). "It's early afternoon. We have tons of daylight left. Bound to be gas in one of those vehicles."

"We should put it off till tomorrow, hunker down and form a plan," Mary states.

"Agggh, that's a croc-o-shit!" Carlos interrupts her. "Same shit. Different day, Kansas. I'm with Carl's plan. We go now; in two's, inspect the closest vehicles at a motoring pace. Be back before it gets dark. Easy."

Mary puts fingers in both ears. "Blah, blah, blah, blah, blah," she retorts, "it's just words, Carlos."

Mouth open. Carlos tilts his head towards the Yooper, about to respond—

That's when—

"Carlos is right," Carl agrees (it's the second time he'd stuck up for the guy, and the Midwesterner knows it as his eyebrow raises in acknowledgment to the words of support). "Okay. We work in pairs. It's how it's been from the start. We'll take the empty jerry cans and be back before sunset."

"I'll go."

Everyone turns at the voice. The ex-Marine is now standing in the afternoon sun. Fedora shielding his weary eyes—hip flask finally stashed away. A slight drunkenness to his stance.

He grunts, "Got all the free time in the world."

"You're not under any obligation to go on this mission!" Mary replies. "You're not a Marine now, and we're not civilians who need protecting, either!"

At this, Deckard nods, partly grateful because he didn't want to go, and because he was still hungover from the bar, and it didn't help that his hip flask didn't contain the refreshing taste of aqua blue too, but a nice 25year Scotch instead. He takes a seat back in the jeep.

***

That's when—

Jed swallows hard. "I'll go," his voice as timid as a mouse's squeak.

And then it's on. Everyone reacts. Everyone stares at the teen with awe.

He nods slowly, raising a hand like a student answering a question. "It was my fault we're in this situation. It's only right I should make amends."

He has a look of a man—no, a boy—who wants redemption. Needs it more than anything in the entire world.

Carl is silent for a moment with an uncertain look etching across his face. He couldn't criticize the teen for trying to make amends for the screw-up but couldn't risk another screw-up of Biblical proportions threatening their livelihoods. He reacts: moves forward, hands reaching out. Jed doesn't flinch—he stands his ground, waiting for a thump or a push of some kind—it doesn't come, and Carl's hands land on his shoulders.

He grips. "I just don't think you're up to it, Jed."

"I am," he mutters. "Let me do this, Carl. Please. Let me redeem myself. Please?"

Carl stands there listening to the teens pleas of redemption, his mouth open, but no words formulate.

***

As the stand-off continues—

Deckard sits in the front of the jeep, takes off his hat, and begins to study the dynamics of the group. Sees leadership in Carl. Sees a reflection of himself in the kid, just a little, but deep down knows it's the kid's parents' Army genes passed to their offspring that make Carl who he is; a resilient leader in a time of crisis.

He sees compassion in Mary, the way she takes care of Jed under her wing like a protective mother looking out for her cub. And honesty may make her sound conceited, but it's honesty, nonetheless.

He sees the half Asian, half Texas Native girl, Naomi, who has taken a bullet in her shoulder from a close friend. Knew she had bigger balls than most of the men he'd fought along within his military life.

Jed was still a child, the youngest of the group; childhood cut short by the zombie apocalypse. He feels pity for the youngster, it wasn't his fault; he was dragged into a world of pain and real-life nightmares where the nightmares will actually eat you alive. But the youngster, well, he owned this mistake with the gas. He wants to make it right. It was a grand trait to have as a human being.

And finally, Carlos Haseltine, a mouth with a grudge, a loose cannon waiting to go off. Knows the guy is the catalyst for bonding the others when there's always a common enemy: Even though the guy grinds hard on the nerves of anything with a pulse. Deckard knows he'll have to keep an eye on the Midwesterner just in case he finally goes rogue and stages a *Coup d'état* and tries to overthrow the current regime that presides over the group.

Deckard refocuses back into present time, looks at the current chief with his hands on the teen's shoulders just as he hears—

"I'll go too."

The voice belongs to Mary.

"You stay here with Naomi," she says, gesturing to Carl. Mary knows he wants to stay and protect her. Plus, she knows it'll be good for him to be apart from Jed. "I'll take Jed with me, and together, we'll scavenge for gas."

"Pardon?"

"You heard me!"

He did.

Carl was about to resist, when—

"*Aagghhh*, screw it, Fearless Leader. I'll go too," Carlos says, reminding them all he was still part of the group. "Feel I need the exercise stuck behind that damn wheel all day. It'll give me a chance to limber up and stretch my goddamn muscles." And the Midwesterner begins lifting two empty jerry cans, one in either hand, like a bodybuilder pumping iron in a homemade gym. (It draws a look from everyone.) "What! Can't I volunteer now?" he aggrievedly adds.

From the side, Mary turns to Naomi and whispers, "There's something I thought I'd never see Carlos do!"

They both nod in agreement.

"That's how I roll baby," Carlos happily jests, a smile forming across his face. "Never know what I'm about to do, do ya, Kansas?" And he purses his lips together and blows a kiss at both girls.

The nauseating gesture makes Mary feel queasy, but she keeps quiet nevertheless.

On the other hand, Naomi is used to nasty boys from her state. College lads were always trying it on with her from an early age. (It was always the Asian thing that got them: interpret the stereotype of the Asian girl as 'easy girls.' It was an argument, equally unfairly put to her because she had Asian heritage. Straight up: Why are we even talking about this? The very premise of the question is racist, sexist, and misogynist, she stated in an online forum. That post had received more than 4 million views in her last year of high school, 356,000 followers, and close to 90,000 responses later, the topic was still going strong before the end of the internet. It was a proud moment for Naomi and brought a new wave of women's movement across her uni campus when she finally graduated from university.)

"Mary's right, Carl…" Carlos declares. "You searched the deserted bar. Look what you found: a flamin' Marine. It's my turn this time. I'm sure I'll turn up with a couple of smokin' hot babes from Miss Salt Lake Playboy Mansion"—he snorts at his own unfunny remark—"anyway, we'll be back shortly, dawg."

"There's no such thing."

Mary's words bring an uneven smirk to the Midwesterner's lips. "Sure there is, Kansas," he replies, and that smirk steadily grows.

Carl held looks with each of the group. He knows the decisions made. Then he locks eyes with Carlos.

"Rock, paper, scissors?"

Carlos turns to their fearless leader. "What are you, ten?"

"Good point!" Carl answers quietly a little red in the cheeks.

Naomi and Mary are both silent for a few seconds. Finally, both burst out laughing, Jed too (it was the first time they had done so in a long time).

After a moment of laughter, Carl turns to the teen. "Okay. It's settled"—he gulps back doubt—"I believe in you. But it's a team game. No going gung-ho out there." (Jed looks over the moon by the acceptance of Carl agreeing to let him go on the gas-run, and he beams back brightly.) "Don't screw it up!"

Jed shakes his head at the warning.

"Good," Carl mutters, happy that the teen will not step a wrong foot out-of-line. He turns to the others. "Guys, hopefully the closest vehicles will still have fuel in their tanks." (It is wishful thinking on his part.) "But we know gas expires and evaporates over time, so you might have to go further afield." He examines his friends again, makes sure they know what to do.

***

Five minutes later—

The three explorers, Mary, Jed, and the self-appointed expedition leader, Carlos, were walking away from the rest of the group towards the convoy of armored Humvees and the longest 'tailback' in history, all in the hope of finding a tank full of gas.

"Be safe, all of you guys," Carl hollers. "If you have to travel further, try to keep off the main Interstate and watch out for Grabbers and Creeps. Don't be stupid. If you wander into trouble—just get yourself quickly and as far away as possible! Understand?"

"Sure, dawg," Carlos answers with a firm hand thrown up in the air like the rebel, John (Judd Nelson's) character at the end of the *John Hughes* classic 1980s film, The Breakfast Club. He carries an old gray sports bag with an assortment of practical tools for siphoning gas.

Behind him, Jed assertively nods back—he holds the two jerry cans, one in each hand.

"Be safe!"

"We will, Naomi," Mary acknowledges her friend with a smile and a wave. Her yellow rucksack bobbing on her shoulders like a 'Minion' from a Pixar film.

Deckard still sits inside the jeep, watching as the three of the youthful group disembarks on a quest to find fuel. (It reminds him of the 70's game Boot Hill, the western-themed role-playing game. It was marketed to take advantage of America's love of the western genre. And at the same time, never reached the same level of popularity as D&D and other fantasy-themed role-playing games.) The childhood memory was a hidden gem of his and brings a weary sigh to his dry lips. He takes his flask out again and takes another sip of the strong liquor; he knows the day is going to be a long stretch at best. Knows he needs a nap too, and kicks back across the seats.

PART THREE

SALT LAKE CITY

22
ONWARDS TO THE EMERALD CITY OF SALT LAKE

Mary, Carlos, and Jed stop an hour past the armored blockade; going further than they'd like to have gone in the first place. They had to because the vehicles in both lanes were run dry of gas, while others ran on diesel.

Behind them, the Great Salt Lake was peaceful and blue, so quaint and calm below the hot afternoon sun, even the ducks were back in the sky—flying to somewhere or to nowhere—presumably scouting the three alive members of the last human population that weren't intent to catch and eat them while they were still—quacking alive.

Opposite the lake, a steep mountain range waits, covered in native plants and trees sweeping upwards to its peak. But where Interstate 80 ran along the tip of the lake—the roads were no more. Craters the size of suburban houses littered the landscape. Rusted wrecks stretched until the edge of the universe.

"It looks like a war erupted!" says Jed. The teen gazes at the deep craters either side of the former Interstate.

"Salt Lake must have been a heavily infested Black Zone!" Mary adds, observing a mountain of twisted wreckage; the former vehicles scattered across the dense thickets of scrubland not far from the hot, blackened, pot-holed asphalt.

"So fun to have my apocalypse buddies sharing their thoughts aloud," Carlos quips, keeping his hand on his sidearm. "Yeah, you're on the money, Kansas."

"What's a Black Zone?" Jed asks.

The Midwesterner is way too busy scanning the open stretch of land for Zs to form an answer. It's left to Mary to answer the teen's inquisitive question.

"In some cities when the local authorities couldn't control the outbreak anymore and when huge herds of dead controlled whole swaths of land, the State Governments decided to launch 'Project Takedown' to incinerate the area instead of trying to save the population. The residents of some cities just refused to evacuate even when the country was escalating into turmoil, and when they finally realized the dead were shuffling over their lovely tidy lawns to get to their front doors… it was… way too late!" she sadly adds.

"Yeah. The military felt it necessary just to bomb the shit out-of-cities. Regardless if you were dead or alive at the time." Carlos' words were blunt, like a lead pipe used to bludgeon a snitch to death.

Seconds go by—

"I remember watching the news broadcasts; wondering just where exactly do these cool Military Operations names come from?" he continues. "And who personally approved every operation name before it was carried out?"

"Wait! Wait! There must have been hundreds, if not thousands of cars escaping the city? All filled with *families*—" Jed stops himself short. Memories of his own family coming to the forefront of his mind. But his words add a dark, demonic, warped realization to reality as he gazes at the twisted, metallic shells: each vehicle containing incinerated skulls and bones.

"Yeah, Jed…" Carlos says sourly. "And with them—our bloody fuel too!" And he picks up a steady pace, marches onwards like a man with a purpose.

***

They decide to veer right, long another stretch of road; leaving behind the vast shoreline of the lake. There were more rusted cars along the two-way road but not as half as many as there were on the demolished, graveyard of the Interstate. The afternoon sun is set high in the sky; its rays burning brighter as they walk further and further away from their friends.

Then it hits them like a tornado across the fields of Kansas.

In the distance, a scene straight out of The Wizard of Oz comes into view, but this was no Emerald City from the famous 1939 fantasy movie. Salt Lake City—The Crossroads of the West—now stood like a primitive civilization at the edge of the world. They could see the devastation and broken structures littering the city skyline and beyond. Avalanches of brick and glass piled high. What took everybody back in surprise was a polar opposite of views; just east of the city's downtown, Grandview Peak, the mountain ranges looking almost like those pop-up books from when you were a child; you often could reach out and grab them. (Grandview straddles the Davis and Salt Lake County line), and beyond, the Wasatch Mountain Range is the defining characteristic of Northern Utah. Its rugged peaks, once the epicentre of outdoor recreation for its residents; its canyons, a vital watershed to the population centre of Utah. But there were no people left to enjoy the great outdoors, to hike and climb the mountain trails and no person left to drink from the city's water supply.

"Oh no!" Mary says, covering her mouth with a deft hand. "It's a ghost city."

Jed sees a few standing corporate buildings in the broken, central CBD, which had survived the aerial strikes of yesteryear, but each had signs of decay—*even* from a great distance.

Carlos exclaims: "Yeah. A totally fucked up X-Rated Disney version." He tilts his head, looks into an empty car: a skeleton stares back, the jaw broken in two. New teeth had started forming at the back of the mouth. *A suped-up Creep with gloriously sharp teeth to tear the flesh from my limbs!* And the thought makes him sick to his stomach.

***

The dead were not your average zombie the human population had come to believe, even since the word 'zombie' came to fruition. Yes, the majority were slow and cumbersome, portrayed so elegantly and grotesquely in the *G. A.*

Romero films and the *R. Kirkman*-led AMC show The Walking Dead all those years back when TV and the cinema were a pleasant cultural distraction for the masses.

They were fast, too, no doubt, and reminded everyone of the Infected in 28 Days Later and World War Z (the movie and not the book), always running amok, eager to catch the living in a sprinting race.

Somehow, though, some of the dead were different, they had evolved, mutated and grew extra sharp teeth in the back of their mouths. And unlike a mammalian jaw that is built for brute force, these dead had more in common with specific reptiles. Take a snake's mouth; it is rigged with tendons, muscles, and ligaments that give the jaw a gymnast's flexibility. One of the enduring myths about snakes is the feeding mechanisms; the idea that the jaws detach. In fact, they stay connected all the time. The two lower jaws move independently of one another. The quadrate bone is not rigidly attached to the skull, but articulates with the skull at one end and is therefore freely moving. However, the jaws on these metamorphosed zombies do dislocate, allowing for extra teeth to grow. And when it feeds, the mouth will continuously open and shut, forming new teeth to replace the old.

The disturbing process had formed another unimaginable terror into the human psyche.

Carlos pulls himself together, shakes the nightmares away, looks further up the road, and sees the continuous stretch of abandoned vehicles: these ones didn't seem to resemble twisted wrecks like the ones before. "Let's get moving," he commands with authority. "Plenty of cars still to search for some gas, boys, and girls."

***

When they are further down the road, Jed apologizes. "Sorry about forgetting to fill the jerry cans, guys. I am… sorry. You guys know, right?" he is straggling behind, dragging his feet like a teenager on holiday with his parents.

Mary shoots him a furious glance.

"Shut up. It's over now."

"I'm really sorry, Mary. I am!"

Apology after apology. The sweltering heat made Mary thoroughly annoyed, and she couldn't help but notice that after they'd left the dismantled Interstate and headed along the road nearing the first suburban reaches, Jed had gone on and on about how tired he was and how he was sorry for what had happened. The teen was getting loud, and that made Mary nervous because with loudness came the dead.

Life is too short to argue with stupid people, she thinks. "If you want forgiveness, fine. I'll give it to you. You're forgiven."

Jed lowers his cap and apologizes again. "Mary, I'm sorry. I truly—"

Carlos is utterly fed-up and interrupts the conversation mid-point. "Okay, you two. I swear… will both of you just shut the fuck up and keep your eyes open and focused." He was getting annoyed and didn't want to end up like a 'Human

Happy Meal' anytime soon. "Keep close, keep in a tight unit!" he says, edging along the guardrail. "Don't fall too far behind when we search the upcoming vehicles, 'kay!"

Mary throws a look back over her shoulder for a final time; she's utterly fed up with the teen's constant apologies and stomps ahead, taking the lead. "C'mon then," her words flow forcefully outwards as she passes the Midwesterner in third gear. "If I hear you scream… I'm not coming to help."

"If you hear me scream, then you'd better fucking run," Carlos curtly answers, raising two passive eyebrows.

"Can you not be a big pain in the ass!"

"I can be a big pain in your ass if you let me!"

Mary shakes her head and rolls her eyes at the inappropriate comment. Remembering the #MeToo Movement ten years or so ago. "Sorry, were you saying something? I heard words, but it sounded like utter shit coming from a fucktard's piehole!" she retorts, ignoring his lewd remarks. *Utter shithead!* She thinks, and turns to say, "One final point!"

"I'm listening."

"Do you ever stop and listen to yourself?"

Carlos laughs. "Nope."

"Not even a little?"

A silent pause. "Not a chance."

Mary shakes her constant headache away that is the Midwesterner's voice—grasps her pistol. (*I could end him right here, shoot the moron dead. Nobody would ever know! I could say it was an accident,* the thoughts resonate through her skull like hand-grenades, but deep down, she knows that lie wouldn't cut the mustard. She was no killer, and her 'whole mood' feels as if she could overthrow his entire shitty-nonsense), and she marches onwards.

Behind, Carlos smirks, bobs his head like one of those 'Bobble Head Dogs' car dash ornaments; he's unsure of how exactly the day has brought him and Mary on an adventure together, but knows his work is complete: he's pissed her royally off.

Now, he follows.

23
SLIM PICKINGS

The first intact car was empty of gas, engine—*dead*, of course. Carlos goes to the second; pops the tiny fuel door from the front compartment of the rental car. Shades of blue in the interior upholstery. The faded rental sticker is still on the dusty windscreen: it says Ally's Rental Shack, Beaver County. He goes around to the side of the rental and takes a suction pipe which was, in fact, a green garden hose reel cut up at a certain length from that same gray gym bag that clings to his shoulders like a spider-monkey.

Jed comes up from behind and sits a jerry can by his feet, undoes the cap. "Here," he says.

Carlos feeds the length of the pipe into the tiny hole of an early 2000s Ford Mondeo. Deeper and deeper it goes. Secondly, he creates a loop in the hose, such that the other end is facing upwards, (this helps control the gas flow better while sucking). Finally puts lips around the end he's holding—*the little* dark hole welcoming his mouth.

(Siphoning gas involves simple principles of physics. The air is sucked out of the pipe dipped in the tank, creating a vacuum. The gas then flows into the hosepipe to fill up the vacuum. It falls into the container from the hosepipe under the action of gravity. As fuel in the tank becomes lesser, it creates a new vacuum, which is filled up by air rushing inside from the tank opening. This air applies pressure on the gasoline, making it continuously flow into the pipe, until the hosepipe is raised high enough so gravity can act in the reverse direction.)

Carlos sucks and sucks like he's trying to earn a living on a dark, street corner.

No such luck. The well's dry.

He takes the hose and walks.

Jed follows behind with both cans.

Further and further they go, trying a variety of vehicles. *Pop! Pop! Pop! Pop! Pop!* Station wagons, sports cars, Winnebago's, and beat-up old trucks—*all empty*. (Some modern vehicles came with a siphon-proof filter in the gas tank. This consists of a metal flap which clamps shut and prevents any hose from entering the tank.) To siphon gas from such a tank, Carlos holds the metal flap open using a long object: in this case, he uses a red-handled screwdriver he'd looted from an independent hardware store some while back.

Almost all the vehicles along the two-way road are empty, except for the occasional, rag-and-bone of the former owner. Some cars and trucks have camping gear, suitcases—faded and torn over time—and attached to the roof racks, others with valuables and stupid-ass items such as game consoles and electrical hardware. Anytime they passed a vehicle, they would stop and search like jackals, through empty rucksacks and suitcases if they could reach, searching for food and water, and the rare firearm. It was slim pickings, what was of any real value had already been picked a long time ago.

"Another fuel tank dry," Carlos grumbles. He kicks a beat-up Ford Corolla's tire—*hard* and direct, the crumbling rubber breaks underfoot like a mud cake left out in the sun. "C'mon. Let's move!" He signals for the others to venture further along the stretch of road where the vehicles became even more compact. "Don't wander too far. Stay in talking distance."

But it was dangerous.

Sometimes there were drifters (humans that lived out in the barren wastelands alone and away from the big, populous zones). At other times, the drifters or 'roadies' as they had become known, hid in or under cars or lurked in the tight corridors between them; ready to kill unfortunate souls walking by or even worse.

***

A while ago Mary was moving with a scavenging group on a tailgated road leaving the city of Columbus before she became friends with Carl and the others. She was talking loud, louder than she should have been, and not focusing on her surroundings, when a 'roadie' - an old man with a gray beard—lunged from beneath an abandoned RV, catching hold of her feet and biting into her ankle like the undead. Luckily the tough leather of her hiking boots saved her from an infection from the old crooner, and the others in her group took care of the man with a bat to the head. Afterwards, Mary made sure she was aware of her surroundings at all times and didn't walk so close to another RV again.

***

Carlos, Mary, and Jed were motoring through abandoned cars, always careful not to open locked doors or obscure windows belonging to vans or buses. That was the biggest fear, getting clawed by a group of ravenous Zs as they piled from their filthy prisons, just to make you a meal-on-wheels.

With a sweaty crotch, Carlos pulls to a stop where the road began to curl around the first abandoned neighborhoods of derelict houses where 'Project Takedown' hadn't made much of an impression on the outer suburban reaches of Salt Lake City. Parks and a prominent complex appear on the edges of the road. It was a shopping center which appeared to be in the aftermath of a post-Super Bowl riot.

Ahead of them in the southbound lane were a tangle of vehicles all facing north. The drivers fleeing the city tried to take advantage of the less crowded roads rather than escape on the two primary Interstates that fed the city. That was until a petrol tanker had lost control and had buckled and was now laying—its burnt out shell—on its side across the lanes (presumably, that was why the first stretch of the road was empty of vehicles because of the accident). Behind that, a couple of public buses had apparently swerved to avoid hitting the tanker and had gone up onto the guardrail, where they'd become stuck; the passengers roasting inside. Some skeletons were still sitting upright in the charred seats. Then the rest of the fleeing vehicles had stopped—bumper to bumper—and bottled up like too many women's tampons being discarded down a toilet.

They eventually rested for a few minutes. The road was eerily quiet. The sun bearing down from above with unbearable heat.

24
SOUNDS OF THE HUNGRY

The five-minute break is broken by a distant growl. To Jed's horror, he freezes by the nightmarish sound coming from behind. Mary sees the change in his face; the mellow adolescence of fear. From awkward to frightened within seconds. "It's fine. It's nothing, Jed. We're safe," she says, reassuring the teen and more importantly herself.

With Jed reassured by Mary's words, he puts down the jerry cans, starts to leap the barrier into the southbound lane to a red Lincoln Navigator; it reminds him of his old family car when he was much younger, except the driver's door was missing. *The driver probably had run screaming from whatever unholy terror was coming his or her way,* he grimaces at the thoughts. And in no time at all, he gives a quick search of the vehicle; checks the backseat first in case of 'lurkers.' Coast clear, he finds the keys still in the ignition. Hesitates for a moment, not knowing if the engine will start. "Bingo!" he says as the engine turns over and over. "Hey! The tank is full, guys!" and the vehicle emits a low groan of triumphant joy.

"Good work," Mary calls back. She looks over and sees him waving at her from the doorless driver side. *He still looks miserable,* she assumes, but Jed was doing his best and seemed happy that he'd found some fuel for the group.

Carlos looks to Mary, eyebrows raised. Sees how the Yooper was—puppy-eyeing the teen—and says, "It still doesn't make good for Jed making a complete dick move back at the bar, Mary!"

She finds him standing by a black Sedan, walks up to him, finger pointing at his chest. "At least it's a start," and she snatches the length of hose from his hands, picks up a jerry can from the asphalt and begins to climb the barrier to join the teen by the Lincoln.

Jed finally clicks the engine off (if the vehicle wasn't stuck in the worse tailback in history, they could have just taken it, driven it all the way back to the rest of the group). He pushes the fuel door button open and begins to move around the vehicle ready and waiting for Mary to siphon the gas.

Suddenly that distant sound Jed heard a few minutes earlier had become louder; it sounded like someone was hitting a hollow object against metal.

Mary hears it too. *Ting, ting, ting.* She gazes back just in time to witness Carlos pulling back a fraction. With one hand, he removes his sunnies, and with his other, reaches for his Glock. As she searches his face, the Midwesterner wore the same expression as Jed had a few moments earlier.

Where they'd just come from was a slow-moving zombie about three hundred yards away; it had something long and shiny in its crooked hand, like a crowbar, and every time it moved between a vehicle, that metallic sound rang again.

Ting, ting, ting.

"Only one Z. Nothing to worry about," Carlos states in a commanding voice that injects a rigid-sense of relief in the others. He feels a rush too. It channels into his limbs, a no-holds-bar-full-of-power. "Keep siphoning the fuel."

Jed: "Will do," and the teen takes the hose from Mary's grip and begins to feed it into the Lincoln's fuel tank.

"I know there's nothing to worry about," Mary cautiously adds. "But it's making a helluva noise! What if it attracts others?" She waits for a reply from Carlos, any reply: he doesn't answer.

***

There are three types of zombies:

Type A: Shufflers, what we've come to regard as the classic Romero Zombies. Slow moving flesh-eaters that shamble about the countryside clumsily stalking whatever humans might be unfortunate enough to stumble into their path.

Type B: Runners are fast, from the more modern movies. These zombies are terrifying because of how animalistic they are. They will jump through windows, run relentlessly, and tear themselves apart without slowing or hesitate to get you.

Type C: Creeps, the new breed of dead, who mouth tears apart, creating new teeth. They are fast and direct and just from one bite will transform the living into one of the new nightmares that plague the earth.

***

In Mary's thinking, she didn't make any assumptions. All the human doubts, questions, hesitations, and fears are entirely removed. She assumed all the dead were high-speed-new-breed zombies… and if they turn out to be slow… all the better.

"What the hell, Carlos?" she asks. "You gonna answer me?"

He waves. "Don't worry. It's just a slow-mo corpse," he says, filling Mary with calmness.

Then she walks away.

Mary helps Jed with the fuel from the Lincoln; it was slow at first, but the petrol starts to flow up and around the bend in the hosepipe. Before it reaches the end, Jed takes his mouth away, applies pressure with his thumb, and pushes it into the open jerry can: and the liquid begins to fill the container.

He's excited, ecstatic.

They both share a laugh and a loud giggle of achievement.

"Guys!" Carlos hisses. "Be quiet, or you'll *attract*—"

That's when—

"Whatcha, say?!" Jed mumbles, popping his head from behind the Lincoln to receive an answer from the Midwesterner but was greeted by the sight of a Creep in ripped hiking shorts and a faded and ripped shirt rushing from the side. Its eyes were black pebble stones set into a sunken and swollen face. Lidless eyes; void of emotion, lipless mouth, teeth bared and just hungry for the teen's tender flesh.

He freezes—

It's all Jed can do—

At the exact same time, both Carlos and Mary raise their weapons, aim vaguely, and fire from either side of the guardrail. The Creep's body propels backward first, frontwards secondly as both bullets enter the forehead, throwing a wave of cranium and brain-matter onto the vehicle's body.

Bullseye.

Jed slides down the Lincoln, clammy ass-crack stuck to his shorts. He bites his tongue, tastes blood. Mary rushes to his side, asking if he's okay and unhurt? Jed just nods his head to both questions, it's the only thing he can do, and the gesture is universal.

Jed stutters. "D-did, you get it?" The coppery taste of blood fills his mouth.

***

Carlos jumps the rail and goes to the teen's side.

Goddamnit.

Goddamnit.

"You're one lucky kid, Jed," Carlos says. He shakes the daze out of the teen like he's shaking a money jar full of pennies. Looks at the ever-worried face of Mary who stands by his side. "Yeah. We got it!"

"G-good."

Mary: "It is fine, Jed,"—her hand clasps the teen's shoulder—"It didn't get you. You're alive."

"Okay. Lesson today! And I think I speak on behalf of at least the entire group of people here when I ask, can't you guys just shut up and keep your emotions in check and keep your volume at decibel-stop-the-fucking-talking-too loudly?" Carlos awaits an answer from someone or both. None come. "Or haven't you learned anything from the 'A-Z of How To Survive a Zombie Apocalypse' yet?"

Mary gulps back hard and apologizes for both of them. It was the correct thing to do, even as apologizing to the Midwesterner was searing a black hole into her gut like a cowboy's iron on the hide of a cow.

A scuff of a shoe.

A rattle of iron on iron.

Then—

Carlos doesn't get the time to form a reply or pull a noteworthy smirk—

Another 'noise' some way off—

That noise has joined the first Z, which was making the metallic noise against the guardrail: it was attracting other infected from the surrounding area, drawing in each like damp from the cold. More sounds, thick and fast: groaning and moaning coming from former citizens of Salt Lake City.

"Guys—we've got trouble!" Mary calls, peeking through the Lincoln's dusty windows. Off in the distance, she can see a pack of infected advancing between the vehicles, just Zs, no fast-moving Creeps like the—shorts and ratty-tatty shirt—from a moment ago.

Carlos peeks too.

Now the Infected are everywhere. Ten in a group, all shambling towards their next meal ticket. An open-air picnic. A chow-down in the afternoon sun. *Damn it!* He grumbles at their predicament, then sees the abandoned neighborhood off in the distance. *There must be plenty of hiding places there?* he assumes. *If only we could reach it!*

Mary asks: "Now what?"

"We fucking skedaddle, Kansas," he replies, throwing a hand up like a signpost directing the way to the nearest neighborhood.

Meanwhile, Jed removes the hose from the can as petrol starts to overflow onto the road just as another shuffler comes into view. A one arm-skull on a stick with lidless eyes stares down at the teen from above.

Then the rapid *POP-POP-POP* of Carlos' handgun brings the Z down. The headless zombie crashes to the floor in a heap of brains and black ooze. Another comes around the corner. An older man, gaunt and hanging cheekbones with gray hair, limping, and a stinkin'. *POP!* It drops, and Jed crawls backward—crab style—from the slump of the body hitting the ground just in front of his face with a *thud!*

"Is it dead?" he bellows.

And yet, the wheeze of the zombie answers the teen's question. Its limbs spasming vigorously. Then he sees the pack of zombies coming closer along the road: moving in for the kill.

"We have to go!" Carlos yells. He grabs Mary's hand and pulls. *"Run! Don't get fucking eaten!"* Hammering home their dire situation.

Jed pulls out his Bowie knife and stabs the fumbling gray-haired Z in the head: it stops moving. Then the teen's up and running, 'track' and 'fielding' towards a nearby slick road.

"The gas! What about the gas! We can't just leave it behind."

With Mary's hand clenched tightly in his hand, Carlos hauls her along, through the maze of vehicles, steadily following Jed towards the slip road.

"Forget about the damn gas!" he retorts. "The jerry cans can't feel a fucking bite! But I bloody can if those Zs start to get the munchies," and he tugs Mary harder, making her move faster.

25
REGRETS

"They shouldn't be taking so long, Carl!" Naomi says, matter-of-factly. She sits in the back of the jeep—arm out of the sling, constantly chatting like a red robin at the beginning of spring. "It's been two hours!" Carl's eyes keep drifting upon Naomi's while checking her wound over, wondering if the world was different would they be together. "Carl! You listening to me? I can't believe you're just carrying on like everything's so… normal."

He'd listened to her complaints about the way he'd acted towards Jed. She'd used the expression to describe him as *'Just fell off the turnip truck'* and heck, he didn't even know what that had meant? Others too, such as *'Friendly as a bramble bush'* and

'*Y'all makes a hornet look cuddly.*' He figured she was calling him mean on those two!

But he understood: 'You're a total dick, Carl,' that phrase he's familiar with. The Native Texan had stuck up for the teen like a badass defense lawyer fighting for a death-row prisoner's freedom; she was so good, she could have had another profession instead of a wedding planner that her former life dictated.

She leans closer to him, temper flaring. "Are you listening! The others are taking a long time, Carl. Too damn long."

His daydreaming ends.

"Everything takes longer now." He looks at her. "Just can't take a walk down the street to your friendly 7-11 anymore, Naomi."

Her mouth whirls open, but no words escape—

Carl felt his body instinctively react before he consciously heard the distant but familiar echoes of gunshots. He instantly found Naomi's worried eyes.

The bickering had stopped.

It was time for Round Two to begin.

26
RUN FOR YOUR LIVES

Several minutes later, and at a sprint, Carlos and Mary eventually made it to the suburban jungle of former homes. Down one street, burnt-out-wrecks fill the once quiet tree-lined streets as they ran for their lives. A local News helicopter sat submerged into a looted corner store. Two hundred yards and they fled across a deserted parking lot and darted between two buildings as the pack of Creeps relentlessly gave chase.

Suddenly Mary stops. She hooks-a-wink back over her shoulder, checking on their nightmarish pursuers. Black-oozing bodies and sharp teeth give a steady and limpy chase.

"Why you stopping?" Carlos yells, breath catching in his tight chest.

"W-where's Jed?"

"I don't—" and he stops mid-sentence, looks left and right; the teen was out of sight, long gone. *Shit! Where's the toad fled to?* he queries. The constant *thump* of mangled footsteps pounding closer. "I'm unimpressed. That pompous little shit has left us for dead!"

"You're not happy?"

"No. I'm livid. Wait till I get hold of him."

"What do we do now?" She moves closer to Carlos, reaches out as she speaks. Carlos takes her clammy hand.

"We'll just carry on," he says. "Jed wouldn't—*shouldn't*—have gotten far!"

"If we can't find him? If he's lost? Or *worse*—" the words freeze in her mouth, she doesn't want to think what possibly could have happened to the teen.

"He'll be fine, Mary," Carlos sharply answers, squeezing her hand tighter. "We'll find him!" She glares back—eyes unsure. "We will."

"Well, in that case, lead on."

***

Mary allows Carlos to pull her through alleyways. Further on, they trundle between buildings like out of control supermarket trolleys down aisles of shelved groceries—out of breath and into a road. A sign reads Elm Street. Three Sheriff Office patrol cars (two Ford Utility Interceptors and the other, a Chevrolet Impala 9C1), are bumper-to-bumper barricading the entrance to a small street; the residents of the neighborhood had made One Last Stand, it seems.

Trees line the once pristine footpaths.

Near the end of the street, a voice screams like a teenage girl—*vocals* extremely high.

"C'mon, you two! This way! Hurry!"

Beyond the patrol cars, at the fifth abandoned house along the street, standing on a porch outside of a blue door, Jed is frantically waving his hands aloft like a scarecrow keeping birds away from the farmer's crop.

Mary and Carlos shimmied over a bonnet like cops from a 70s tv show, following the teen's invitational wave.

The neighborhood is in good condition, considering DIY was at the bottom of the homeowners to-do-list. Houses in a cul-de-sac, each a single floor property with flowerbeds that are over mulched and shot through with mushrooms, weeds and un-mowed gardens. A long time ago, the gardens were postage-stamp properties. These aren't poor houses, but these aren't luxurious houses, either. Middle-class suburban Utah homes with just enough mortgages and bills to keep the—former—homeowners in work.

The once lively neighborhoods of Salt Lake City are defined, as much as anything else, by the houses in them. And these, in turn, are defined by their architectural styles. And the cul-de-sac of properties incorporates design elements from different periods such as basic elements from the Pioneer Period (the garage style is humble, brick and stone, and stretched out), with details from the early twentieth century in the main frame of the buildings (and are less visible, informal and straightforward, and less intrusive on the landscape). Each bungalow has low-pitched roofs with wide front porches and dormers facing the street.

This particular bungalow has a paint-peeling white picket fence out front; a small iron gate that cannot be undone due to twisting weeds keeping it from use. The porch is timber—water damaged—the wood walkway wraps around the property: the house looks okay.

Moments later, they pull the screen door open.

Mary jolts a little when it *rattle-bangs* in its ill-fitted frame.

They are inside the safety of the four walls just as the pack of zombies starts to scramble over the blockade. Jed immediately shuts and locks the front door; one lock follows another, firmly behind his friends.

He breathes a sigh of relief.

27
THE HOUSE ON ELM STREET

It's dark.

"Okay, see? We made it. We're okay," Carlos banters. "Hey, how are you feeling?"

Mary stumbles back against the wall of the hallway for a second, a hand covering her mouth; she wasn't going to throw-up but came close to vomiting a black stream of yuckiness into his face. She replies, "Only half dead."

"Well… twice as good as before, right?" he jokes at her expense.

Mary breathes hard, can't see the amusing angle; keels over at the waist like a drunk in an alley.

"Just breathe, breathe from your abdomen," he says, gesturing to her. "Deep, long breaths."

She mentally checks her breathing—slows it down. *Okay, I'm fine,* she thinks. *Just peachy!* She leans back against the wall, slowly panting, internally shouting at herself to pull herself together. Then she looks at the Midwesterner who is now looking at Jed; his face is flushed red, but more importantly, it seems like his head is about to explode and fill the dark hallway with red-hot lava.

Carlos pushes Jed up against the wall. "Never do that again! Leave us for dead!" his voice above a whisper. He's hungry for blood. "Understand?"

"Umm."

Mary notices the teen fidgeting with his cords again (reminds her of when Carl 'beat up' on him earlier). "It's fine," she says, hand on the Midwesterner's shoulder. "He knows!" She focuses on the teen. "Don't you, Jed?"

Carlos gives her a look that conveys *what gives you the right to touch me, princess?* And at the same time, understands how he's acting towards Jed is wrong. He does the civilized thing, which is a rarity for him and says: "Okay, I get it. My bad, Jed. Didn't mean to beat up on ya, dawg. We cool?"

Jed nods a comprehensive nod.

"It's fine. I'm sorry too, Carlos. I just wanted to get out of there—away from the d-dead."

"I'm just saying," Carlos says, giving the teen a bro-punch in the shoulder. "Me too. Listen, things are different, knucklehead. You just can't run off like godforsaken Lassie on a mission!"

This is one for the record books! Mary thinks.

The teen nods again; takes the Midwesterner's cautious words on board. "So, hey, listen, I stumbled upon this house! It's empty. The door was unlocked. I tried a few other houses before… er—*no luck.* All bolted and locked."

Mary and Carlos look at each other, both in solidarity agreement; Jed has done well finding the abandoned property in the isolated neighborhood in the mix of being chased by a pack of ravenous Zs.

Mary: "You did well."

A twinge inside of Carlos. "Yeah. Did well."

Jed smiles. Twenty seconds later. "Now what?" he asks and starts to scan the darkened hallway of the abandoned property.

***

Outside the house is like an oven.

In here it is dark and cool, at least.

That's when—

A low *creeaakkkk* bleeds from the shadows—

It sounds as if someone is sneaking down some bare, wooden stairs at the stroke of midnight. But there are no stairs in this house, just a long stretching wooden corridor.

The unnatural sound, possibly amplified by a loose floorboard or two, makes Mary nervous. She spins around dramatically. *"Shit!"* escapes her mouth before the vase rolls off the small mahogany side table that sits by the door. (The slow look of fear spreads through the group like a bout of chlamydia through a retirement center as the inevitable happens; the vase shatters onto the wooden floorboards; the once peaceful quietness of the house magnifying the loud sound a hundred-fold.) "What was that noise?" she wonders, eyes panicking.

Fear transforms and envelops them all.

Silence unfolds for a second longer in which it seems to stretch a millennium.

Carlos' instincts take over. "Jesus! *Fuck!* Shall I just paint a target on our backs!" he curses, and takes aim with his Glock; his finger lying straight across the finger guard, he starts to scan the hallway for movement. "If. We. Have. To. Make. A. Run. For. It…" Each word escapes his lips quietly. (What were they going to do? Where were they going to run? Back outside with the pack of the undead? *Who knows if the fucking house is still inhabited?* He mind-swears to himself.) He doesn't finish the sentence. Instead, he sees shadows looming across the wooden floor. But if there were any residents left dwelling inside the house—alive or dead—they would come to greet them. *Right… about… now!*

Seconds later—

Nothing.

Jed mumbles quietly: *"We're alone! We're alone!"*

"Thank God!" Mary replies, her hand cusps her own weapon.

Carlos sneaks further and further into the house, Mary and Jed slightly behind. The floorboards remain silent; no squeaking or loose boards in the abandoned property. Another step and Carlos gazes through a set of open doors that lead into a large lounge. The shadows forming across the hallway floor were coming from the curtains in the big bay window fluttering like sails on the ocean in an afternoon wind. Someone had left the window open.

"Clear!" he whispers, sweeps the room of any sign of life.

Jed: "Now what?"

Mary rubs her eyes. Stretches. "We rest."

Jed: “Sounds simple.”

Mary: “I like things simple.”

Carlos: “You’re simple, Kansas.”

She sighs. “A lame comeback.”

He pauses. Looks at the Yooper. “It wasn’t supposed to be a comeback. Just reality.” And Carlos takes a step into the eggshell-colored lounge.

Ornaments decorate shelves below a large mirror on the far wall. Furniture too; a mix of side tables inserted into one another; smaller ones beneath large ones and so on like Matryoshka dolls (Russian dolls from the Motherland). A flatscreen TV and two dusty crème couches made the room seem almost normal.

“I’ll make sure the Zs are off our trail. I’m hoping this shitstorm will be over ASAFP (As Soon As Fucking Possible!), so we can go and retrieve that fuel we left behind…” His voice is in wise-Jedi mode. Carlos approaches the bay-window; grasps the thick fabric, and peek-a-boo through the curtains and out into the street. “Before high-tailing the fuck out of Dodge.”

“Yeah. OK. Love the plan.” Mary chews on her bottom lip. “What’s on the other side?”

Something: *“Ggguhh!”* groans back.

Carlos turns around; his face reminds her of getting down wit’ Droopy-D. “That’s not your ‘anything face’ it is more your ‘there’s a problem’ kinda face.”

It doesn’t take long for Carlos’ positiveness to turn dismissive. “Agghhh, there’s a slight problem, Kansas.”

Mary comes closer; peeks through the fabricated shield that protected the window like a poorly constructed barrier at a U.S Consulate in the Middle East, and stares through the grimy glass. Off in the distance, across the overgrown garden and further up the street, the pack of undead that had gathered on the freeway had dwindled to half. But the pack was far too many for them to escape through. Even if they managed to take down half-a-dozen, the other Infected would be on them in no time.

That’s when—

Mary sees what Carlos has just seen—

The Creep’s skin was yellowish and covered in dark red blotches, and once—brown or blue eyes—were now filmy and black. Hands rigid by its pot-bellied side, fingers tensed. But its mouth was opened larger than its own body to reveal a set of gnarly, sharp teeth. The lips closed, fusing back together for a short time before ripping apart to form another nightmarish grin.

The tatty Z stood outside the garden gate sniffing the afternoon air: sussing lunch out.

Mary gulps back: *“Don’t make a sound!”* Her frown a curved blade. Her trembling hands still have the fabric of the curtain gripped tightly. She shakes, continues to shake like her hands are reciprocating saws.

Carlos remains quiet; still as a still-life in an art class. “Kansas?” he hisses, noticing her hands vibrating. The heavy fabricated curtains shaking like a fat man on a dance floor.

“Ohhh!” she says, finally letting go.

Then, after the eternity it took for the sound of the slumbering to pass, their moans faded. There was silence.

"We're dead if it caught our scent!" she silently mouths, shifting uneasily from foot-to-foot before taking one last peek at the Creep through the curtain. It snarls at nothing; its mouth chomping shut and slowly wanders away—leaving the property behind, and most importantly, them alone.

***

Several seconds later, Carlos waltzes past her and gently reaches up and pulls the top window shut; both catches *click* into place. He draws the curtains, pulling himself and Mary away from the window. It doesn't take long to realize they are alone. "Where the fuck is Jed?" he asks, mystified why the teen wasn't where they'd left him.

The room was empty. The teen had disappeared again.

"I swear we need to keep that damn kid on a freakin' leash."

"Jed! Jed! Where are you, Jed?" Mary whispers for the third straight time.

There's a movement—

Carlos levels his Glock towards the hallway—

Mary does the same, imagines a hundred different scenarios: none of them good, and all involve the dead—*former*—owners of the bungalow coming to greet them.

"Carlos… you… think… that's… him?" Her words catch between each breath.

"Mm-hm," he retorts, voice shallow. Cursing seconds later as Jed wanders into view like a misbehaving toddler playing a game of Go Hide and Seek with unsuspecting parents.

They both lower their weapons.

"Shit! Fuck! I nearly blew your goddamn head off!" Carlos snarls. "Why you tip-toeing around the house like the killer from goddamn Cluedo?"

"Where'd you go?" Mary asks, much more politely.

"I was searching the kitchen." The answer comes out of the left.

"*Damn!*" Carlos exclaims, infuriated by the answer. "Least give us warning before you swan of next time, knucklehead!" He holsters his weapon. "You're a fucking idiot, Jed. Fact. Lock and stock. You'll get us all killed if you pull any more of your immature stunts!"

Mary shakes her head at the Midwesterner's words but knows he's right. Turns. Eyes the teen in utter hopelessness. "We need to stay close together. Have each other's back!" She moves closer—gun away—and holds his face in both palms. Staring into the teen's Bambi-laden eyes. "Don't you dare scare us like that again! I mean, ever!" Mary brings him closer; hugs him firmly.

Carlos stands behind, cursing Mary silently for encouraging him. But lets it slide.

Jed feels the warmth of love spread through his body and locks eyes with hers; realizing something both striking and comforting; Mary reminded him of his eldest sister, Audrey. (She was always protecting him.) He stammers for a response. "Oh—*I'm sorry*, Mary." Apologizes. "I-I—*thought* I should make myself handy, you know…"

"I don't follow?"

"I wanted to see if the backyard was all clear. So we could make a break for it through the kitchen and hopefully through the neighbor's backyard."

But all of that running off doesn't matter now, and Mary shifts from the embrace and pulls away. "Is it?" she asks, matter-of-factly. "Is it clear?"

"The garden's empty, but…"

The silence stretches. Mary can't ignore the waiting any longer. "But what?"

"The neighbors haven't exactly gone on holiday!"

"*Soooooo*… we're stuck between Zs out front and neighbors from beyond the grave out back?"

The teen nods at her question.

"That's fucked up," Carlos says, feeling his hairline; his t-shirt secondly. "Great. Topping the fucking day off, I've gone and dropped my sunglasses."

Mary, standing in front of the Midwesterner, squints in a mirror that hangs from the wall. She looks at herself. A mess. Jed a close second. An equal mess. Finally, Carlos. *Jesus! All he can think about is his goddamn sunnies!* The notion sounded ridiculous with how the day had planned out. A totally hopeless thought. She ventures: "We'll get you a new pair."

He chuckles at her remark. "Sure, will, Kansas."

Carlos begins scanning the egg-shell walls of the lounge; photos of wives, husbands, and children all smiling back. Some are taken on the pebbled shores of a lake: blue water glistens behind the family of four African Americans. Others on a beach. One with the wife on a horse. He wonders what had happened to the inhabitants of the house. Did they escape? Were they trapped in the worst possible tailback in history? Or did they make one Last Stand—like the residents of the Alamo—before the inevitable came—and a bloodthirsty end came to all the folks of the barricaded street?

It seemed the residents had taken the last option and had sadly failed in staying alive.

Mary collapsed onto a small, red leather footrest. "I assume we have a plan B and that it progresses beyond this exact moment in time?" Her words said so bitchily. Like it gave her pleasure in their dire situation.

"I try to take it one step at a time, Kansas," he answers and slides back down the couch, his ass smacking against the carpeted floor.

"Do you really?"

"Yeah. A step at a time."

28
ECHOES OF GUNSHOTS,

Deckard manages to pull his custom-made boots onto his feet as the far away shot rings in the distance. He is instantly up; his weary soles fully rested, and his sleek western jacket hanging on the jeep's side-mirror. As a combat veteran; he'd developed almost genetic survival skills since the end of the world had come around. Before even; in Afghanistan. Two tours of the Helmand Province. Hell, he was even present at the toppling of Saddam Hussein's statue in *Firdos Square* in Baghdad shortly after the invasion of Iraq in 2003.

Like the Texan, the former Marine was razor sharp when it came to gunshots.

Naomi: "That's—"

"—Gunshots!" Carl concludes.

"Affirmative, kids!" Deckard says, swiftly moving to the top of a hill. He surveys the horizon through his army-issued binoculars for the rest of the group. He zeroes in on the armored convoy. Nothing. Past the tailback until he reaches the point that the road bends around a craggy-mountain edge. Still no sign of life. No dead, either. No nothing.

Carl follows in the man's tracks. "Any luck?" he asks, reaching the top.

"Nah, kid. Can't see your friends."

Carl gazes through his own binoculars; circumnavigates the surrounding area.

"Our friends are in trouble. Do you see them?"

He doesn't know how to respond to Naomi's statement, doesn't know what to do at this moment? Should they wait and see what has happened? Or branch out and try to find their friends? It'd be foolish to try and navigate the roads by themselves, going closer and closer to the main city considering it was a Black Zone back in the day. Carl is apprehensive in what they'll find. But a part of him knew, if the others had run into trouble, they would find a way out of it as quickly as they'd stumbled into it.

Naomi narrows her eyes. "Carl? We gonna go?"

"We… wait!" he answers, his voice void of emotion.

She sneers. "Seriously?" Her voice erupts. "Christ, Carl, why aren't you communicating?"

And just for reassurance, Carl looks at Deckard for support.

The big guy stares back. "Your call, kid."

Carl quietly nods.

29
BACK IN SUBURBAN HELL

They waited until the dead got bored and left the neighborhood, (but the thing with walking corpses; they never got bored, and if the dead did somehow manage to find boredom as did the three survivors holed-up in an abandoned house on the outskirts of Salt Lake City, they weren't in a hurry to arrive home, go on Facebook, create a profile that clearly stated that *I am really bored of being an undead prick).*

An hour later, Carlos was lounging on the sofa in front of Mary while watching Jed twiddling his fingers, thoroughly annoyed, wondering precisely how long they should babysit this situation instead of striking out and trying to do something else. Finally, he's bored enough, stands, goes to the bay-window and parts the curtains. The view through the glass was still buzzing with Zs, while the Creep moved steadily down the street, lurking at every corner, reacting to every sound. While the 'Shufflers' were back at the barricade like a line of fucking scary-ass scarecrows. Up above, Carlos sees the sun moving across the sky and knows they wouldn't be able to make it back in time to the group before nightfall, even if they could escape the horde-of-undead camping outside for the long haul.

"That's it, I've had it," Carlos says, leaving the window behind. He heads towards the hallway. What else was there to do?

"Carlos?" Mary says, lurching from the confines of the couch. *Jesus! He's gonna make a run for it, and leave us behind.* "Come back!" her voice louder. "You may be a huge pain in the ass but… but we need you."

"Shucks. Don't worry, Kansas; I'm going nowhere, just exploring. See if there's something of value!" he calls back, shouldering her a smirky glance.

"We're not splitting up?"

"No," he chuckles. "Just… taking a look!" and he trailblazes ahead, totally ignoring what he'd said to Jed about running off on your own a while ago. "I'll take point. You guys follow." The Midwesterner liked being in charge, as though it was his God-given birthright like Jafar in Aladdin, he had to be Top Dog and rule the Kingdom.

"Yeah, okay," she replies, peering down the passageway like she expected zombies to pop-out from the walls like people-in-scary-ass-costumes-at-a-haunted-house attraction.

"Mary!"

"C'mon, pull yourself up!" she says to Jed. The teen levers himself from the floor, barely lifting his feet. He was imitating the slow, shuffling posture of a zombie, and together they followed.

***

Carlos noticed the house was in relatively good condition since being abandoned, even the dust seemed to be at a minimal-count. He waits by the first door for the others, with his Glock ready. “Ready to play what’s behind door number one?” he asks.

Mary murmurs, not too confidently, “No. Yeah. Probably.”

“That’s a terrible answer, Mary,” he replies, and pulls the handle down, gun on the trigger; the door opens.

The first room is a small bedroom painted baby bird blue. It was obvious it was a little boy’s room. Toy trucks and ABC books littered the fluffy floor. On the bed was a blanket that would have been soft if it wasn’t so old. A half-boarded up window sat just above the bed, the glass below—smashed outwards (they decide to leave the room and never enter again). They re-entered the hallway, and Carlos by-passes the next three closed doors and immediately ventures towards the end where the kitchen was situated.

Mary gestures with hands outstretched. “Where are you going? I thought we’re supposed to be doing this task together, Carlos?”

“You’ll be fine, Kansas. Anything moves, then pump it full of lead. Also… holler! If not—” he doesn’t finish the sentence, and before Mary can form a reply, Carlos disappears into the kitchen.

Jed asks: “Should we wait for him?”

“What? No. We’ll be fine. C’mon,” she replies. “Let’s go.”

***

They took a leap of faith, crossed the hallway, and opened another door. Colors from the outside world splashed through crimson curtains. It was also a bedroom, but this one was clean. Mary decided that this must be a teenage girl’s room. Torn boyband posters adorned the walls, and a tall bookcase stood in one corner with books full of horses and other animals. An oak wardrobe partially stood open, and Mary found gorgeous, colorful dresses. The colors had faded slightly on some of the dresses, and Mary saw why. A beam of light shone through the curtains and had fallen on the long-forgotten occupant’s threads. On the bedside table, a book waited for its former owner to come and read it. Mary moves closer, reads the cover; A Wrinkle in Time, written by *Madeleine L'Engle*. She’s read it before, it was a great story, and Mary realizes she’s the unearthly stranger that appears at their door, knowing she’d been blown off course. She takes that book and slides it into her rucksack.

Next up, they enter the master bedroom. The room was also empty. A king-sized bed with warm colored covers took up the majority of the space. Throw pillows, and sleeping pillows and every other imaginable pillow snuggles against the dark-wood headboard. A walk-in wardrobe stood open in the corner, and an ensuite stood adjacent.

Mary finds stains covering the carpet, which led into the ensuite. It took a second to understand what the dark spots on the floor were; the bloodstains were hard to see against the dark carpet, but they were there just the same. She tries her hardest not to seem afraid, doesn’t jump back, and focuses on the ensuite door.

"H-how does this work?" Jed nervously asks. He stands behind Mary with his hunting knife out. "We should get Carlos!" he proclaims, nervously looking down the hallway for the Midwesterner to show his face.

"No. Don't worry," she says, face brimming with a smile. Nervousness had taken a back seat. "We'll be fine. You got my back if a bathroom full of Zs jump us?" and she unsheaths her sidearm. "Here! Aim for the head"—she taps her own skull between both eyes—"drop 'em with a blow to the forehead. Right?"

Jed bites his upper lip, trying to form a reply and finds his mouth is as dry as the Arizona Desert. At the same time, wishes he had a pistol. He peeks-a-look back into the hallway; still no sign of Carlos.

"You ready?"

"Not at all," he answers, keeping close. His hand slightly shakes, and the curve of his hunting knife glittered away.

Mary pauses for a second.

Breathe in, breathe out, she tells herself. *One, two, three. Ready!* And she slowly turns the handle; the first thing to hit her is a pungent smell that smelt of old mothballs and decaying beavers. She raises a hand to shield her nose and was too shocked to speak—

Inside the ensuite lying on the floor, an arm—just an arm—and nothing else. The flesh had decayed away long ago, leaving the remnants of bone and rag combined. Dark blotches decorated the once clean tiles. Dry, bloodied handprints adorned the white walls, floor, porcelain sink, and toilet, and also around the smashed window frame: someone or something had gotten out.

Mary curses. *"Shit!"* she chokes down fears and peers into the bathtub, her hand still covering her face. The decayed, curved body of the arm's owner stared back at her. Mary spastically jerked backward—gazing steadily into the skull's sunken eye sockets. In the skeleton's bony grip lay a revolver, and in its skull lay the bullet. Beneath the body, the body's oily fats had congealed into a sticky and solid greasy film.

Mary stands for nearly a minute looking at the light coming through the side of the skull, and long enough for Jed to ask her what was happening.

"Mary, what is it?" he questions again. The teenager had stayed outside the ensuite, ready and waiting for oncoming danger. The threat never materialized. But he still smelt that pungent whiff-of-death.

"Don't come in," she gasps.

He realizes Mary's voice has changed and wary of the command, and eager to obey, the teen freezes.

She leans into the bathtub, grabs the revolver, but the skeleton's grip was firm. With the butt of her gun, she brings it down, smacking the bony hand's tight grasp. *Yuck!* With a *crack*, the former owner relinquished its grip. She checks the chamber; one bullet spent, but otherwise, full. (She blinks, and a small glitter pings from the bottom of the tub, half submerged in the body fat and dried blood; it's the ammo casing.) Without pause, Mary says: "Let's go." She reverses like a car towards the door. The whole scene makes her nauseous. Finally shuts the door. "Here," she says, turning, "take it!" and hands Jed the Smith & Wesson Model No. 2 revolver. "Nearly all the chambers are full. Make sure every shot counts when you come to use it. Don't lose it this time. And don't shoot yourself, either!"

Jed reacts instantly.

"Whoa!" he says. He was itching to get a gun again since he'd dropped his last firearm back at the silo. "Thanks, Mary. I won't." He stores the over-sized pistol inside his empty holster. It's a bit loose, but otherwise won't fall out, and it makes him feels safer, and at the same time, a bad-ass cop.

Before the teenager knows what's happening, Mary ushers him out of the master bedroom and back into the hallway, all the while Jed wanting to know what lay in the ensuite. She needs a moment away from the body, the smell, the skeleton in the bathtub; hole in its head, laying in the firm, fatty juices like a piece of turkey left over from a Thanksgiving dinner.

Mary shuts the door, plants a hand onto the hallway wall, breathes in and out. *Jesus! Sonovabitch, why did I have to see that image? It'll be branded into my memory forever.*

Eventually, she looks up—

Carlos is standing at the end—

"I was just coming to find you guys," he says, looking at Mary. "Fuck's wrong with you? Everything 'kay? You look whiter than usual!"

She nods, doesn't even mind the Midwesterner's dry sense of humor. "I'm fine. But the room"—her head tilts to the closed door—"is off limits until we're gone."

Carlos understands the command. Deep down, knew she had walked into a hellhole-of-a messed-up-situation. He too had stumbled into rooms he'd never wished he'd entered in the first place. The horrors of those images burning a mental template into his memories.

He quickly changes the subject. "Guess what I found?"

30
FRUSTRATIONS OF ANGER

Back at the jeep, Carl gazes at Naomi. Her jet-black hair still held mud from the grounds of the silo. But her delicate facial features only reinforced Carl's love for her. The Texan stares back at him with eyes the sizes of asteroids. He sees the fire burning brightly behind those eyes; senses the willingness to form a search party all by herself and go find their friends from whatever unholy mess they'd found themselves in.

They sit on the brow of the hill beneath a shaded tree, overlooking the trail of abandoned vehicles that stretches for miles in one direction.

"We should have gone and searched for them, Carl," she says forcefully. "Not idly sat on our backsides waiting for them to wander back like family pets. You heard the shots! *God* knows what might have happened out there."

Naomi had been pacing up and down the hot tarmac for what felt like forever worrying about her friends. And yet, they never left this spot to search for them. Eventually, she joined Carl on the brow of the hill and had been there ever since—checking and re-checking through the binoculars. Zooming in. Zooming out. Scanning the clogged Interstate for signs of life.

Meanwhile, Carl had time to think: recalculate his decision not to go searching for their friends. Did he make the right call? If the tables were turned, would Carlos, Mary, and Jed leave them out there in the middle of nowhere? (Thinking about the choice harder, he realized Carlos probably would have, but Mary and Jed would have come straight to their rescue.)

"Oh, come on! After all, I—" He pleads his innocence like Ned Stark up on the gallows just before he came to a messy end. "What more could we have done? What more can I do to prove—"

"You didn't need to prove anythin' to me, Carl," she answers. "They're our friends. They could be in trouble. I…I just expected some leadership from you, cause—*well*, that's your thing! Your ability. You lead us all in times of trouble… like we're a team. No. Like family."

She waits for Carl to comprehend how literal her words are.

Several seconds later, he doesn't seem to get it.

"Damn it, Carl! We could have done somethin' when that option was on the table. When we still had choices to make."

"I'm sorry, okay," he interjects. "What good is it if we went and tried to find the others? We have no way of knowing where they might be. They could be on their way back for all we know. Taking an alternative route." He swallows a hard knot at every question asked. "We might have passed them on the way—It will be getting dark soon…" The list stretches and (he knows deep down the reasons for not going sound like lame-ass excuses). He offers her a hand.

"Bah." She waves him off with her uninjured arm. "Two hours! Two goddamn hours," she takes a breath, finally releases her anger, "we have been sittin' on this goddamn hill waitin'—*no*, hopin' for our friends to come back to us with fuel. All of them safe and in one piece. So we can go on our travels! But you were wrong in making that call."

Carl didn't move. He felt like he had during the drive away from the exploding silo before they ran into the ex-Marine at the abandoned bar. When Naomi had been shot by Mary. He felt useless, unable to address the situation, to find a way out of the mess. It was a life-and-death situation. That was a strange thought. And he felt the same now.

"Naomi!"

"What?"

"Mary's a survivor. Jed is a survivor. Carlos… well, he's a dick, but he knows how to survive when the goin' gets tough. They're all survivors of a shitty world we happen to live in. But they will survive. You just have to believe."

She shakes her head. "We should've gone!"

He finally concedes the truth. "I know."

They sit silently on the hillside, gazing into the distance. The sun was hanging low in the sky above their heads; it would be dark soon, and Carl knew that they could never make it back to the jeep by nightfall—if they went searching for the others now. He wondered if the others were okay. If they were cornered. Trapped. Injured. Or worse? Wonders if they'd managed to claim an empty house in the 'ghost city' for the night. Carl knew that the situation would drive Mary completely crazy—*sheltering* with Carlos for the night while hiding from the dead.

But he hoped for a 'silver lining' outcome. And he hoped Naomi would forgive him too for making the wrong call.

***

Seconds later—

"Sundown coming in a few hours. We better start preparing camp."

"What?" Naomi says, looking up at the figure beneath the branches of the Balsam Poplar standing on top of the hill. "But… the *others!*"

"What else you want to do, missie? Go back out there in the dark?"

Naomi looks at Deckard. Turns back to Carl; eyes probing his flawless diamond eyes for backup, an objection to the ex-Marine's questions. And Carl was looking back. Two seconds Three seconds. More than ten.

"Deckard's right," he agrees. "We have to settle in for the night. Make camp. And in the morning… at first *light*—" Carl leans into her and tries to take her hand. But Naomi pulls away, fingers slipping from his grasp.

"Crap!"

All heads turn towards her, and Naomi stares back at them as the only speaker-of-sanity.

"It's what's gonna happen, Naomi. End of convo." The words escape Carl's lips harsher than he'd like them to.

She gets it. Knew Carl was correct—still, the notion of leaving their friends out near that abandoned city at night didn't sit right with her. Plus, the Texan was pissed at the lack of leadership Carl had shown all those hours ago. She gets up and storms down the hill towards the jeep.

“Naomi!” he yells. “There’s nothing we can do!”

“No. Not now. But earlier, we had a chance.”

(Door slams.)

31
THE TALK

"Well, that was an interesting development," Carl murmurs.

"Let her be, kid!" Deckard says and plonks his large frame to the ground. He scuffs his boots into the green grass; stumps up a tuft of dirt like he's digging at the beach with a shovel. "Time apart will make both your lives loads easier!" and he tilts his fedora; tiny specks of dust drifting in the evening sundown.

"Huh!"

He explains: "Fuel needs oxygen to burn. Take one of those components away, i.e, you or your lovely Asian friend—Naomi—from the equation and the situation will solve itself. Don't be quick on the draw, trying to make everyone in your life happy, kid. Sometimes in life… you can't remedy that action. And in this life, we've been dealt with…" (*Choices are shittin' scarce*, he thinks), but says, "*Heck*, choices are based on 'here and now' decisions. You made the right call. You have no idea where your friends might be out there!"

"I don't." He crosses his arms and leans forward in a straighter sitting position. "You're right, Deckard."

"You're a quick kid. Fast. Caring for the ones you love. You're a natural, born leader. The choices you make will make you into the leader you are now. Don't beat yourself up. It'll all work out in the end."

A moment passes, and Carl gazes at the darkening sky, a flock-of-birds (*maybe the ducks Mary had seen earlier?* he imagines), flying westerly over the great lake. The same way they were. Carl didn't know if it was a good omen that the birds were traveling in the same direction or not. But he hoped they weren't fleeing a horde of ravenous Zs coming from the former city streets. He takes a deep breath, understands Naomi was—*still*— furious with him for not going to search for their friends. But he'd made the decision to stay with the jeep. Wait for the others to return. He'd dealt those cards for both of them like a dealer at a blackjack table, Deckard too, and exerted the leadership which needed to be shown.

What else could I have done?

Deckard leans forward. "On your travels, kid, you'll let some people down for sure, but you won't fail them. Never. *Ahhh heck*, it'll all make sense sooner or later." He offers the silver hip flask. "It'll make you feel good, kid. Strong also, like a magic potion. Trust me. Take a swig and relieve your burdens for once. If not, and you hold on to your group's problems, they will eventually drive you insane. Or straight out, kill you."

Carl takes the small silver metal hip flask. Drinks, not *sips* like he's supposed to, from the small opening. He coughs and splutters, washing the dust from his mouth with a swig of whiskey. "You're kidding me," he chokes, the sharp aftertaste burning the inside of his throat. "This… stuff… it'll kill me before my group's problems will!" Carl feels he'd taken a swig of flamin' sambuca in a trendy Westside bar. He persists, takes a sip this time, and the elegance and class of the whiskey strikes.

"Talisker Scotch Whisky," Deckard says, taking the flask back from the kid's grip. "Those damn Scots knew how to fuck with the English and also brew a decent drink." He explains further: "This scotch captures the Scottish spirit, their mighty Highland strength well with its bold taste and brand attitude. Captures their spirit in a bottle of hard liquor."

Carl admires the ex-Marine as he takes a gulp, noticing the man knew how to handle his drink.

"When it was finally released to the general public, this particular Scotch whiskey caught on around the world like wildfire." Deckard let out a short, unapologetic laugh. "Just like this plague, hey kid!"

Carl looks to his guest.

"Loving someone means protecting them from themselves, kid. You did the right thing with your friend staying put; who knows what might have happened to the rest of your group so close to the city. And with night fast approaching, you wouldn't have been able to make it back in time." Carl listens intently to the former Marine's words. "The best thing for all of us—*ride* it out until morning. If they're not back, we'll go searching for your friends and the fuel at sun-up so we can carry on with our journey to Portland!"

Carl nods at the promise of help. Knows it'll be faster too having more feet on the ground. More souls in the search party. "Did I make the right call by not going to search for our friends?" His eyes scan Deckard's.

"Please don't, kid."

"Please don't, what?"

"Okay. True fact," Deckard says. "When I was 15, I thought it was a good idea to paint a self-portrait for a school art project that featured half my face like a Jackson Pollock." (Carl's eyebrows rose; knowing the work of the great American artist.) "I like to remind myself of this because I thought I was a sensible functioning adult then, too."

This wasn't entirely correct.

"What do you mean?"

"We've still got a lot to learn, kid, even in this new world that continually surprises us." Deckard hands him the flask again. "Stop self-doubting yourself, kid. Your friend will come around. It'll just take some time for others to see your point of view. That girl has got that tough Texan spirit embodied throughout her the same as this darn, fearsome Scottish whiskey. It never goes away. She'll be fine soon."

Deckard hands him back the silver flask.

***

Carl found himself smiling. "Okay," he says. "I believe you. Naomi will recover. We'll find our—*my*- friends in the morning, and get out of this mess. Can continue to Portland too." The talk with the man had done him a power of good, and he takes another swig of the Talisker Scotch Whisky. But deep down Carl's still apprehensive about the safety of his friends.

He gazes at the former Marine. A few hours ago, he was ready to end the life of the 'drifter' back at the bar. But now, after getting to know the guy, for all of his help with restoring the jeep, Carl likes Deckard enough to trust him. Or to open up to him with his own problems.

Carl looks at Deckard again; he was cool, a lot cooler than him. Not just his choice of clothes or firearm. Maybe it was all that military training. For a moment, the Marine reminded Carl of his father. Always trained and ready, waiting for action, intelligent. Always strong enough to protect his family—the ones he loved—from crises because he believed in it. Carl realized the Oklahoma local was full of irrefutable logic and was like a hardened version of Gandhi.

Then it hit Carl, he realizes he is more like his father than he'd ever imagined. "Hey, did you really draw yourself using the style of Pollock?"

Broad shoulders shrug, and Deckard looks across at the millennial, caught off guard and gave a yes just as the question begged to be answered. "Sure did," he replies, and five seconds go by. "Threw that paint around the canvas like I didn't give a shit who it landed on. Got A+ in art class, though."

The image brings a warm smile to Carl's face. He gives back the hip-flask.

"When first light hits, we'll go find your friends and bring them safely back." Deckard takes the flask, raises his large frame off the ground. "Let's make camp before it gets too late, kid. We don't want any surprises during the night if we're not probably prepared."

Carl nods and follows, leaving the hill behind.

32
BACK AT THE HOUSE

There was once a time when local preachers standing on street corners predicting the apocalypse would have been deemed crazy. Shoppers would cross the street to avoid the ranting-archetypal-banner-waving man loudly proclaiming 'the end of the world is nigh' and 'God loves no sinners.'

Then there were as many as three million Americans who fell into the category dubbed 'prepper.' People who made detailed plans for the end of the world as we know it. The preppers were an ever-growing group of survivalists who took extreme measures to prepare for a major catastrophic event (there was even dedicated TV shows, and Web series on the subject too).

One man from Las Vegas kept 4,000 goldfish in the deep end of a vacant motel swimming pool which he planned to eat when a massive solar flare 'knocked civilization back to the Stone Age.' While an Ohio couple living in a gated home with 85,000 rounds of ammunition had enough food to last half a century. Then we had bullet-proof and bomb-proof bunkers being constructed in the Arizona Desert for the wealthy elite, and there were countless others too in each and every state.

Also, whole websites run by groups such as Survivalist Summit America (SSA), and the American Preppers Network (APN), who dedicated their time, cataloged how people were planning for the worst-case scenario. (More than 300,000 people in a single month visited another movement's website, *survivalblog.surviveatalllowcosts.com*, which catalogs what people needed to buy and made a smacking profit by selling those goods to the hungry masses.)

***

That's exactly what Carlos had found in the garage.

Shows them the water purifier system by the door that collected rainwater on the roof of the bungalow which fed through the main house into the garage. Clear canisters of slowly evaporating water sat next to the system.

He says to the others as they search crate after crate for goodies like bargain hunters in a backyard sale: "When the worst happened, and it became apparent the U.S. Government couldn't provide for everybody and the realization the country was about to fall and crumble to a zombie epidemic of biblical proportions, prepping became widespread."

Jed shifts his gaze to the Midwesterner as he fumbles through a large plastic container: food galore greeted his hungry eyes. Vegetables. Fruit. Beans, all in easy-to-open cans.

"Whether you're expecting Doomsday on the West Coast or live in Tornado Alley. These people had a proper prepper's pantry. I mean, they knew what to do, how to prep for the worse scenario imaginable."

Then there were the camping supplies: two stoves and a cache of wind-up flashlights. And an abundance of candles too.

"Having a light source that doesn't require batteries or fuel is a good backup to have," Mary adds. "And oil lamps are much safer than candles, especially when there is no electricity," she points at the extra light source in another box.

"Yeah, Kansas," he acknowledges with a curt nod. "Sure come in handy."

Three 'Bugout bags' prepped and ready to go sat in the back of an empty teak Buick Enclave. Other bags and packs for other purposes like car kits and first aid kits sat around the vehicle.

In the far corner, Jed found an old crank radio in need of repair and a CB radio sitting on a workbench. The teen always wanted to find a crank radio; it was on his survival list and an ideal addition to every emergency kit. The find brightens his young face, and he proceeds to go through the spare parts scattered on the bench to fix the CB radio.

Mary found extra clothing and boots. *Having some extra clothing was always good to have, even if it's just 'SHTF clothing' and they even put 'em away in a storage bin for emergency use. Smart people*, she's glad, and rifles further through the clothes, finding a pair of tracking boots that fitted her nicely and decided to throw her worn sneakers away. "The family sure wanted to be prepared for disaster when it struck!" she says of the cusp.

"Yeah, it seems they wanted to be able to keep themselves safe at all costs," Carlos answers. He'd also found some nice new footwear.

"Which didn't exactly go to plan, though!" Mary quietly whispers to herself.

The image of the skeleton lying in the bathtub with a bullet through its skull lingers in her mind a moment longer before she tucks the disturbing thought away like a secret in a box beneath her bed which she didn't want her parents to know. The Midwesterner doesn't hear her, and she continues searching for a change of clothes.

Then there were the canned and dried supplies: stacked and stored in Tupperware on shelving units that filled an entire wall. Survival knives, kitchen knives, and other kitchen utensils that hadn't been sorted into a box. Three automatic rifles and a cache of ammo were just lying on the concrete floor, ready to be packed away. Then there were the fuel cans piled high by the garage door; each with premium golden gas.

The whole garage was like an 'Aladdin's cave of treasure' waiting to be carted away on a magical fucking flying carpet.

***

A while later, Mary and Carlos left Jed in the garage at the workbench; the teen was happy enough with his new toy, and at this rate, wouldn't run off into trouble. They ventured back into the house through a small passageway and into the hallway and checked out the final unopened door. It was the main bathroom; this room had nobody in the tub and was pleasantly nice; a shower, double vanity, a porcelain-styled-freestanding bathtub greeted them. Pale greens walls and a tiled floor, but no running water.

They finally settled in the kitchen where the cupboards were bare, except for the usual: plates, bowls, and cups that lined the shelves, and they guessed everything that was of value was now packed away in the garage.

Seconds later, Mary peeks through the boarded up rear patio doors—just as Jed had earlier—which feeds into the backyard. Six-foot wooden fences thick with heavy scrubs ran around the perimeter of the garden. On all sides are neighboring properties surrounding their 'fortified hideaway' in not-so-welcoming paradise, and to escape, they have to clamber over the fences and into hostile territory.

All hope fades, and Mary's smile subsides as she sees broken planks in the fence. Between each splintered piece of dark wood, she sees a hand reaching through; the fleshy fingers curling in a desperate plea for aid. Mary stares in horror as the hand is slowly followed by the arm; the flesh loose, catching on the wood and rotting away in chunks. Through another fence at the back of the property, she sees the unmistakable shadow of a figure. But it wasn't a helpful neighbor with freshly home-baked cookies and a smile.

It's a Creep. (*The middle-aged former neighbor,* she's guessing.) It stops for a second longer, sniffing the air like a wolf tracking prey. Its jaws opened wider than its body would allow; its mouth tearing at the sides before fusing together again as it shut its hideous food-hole and trundled away.

"We're fucked," she curses aloud, plonking her bum down on a stool. A steady submissive gaze cast to the floor.

Her words catch Carlos by surprise, and he sits down by her side on another stool at the kitchen island bench. "Nothing's ever easy, Kansas."

She looks up into the Midwesterner's eyes, his words were spot on. She can't even think of a snarky 'comeback.' All she says: "Right."

He looks about the kitchen: copper pans hanging above his head. Integrated cupboard space. LED lights in the snowy-colored ceiling. He feels the granite top; a sleek feeling beneath his fingers. "Helluva fancy kitchen," he whistles. "Could have fitted my entire Lower East Side apartment in this space!" A cheap snort of amusement. "With plenty of room to spare for another block or two."

They sit at the nice island benchtop, in the fancy kitchen with its boarded up windows and doors keeping the undead at a safe distance like Mr. and Mrs. Haseltine (the perfect image of an 'all-American family' but doesn't fit the generational and societal 'white picket fence' stereotype no more).

"Mine too," she adds, and they share an unfamiliar smile with one another. "*Sooooooo,* now what?"

"I guess… we make ourselves at home."

33
DUSK UP

It was still twilight, but the sun had taken all the warmth with it. Priorities such as finding a decent patch to set up house—for the night—and preparing dinner kept them busy.

Luckily, where they stopped, just off the side of the interstate, a thick bracket of bushes offered them protection from one side. While the hill with the tree atop sat in front of them. The jeep lay across the opening of the small roadside clearing, shielding them like a wall. It was a solid encampment. They hung two zip lines across the only opening that allowed anybody into the camp. The wires, one at shin height and the other at mid-waist were fastened to the jeep at grill and wing-mirror respectively and stretched to a nearby tree, another Balsam Poplar around its round base; its dark green leaves above, and lighter shades below added shelter as the night was cold and gentle.

Naomi prepares a small fire; big enough to cook on, but at the same time small so the flames wouldn't draw uninvited intruders into their encampment.

Deckard, who had lived on nonperishables for longer periods than some astronauts was amazed that the tin of mixed beans never tasted so damn fine when cooked in the Texan's aluminum pot.

"Fine grub, Naomi," he says.

She takes that compliment and tucks it away for later. "Only the best à la carte meal will do, y'all," she replies in a moderate to happy tone. "Choices are a minimum tonight." She stirs some beef jerky into the steaming pot. A splash of herbs also. Goes to scoop the beef and beans broth up onto a tin plate that balances on her knees.

Carl wants to help out—goes to grab the tin plate for her. "You need a hand!"

"Trying to be funny?"

He doesn't realize his words come out dumb, also a touch rude.

Seconds later—

"Naomi, you okay? About earl—"

"Carl, stop giving me arguments so easily; they might come back and hurt you!"

"I just wanted to apologize."

"Right, because an apology is what you think I want to hear round 'bout now?"

"Yeah. Yes—that's exactly what I think you want me to say."

Deckard listens carefully. He sits in the path of flying arguments coming from both sides of the coin. The Marine is also tired of the two kids, and at that very moment, feels like he'd never left school and is the third wheel in a lover's squabble in the mix of a sleepover. Finishes the rest of the food quickly. "It's gonna be fine," he murmurs, setting down his plate to the ground. They both stop arguing in front of the ex-Marine. "Your friends are safe in some secure building they found for the night. It's a shoo-in!" His words bring added clarity between the sparring boy and girl. Next, he gets up to leave. "I'll stand on watch," he says, not offering much of a chance for objections. "You two will be okay?"

Carl nods for both of them.

"Sleep tight."

Naomi says: "Will do."

Carl says: "Wake me when you want a rest, Deckard. Okay?"

"Affirmative, kid. Be seeing you in the early hours," he replies. Leaves Naomi and Carl snuggled by the flames of the rescinding fire.

***

A damp chill grips the air, even in the middle of the Utah summer. The days are hot and long, while the night brings about a ghostly chill to the skin, like damp set into the bones of an old house for the long haul.

No seasons of the year were ever normal anymore.

Deckard does his jacket up tight beneath his grizzled chin. Scratches an earlobe and ponders the long day. Knew he'd traveled a great distance. Found companions he believed he could trust once again. But also, knew the kids needed protecting from the horrors of the world, and from themselves, it seems. He's unsure he wants to be the lion of the pride. The bear father looking after young cubs trekking all the way to Portland, to salvation.

Huh, he muses at the word. *Jeez, these kids must believe in this shit real bad. Bad enough to travel across the unknown states of Good Ol' America to what... endless possibilities of unknowns?*

He does a quick circuit of the grounds; checks, re-checks the perimeter. No signs of the dead. Goes back up the hill, sits underneath the tree for shade. He has a perfect 360 of the surrounding land. Every square mile of geographical delights. He has an itchy back and uses the trunk of the Balsam Poplar as a scratch post; the tough bark itching that itch. (The tree is uncommon to the area, just like them. Just drifters trying to find a way in the unfamiliar world.)

Itch finally satisfied, there he sits, ponders, and waits till dawn.

34
CARING IS SHARING

With night drawing in, and the darkness sweeping the city, they decide to get comfy in the lounge after barricading the bay-window with an abundance of furniture; the house seemed secure enough, front and back locked down like Fort Knocks securing billions of bullion for the wealthy elite. A maximum security prison in the middle of a riot. Nobody was getting out. More importantly, the dead weren't coming in.

Mary sat back on the couch, munching one of the dehydrated fruit bars they had found in a box while Jed was in the garage cataloging supplies. "Why do you keep beating up on Jed, Carlos?" she asks. The Midwesterner sat opposite her with two cans of tinned peaches between his new threads, and two small candles beside his feet; small flames casting light into the dark lounge.

"He needs to learn that you can't keep on screwing up in this world. It's not like before, where if you made a mistake you'd get a slap on the wrists. A pat on the back while someone says 'It's okay, just don't do it again'. It just doesn't cut the mustard anymore. In this world, if you keep on fucking up, you'll die, and others around you will die too. There are no second lives. No pause button like… in a PlayStation game. No restart mode."

"But—"

"There's no but's, Mary. We've all learned the hard way not to make mistakes. And Jed has to learn as well."

There was a dynamic power struggle beginning to emerge from the room, and Carlos didn't want to lose the argument. (Hell, he didn't want to play second fiddle to Mary also.) He grabs another pear; between thumb and forefinger, pinches the slippery fruit between digits and eats.

(Munch. Munch, munch.)

"At specifically what time did you become aware that you'd become such a Grade A Social Dickhead?" she asks unashamedly.

His lips turn into a tight smirk. *Munch. Munch, munch.* He glares hard back towards her. "The same reason many of us struggle, Kansas…"

"Let me guess, mommy and daddy didn't love you?"

"No, they loved me," he retorts.

Mary lounges on the couch like a mermaid lazing on a rock inticing unfortunate sailors to their deaths. "Are you going to cry, Carlos?"

"Screw you, Mary."

Mary leans closer, peering into his eyes; the flames casting shimmering light onto his upset face. "No, tell me. I want to know," she persists. "How does a kid who's loved by his parents turn into the biggest dick in the world?"

That brought silence to the room.

Carlos sticks another peach in his mouth. *Munch.* Swallow in one. Gulps. Thinks for a second. "It's a funny story," he begins. "My life began with the same flash-bulb crack that would accompany any first child of two of Indiana's most prestigious country singers, John 'Moony' Haseltine and Loretta Ashley Moore. My parents had a catalog of razor-sharp rhymes stretching across several albums, three solo albums apiece and a duo album. They were both 'Hoosiers'…"

Mary tilts her head like a dog looking at another dog performing a trick on television, but doesn't understand how that dog is so miniature.

"Huh!"

He gets it, by the look on Mary's face, she doesn't understand the meaning of the vague word. "Yeah. Okay. A 'Hoosier' is defined as someone who helped shape the cultural identity of Indiana or someone whose identity was shaped by the state."

"Ohhh," she declares at the unknown fact.

"When two celebrities do the deed, someone like me is the result." Carlos finishes the last of the peaches and tosses the can away (it bounces once on the carpet and stands upright). He continues calmly retelling his childhood to Mary. "How I remember, when I was born, my mother was given an anesthetic by the nurse because she was allergic to epidurals. Consequently, she was unconscious. Now, my mother was a beautiful woman—*she* was beautiful into her 60s until she died. Of natural causes!" he adds for the sake of his memory. "So at 42, she looked like a Christmas morning. Delightful as ever, Mary. All the doctors in the delivery room were buzzing around her pretty head, saying: 'Oh, look at Loretta Moore asleep. How pretty she is,' and she was a stunner too. In the meantime, my father, upon seeing me start to arrive into the world, and his beautiful wife unconscious. Well… *fuck,* he does what he does best. My father faints—*hogs the spotlight* away from his first born son and my sleeping mother. So all the nurses ran over saying: 'Ohhh, there's John Haseltine. Let's go look at him, the crooner (*and he was a ladies' man,* he thinks *a right, vengeful womanizer*), on the ground and unconscious.' So when I arrived, I was virtually unattended in that small delivery room in the middle of F-you Jerksville Corydon."

"Holy shit! Were you some kind of 'The Partridge Family tribute act?' touring towns, singing, and performing!" Mary absentmindedly hollers as she chews her fruit bar.

Carlos shoots her a smug look of annoyance—*grinds* his teeth together. "Yeah. A family dynasty." Gives a quick middle-fingered salute to her and carries on. "During my life, I never showed a glimpse of show business talent. None. Zero. Zilch. My brother did; my sis too. Thirteen years later, my Pa famously left my Ma and his kids for this other, younger woman. His goddamn music producer. In the court documents it cited 'Irreconcilable Differences,' and I'm like fuck me when I finally found out. An attorney for my mother told the Local Press at the time that the decision was made 'for the health of the family.' She also asked for physical custody of us—13-year-old Carlos, 12-year-old Devin, 10-year-old Keri. My father never objected to this condition."

Mary sat thoroughly engrossed, listening intently and eating another snack bar as Carlos spilled his life story to her like he was talking to a shrink regarding the many underlying problems that made him into a functioning but somewhat, faltering adult.

"My mother and my father were Indiana's sweethearts," he banters. "They literally received that tag throughout the state and beyond. Even my parents sort of went along with the assumption that they were a good couple. In the beginning, they probably were, but when they had children, they probably weren't a very good couple. So, with a career to maintain, my mother could not put her entire focus on her children. She was away so frequently that my sister, brother, and I took advantage of her time at home anyway we could."

Mary found herself shivering as she listened intently to the Midwesterner talk about his childhood; layers and layers peeling away like an emotional banana skin; one slip and he'd be falling onto his backside crying.

Carlos sunk further down the wall. "Mary, I grappled with the notion when I grew older that my mother 'belonged to the world and to her fans,' as much as she belonged to her children." He takes a deep breath. "Whenever we went out as a family to the cinema, restaurants et cetera… we were constantly interrupted by so many fans that it was not like having private time with her, anymore. People walked over my younger siblings and me just to get to her. And no, I didn't like it. And I didn't like sharing her." Carlos pulls the lid from the second tin of peaches; it peels back with a metallic scrape. "When we went out, I overheard people saying, 'He must think he's so great because he's the eldest son of John Haseltine and Loretta Moore!' And I didn't like it; I was just a kid, and it made me different from other people, other children and I wanted to be the same. My brother and sister were fine with everything, though—they were *lucky* enough to get the good genes and started singing too. But I knew I could never be like her or my father or even follow in the footsteps of Devin and Keri"—he groans a frustrated moan—"I have been trying to make up for that fact ever since."

Mary slides off the couch and joins Carlos on the floor. "Jesus. Carlos—I didn't realize…"

He looks up, caught off guard by her sudden movement towards him like a snake to its charmer. "Don't beat yourself up over it. If you weren't born in or around Indiana, you wouldn't know me from your average Joe." A short burst of laughter follows. "Kansas, why am I telling you about my fucked-up childhood!"

She shrugs. No answer comes.

"Why do you keep on calling me Kansas? I'm not even from the Sunflower State."

He shrugs. *Because your face radiates warmth,* he thinks. *WTF!* And wonders where the thought had come from before shaking the unwanted notion away. No answer comes.

Mary waits for a cocky comeback.

Seconds pass and Carlos begins chirping away regarding his past like an edgy parrot divulging its master's secrets.

"That's why I skipped Corydon the first chance I got and ended up living in Manhattan on the Lower East Side. The corner of Orchard and Rivington Street. Seemed like a good place to vanish from the world where vacant storefronts dot the streets, and beloved institutions seem to vanish every week." Reminiscent at the metaphor. "Never looked back, though. I never regretted leaving either. I forged my own path in the world, my fortune, and glory… and I was happy. That's what counts in life."

Mary gazes at the annoying prick of a Midwesterner. It's the first time she's seen beneath his hardened exterior. *Don't feel pity for him,* her own mind whimpers. They had never truly gotten on, and in retrospect, Mary wished they were much closer than they really were. Friends maybe, instead of constant frenemies. Carl was still a dick, but he'd always put the group interests first and foremost in front of his own needs when Mary thought about everything that had happened since they'd first met. *Damn it. Too late!* Her lake of sympathy begins to cascade at the edges. Spills into little ravines and slipways of guilt.

Carlos' head is pounding. His emotional rollercoaster of childhood unfolds for all to see: namely the one person on Earth he didn't want to show. He glances around, half expecting and hoping to see a Z tearing through the floorboards before dragging him down to the depths of Hell. He's out of luck. No zombie. No escape from the emotional rollercoaster of his life.

She moves closer. "Family… it's never easy, right?"

"Sorry, sorry. Okay. I let my emotions—get the best of me. I got heavy on you there. Um, stupid, I know."

"No shit!"

Carlos feels a tear free-style his cheeks and chuckles nervously. "Gotta go check on Jed"—he takes the convo in a different direction—"that kid has been a long time down in that basement. He's probably found an old Hustler mag and 'stroking the pony' as we speak."

A strand of hair fell in front of Mary's eye, and she pushes it back beneath the yellow headband. "Go! Knock yourself out," she says, sitting up (no pun intended). "I guess he'd rather have you finding him 'touching' himself than me!"

"Nah, I'm sure he'd rather see your face than mine, Mary," he quips.

She fakes a smile—*shivers* at the thought of the teen with his dick in his hand. "*Ewwww*, Carlos. I quiver at the thought!"

"He's fifteen, you know. Puberty kicking in. It's all biology."

"He can keep his biology."

They share a laugh.

He says: "I know you don't like me."

"I do."

"Huh…!?"

"I did. Er…" Mary stomps a nervous foot. "You're just… such a big idiot most of the time."

"What?"

"You know what I mean! The way you act all hard like you have armor-plating attached to your skin. Transparent too! In a sense that you don't give a fuck about anyone. Just care about yourself."

"I suppose that's fair. It takes me a while to let people into my circle, Kansas." He finds comfort with them shooting the breeze like they have never done before. "I know. I can't change."

"I agree."

And they laugh. The heavens laugh, all the worlds and underworlds join in too.

35
PILLOW TALK

"Hey!" Carl whispers. He peeks into the back of the jeep through the opening between the front seats. "Can't sleep?"

"No. Weak. Bored of not being able to help," she says straight away. Considers for a moment how rude it comes out, more profoundly, more importantly, she says, "I'm worried, Carl. Worried for our friends out there all alone in the middle of the city."

Carl couldn't really see in the dark, but he stuck out a hand in the general direction of where he thought Naomi's hand would be. She stuck out her own hand to meet his. Fingers clasped gently together.

He blinked again, could see the outline of her body, her face not a meter away. The scent of strawberries in the night. "It's all gonna be okay," he murmurs. "You will get your chance to help first thing tomorrow morning. We'll leave at first light. Go find the others. Okay!"

Naomi doubts for a second if Carl really means that promise.

"But first, you'll need to rest."

"Sure."

The words are all she needed to hear to make her feel content. She drops back into the upholstery rear seats, tuckered out from the day's events. She still has hold of Carl's hand. It feels nice, strange, but reassuring at the same time.

"Night Naomi."

She falls asleep even before her name is whispered.

36
WHAT MAY COME

"What? You've been staring at me for far too long."

"Can't a man look at a beautiful girl without the third degree?" Carlos replies, and rounds on her, kissing her lips. At that exact moment in time, two worlds collided, and a universe exploded in a heartbeat.

Then she jolted back to see the aftermath.

"Tell me I'm hallucinating, Carlos? Did you just kiss me?"

"*Uh...*" words were hard to come by for the Midwesterner.

"I take that as a yes. Why?"

"It seemed… the right moment," he gulps back doubt before his cockiness returns. "I mean, it's not a shock, you are a stunner. And, well, I am dreamy. Try to control yourself, Kansas."

Mary made sure to swallow first. "It did. I mean it does, I think so!" she counters, unsure if she was making sense. "Do you always drop lines on women like that?" Then she laughed gently.

Always, he wants to say but actually says, "No. Course not." Carlos cast his eyes to the carpet like a 14-year old receiving a compliment from a secret crush from a school mate.

Mary sits still, painfully trying to avoid eye contact with him too.

Carlos gives her a look, a look that conveys *hey, I'm sorry I just kissed you!*

There is no getting away from the Big Elephant sitting in the room. The hormones rising above restricted levels; radiation at a critical mass; bursting at the seams like a flower ejecting its pollen to a close up buzzing bee. It's not random; it's not a fluke. But circumstances do make the difference in this situation. Magnetic Infatuation at its best. Physical attraction having a purpose. Was there a deeper meaning working behind the scenes?

What happens next surprises both of them.

She's on him like a rash.

A good rash; like brushing up against an itchy leaf. Not an STD itch, where you'll be treating that itchy itch with a course of antibiotics. In a flash, their clothes are strewn across the floor. Carlos is beneath Mary, tasting the inside of her mouth. A kaleidoscope of truths spills from the bowels of something which should—would—never have happened in a previous life. They continue as first-time lovers exploring the boundaries of endless possibilities.

The room is dark, went considerably darker when Mary blew out the candles.

PART FOUR

RESCUE PLANS

37
SLUMBERING TEXAN DREAMS

Naomi was in a deep slumber, dreams of 'The Lone State,' her father, and uncle on horseback hunting wild hogs filled her sleep. Except the pigs were not your average scavenger types. Instead, they were built as large hogs, had the same posture too. Snouts down to the ground, small tusks, but the faces were that of the dead. Hungry, ravenous Creeps which are intent on gorging on human flesh. Mouths opening wider than their little bodies would allow. The sounds of *Oink, oink, oink* getting louder. And there she is, standing on the brow of a hill at the edge of her father's farm, weaponless, defenseless as three hungry Z-pigs charge—*ready* to devour her whole. *Oink, oink, oink,* the sound of the charge. She tries to turn, run, but fear freezes her to the spot. Death bores down on her.

It was crazy, the whole damn dream was a diabolical nightmare.

Oink, oink, oink.

She stirs, tries to wake from the deep slumber—

That's when—

Carl put a hand on her good shoulder, started to shake.

"*Naomi!* Wake up. *Wake up!* Naomi?"

"*Uh-huh!*" she mutters languidly, opening her eyes, the morning light cascading through the windows of 'Priscilla' trying to rub the waking world off them. She is sweaty but relieved her nightmares are over. The Z-pigs are nowhere to be seen. "What's happening?"

"It's our guest. He's gone."

For a moment, she doesn't understand. "Guest! Huh?"

"Deckard. I can't find him. Anywhere."

"Y'all kidding?"

"No."

"Did he take anything?" she says, hoping their supplies were still around the campsite, attached to the jeep too. The theft wouldn't be all surprising given the situation of the human population nowadays, but the way in how the plan was executed, could have come straight from a crime novel.

"No."

The one word answer satisfies her doubts. At the same time, she takes a breath, winces as her shoulder hurts again. "I don't understand. Deckard was here when you guys changed shifts last time, and we didn't get to sleep until early morning. Where could he have gone to?"

Carl doesn't know how to answer that question.

Sure, the ex-Marine had been with them throughout the night. They had taken it in turns to be lookouts. A few dead had come around the jeep during the early hours, but nothing they couldn't handle. Just isolated shufflers: classic 'Romero Zombies,' stalking the countryside, and a crawler: a half-bodied redhead who'd managed to crawl beneath their intruder system, until it had started clawing and biting at the door, trying to get into the jeep to devour them. Deckard had put the Z out of its misery by crushing the skull with a rock and disposing of the body on the roadside.

Carl had lost count how many times he had woken up not knowing where he was.

One time on a 'supply run,' a few months back while they were still living at their former camp, Carl woke to find himself alone, the rest of his team had simply disappeared into the night. He never knew what had happened to them. But he hated to think Deckard could just have disappeared with no signs of a struggle.

"Is his bag still here?"

Carl slides back out of the vehicle, a moment later returns, holds up the ex-Marine's duffel bag. Naomi arches up, using her good arm as a lever and stretches upright working her stiff joints, doing a panoramic view out of all the windows: still no Deckard, no military pose atop the hill. She sees Carl holding the fabricated bag in one hand, though. In the other, he pulls out two handguns, and small white boxes of ammunition and lays them on a nearby stump.

"Sweet tooting soldier of America's former gun-loving policy. He's hauling around an armory." The tasty words escape the Texas Native's lips, as she clocks two military-issued M9 Berettas; it's the new standard. "He just took off alone?"

"I guess… to go rescue our friends."

"What makes you so sure, Carl?"

He points to the cache of weapons. "Deckard wouldn't just leave these here for us to enjoy."

She nods at the statement, realizes Carl is correct. *Guns are hot commodities nowadays and leaving all these weapons here would be an awful mistake.*

"Plus, I have a gut feeling."

She laughs at the comment. "Funny," she says. "There are lots of guts around nowadays."

"Yeah. I know, Naomi."

"Should we go after him?"

"He's got a head start on us."

"I know," she answers, but thinks *how hard it'll be trying to track the trained Marine down.* Considering the argument they had yesterday, she is inclined to say yes to her own question, *and let's double-quick step to it.* Doubts surface, though, and Naomi knows it'll be risky venturing into the city just the two of them, especially as they have no idea where the others would be?

Carl plops the duffle-bag to the ground, places both Berettas and ammo packs back inside like presents in a Christmas stocking. He takes her hand, she doesn't resist, and together they leave the confines of the jeep and venture up the hill with the lone tree atop. The morning was chilly; still no sign of Deckard though.

Naomi squints hard; taking in the view afforded to them by the low morning glow of the sun creeping into the distance. "This situation isn't getting simpler!" she says. "I wish everybody would stop disappearing." She touches her injured arm in frustration. “Damn trip should’ve been easy, Carl. You said it would be easy.”

“Yeah. I know.” *Circumstances change.* “The world’s not in the mood to make it easier for survivors, Naomi.” (Inside Carl’s head, a little voice laughs at the statement.) “But we’ll get ourselves ready and go find our friends.”

Naomi smiles that Texan smile again.

38
GOOD MORNING SALT LAKE CITY

Mary jolts awake, ripped out of an unwanted nightmare involving something terrible happening to the people she loved. Her family never making it out alive from her home town was always at the forefront of her mind. She and her mother's last live chat before their family home became overrun. She always had those dreams, and now, their dire situation had heightened them.

Mary didn't remember the details of the dream but didn't need to. That was the only nightmare she ever had. She was shocked she had eventually drifted off, especially with where they were. These could be her last moments on Earth, and her body decided to sleep through them. But she was glad she'd managed a few hours of sleep considering what had happened with Carlos.

She yawns, rolls over on the blanket they'd unpacked from a hallway cupboard—used it as a shag-rug to some degree (well in every possible angle). Carlos lay next to her asleep, he'd nodded off after their unexpected passionate night together and hibernated like a bear during the winter months. His shirt hanging over the edge of the couch and his pants in the hallway. Likewise, her clothes. Five minutes later, she looks down, hiding a smile. In her hand, she toys with the Rambo-style bandana.

Seconds later, Mary sits up again when Carlos tries to kiss her cheek. "Hey!" he says.

"Hi."

"Well played last night, sweetcheeks."

Her face turns into an unwanted frown.

"Jesus, you had to go and spoil it."

"Huh!

"It wasn't a bleedin' game."

"You. Me—" Carlos begins to make inappropriate hand gestures confirming what they did during the night and again in the early morning. "Makes two, babe. Team sport. Gold medals all around."

"That was fucking rude. I'm done."

Mary lurches up from the floor—tugs a cotton sheet from beneath Carlos, wraps it around her like a Roman leaving a bathhouse—leaves the Midwesterner and his torrid mouth behind and goes to freshen up in the bathroom.

***

No power, but light shimmies through the skylight and into the bathroom, letting the early morning punch through with a boxer's mean right hook.

She sits on the toilet and pees.

Jesus, did any of that happen? She tries to remember last night. *Think fast girl!* The eating, the talking, the fucking. The emotional rollercoaster of the

Midwesterner's past unraveling itself like a red carpet of untold truths. The memories are real, not some distorted vision mixed with unreality. But was she ever there at all? He told her he liked her. *Or, was it the other way around?* She's unsure. But one thing was certain—they ceremonially bumped-uglies. Did the naughty like two forbidden teenagers shagging behind their families' backs. Two colleagues getting it on after a late night out.

She goes to the sink, washes her face with a 2ltr bottle of water from the garage supplies. One of many they'd brought into the bathroom the previous night, along with some other supplies. Cleanses her face, skin, and armpits. Naughty parts with a damp flannel. Unpacks a toothbrush and toothpaste—offering simply white natural fluoride goodness (*sweet mint*, a luxury, she knows), and begins to vigorously brush. Looks in the mirror; her weary reflection stares back. Swallow. Spit. But every action reminds her of last night.

That's when she staggers back, drops the sheet—

"You're awake?"

The voice damn near gives her cause to pee again. It's not Carlos nor the dead either. "Jed?" she asks, genuinely surprised and instantly bends down, hooks the cotton sheet with both hands and covers herself like it's a magician's cape. *Nothing to see here.* Hopes the teen didn't see an inch of flesh; a glimpse of side-boob.

The teenager fills the bathtub. He rocks upwards from beneath a cover, a pillow too—minus case—puts his hands on the side of the tub and grabs the edge while smirking a cheeky teenage smile seeing the wonderous female body for the first time.

"You two had an adventure last night." (The statement jolts Mary to her core.) "I won't tell."

She says, "Jeez, thanks." Thinks a little harder. "Didn't mean it to come across as a bitch. Sorry to force you to sleep in the tub. Comfy?"

"It's okay. I had choices, but the bathroom walls were…" He sits there in the bathtub, knees bent tight against the porcelain side trying to think of a response, finally settles on: "Much more soundproof than the other rooms."

Mary can't help it. She laughs at the teen's answer. "Good option," she replies, finishes brushing her teeth, gargles with another bottle of delicious H2O, and takes herself and (what remains of her dignity), from the bathroom. "Sorry," she says one final time by the door.

Jed just throws up a hand: nothing more.

39
SHITTY LAID PLANS

It seemed everyone had to go to the loo one final time. The essence of a civilized pee or poop—top of everyone's agenda of normality.

While Mary used the bathroom, Jed and Carlos moved the treasure-laden rucksacks towards the front door. They couldn't take everything they had found in the garage, just the necessities: easy-to-open cans of food, fruit bars, and some bottled water emptied into three handy metallic canteens. Two of the rifles and extra ammo, and more precisely, two full cans of fuel. Jed had made room for the CB radio too but didn't tell the others about it, (in case they thought of it as non-essential junk).

While Mary used the bathroom for the second time in as many minutes, Carlos peered through the curtains in the lounge, re-checking the street for signs of the infected. He couldn't see any Zs or unwelcomed neighbors and felt relief flood his system, just as the relief had flooded his system when Mary had returned to the make-shift bed on the lounge floor earlier and acted like nothing had ever happened between them. He didn't feel cut-up regarding the sexual snub. Wasn't gonna cry. Or needed a couple counseling session, either. Hell, it was fun while it lasted, he'd thought, and moved on with his life.

He moves to the hallway, hears a toilet flushing, and a few seconds later, Mary exits the bathroom—*tucking* her clothes into her pants. She shrugs as if to say *what, I'm a girl, I needed to go again, dick.*

He gets it, *when will we ever find a clean bathroom like that again?* He asks: "Ready?"

"Uh-ha." She picks up a can of fuel, while Jed shoulders the second rucksack of supplies in front of her.

Carlos opens the front door and closes it again.

"I'm confused," she says. "What are we waiting for?"

"The dead to move!" comes back the reply.

"Still out there?"

"I'll give you a solid A+ for your intuition, Kansas," he quips. "A fucking F-for the stupid-ass question. Course they're still the fuck outside! Why'd you think I shut the damn door?"

She screws up her face as if to say *screw you, I was just asking.* She goes back into the lounge, peeks through the curtains. Up along the tree-lined streets, shambling movement catches her eye. "Shit!" she hisses. "We need to move. Can't just stay in this house forever." But thinks, *we could, with so many supplies gathered underneath this roof. A defensible position. Solid walls. We could last a whole year. Maybe longer?* But then her friend's faces: Naomi, Carl, even Deckard's gritty features punch through those selfish thoughts.

"Maybe your constant flushing attracted the infected back?" The question sounded silly from the Midwesterner's mouth. But was in fact correct. He looks at Mary. "Oh, goody. Killed by sewage full of your crap! Nice, Miss Kansas."

"Oh, totally!" she retorts. "It's not just my shit in the loo!"

"You flushed?"

"I had to. You left the bottom of that toilet an utter disgrace. I've heard of dirty bombs, but what you left behind—it was effing ridiculous!"

Jed pipes into the convo: "Guys, you hear what I'm hearing?"

Mary and Carlos fall quiet, listen as moans and groans got louder by the second.

Carlos: "Why the fuckety fuck, fuck fuck, can't we get a goddamn break once in a while!"

At the same time, Mary and Jed stare at Carlos. Silence washes back and forth between them like waves at a beach.

Mary says: "Plans?" her voice rising high. "Guys?"

That's when—

"I'll do it."

"Do what?"

"Be a fucking Uber Eat treat for those Zs outside." Carlos chuckles at the ludicrous thought. Remembers a happier time when he used to order out food from his dive-of-an-apartment, and some sucker would go fetch his dinner at insane times of the night.

Simpler times.

The suggestion makes Mary laugh. She thinks he's joking. Then she sees no smile. No hesitation. Just a serious glare. This gets her attention.

"No, no, no way," she says. "I'm not leaving you alone."

"No choice, Kansas. I don't like splitting up the team," he shrugs at the statement. "I'll make a diversion for you two. Give these brain-feeders some exercise and be a moving meat wagon to chase. At the same time, it'll create an escape route. You two can take the supplies. Get back to the jeep, to the others." To Jed he says: "Remember, get to the Interstate. Don't stop for owt. This isn't a video game; we don't get any extra lives! Get back to the others pronto. Understand?"

As Jed nods in acknowledgment—

A part of Carlos realizes the plan is crazy, but another part of him knew this was the only way to save them both, hopefully, himself too.

Mary doesn't care about the Midwesterner's insane plan. She wasn't going to let him go outside alone on a—suicide mission—to draw the remaining dead away from the house, and more importantly, from them. Not now, not ever. Not for a billion dollars. Not if her life depended on it. *I can't let him throw his life away... for us.* A shiver runs down her spine with tiny spiders' feet. "I don't like it... this plan... it won't work." she protests. A pin-prick of doubt. "You're not going to make it."

Carlos felt the monumental weight of what he was about to do pulling down his shoulders. The suicide run of all suicidal runs.

He went through the plan in his head: sprinting up the street while distracting the Zs second, hoping there was only regular dead outside instead of any Creeps and their scary, wide mouths full of teeth. Fighting, blowing some heads apart with his Glock. As strategies go, this one actually seemed to be the worse plan he'd ever come up with.

He finally says to Jed, "I'll be back," in his ultimate Terminator voice. Turns to Mary: "I promise I'll make it, Kansas." Unloads the rucksack of supplies onto the carpeted floor, and looks at both of them. "You guys will have to carry my load as well. Be heavy. But… I'll meet you guys back at the jeep. Stay safe. Survive."

The look on Mary's face tells Carlos she was looking at a dead man, if not a seriously crazy individual, for even trying this insane stunt. Deep down, it gives him a crazy sense of belief.

Mary lets go. Knows there's no point in trying to talk Carlos out of the shitty plan of shittiest plans ever. Instead, she throws her arms around his neck. "Be safe, and don't fuck everything up! Okay?" She wants to say more, but sadness darkens her eyes.

Carlos gives a short laugh. "Technically, we're in a fucked up state already. I'm just trying to find a solution to get us all out of a messed-up situation." He wants to disguise his fear from the others, and produces a 'movie star's,' smile. It works, and deep down, he is glad his emotions didn't show through his hardened exterior.

***

He opens the front door first, the shutter secondly. A blast of morning freshness takes his breath away. Outside was the sound of wind whistling and the sounds of Zs moaning while taking an early morning stroll just as they had done once when they were regular citizens of this fine neighborhood.

It's then—

A *C*reep rushes through the overgrown lawn towards Carlos. A mane of hippie dark hair cascades across its face. A half-collapsed nose bends to one side. He pivots, Glock out, steadies and fires. *Blam!* Hippie Creep takes a bullet into the forehead and drops from sight in the garden's high grass.

Just more fertilizer, Carlos thinks and hollers: "I'll be fine. Go. Get inside," and he runs, jumps the garden gate in one go.

***

Behind, Mary wants that door closed and locked again; to have a barricade between herself and Jed and whatever was waiting outside. Instead, she freezes, watching the Midwesterner sprint the street like a 100metre athlete towards the end of the road where the local law enforcement cars were barricading the entrance to the desolate cul-de-sac.

"C'mon, *you shitheads!*" he continues to holler. "Come get your meal on fucking wheels!" his voice drawing the dead away from the street, and more importantly, the others.

Mary finally shuts the door. "Carlos, you're one crazy bastard," she mutters softly, before making her way back into the lounge, grabs the 'Bugout bag,' and begins to lighten the load—*prioritizing* what she can and can't carry. Finishing rearranging the gear, she turns to the teen. "You ready?" Jed nods solemnly back. "Good. Let's go."

Twenty minutes later, they were out on the porch again with as many supplies as they could carry between them. Carrying both rucksacks, lighter by a few pounds of essentials (Mary carries her small yellow backpack across her chest and one hunting rifle, the other is just too much to carry), and more importantly, between them, the two jerry cans of fuel. The overgrown garden gently swaying in the morning breeze. The street is clear of the lifeless corpses; the dead following Carlos on cue, (the Midwesterner's plan coming to fruition).

She stops by the gate; the rusty letterbox sits to one side of the path. Mary peeks up and down the street, looking for him: no sign. *Hope that dipshit will be okay.*

Up and over the gate, they slowly make their way to the end of the street. Edging through the line of abandoned cop vehicles.

Mary looks around one final time. A breeze carrying the distant echoes of groans. At the same time, she swears she can hear the Midwesterner's voice hollering: *"Yippee-ki-yay, motherfuckers! Follow me, you bitches!"* Suddenly, she has a sudden stab of fear that she might just never see Carlos again.

Time to skedaddle.

40
REFRESHING MORNING WALK

Mary and Jed make it safely back to the former Interstate away from the first suburban reaches of former homes within half-an-hour. There is no sign of Carlos or the dead anywhere when they finally reach the Lincoln. The red jerry can is full of gas to the rim, while the garden pipe and sports bag sit by its side (they had to leave the gas because they were already overloaded with equipment).

Mary also found the Midwesterner's ray bans on the ground; they weren't cracked or even damaged, and she'd picked them up as a safekeeping, to give back to Carlos on his return.

As they saunter onwards, the Yooper is worried for the Midwesterner; no matter how much he'd annoyed her since they'd first met. How much he was a dick to her and everyone else he'd ever come in contact with. There was a heart under that chauvinist exterior, and she was going to miss that big Indiana Lug if he didn't make it back alive from his far-fetched scheme.

The cool morning heat with the clouds keeping the warm sun at bay held for a while, but the weight of all the supplies began to take a toll on their muscles as an hour stretched by.

Jed was quiet for most of the trip, but as his feet got sore and his muscles felt the strain of carrying a can full of gas and a rucksack of supplies, he started to get cranky.

"Are we there yet?"

"No."

"How far is it?"

"Not long."

"Really—"

"Jed… so help me! I know you're tired. I know we've got a helluva lot of supplies to carry. I'm tired, but we have to keep on moving, because…" Her words catch in the back of her throat. She gulps back a mixture of grit and despair. "Because… Carlos gave us this opportunity… a chance to escape. He's counting on us to get back to Carl and Naomi. We need to make that opportunity a reality. We have to!"

"I need to stop."

"Shut the fuck up, Jed!" she snaps. (He falls quiet instantly, *jeez, what did I do to deserve that insult?* He questions her with a wide-eyed Bambi glare.) "I just need—*please* give me a minute. A couple of seconds to… to think!" she adds, instantly regretting the outburst. Shakes her head. "We'll stop soon. Okay!"

He murmurs, "Okay." But keeps fidgeting, irritated and uncomfortable with the extreme weight.

She notices the teen putting on a brave face; carrying all this gear was never going to be easy. Stops him with a hand on his shoulder. Drops her jerry can, and bends at the waist to re-fasten the straps on the teen's heavy rucksack. "I know it's heavy. Sun is hot. But we need to carry on!" He nods at her wise words. "Here," she says, "equal distribution of weight. Both sides of the hips. It'll help. Trust me." And Mary remembers a year she'd taken out before she had attended university and gone backpacking across South East Asia with another friend. Traveled like a mule, with a large rucksack on her back, and a smaller one strapped across her chest. Just like she was doing now, but now it was easier of course because she knew how to evenly adjust the weight of both bags.

"Thanks. Feels better." And Jed starts walking; the weight on his shoulders evenly spread. Moments later, "Everything's gonna be okay," he says softly. "I mean… with Carlos. He'll be okay."

"You keep saying that."

"I have to. I have to believe in these miracles. You guys are all I have left in the world now. You're all my family… even Carlos."

She jerks a look over at the teen. Mary gets it. She understands. *We are each other's family. In it together till the end, or hopefully until we reach Portland.* The words converging inside make her smile and at the same time, sad. "You keep pushing me a lot, Jed."

He replies: "Because you can handle it."

She surrenders a chuckle, and they keep walking beneath the increasing heat.

41
SHITTIER PLANS

Carlos limps painfully towards the metal graveyard; in the distance, the bombed freeway was in touching distance. The beginning of the day was turning out to be a very, bad day, indeed. He struggled to recall why he thought it was such a great idea volunteering to be the guinea pig in a shit show of a sideshow. *Yeah, couldn't let Mary and Jed get trapped like rats in a trap back at the house*, he concludes. Carlos wished he'd never volunteered to lead the pack of zombies away from the neighborhood of 1,000 corpses in the first place, and especially on his own, but he was curious to see how his plan would turn out.

And those forty-five minutes turn out to be some of the longest forty minutes in the history of minutes.

Carlos tried to outrun the pack first, maneuvering through backyards and then down alleyways that fed on the backyards of abandoned houses. Once, Carlos thought, *damn, if I keep on running like this for another week I'll be able to win a fucking marathon!* If only marathons existed.

He tried fighting them off one-by-one every time he bundled around a corner after catching a quick breath. But the pack refused to give up chasing their meal, and Carlos ran and continued to run from the dead. It was all he could do. Every time Carlos thought he could catch a break, some feral zombie would stumble out of nowhere and try to take a bite out of his shoulder or calf. Carlos was lucky half-a-dozen times; he was the luckiest sonovabitch in the whole universe.

But eventually, his luck ran out when he ran past an abandoned convenience store. Carlos should have been more careful but didn't see the hands reach out and grab him from behind an overturned trash bin, and he found himself tumbling to the ground with the sound of a rib breaking. Then a moment later, the Creep was upon him. It used to be an old man, snapping wildly with its sharpened teeth. Hips gave out twenty or so years back. It crawled across the ground; grayish skin clung from its face, and every time it took another bite, Carlos saw the mouth fuse together before it ripped apart to form another evil grin. At least it wasn't a fucking Clown Z, he thought. He fucking hated clowns when he was younger, and the combination of the zombie apocalypse capitalizing on his longstanding love-hate relationship with clowns made the world a far terrifying place.

Grandpa Z was strong; considering it was decomposing and had only its upper body operating. Carlos eventually found his gun, shouting, "Die shitbrains! Die!" and blew that old fart to bits.

Eventually, Carlos made it to the Lincoln where the pack of infected had originated from yesterday. It was clear; no signs of the Infected anywhere. It was a relief. He could still see both jerry cans on the road; one attached to the vehicle, the other just discarded away like a piece of trash. *How ironic?* he thinks, *now I'm back where I fucking started!*

He holds his lower abdomen, the simple act of breathing hurt his badly injured ribs.

Carlos keeps telling himself: "Keep it together, you can make it." Then he hears those moans and swings a look behind.

A staggering swarm of undead was sauntering up the side ramp towards his position. The undead clogging up the road like an unflushable monster shit in a loo. Twisted necks and outstretched arms, hungry mouths pined for fresh meat; particularly Midwestern All You Can Eat Buffet Ribeye Steak.

"C'mon! Fuckoff!" Carlos yells. "Give me a break, you undead bastards."

42
SAFELY BACK AT CAMP

Carl clasped his hands together and splashed the cool water over his face, pausing to let the beads of water drip off. The refreshing water was much needed, serving to wake his body up from an uncomfortable night of restlessness. The thoughts of his companions stuck somewhere in Salt Lake City. In mortal danger. Deckard disappearing sometime in the morning without a clue. He stands up, his back aches, his neck aches, his legs are still spent from the constant traveling of the last few days.

Another splash to his face was enough to hear voices in the distance. Real human voices were advancing to their position. Then Carl hears Naomi's excited voice from behind. He turns and sees her standing on the brow of the hill with the binoculars at eye-level. The tone of her voice was all that was needed to put his stomach into knots of relief. He knew instantly who she'd seen; the others on their way back to the camp. He walks—now—running towards Naomi's excited voice, but the scene that meets Carl's eyes breaks his heart.

Running to meet them, Naomi calls: "Thank God you're alive, Mary!" She has her arms around Mary's neck in a great Texan hug in no time at all, momentarily forgetting about her injury. After a moment, the Asian girl winces back, her shoulder throbbing. "My God where the hell did you guys get to? Did you hunker down for the night? We were terrified that something bad had happened to you! What kept you so long?"

"We got ambushed by a pack of Creeps and spent the night trapped in a house. It was awful."

Naomi nods. "That's my girl. Fear is only a problem if you let it stop you, right?" and gives Mary another Texan hug. She gazes over and sees Carl hugging Jed, but instantly knows something is wrong when she hears those words: "Where's Carlos?" tumbling from Carl's mouth.

Mary breaks from the embrace and nervously looks at Jed then towards Carl. After a short silence. "He—we don't know *where* he is!" she claims.

"So, what happened?" Carl presses. "Where's Carlos? You're wearing his sunnies!"

Mary pincers the black-framed glasses between forefinger and thumb. She tries to remember every last detail of the past 20-something hours trapped in the house on the outskirts of Salt Lake City. Tries to convey as much information to the others. The Lincoln on the clogged up freeway. The race through the suburban streets. Finding the house on Elm Street with all the supplies gathered in the garage. Eventually, she gets there; barely audible last words. "Carlos—he saved us!" She ropes her hands through her hair and takes the Midwesterner's glasses off, undoes the heavy rucksack; it drops to the floor with a thud. She stares back at the road they just marched through the morning heat. "He goddamn saved us back in the city with a dumb plan." Several seconds later, her heart thuds. "What if he's hurt? What if he's—" Mary wonders.

Naomi moves closer to her friend, throws a reassuring arm over her shoulders. "He'll be fine, Mary. He may be hurt. But knowing Carlos, he'll get back to us one way or the other," she says. "Besides, he's one lucky shit."

The Texan's words don't bring relief to the Yooper's system, but a sense of dread spiked evenly with fear. Mary turns back one last time to the road and waits.

43
RESCUE PLANS

Carlos sees the pack of hungry Zs staggering up the ramp, getting closer with every passing second; the scent of blood and his sweet, glorious sweat in the morning breeze enticing his new found friends to a bowl of human gumball. Now they were slumbering between the abandoned vehicles which clogged the freeway. They kept coming; with eyes front and jaws snapping too, and black bloodied teeth and hands outstretched. Carlos wasn't thinking about his sacrifice at that moment, but he hoped he'd given Mary and Jed the pep talk they'd needed back at the house. Hoped they were long gone from this road of despair. The Midwesterner takes a long full breath like a diver; he knew the day was going to get a lot shittier before it got better.

Then he hears running—

The smack of heavy boots on the asphalt—

A quick look over his shoulder—

The remarkable thing now was emerging over the abandoned vehicles; a figure for which Carlos didn't even have words and was only able to punctuate with "Holy fucking Satan's testicles." His words dissolved into a gurgle.

Deckard came pounding along the road, through the tailback, his heavy feet leaving the asphalt with a buoyancy of a spaceman's jump on the surface of the moon. He was picking up speed like a hurdling athlete in the middle of a race. Then he was up, clambering over a bonnet with a revolver clicking into action, looking like an extra from a John Woo action classic, his jacket fluttering in the morning breeze. The former Marine began to fire short control bursts. Each shot cracking the morning air. Each shot slamming hard into a zombie's forehead. "Get your dick out of your hands and move your lame ass, Carlos!" Deckard yells, unleashing another shot, and another Z's head explodes with a firecracker effect. Black ooze and bone chip flying through the air, dazzling the other undead spectators. But they kept on shuffling forwards, eager to catch the moving breakfast buffet that was Carlos' ass.

Carlos wasn't going to give up. Not now or ever. He wasn't going to become one of them; slouching and moaning forever on an endless death march across the land like an uncoordinated strike for better pay and work incentives. He was barely up on his feet when a fresh Z came in for a charge. The Creep was fast, and Carlos knew it must have recently turned. This man hadn't been dead for more than a few months by now, and the nimbleness of the creature sent fear shivering through the Midwesterner's spine as the creature's jaws opened wider than its whole body.

Chomp. Chomp. Chompty chomp.

He stands at the ready. Defensive position. Hands up, palms out. It charges and Carlos edges out of the way just in time to stop the monster's lunged attack, grabbing it by the shirt and forcing it down to the ground with a knee to the back and holding the dead man's hands behind his back. The retro-game 'Streetfighter,' instantly came to the forefront of Carlos' mind as he implemented the flawless move on his undead opponent.

Mwah. Mwah, mwah.

The Creep's mouth clamps shut; opens again, chomping at the human's heels as Carlos tries to take out his gun and pump a round of lead into its crumbling cranium. No such luck; the Glock escapes his grasp, spins across the floor like a ten-time salsa dancing champion.

He turns just in time to witness—

Deckard shouting, "Time to meet your maker!" The ex-Marine was fighting off two elderly ladies; crusty stockings and undergarments on show.

Carlos goes back to his own problem and starts kicking the Creep's head again and again. Finally, he hears a *crack.* With a splatter, the cranium gives way, leaving a large blob of blackened ooze on the hot asphalt.

The body dies for a second time: no extra lives, no returning from the grave.

Carlos had completed his 'finishing move.'

***

After disposing of the two zombified-grannies, Deckard turns back to Carlos and is relieved to see the Midwesterner has beaten the fresh zombie into a mushy pulp. "You unhurt?" Deckard rasps.

"Sure… shitty… sure!" Carlos acknowledges between breaths. Jests: "My Knight in shining armor."

"Yeah. Except you're no damsel in distress."

"Don't worry, I'm not gonna repay your kindness by hitching my legs up behind my head so you can see my shiny crown!"

It's then Deckard inclines his head, notices Carlos holding his lower ribs.

"You injured?"

"It's nothing, Marion. Took a tumble like a stunt man!" he exclaims, bending over at the waist to pick up his gun he'd dropped. "Fuck." *Breathe. Just breathe.* "Ahh."

"I've been in enough scraps in my life to realize when a man's broken a rib, bud. We need a ride away from this road-of-death!" Deckard says, surveying the clogged lane. "You ain't going to make it back in one piece if another pack of infected come our way." He scans the vicinity for an opportunity for them to escape. "Catch your breath. We're getting outta here in a few minutes."

"Don't wanna be a buzzkill or anything, but, you have a plan? A goddamn plane? You gonna fly us outta this fucked up warzone?" Carlos sarcastically jests. "Are you planning to give me a piggyback? 'Cause I can't run."

"No. Drive. Dumbass! One of these cars must have some juice left in its bowls."

Those words bring a sudden confused look to his face; and silence of a good kind, as the Midwesterner's mouth is empty of comebacks. Then the sounds of the dead blew through the air and a cold, chill sweeps through his system. "Okay!

I'm all for that plan," he replies. Something glints in his minds-eye. "The Lincoln. The fucking Lincoln—It has gas!"

"What you waiting for, bud! Get in!" Deckard orders, dashes to the driver's side, clicks the ignition on. It splutters into life. The engine turning over. Under a quarter of a tank flashes on the panel. "We're driving out of this shitty place of inconvenience in style, riding to safety like the goddamn U.S Cavalry."

Carlos springs into action, goes to the open jerry can filled with the gold liquid. The red can stands in a puddle of gas where it had overflowed yesterday. He finds the cap and screws it back on top. Locks it. Next, fetches the little screwdriver delicately perched in the gas cap and throws it and the measure-of-green hosepipe both into the sports bag on the floor by the back tire and begins to lift both.

That's when—

The Midwesterner felt movement close behind, mutters, *"Oh fuck!"*

From behind, a hand grabs his shoulder and Carlos pivots off balance. From nowhere, a Z has hold of his top. Another crusty-lipped old-timer with sunken eye sockets of blackness and roadkill breath. *Is a Cocoon convention in town?* He thinks, remembering the classic 1980s sci-fi, fantasy film starring 'Mr. Nice Guy,' *Steve Guttenberg*. It yanks harder. *The bitter end!* He zeroes onto the Z's black eyes (just like the actor's career after those funnier years in the limelight).

Tap, tap, two gunshots later, and the zombie drops to the floor, headless, mouthless and motionless.

"Bud!" Deckard says, not sure if the Midwesterner's listening. "Carlos?"

Carlos grits his teeth and sweeps the gore off his clothes to confront the inevitable conclusion: he has to throw away a second pair of comfy clothes in two days.

He focuses back on the ex-Marine standing by the side of the car; the revolver an extension of his arm straight like a javelin. Deckard looks back at the Midwesterner; a grin forming on his grizzled chin. "Waiting for an invitation? Or you want a ride from this hellhole?"

He just stares. "It could be worse, of course," he remarks through a bitter smile.

Deckard wonders, genuinely astonished by the Hoosiers' positive attitude to the life-threatening situation. "It could?"

"It comes from a deep, intense energy building up around my groin, and a stroke of lotta luck, Marion."

Deckard shakes his head, and chuckles tolerantly, "Luck! You're full of the good stuff, Carlos. Now get your ass on board!"

Carlos unsteadily picks up the jerry can and sports bag and hoists them into the back of the Lincoln like an Olympic shot-putter for the second time of trying and 'shotgunned' the passenger seat. The car's upholstery is beige. Empty water bottles form a sea of plastic in the rear compartment, a few crunched bottles drift beneath his seat.

***

Then the engine cuts—

Deckard twists the key in the ignition, but the engine sputters. It turns over, again and again—*glok-glok-glok-glok*—but never starts.

"What the fuck, Marion?" Carlos yells seconds later. "C'mon, let's not be the dead's chow-down. Punch it… AFASP!"

"I'm working on it, bud!" The Marine barks as though he's giving commands again to a junior. His foot taps the gas pedal.

Dead behind. Forty feet away, maybe less-bodies, limbs, feet, but the onslaught of the dead march towards them like an unstoppable hungry army of locusts from Biblical times. Marching, stuttering, but never stopping with a grim determination and an eerie purpose gleaming back in cold, black eyes.

Carlos sees the hungry army grow from his side mirror. *A call's going out, and dinner is back on the menu again,* he muses. "Go! Go! Go!" he yelps. It's a terrified, hoarse shout from his belly. His colon tightens. His rib hurts. "Move!"

The Lincoln rumbles into life. The engine shudders and roars into a frenzy. Deckard throws the unit into reverse—backs into an old Ford Mustang. The classic kicks back again and again as the ex-Marine keeps piling into its chassis.

All around them, the sounds of the hungry, former inhabitants of Salt Lake City converge closer, literally at biting distance. "Carlos," he says. "I'm not sure we'll—" Then enough space was created for the Lincoln to squeeze from its tight confines. Slip beyond its noose.

Freedom was in sight—

Carlos screams: *"Let's go!* Fuck these *dead A-holes*, Marion!"

The infected were now washing in from behind like a tidal wave of rags and bones. Continuing their death march. Ten, then twenty, slow, slumbering bodies filling up every available nook and hole the clogged freeway offered.

With specialized driving skills, Deckard sticks the Lincoln into first and floors the gas; the car bursts forward; their escape vehicle found enough momentum to drive up over a trailer that had come loose from another car and had formed a ramp up and over the side-barrier. The vehicle shook as the chassis scraped along the concrete barrier, sparks spraying everywhere like a firecracker effect. Deckard fights with the wheel—eventually won and just as a nightmare horde of undead descended upon them, they were screeching away across the scrubland.

Carlos winds down the window—aims his Glock like a bank robber aiming fire at the trailing Feds. Steadies, and fires. The bullet hits its target, and where the gas had spilled from the Lincoln's thirsty belly yesterday afternoon onto the asphalt, what remains of the puddle catches fire. It takes a moment, but the Mustang catches fire too. Several seconds later, and the fancy vehicle explodes. Ignites into a fucking fireball. And the screams of the dead are set on fire.

Carlos hollers in delight from the front seat by the grand show.

Behind, walking torsos of flame begins to burn in the morning sun, and almost simultaneously draws the rest of the dead to the Bonfire-of-Death.

"What just happened?" Deckard asks. "What the hell did you do?" He was in the middle of the sentence when he notices there is no need to shout. He feels they are safe even before he registers what happens.

Carlos offers a small smile. "I ended them before they came for us later on."

"You sure did, you cocky bastard," Deckard replies. Further across the scrubland away from the freeway. "Hold onto your socks!" he says as the Lincoln hits 80mph. He wears his seatbelt—safety first—considering the driver's side was missing a door.

"Okay, that was a fluke."

"Yeah. A fluke of nature. That's what you get when you live your whole life as a Marine. Perfect situational awareness skills."

"Fuck that shit," Carlos clarifies. "Well, it went to plan, nevertheless! Which level of crazy is too much for you, Marion? I'm just curious."

The Marine doesn't answer the question, just keeps his hands on the steering wheel circumnavigating the rugged landscape.

"I think this could be the sign of a beautiful partnership, don't you?"

"Partners? More like a glorified ride-along," Deckard murmurs. "Don't get too attached, bud. We've got a long way to go before we're away from trouble."

"Yeah. You're right. Hey, what a difference there is between coach and first class!" Carlos whistles and sits back into the seat, holds his broken rib and blows a satisfied breath.

He stares through the open window, catches the fresh air.

A pocket of dust.

The relief that his shitty plan had come to fruition.

44
REUNITED

"It's taking too long."

"It takes as long as it takes, Naomi!" Carl says while clearing away the remnants of the previous night's camp like a tidy camper. Sticker achieved. Merit earned. "Deckard will be back in no time. Carlos too."

"You seem overly sure."

"I am. It's a gut feeling. The world has moved on. People too. A few keep pulling the wagon of progress along the roads of prosperity while the rest just don't give a damn shit for the living. But Deckard seems genuine. The man's intent as any good-natured person once used to be." This, Carl thinks, is what it comes down to in the end.

Naomi stands wordless, just stares at him before turning to the others.

Jed and Mary sit together on the cusp of the hill; sheltering beneath the single, solemn Balsam tree. Mary keeps looking through the binoculars waiting for the Midwesterner's return. While the teen nervously scuffs the soles of his trainers through the grass. They wait and wait—not budging from the spot—an hour has gone by since they'd returned to the jeep.

"Dandy…" Naomi begins to say, sure to imply how little okay everything was.

That's when a call comes from above—

Both gaze up at the hill and see Mary standing straight as a lighthouse watchman gazing across an ocean at that missing ship. "I see something, guys!" she yells, pointing at a fast approaching specter in the distance.

Carl and Naomi race to join the others.

Carl steals the binoculars back. "You guys! See what I'm seeing?!" he says in disbelief. "Who the fu—I mean, what the fuck!"

"What do you see?" Naomi hollers as the unmistakable sound of an approaching vehicle saunters across the landscape. It approaches the barricade, zooms in-and-out of other vehicles and narrowly passes through a tight gap and continues to where they are.

Mary murmurs: "Carlos!" She's positively thrilled.

***

Mary stops in front of the wrecked Lincoln, sees the ex-Marine behind the steering wheel. He clicks the engine off and just sits. Then another figure exits from the passenger side. She feels a gaggle of excitement, relief pumping through her veins and stares at what seems like a ghost returning from the grave for what feels like an eternity and then some more. "Big ideas with no follow-through will get you killed, Carlos."

Carlos gives her a look. "I'll have you know, I have plenty of follow through."

"I was scared you weren't gonna make it."

"Thanks."

Her jaw drops open. "Thanks!"—the word punctures her throat in sheer annoyance—"is all you can say?"

"Want more? Fine. Okay… I was shitting myself out there. Wondering how long I could keep those Zs on my trail, so they weren't trailblazing after you guys." Then a smile forms. "I wasn't gonna miss our road trip across the goddamn infected States of 'Merica. Not a fat chance in sweet old Hell, Kansas."

She tries to think of a sarcastic answer for that and fails. She pauses if only to appreciate the fact that her bitchiness hasn't subsided one iota for the Midwesterner. Mary lunges towards Carlos, grabs him by the blood-splattered collar, and during that split second of transition—an embrace to end all embraces follows. She feels herself fall into his muscles.

"Miss me, Kansas?"

The question lingers.

"No," she retorts cheekily. "As if."

"Knew it."

"No holes in ya?"

"What! Nope."

"Good," she clutches something in her hands. "Got you a present…" and hands over the glasses.

"Huh! I don't—*how?*"

"Found em' laying on the exit ramp when we finally left the neighborhood behind."

He catches Mary smiling, which feels like a little flirty smile. It was. "Knew they'd see their King again," he smirks and places them above his hairline.

"You're so full of shit, you big lug," she smirks. "Hey, you saved my life today. You may be a total ass half the time, but I need you. I mean—*we* need you. The whole group. We all need each other." Mary then wraps her arms tightly around the Midwesterner's neck. She hugs again, embracing for what felt like an eternity. She felt strangely good upon thinking she was the first person ever to touch another living being in years. But this time, he pulls away; his ribs throbbing with pain. "You okay?"

"Injury. Ribs. Broke. I think."

"Jeez. Soz."

"It'll be fine. No worries, Kansas. Just need to rest."

***

While Mary was staring at Carlos with eyes full of emotion, Naomi and Carl stand side by side, flummoxed at the strange arrival of the remaining group members in the shell-shocked transport. Deckard exits the vehicle; his trademark long black jacket covered in dust, his tanned fedora still on his head. The big Okie stands next to an excited Jed like a parent keeping their child on a leash at a theme park.

"We thought you were dead! I'm so glad you're not!" the teen jubilantly adds.

Carlos breaks from Mary's embrace. "C'mon, Jed. It's time you understand how the world works. It's time you learned that no 'meat bag,' would ever get the better of me."

The teen takes a couple of moments on that thought, then laughs.

"Of course you survived. You're too stubborn to die, Carlos," Carl says, moving forward. He sticks out a hand.

"Too right, dawg," Carlos takes the gesture, shakes for a minute.

After, Carl turns towards the former Marine; he was both happy and angry. Glad that Carlos had returned in one piece but upset the Marine had left—alone—in the first place to go and retrieve him. It was supposed to be all of them going to their friend's rescue, not just the Marine.

"You didn't need to do this by yourself. You didn't owe us anything!" he says, almost forcefully.

"I know, kid. But since the end of the world came around, I've always learned to watch and wait. Evaluate any situation that puts someone else's life in danger. I knew you and Naomi would do whatever it took to go and find your friends, but the risk would have been overkill. You welcomed me along on your trip, and I thought it was only right to repay your kindness."

Carl looked around his group of friends and knew the ex-Marine had made a radical decision that had ultimately paid off, and everyone was grateful that they'd run into him at the bar in the middle of nowhere.

Carlos takes another deep breath, his chest filling with pride. "I owe you my life, Marion. I didn't believe you could be trusted. But I was wrong. Wrong. I'd always thought of the Marines… as stupid, testosterone-driven jarheads…"

"Jesus! Carlos, the man's just saved your life, and you insult him!" Naomi says with a slack-jawed expression. Rage rising—

"I'm not offending the man in any way, Naomi! It's just a fact!"

"You are offending him… and in many ways, Carlos!"

Carlos jerks his head. "Just to be clear… I got nothin' but respect for the forces, dawg."

"Funny. I agree, Carlos," Deckard muses. "The Marines never had a reputation for being stupid. We had a reputation for doing what none but us could do."

"Sometimes you need someone who relies more on physical and mental toughness, not educational prowess. The Marines were that someone. Still, are."

Carlos: "No, shit!"

"No, shit, indeed. I had a friend who was in the Air Force. He had a cushy desk job. Pen-pusher and a typewriter back in the day, and an A+ average in calculus. I said to him, "I will take being a Marine and getting an E- in algebra and being able to walk 26 miles with the weight of all 'Your World of Self Help books,' on my back. And your perfect 4.0 GPA won't help you stay on a rope on the side of a helicopter when you drop into enemy territory. Calculus never saved my life."

Carlos: "The Marines did?"

"I'm not kidding. Being strong mentally and physically helps me every day, and we were some of the most mentally tough people that you will—never come across again. True Marines—not the goofballs that want the uniform so they can get girls. I'm talking about the guys that have the blood of the first pioneers running through them anytime they put on a uniform."

Carlos laughs the hardest at the ex-Marine's words. Jed would never look at maths again in the same way, while Mary, Naomi, and Carl look at each other in awe.

Afterward, everyone felt the need to hug Deckard for what he had done. Then Jed saluted the man, and everyone stopped and stared at the teen for untold seconds.

"Put your hand down, kid. You're not in the armed forces, and I'm not your designated leader, either," Deckard says quite forcefully. "So stop saluting me and don't even think to call me 'sir' or 'shit' like that again. I'd rather be called Marion for the rest of this goddamn trip!"

Jed lowers his hand, anxious he'd upset the Marine. Then the teen glances back at the man after studying the floor for what felt like ages, and finally says: "No, sir." (And everyone burst out laughing.) "Oh, God! I'm sorry. I'm sorry—Marilyn!" and quickly apologizes. "I mean—Marion."

"What the fuck, Jed!" Carlos utters. "Marion said, 'don't call him sir,' and what do you do? You call him, sir!"

"There's no hope for him," Naomi says in a juvenile response, smiling at Carl.

"I believe you're right," Carl acknowledges with a nod.

"It's alright. I'm just pulling your strings, kid," Deckard says, and a grin plasters his face. "Just… Deckard will do from now on. Understand?" And Jed found himself instantly standing to attention. Seconds later, he lost the military pose.

And it's then Deckard turns, eyeing the rucksacks and two gas cans warily. "You kids had time to go on a shopping spree back in town? What do you have in there?"

"Oh, you know… everything!" Mary answers. "Found an abandoned house laden with supplies. Clothes, water, food, and gas—"

Deckard: "Guns?"

"Uh-ha."

"How many?"

"One high-powered hunting rifle… plus ammo for this gun and the shotgun. Had to leave an extra rifle back at the house. Extra Glock ammo too."

"Make that two weapons!" Jed corrects, showing everyone the Smith & Wesson Model No. 2 revolver that Mary had given him back at the house. (Deckard frowns, slightly impressed with the youth and his Dirty Harry styled-cannon.) "We took what we needed. What we could physically carry, but the garage was jammed full of supplies. Enough to last a family of four for a year or two, at least!"

"Shame," Deckard muses. "Undisturbed treasure troves of supplies are always rare these days."

“Survivors?” Naomi asks, the innocent question coming from nowhere.

Mary took a moment to compose herself, failed.

“Hello? Mary?”

Carlos intervened and spoke for her. “Gone,” he says. “The inhabitants cleared out yonks ago. Just the dead hanging around like gangsta pimps to an uninvited street party.” Hunched his shoulders and hands on show to everyone. “We were lucky to find the place at all given the circumstances of what we were up against!”

Mary was still quiet; her mind drifting back to that bloodied bathroom with the corpse. She hears the Midwesterner’s words, glad Carlos had taken the lead.

Naomi eventually nods, satisfied with the answer.

With all the standing around, Carl assertively says, “Okay, I think our time in Salt Lake City has come to an exciting end. It’s time we moved.”

Everyone agrees.

He starts to give orders to the rest. Jed and Deckard got to work on the gas supplies, refilling ‘Priscilla,’ and siphoning the last remaining droplets of gas from the Lincoln’s tank. Naomi helps him with the rest of last night’s camping gear; untethering the wires around the encampment, clearing away pots and pans, etc. While Mary and Carlos inventoried their supplies next: Considerable ammo for the shotgun, hunting rifles, and a range of small handguns. The only weapon that had a limited supply of ammo was the gun Jed was given by Mary back at the house. Five in the chamber of the revolver, an extra ten found in the garage in a small box; fifteen shots in total; one for every year the teen had been alive. They had a selection of food, though, ranging from nutrition bars through to cans of easy-to-open peaches and other canned vegetables would join the everlasting supply of beef jerky they had on board the jeep; the extra ingredients would make the evening dinners taste a lot better. An abundance of packaged dried fruit and raisins would make an excellent breakfast also.

The packing bit was troublesome as some equipment had to be dumped to make way for the extra supplies gained but was relatively quick nonetheless as they quickly decided what they could dispose of.

Finally, they were set.

The wind whipped across the small hill with the Balsam tree on top. Its leaves fluttering, hissing and shaking. Above, clouds like cotton-candy sweep across the blue sky. It was time to depart.

PART FIVE

LEAVING UTAH

45
GOODBYE AND THANK YOU VERY MUCH, UTAH

After finally saying goodbye to the ruins of Salt Lake City they continue along the Lincoln Highway heading west past ghost towns and old mining settlements which were used by nineteenth-century pioneers. Carl took over driving duties, Naomi as his navigator up front. Behind, Deckard, Mary, and Carlos sit together like squashed condiments on a supermarket shelf. And Jed rides pillion again.

Later, a fun roadside surprise came into view.

They see an odd shape towering above the interstate on the north side. It looks out of place. What they see looks like a large concrete tree. But is in fact a sculpture. The Tree of Utah (also called) 'The Tree of Life' is a sculpture by Swedish artist Karl Momen. It stands 87 feet tall and was dedicated in 1986. Reportedly, the artist had a vision of the tree while driving across the Bonneville Salt Flats and was inspired to create it, financing the project himself to bring bold color and beauty to the stark, flat, salty landscape (it kind of worked, the gang agreed).

Unfortunately it appeared three of the spheres has fallen and broken in two. No one would be around to fix it, and they continue west on the I-80.

During the afternoon they eventually cross another state line, leaving behind the husky sands of Utah and Mormon territory and into the natural landscape and predominantly arid ecology of Nevada.

They bypass population centers such as West Wendover on the cusp of State lines which sits on the western edge of the Great Salt Lake Desert. And Elko, the former city straddling the Humboldt River (where there was no state income tax, the property tax was low, and sales tax was low; a great place for a business and a home—a fact the once living locals were proud off, in the pre-zombie-infested state).

Interstate 80 was relatively car-free; the long stretches of road desolate of former vehicles and no signs of the living. Keeping to tracks and smaller roads where possible. The roads Carl picked were often gravel or dirt. But the truth was you couldn't avoid all signs of humanity or classic Romero-esque activity. And once or twice they saw the undead shuffling through vegetation and through the Nevada countryside. Sometimes where the roads were washed-out, in disrepair or straight-out impassable, they had to bite the bullet and travel through a few sparse population centers. Varmy, the former gold-mining complex with its solo Pump Station and Post Office. And Golconda (the community was named after the ancient diamond mining center of Golkonda in India). Most of the small town's buildings were from its mining heyday; a train depot, several hotels, and former homes now stood desolate and abandoned. Both were minor stops on I-80, like the jeep's six human inhabitants; just extras in a new world.

***

A stop later on the Dwight D. Eisenhower Highway by some old farmer's fields, and after a debated conversation between the boys and the girls, they decided to head towards Reno and take the coastal roads all the way to Portland. The change of scenery and fresh salt air would add a great deal of relief over the previous, stress-filled days.

"We haven't seen signs of the infected for a while," Jed says as he takes in the scenery through the windows. Jed never liked to say the word 'Zombie' out loud but knew they were the real deal, especially from past experience. Escape from New York was just a distant memory, but still live on in his dreams. "How come we haven't seen any large infected packs?" he ventured.

"Unless they hear or smell something that draws them, they tend to stay close to home," Carl explains.

"Home?"

"You know… to the places, they used to live and work."

"Why?"

Carl couldn't think how to answer that straight-to-the-point question. It took him a few minutes dithering over a reasonable response, and before he knew it they were driving slowly through the outskirts of the city of Winnemucca of Humboldt County, previous population: 9,000. "There are a lot of theories," he guesses. "But the one that stands out. The one that some scientists came up with at the beginning was that the dead lacked the intelligence to think that there's anywhere other than where they're standing. That's why a lot of time you see them motionless; they'll just stand right where they are until they hear or smell something. At the beginning of the outbreak, you would see the whole swarms of Zs moving across the countryside."

Naomi adds: "Because everyone had the same fundamental survival instinct, y'all. Fight or flee. That same silly notion that maybe other cities were free from infection! And all those hordes of fleeing—still alive—Yankees fled for their lives, desperate to escape their walking nightmares of former friends, work colleagues and family, but always in the same direction"—she rolls her eyes in despair at the silly survival instinct that most Americans had back then—"from one city to another, and always in big groups."

"But the infected eventually caught up to those groups," Mary edges into the convo.

"Correct, Mary," Deckard agrees with the life-long Yooper. "Or there were already individuals infected in those groups fleeing the large population centers. People with bites and wounds hidden from friends and family—until they died and reanimated as a corpse—and turned every last man, woman, and child in those unlucky groups into walking stiffs." *Just more meat for the grind,* the ex-Marine muses to himself but doesn't add his thoughts to the discussion.

"When there were no large groups of survivors to chase anymore, all those hordes of Zs just settled where 'humans' used to live and work," Carl concludes, looking both ways across an intersection, and he eases off the gas, slowly moving the jeep through the quiet streets of former homes and buisnesses.

Some buildings teetered with cracks, others had bullet holes in the walls, and grass grew from broken walkways. Surprisingly, the city of Winnemucca (named after 19th-century Chief Winnemucca of the local Northern Paiute tribe), was void of any life and spiritual life of the former tribe's ancestors, and Carl was extremely happy. The empty roads. Empty supermarkets and cafes; the former hustle of life ran through his mind. *No one is around? Not one single living soul, nor undead body?*

And everyone watched and pondered as the city sailed by.

***

Jed gazes at the pretty town and sees plastic bags blowing through the roads like tumbleweeds, and re-focuses his attention to the front of the jeep. It took a moment to realize what he saw off in the distance. Several short seconds later, he realizes no one else is paying attention.

"Living dead!" he calls rather loudly.

"Fuck me, Jed!" Carlos mutters, slightly annoyed as the teen's high-pitch words vibrates through his eardrums. "You're not fourteen anymore; you can use the flippin' Z-word!"

"No. *Look!*" he replies loudly, throwing a hand forward past the Midwesterner's earlobe and points to the front windscreen. Carlos opens his mouth; wants to berate the teen for yelling in close quarters again, but no words emerge as he looks down the straightness of Jed's finger. The Midwesterner then sees the sea of darkness, soaking up the distant highway.

At the same time, both yell: *"Stop!"*

Carl instantly pulls the jeep to a rolling stop in the middle of the street; tires screeching to a halt, engine quietly rumbling.

Deckard is out of the jeep in no time, his military-issued binoculars up, his vision focused on the oncoming danger. The others following suit. "It's a swarm, kids, and a big 'un," he declares. "Probably… a few thousand strong. Here! Look for yourself! It's a shitstorm of the dead, heading our way!" he details what lay ahead in their path, handing Carl the steel binoculars.

Carl takes the binoculars. They were built with military-grade precision and optical quality, proven in every theater of combat. Carl focuses the lenses and sees the horde-of-dead advancing towards them. It was like watching a slow tsunami rolling over and over the countryside, never stopping, never decreasing, just consuming.

Carlos takes the binoculars from the dashboard; gets into the action. "Holy shit! It's like Mardi Gras has come early this year!"

Jed: "Is everyone dead?"

Carlos: "Fuck yeah, every last one of those walking blood bags is as dead as the opening act of an Academy Award Ceremony."

Deckard nods affirmatively: looking every inch like a veteran commander on the verge of an oncoming battle with insurgents in the hellholes of Afghanistan. "As dead as our asses if we keep to this road. We need another route and quick!" he adds with haste.

The air is humid, the asphalt hot and sticky beneath their feet like a moist cake. The smell of death does not take long to hit them. It's not overpowering, but it's there at the tip of their noses. Roadkill mixed in with rotting flesh and excrement. Remnants of the advancing horde stinking up the tailwind of a light breeze. And the *buzzing* of flies too, thick, bloated black specks hovering above the pack of the dead.

It's left to Carl to get his assortments of plastic maps out again. He starts searching for the right page, flicks with his stiff fingers through the plastic and some-what tattered maps of former states. Blue lines. Red lines. "C'mon," he says to no one in particular. "C'mon, we need a viable escape route."

"What are they following?" Jed quizzically asks as he—now—peers through the binoculars that Carlos gave him.

The main group of dead formed along the highway, while smaller clusters seemed to populate across the countryside. Occasionally some would get stuck behind trees, and from behind, other dead would walk past to take their place in the dead parade of hungry, lost souls.

"Huh!?" Naomi says, throwing a glance towards the youth.

"They must be following something?" he says, the question is in the open for anyone to answer. "Otherwise, the dead would be immobile like you guys explained earlier."

"I don't know, Jed! Maybe they're chasing some wildlife that's brave enough to come back to the area." She shakes her head in annoyance to Jed's silly questions, turns back to the others gathered around the map covering the bonnet. "Right, quick. Where to, y'all?" she asks. Naomi's tough Texan accent was shining through ten-fold as she scans for an escape route.

Jed looks frustrated but continues to look through those binoculars.

"If we double back to Melarkey Street!"—Deckard points to an intersection dead center on the map—"keeping on this damn road! See?" (Each study the isolated section of the map, where the ex-Marine's finger trails.) "It will lead us straight under Highway 80 and across this small river and right outta town away from that oncoming 'Deathmarch,' heading our way!"

"I don't know!" Carl second guesses the choice of the man. "It takes us in a completely different direction to where we want to go!"

Deckard nods, leaning towards Carl. "When you're in the field, operations change all the time, kid. You just have to bite the bullet, and deal with the situation." The Marine gazes at Carl with a tough look expression forming underneath his fedora, then continues: "Sometimes, we have no other choice than to take plan C when plan A is outta the race. And plan B is nowhere to be seen. Understand?"

Mary says to Deckard, "I'll agree with that assessment." Turns towards the rest of the group. "If we can't continue onwards to Reno and the seaboard, let's just take the alternative route, guys. It'll be a far better choice than heading straight on through a barrage of ghouls."

Carl: "I understand that—"

"Carl, that zombie horde is too large for us to get through!" Naomi states, taking Mary's side. Both stare at him. "We don't have time to form a discussion group. We should just go."

Carl stands between the two girls, frowning, the rest of the group looking to him for a clear answer (he figuratively sits on it for a minute).

Carlos agrees with the others. "I don't need to hear it's a good plan either, dawg. Just that it ain't the worse plan I've heard all day."

Carl feels fingers delving into his mind, poking about trying to pull the lever to form a response. All the while, he listens intently, as is his way. He takes it all in, thinks, *plans always change. Get use to it, Carl.* "Good enough," he finally agrees.

Twenty seconds later they were tearing through the streets of Winnemucca away from the horde of undead, and four blocks later passing underneath Interstate 80 and over a small river and onto Veteran's Memorial Highway.

46
RESTSTOP

Winnemucca's epicenter with an onslaught of walking corpses descending on the deserted town like a Mardi Gras street party was just a distant memory as they now traveled past Steens Mountain which was located in the southeastern part of the U.S. state of Oregon, located in Harney County. It was some of the wildest and most remote land left in Oregon: an untouched gem of avocado-green backdrop beneath a light blue sky and candyfloss clouds. Once or twice, the girls saw Rocky Mountain elk, pronghorn antelope and bighorn sheep traveling together along the side of the road. (The animals didn't shy away from the vehicles of humans. Instead, the creatures formed a military formation; a necessary battleline of protection, as if they were in an armored convoy and had made this corner of southeast Oregon their home since the end of the world had brought a new kind of tourist to town.)

Carl stuck to the Oregon Route 78 following migratory birds traveling the Pacific Flyway using Harney County as a rest and refueling stop and soon passed the community of New Princeton (an unincorporated community), before they eventually rolled to a stop in the small city of Burns. Remnants of an old county fair adorned its dusty litter-ridden streets, with dry fountains and feral dogs too. Its dying, and stunted trees, strips of brown grass and desert-colored buildings made an instant Mad Max-esque kind of place. Just north of the city, the Burns Paiute Reservation (sat on 770 acres of prime real estate land).

As they searched an empty drug store on North Broadway Avenue, one or two dead came out to meet and greet them like former helpful locals. A few cracked skulls and bottles of aspirin later, the road was cleared from the dead and the remaining shelves empty of supplies.

***

Then it happened—

From nowhere, an unexpected storm rose all around them; like Smaug from *J. R. R. Tolkien's* 1937 novel, The Hobbit, declaring war on all who disturbs his mountainous fortress. The air hummed with *cracking* of lightning, multi-tentacled winds roared from above, beneath, sideways; black, menacing thundering clouds opened up, releasing a torrential downpour on the group of weary travelers below.

Where they'd stopped, this side of town on North Broadway Avenue a four-block residential area off the main street. The houses stood old and solemn on desolate, overgrown gardens. Opposite, the chemist. On the other side of the junction; a 1920s two-story brown building stood alone; a parking lot, void of vehicles, surrounded by waist-high walls, a steel chain-link fence partially open—covering the opening of the lot. A sign above the entrance of the boxed-shaped brick building read: Dolorosa Café, Friendly Vegan Café, 'C'mon in and eat,' was its tag-line.

"I think we should bunker down for the night, kids," the question comes firmly from Deckard's mouth. He stands like an unhappy *Gollum* as big fat drops of rain hit his stubbly chin. "Objections?" His fedora bends at the front as a *tap, tap, tap* of rain hits its rim.

"Okay, guys, Deckard's correct," Carl hollers, agreeing with the man. "It's a couple days drive to Portland, considering if the roads are clear and clean of any hiccups."

Deckard: "Worst-case scenario, slightly longer."

"Okay. So we should rest the night. Recharge our batteries with some decent shelter for a change. Wait till the storm passes."

"Suggestions?" Naomi asks both of them. Together, Carl and Deckard point to the brick building as if they are one sentient being.

"That's food for thought, right?" Carlos says as he stands in his third and final clean tee. All eyes fall on him.

Mary: "What is?"

"I guess there could be worse places to spend the night. And on the bright side, none of us are vegans right? So we won't get eaten if the owners are still around looking for customers!"

She tries to think of a sarcastic dismissal to the Midwesterner's illogical thinking and fails.

Naomi agrees. "Good place as any to hole up for the night!" She shows it with a firm Texan nod. "Chow-down. Rest. It'll do us, grand."

Carlos clucks aloud: "Yeah, beats sleeping in 'Priscilla,' with you guys head-to-toe while the clouds piss on us from above."

"Feel free to jump in any time, Jed?"

"I'm happy with whatever, Carl."

Carlos: "Spoken like a true teen not vaguely interested in any adult's conversation."

The teen was still stood a few feet away, oblivious to the Midwesterner's comment. Just interested in a safe, secure, warm shelter until the storm passed.

"Okay. Sorted," Carl says, assured at the group's unanimous decision. "Deckard and I will go ahead—scout the building. Mary, you bring the jeep into the carpark, pronto. Carlos, lock those gates behind. I see a chain that's trailing the ground." He turns to the others. "Guys, start unloading supplies for the night." He offers the instructions to everyone, and everyone gladly accepts their supporting roles. "Let's be quick."

Naomi and Jed nod back a supportive yes.

Carlos blinks.

Mary frowns.

Everyone scatters—does what they're told to do.

47
DOLOROSA CAFÉ

Some twelve minutes later, the coast is clear, room-by-room checked. Carl and Deckard resurface through the main entrance of the building. Either side of the doorway the windows are boarded up good and proper with plywood and aluminum as though a tornado warning had been issued.

"All clear, guys," Carl hollers from the doorway, waving everyone inside. "C'mon in outta the rain."

The downstairs of the building is a nicely laid out café. "Nowhere quite represents a place like a fine café!" Mary remarks, shaking drops away, fond memories of her former employment flooding to the forefront of her mind.

They drink it all in: and could imagine the once bustling eatery had a crowd of elderly regulars and younger customers once, ensuring a nice welcoming atmosphere to townies and out-of-towners alike. It's spacious, the same bare, brick walls decorate the inside as the external walls. While three large blackboards showing the former menu glisten behind the main serving area; as well as herbal teas, regular teas and coffees, and the best milkshakes in town: chocolate shakes, strawberry shakes and so forth, and toasted sambos, muffins, cocoa–avocado brownie and polenta chips. (Each completely plant-based version of milkshake and lunchtime favorite meal written in neat chalky handwriting, with a stylish author's flourish.) Tagged-up walls all over and even on the furniture, and soft lighting and polished wooden floors (now dusty due to neglect and the rustic premises looked promising—if the world ever recovered from the apocalypse—and if they ever decided to go into business).

"It gives this place a really cool artsy type of vibe," Mary nails the coolness of the space. She likes the style of the café, too, no doubt, but the décor resonates an upper New York bar more than a small town café as she heaves a heavy rucksack onto the cafe's wooden floor— awakening a layer of fine dust.

"I like it. It's cool, hip and funky," Naomi says. (Fond memories of county bars from her home state resonate through her mind.) "Beats having dinner out on the ranch porch with the folks at night. No swatting damn flies or mossies either. Coyotes comin' around pining for food."

Seconds later.

"Agghhh!" comes a voice behind the counter, not as in a scared holler but an excited screech.

"Now, what!" Mary says looking frustrated. "What's the problem?"

Everyone zeroes in—slightly nervous—as Carlos slowly stands. But the tensions are gone, as he grins largely. "Looky what I found. The bar is now truly open for business!" he declares, holds up two bottles of beer (expiry date passed by a month or so). "Kind of a welcome to our new favorite 'home away from home,' girls and boys." Down below, a full bar of beverages sits behind the long wooden counter. "The question asked every day, all over Oregon, 'What is the best craft beer produced in the greatest craft beer state?' What lager goes with that waffle-grilled cheddar cheese n' bacon wrap? What seasonal ale hits the sweet spot on a cold, rainy night? What sour do you love but your significant other can't stand?" And Carlos casts an endearing glance the Yooper's way.

At this, Mary glares back and smiles lightly. Sighs, her fingers reach to latch on to a bottle and instead find his fingers. A connection of flesh for a few seconds—she says nothing, just grasps the beer and takes it gladly.

"You nutjob, I.P.A, rulez!" Naomi rattles off, and goes and grabs the other bottle from the Midwesterner's hands: it is an I.P.A; she cracks the top with a hefty *clunk* on the edge of the bench (the lids spins across the workbench like a dropped penny from a purse and finally stops at the counter's edge). "I'll put it to y'all, folks, let the shenanigans begin!" and she glugs; deep swallows of warm beer drives a long time thirst away. *"Kanpai!"* she cheers, the bottle up high. "The Japanese way for declaring a toast!" (It is not too warm, slightly cool, and the taste still holds.)

Mary takes her eyes from the Midwesterner's smitten stare. "Cheers, guys!" she declares, celebrating with her best friend. *Clinks* of beer bottles follow.

Deckard: "Bottom's up, girls and guys." A taste of alcohol to Oklahoma's lips was the same feeling as breast milk to a newborn baby's mouth; it was what he needed since his Scotch had all but dried up. (It doesn't have that fire-driven effect, but it hits the sweet spot nevertheless.)

Carlos dispenses a beer to everyone from the below counter shelves; a mixture of pale ales and bespoke beers. But Jed's not too keen on the adult beverage, instead (settling on a natural, no sugar, no fun, no thrill raspberry cola), from a tall, standalone fridge.

***

Everyone drinks, everyone sits on the comfy couches, and Naomi says, "It's a good find."

Carl stares at her and finally nods. "Yeah. It is. It'll do for the night while the storm subsides."

"Uh-ha," she replies.

"You okay?" he asks Naomi as she gulps down the beer.

"Daydreaming of sweet gnocchi-pan-fried with butter, and bacon fritters, and a slice of double strawberry cheesecake."

"*Aaannndddd,* I'm hungry."

"What is, gnocchi?" Jed asks behind his cola bottle.

And it brings a roar of laughter from the room.

Just to the rear of the main eating area, an empty kitchen with a long steel galley with a single locked door at the far end; bolted from the inside. At the other end of the café, toilets: empty, but toilet paper is still in place in see-through dispensers attached to the cubicle walls. Upstairs was empty, also serving as living quarters. A lounge, kitchen, small washroom, and two small bedrooms; nicely decorated with double beds, covers, and some sparse furniture sat idly all alone in each room.

As the evening ticked by and the storm worsened, outside, 'Priscilla' sat like an Out-of-towner coming from the 'Big Smoke,' to pester the locals of the small community on Spring Break. Inside the perimeter fence, everyone made themselves at home within the building. Solid walls, barricaded entrances, and a roof to sleep under; camping overnight in the upstairs apartment, (free from the dangers of the outside world and without any Zs to worry about was a great feeling to behold).

The night was long, comfortable, quiet, and full of beers and laughter.

48
THANKS FOR THE BEERS

The next morning came scampering into existence like a Jack Russell biting at the heels of its just awoken master from a deep night-of-slumber, and the gang were back on the road in no time, leaving the confines of Dolorosa Café and the sleepy, slick wet streets of Burns behind, hurtling along the John Day-Burn Highway. Two crates of beer, coffee, tea bags and extra condiments of supplies from the well-stocked café added to their inventory.

As morning rolled into the afternoon, the Vaseline-smudged sky turned once again into bright clear picture-perfect watercolors as they continued north through the Malheur National Forest. (The forest consisted of high desert grasslands; sage, juniper, pine, fir, and other trees where they saw the varying elevations of Strawberry Mountain extending east to west through the center of the forest. 312,000 acres of beautiful forest expanded across Grant, Harney, Baker, and Malheur counties.)

A while later, the road became an utter mess, a rollercoaster of brambles covered asphalt, wooded dunes, hilly trenches of greenery where previous roads were now dried-mud causeways. They drove up a slithering hill, down into murky holes. All around, encroaching pine trees spread for miles and miles in every direction. The inhabitants of the jeep had begun to wonder whether they'd taken the right direction.

"We're lost!" Mary says.

"We're not lost. We're on the correct route, it's just I can't pinpoint exactly where we are at the mo!" Carl replies.

"It sounds a lot like we're lost."

"Mary's right, Carl. It does sound a lot like we're chasing our own tails around the damn yard without a clue where we're actually goin'," Naomi chips in.

Carl got his maps out, assuring the group they were going in the right direction. But the others didn't really see it; the same way one can be in a crowded city and not see that city. Because you can only see the entire city with its streets, and buildings in satellite pictures.

When Carlos started to ask questions of Carl's fearsome leadership; his pioneering spirit of the Ernest Shackleton and Robert Scotts of the world, that's when—

The late afternoon sunlight slanted through the trees as they finally exited the grand, ancient American forest and threw light on Route 395 once again. Four rest stops, three more small population centers, a brief sightseeing trip through Umatilla National Forest and a few hours later, they felt like they were achieving mileage.

"Priscilla drives good!" Mary says, matter-of-factly from behind the steering wheel, she'd taken over driving duties from the ex-Marine an hour ago. "You did a helluva job patching our home up when we first met back at that bar."

"It drives well," Deckard comments from behind her seat.

"You enjoy this, don't you?" Carlos objects.

He's riding shotgun, leaning out of the window like a pet on a trip with the entire family. The CD they had acquired from the café back in Burns blasted an assortment of Nu-modern kitchen swagger and Jazz. Considering the Midwesterner always had taken care of 'Priscilla,' it had taken just one engine problem he didn't know how to fix to shove all the good work he'd ever done back in his face.

It was a hard insult to swallow. A slap on the comical side; an edgy blade to Carlos' largely inflated man-ego.

"Enjoy what?" she asks, trying to navigate around a trailer attached to a late 1980's pale, blue Ford that was stuck in the middle of the road. "Making you feel inadequate?" she says the insult before he has a chance to answer the subtle question.

Carlos sits back in the passenger seat for a second longer, taking in the below-the-belt remark. *I wasn't inadequate last night, babe.* But he refuses to spill his thoughts to the rest of the car. Instead, he resorts to his natural optimism and bountiful charm any time he's cornered with no way out of a conversation. He gives her a look, followed by: "Fuck you, Mary."

She lets out a small titter of enjoyment. "I know how hard this is for you to grasp, and I admire your tenacity and effort. But… you're an asshole. I don't feel bad! And you lack social skills."

"No, shit."

"See!"

"Point taken."

"Guys, guys, guys, what did we say we weren't gonna do?" Carl says from behind.

Mary says nothing. Instead, just concentrates on driving.

"Don't worry, dawg. We're not arguing!" Carlos frankly says, looking past the small gap that separates himself from the blond Yooper. "Mary's just busting my balls!"

Carl is about to respond to the oddly pragmatic response and calm natured words flowing from the Midwesterner's lips when, without an introduction, a lake just happens in front and all around them, as a tree range ended and a sun-blast comes flooding through the last line of pines.

A bright sun glimmers off the surface of the water.

Mary eases off the gas, brings 'Priscilla' to a stop in a small parking lot just shy of the stretch of clear water. Everyone checks the beautiful sight; imagined fishing, boating, picnicking, and hunting were popular activities at the water a long time ago. Next to the parking lot, a faded green sign welcomed them to 'Mckay Reservoir.' The birth of water was located 6 miles south of Pendleton.

There was also a wooden sign, with large text printed on the sign in bold italics saying: *NO CAMPING PERMITTED.* The rot had eaten through the word

NO. But a hundred yards away in a clearing, a strange sight drew their attention. An array of vehicles was stationed in a circle, like the American pioneers defending themselves with their wagons from the Native Indians a long time ago.

There were no hostiles in sight; no Zs either.

No, no one.

"Someone's flouting the rules!" Naomi says, chuckling to her own joke.

But that wasn't even the strangest sight—

"Are we reenacting a scene from Vikings?" Carl exclaims, peeking through the binoculars at the peculiar sight while remembering the historical drama television series created and written by *Michael Hirst* for the History Channel (one of his favorite shows from another time, from a different era).

"What do you see?" Jed demands, the teen's voice inquisitive as always.

Carl explains as though he's a history teacher lecturing to a class of third years on a day trip to a museum. Huge wooden spikes—each half-a-foot apart, each pointing waist height—were piled into the dirt and surrounded the ring of RV's and other vehicles like an enormously armored porcupine (the display resonated survival instincts from an unbeknown civilization).

"Hey!" Mary says. "I'd rather stop and continue tomorrow, in the morning. We all need the rest."

Carl considers options, doesn't answer the question immediately, considering the day was fast coming to a close; a break would be the best option for all of them instead of driving onwards through the night. "Okay." He polled the rest of the group. "Naomi?"

"Dandy."

"Okay with me, Carl," Jed answers.

Carlos nods.

Deckard tips his fedora. "You're in charge, kid."

The evening was drawing in, and the group needed somewhere to spend the night. The discussion decided; the fortress of vehicles would be their home for the night.

***

Carl levers from 'Priscilla' and goes to stand a meter from the hood of the jeep, takes another look through his binoculars at the strange encampment of vehicles and fortified defenses.

"But first thing's first!" Deckard declares as he saunters up to Carl's shoulders. "I'm inclined to scout the area first and foremost. I want to know if the camp is clear from the undead. We don't want any ugly surprises creeping up on us during the night." The Marine surveys the fortified ring of sharpened poles off in the distance. *A solid base for protection?* he muses. "I'm not sure if it's safe or a multi-threat environment." *You always need to think ahead of your enemies if you want to stay on top.* His instincts taking over. "The whole place could be full of Zs, survivors, or goddamn LMOEs…"

"LMOEs?"

"Last Man on Earth. I'm talking Lord of the Flies kinda stuff, kiddo," Deckard shoots back at Jed. (The 1990 American survival drama goes beyond the teen's knowledge of films from that decade.) "There's always one or two in every town, some dude or chick who managed to survive the worse of the shit," he says with determined grit to his voice. "Now eventually reverting to savagery. Nowadays, they're too used to being King of the Dump to share supplies, a safe haven, and the love of our former land!"

The teen's hands instantly go to his new revolver holstered in his gunbelt; an itchy trigger finger waiting to be pulled.

"If someone's in there, we should let them know we mean no harm," Mary suggests.

Carlos gives her an iffy look. "What do you mean, 'mean them no harm?' We're not greeting an intelligent alien lifeform from another planet!"

"It's the right thing to do," her voice edged with annoyance. Mary gazes back at the fortifications. "Well, it can't hurt!"

"Right, I'll just make sure. Hey! Anyone inside?" Carlos hollers, feeling rather cavalier. "Dipshits, Friendlies, Zs, Last Fucker Standing? We would love to spend the night with you, cozying around a bonfire roasting marshmallows!" A few seconds later. "Anyone in?"

A heated voice filters from behind: "What are you doing, Carlos?"

The Midwesterner gives Mary a look. "Told ya, nobody was around, Kansas! We okay?"

"No, we're not okay."

"Okay," Naomi says. "I think I speak on behalf of at least two-thirds of the people here when I ask, what the fuck you doing, Carlos?"

Mary, from her side adds: "I do say your relentless antagonization, is part of the fake façade you use to keep people at arm's length."

He's quiet. Too quiet. Just stares at the Texan and the Yooper which feels like a lifetime to the entire group who wasn't already involved with the conversation.

Finally, he responds: "Nah. Just like to piss people off—is all!"

Deckard says off the cusp: "You're doing a grand job, fella!"

Suddenly Carlos found himself between both girls' sturdy gaze. Naomi and Mary check each other, facial muscles still tense and miffed grins and a certain appreciation ignites between the two girls; they knew the Midwesterner would forever be a dick.

A cough. The tension is broken.

Carl hollers: "We mean you no harm—just looking for someplace to crash for the night!" He edges forward. "Can you help?" No groaning, no *clicks* of gun catches, just another moment of silence stretches like the length of undisturbed water off in the distance. "It looks fine, guys. I think the place is abandoned. We should move."

Carlos looks at him; a lake of questions bubbling beneath his surface.

"How come you so sure, dawg?"

"Intuition."

A frown ripens the Midwesterner's jaw. "No shit!"

Thirty blank seconds later they were still standing in front of 'Priscilla' looking ahead at the motionless and—they suspect—abandoned camp.

Deckard shakes the daze from beneath his fedora: swept the area; expert eyes focusing on the high ground; the top of a Class A Winnebago made a great lookout of the surrounding area. On top, sits a chair and a small, colorful umbrella. "Keep close together!" he warns the rest. "Look out for movement from those windows."

Then Carl turns to the others. "Be careful, guys! Look for survivors; we never know what we will find behind those barricades. Let's try to keep ourselves out of danger."

A group nod of approval erupts—

Everyone starts to advance—

49
ENCAMPMENT OF SPIKES

Carl and Deckard took point; steadying the group with ease and poise. Mary and Naomi took a left with a handgun and a high-powered hunting rifle. While Carlos and Jed took the right side of the circle—with Glock and revolver drawn. Together as a military unit, they moved forward in formation, inching across the grassland one foot at a time.

As they grew closer to the fortifications, they could see remnants of blood on many of the wooden spikes. On others, clumps of hair and chunks of meat that had stained the wooden stakes a dark red.

"It's disgusting!" Mary says. She feels pukey phlegm in the back of her throat, her belly heaving.

Naomi grins. Her stomach was performing somersaults too. "Yeah, you're right, Mary!" But was used to the blood from working on her father's farm back in Texas. "Whoever made these barricades sure knew how to fortify a position. They made an impregnable killzone away from their campsite. Perfect views in every direction."

Mary nods in agreement to the Texan's tough assessment of the encampment.

"Don't forget trip-wired shotgun shells and booby traps!" Jed yells opposite the girls.

"This isn't the time for that X-Box game bullshit, Jed!" Naomi irately calls over her shoulder, yet she starts to sweep the ground frantically in front of her like a U.N. mine-sweeper in the depths of the Congo.

"Jed's goddamn right! Why the hell are we treading into this killzone like eager beavers into their cozy damns?" Carlos bemoans. He pauses to let that dismal image sink in. "Doesn't make sense, dawg!" he continues, making eye contact with each of the five, individually.

No one replies.

They steadily move past the ring of protection, carefully surveying for mines and booby traps and twenty yards later are standing outside the circle of RVs and vans. Wires with cans were strung along the ground from every fifth pole and connected to a vehicle's wing mirror. A flowered Volkswagon Kombi, two mud-splattered RVs, a large slightly-faded chrome Winnebago and three sun-soaked Sudan's sat confined to the circle. Between the bottom of the chassis and the grassy floor, a wooden fence was constructed—no gaps for Crawlers to crawl through at any given time on their bellies.

The fence also circled where the vehicles joined. There were no gaps or openings between bonnet and boot. Smaller wooden spikes and 10inch nails were driven randomly through the fence at varying heights.

Deckard tips his fedora back, inspecting the Kombi. The once hippie van—an iconic symbol for peace-now a desolate reminder of simpler times, had bullets holes decorating the 60s-styled vehicle. "Be careful when we enter kids"—he recognizes the distinct bullet pattern of semi-automatic gunfire—"Whoever's been living in this camp… has had fights against other survivors before."

"Good observation!" Naomi and Mary say in agreement.

"No shit!" mouths Carlos.

A split second later—

The ex-Marine proceeded to climb over the structure with his revolver drawn. A hefty boot later, and he was inside the perimeter. Carl and Carlos slowly follow, making their way into the center like an L.A SWAT team; making sure the coast was clear through each and every window. Then, Naomi, Mary, and Jed followed.

Three minutes later—

"Empty!" Carl says aloud as he checks the last RV of lifeforms, slightly relieved by the fact they'd hadn't run into the previous homeowners, corpses and more importantly, the undead clamoring through the tight doorways of the stationed homes.

He was now looking at a fire pit. It was constructed in the middle of the ring of vehicles. Burnt and blackened logs rested on top of one another. Two picnic tables were strewn around the pit of stones, and a clothesline hung from a pole in the center and stretched towards the Winnebago side view mirror.

"I guess we should look for supplies, guys," he assesses the next course of action.

"Coast is clear," Deckard acknowledges as he steps from the Winnebago's homely interior with a nod. "Affirmative."

Carlos jests: "Ahh, another glorious day in paradise." He turns and sees the girls leaving the compound. "Where you two off to?"

They both turn and answer as one: "Girly chat. Tampons and menstrual cycles. Why! You wanna come along for the show?"

"I'll pass, thanks. Had enough blood and gore in the past few days."

"Good," both girls says, and a split second later, both erupt in laughter. Naomi and Mary strut towards the lake, giggling like 11th graders.

From behind, "Don't go too far, okay!" Carl hollers. "If you need anything, see anything, then fire a warning shot!" Both girls stick up a hand in reply.

Soon the girls are gone from sight—leaving the guys behind to search the campsite thoroughly for remaining supplies.

50
THE UNEXPECTED CHAT

A cache of trees gave away the walking path—wooden slats laid down on top of the earth like train sleepers—leading from the campsite, flowing through tall grass and native plants and the clear waters of Mckay Reservoir came alive. A long deck jutted out into the waters. On the other side, hills and more pines rose in the distance in the late afternoon sun.

Mary canvassed the horizon. A line of trees wound around the edges of the lake in every direction, and a low cloud system drifted westerly like dragon's breath clung across the wide water.

Naomi hovers over the edge of a shallow bank, splashes the cool, cold reservoir water over her face. "Hey, Mary! What are you waiting for; a signal or something?"

"No. What!"

"Your mind seems to be in the middle of the lake than here with me."

"Oh, I ah, don't know." It's an answer, but not a good one. "Just thinking."

"You know you've been quiet. Just wanted to make sure you're okay?"

I'm thinking about Salt Lake City. How we nearly died back in that hell-hole of infested suburban houses. My time spent with Carlos. A stupid decision I'm trying to forget. But something keeps pulling me back to that night. If it was the warmth, the company that the annoying Dickhead offered? I don't know. She says none of that. Instead, she just says, "Yeah, I'm fine. You know… just zombies."

"Not Carlos and his attitude?"

"I, eh—?"

"Hmmm…" Naomi works her damaged arm, rotates slowly. "You guys were trapped overnight in Salt Lake. He must've gotten on you a bit?"

But no answer is forthcoming.

"Hey. You. I'm waiting for an answer, girl."

"On me!" she says, her words more a desperate bleat than anything else. *We were all over each other, like tectonic plates shifting beneath the Earth's crust.* She feels shame over the act. "Heavens do you mean! On me?"

"Hmmm… I guess you two seem less at each other's throats! More… steady, like you two are keeping a secret from the rest of the group!"

Mary looks at Naomi, wondering if that was a statement or another question. "We didn't do anything!" her words come out forcefully. Her lies already unraveling themselves.

It takes a second of realization before the Texan looks at her friend with many unanswered questions boiling to the surface. "Jeez, you didn't, did you, Mary! Bump uglies? Shindig with Carlos? Get down in the hay-shack?"

Mary peers back over the large body of water; a touch of fog was steadily moving across the surface as daylight was looming to an end in an hour or so, and a flock of birds took to the sky from the reservoir's belly. All around them, the nearby trees gave off a sweet, earthy smell of recently burned pine, and in the fields surrounding the shoreline, green blades of grass made a natural contrast against the fortified encampment of metallic cars and rusty spikes that sat nearby.

Naomi studies the lines etched around Mary's eyes. She loved the way they scrunched together when her friend was lost for words. Or lying her tits off.

Mary feels the whole wide world suddenly fall quiet waiting for a response from her lips. The ripple of water. The gentle wind. The birds. The dragon's breath. Her lips forming a big O in response. She remembers the night back in Salt Lake City. The talking. The fucking. The regrets in the morning. No. She was empty of regrets. *What was done, was done.* "It just happened, okay." Her hands tried to communicate something very explicit.

"Sex?"

"Heck, we never really talked about it. The sex just happened. I didn't—I don't *think* of Carlos that way. I don't think I would've done anything with anyone that condescending." The words blossom from her mouth like tulips in spring.

"Don't you find him charming?"

"Charming?" Mary repeats. A soothing breeze from the water's edge caressed her face. And a loose strand of hair dangled over her nose. "Like… brings me chocolate? Waits in the rain when I'm running late for a movie? Eat's my quiche without complaining?"

"Rubs your feet too," Naomi sarcastically teases. "Uh-huh! Maybe his ultra-cold Midwesterner exterior is more charming than you realize? Like a night out on the town, drinking several tequilas with friends, partying on a dance-floor, and then some loser comes over to you, offers a drink, his hand. Dance to a tune or two. But deep down, you know the loser—is just a loser. But you think, 'heck, it's just for one night, huh!' and you continue to dance, bumping up against the loser's rippling frame. Two to three more drinks later, and you ditch your posse of friends—*finally* following that loser home, only to wake up in the morning with a cracking headache and more regrets than you'd had the previous night."

She presses her forehead against her own palm. "Oh! I'm perfectly aware of how charming Carlos can be. But most times… not in a good way either. He has committed to acting like a thundering dickhead on so many occasions to those who cross his path I have finally lost count."

"That's the truth?"

"Truth…" Mary lets the solemn word flow, eventually plucks a blade of grass between forefinger and thumb. "Yup."

Naomi goes on to add: "Damn, he has zero chills, Mary."

The Yooper has her sights on the fluttering wildlife off in the distance as the Texan shuffles a nervous foot through the grass on the bank, accidentally knocking her friend's foot. "We didn't make love that night. Just—just easier to say we fucked the night away—but this felt different. It wasn't the ins-and-outs of the motion. The situation brought us together, but I trembled. That feeling when you first do the deed!"

"Fuck?"

"Uh-ha," her words catch in the back of her throat. "In the morning, though, Carlos acted like a dick. Like always." She continued to play with that thin blade of grass.

"Every man does, Mary. It's a circle of screwing and getting their dicks wet. Then they revert to the caveman of yesteryear once they have finished gettin' their dicks wet."

The more they talked, the more Mary became anxious. She gnawed at a thumbnail. Chewed on her bottom lip—a trait that had traveled all the way from 3rd Grade. Eventually, peered at the tree-lined shores opposite.

***

Naomi can't hack it anymore, and she rotates her injured shoulder again, and again: pain lingers deep from the bullet. Other pain too. "Sometimes, do you ever feel so alone and invisible it actually aches?" she says off the cusp. Her thoughts thundering back to happier times with her ex-fiance before he became dinner for the dead.

The question takes Mary by surprise.

The Yooper takes a moment to gather her thoughts. "Yeah… I mean… I think—sometimes." Then she notices the Texan's eyes staring off into nothing. Mary took her friend's sleeve, realizing Naomi was thinking about her dead ex. "Hey, since I've gotten to know you, you have always been a river of strength. A charge of electric fun, Naomi." A deep breath. "You miss him?"

"Uh-Huh..." Her words are shallow, void of emotion. "A lot… actually. But I think it's about time I should move on with my life. Don't you?" Then those words are punched with meaning and feelings as she waits for an answer.

"Suppose," Mary says. *Heck, she's so strong, this girl,* she thinks. "Only you will know when it's time."

Naomi found her courage now and rested a hand on Mary's shoulder; the pain from her injured arm subsiding.

Mary flicks the grass away like a cigarette onto the ground. "I'll be here for you."

"Thanks, partner…" Naomi lets her words drift. A rustle of reeds off in the distance makes her lose concentration; her trail of thought preoccupied with the sound of footsteps.

"Naomi?" Mary says. "Naomi, you just stopped in midsentence! What's wrong?"

The Texan blinks back into reality. "I just have a bad feeling—" A snap of twigs from underfoot. She immediately shields Mary's mouth with a hand. *"Shhh!"* she whispers. "I think we're not alone."

At this info bomb, Mary's eyes bulge to the size of melons. She mouths back a reply very quietly: *"Let's go back to the others."*

"I don't think that's an option, anymore!" Naomi nods; her hand outstretched.

Mary follows the Texan's line of sight like a sniper, hovering over a target five feet coming from their right. They both flatten themselves against the grass waiting for the person—or dead—to reveal themselves.

Another movement.

"Naomi!?" Mary whispers.

Naomi grips the hunting rifle with her weaker hand, ignoring the Yooper's voice beside her and waits for incoming footsteps; her finger on the trigger, ready to unleash 'hellfire,' on who or whatever was slowly creeping towards their position. Meanwhile, Mary was on her knees—sneaking a peek—through the high grass before Naomi notices her friend has become a comically expendable blond target for whoever was in waiting.

51
THE BONNIE & CLYDE SIDESHOW ACTUALLY (KELSEY & TITO)

"Freeze!" comes a voice. Mary obeyed, hands thrown up in the air like a hostage in a bank robbery. A figure moved from hiding and into view.

That's when—

"Freeze yourself, y'all!" Noami hollers from the ground, taking aim with the rifle with her weaker hand like she was on a shooting range on a Sunday afternoon with her Pa. "Show yourself," she demands.

The figure moved forward from the confines of their hidden position, but the tip of a rifle was still pointed at Mary's head. It was left to a new face to break the deathly stance.

"*Okaaaaayyy*, this is awkward!" a girl says.

"I'll dare y'all to make as much noise as a nuisance coyote on my Uncle Mark's farm, and I'll turn you into a damn scarecrow and drop y'all where you stand!" Naomi grips the hunting rifle's trigger, glaring at where both voices now stood.

Adjacent to Mary and Naomi were two armed figures.

A Latino; skin, beautiful as olive oil, with a black as black man-bun and a shortened rifle—half a barrel was sawn away. While his side-kick, a pasty, slim blond (reminds Mary of an American socialite and wannabee TV star in the mid-2000s) held an M9 Beretta with unsteady hands. They stood shoulder-to-shoulder with one another pointing their weapons at the girls more like a rich, white girl, and her low-paid gardner-in-tow than a fearsome Bonnie and Clyde double-act. Both wore green goose down jackets, and each shouldered a small blue rucksack (what you would get from any All American Dick's Sporting Goods store).

"If you're after a happy ending, then you'll put your gun away first!" the Latino commands. "I won't ask again."

"Yippey-no-fucking-way-on-Earth." Naomi rebukes the offer and lays out the alternative option to the two strangers. "Take another step closer, and I'll pump your face with lead, it'll add another shade to your mascara."

Her offer is on the table now.

The blond kisses her teeth; loving the bitchiness shown by Naomi. "Whoa, whoa, whoa melodrama alert!" she says. "Well, somebody's not being crowned 'Homecoming Queen' are they?"

"Don't go making BFFF bracelets just yet, girlfriends!" Naomi sarcastically blurts back.

The Latino arches his head at the feeble remark, says something to his partner-in-crime. His words—too quiet for the girls to hear—but the blond understands and nods. Ten seconds later, she finally says: "Greeting's y'all!

Friend or Foe?" (Her option of a hug or a bullet to the brain comes with a thick Southern accent.)

The question unbalances both girls for a moment. They're not sure how to answer the blond girl—considering the strangers had them covered with some brutal firepower. A telepathic answer and combo session later, both awkwardly answer 'Friend' at the same time.

The blond girl sheaths her weapon and walks up to Naomi and Mary. "Hiya, I'm Kelsey," she says quite proudly—sticks out a firm, slim hand to Mary (who is still kneeling down in the grass), but her hands come down, nevertheless and she takes the friendly handshake.

Mary notices the blond girl has high cheekbones, light skin, and once delicate hands that hadn't seen a day of heavy strife in her magical-unicorn-realm-of-existential life.

The blond girl extends a hand towards Naomi, as the Texan lifts her body from the ground with her good arm—supporting her own weight—and then she's up, standing opposite the Southerner. Next, hand out, a shake that would break the end of the American Civil War between the two opposing leaders.

Kelsey throws a nod over her shoulder towards her accomplice. "Tito!" (Hushed silence greeted the girls from the gun-carrying Latino.) Naomi and Mary were as silent as the Latino. The blond girl continues, "Normally, a howdy will suffice. Or your names? Either way, it's a polite starting point in any convo!"

Naomi starts by stating her name. "Naomi"—Points to Mary—"That's Mary." (Mary formed a nervous smile—a gritty tooth inducing nervous grin.) Naomi snaps back a grin too.

"Well. Nice to meet y'all," the blond answers. "Tito won't do you no harm. He's like a big, genial bear. Ain't ya, Tito?" Turns to look at her friend (the Latino shouldered his weapon and started moving slowly towards the group of younger girls).

"Okay. But bears have sharp claws; you know, right?" Mary nervously replies; her sidearm itching in its holder to be released.

"Fair do's…" the blond girl says, shrugging the fact away, before carrying on chatting as though they were best buds at a country retreat. "Well… I see y'all made yourselves at home!" She points in the general direction of the fortified campsite. "Hopin' you'd be friendly. Ain't too many of us around nowadays."

"Didn't want to pump your pretty little faces full of buckshot," Tito chips in.

Naomi and Mary feigned a strained smile at one another.

Naomi: "Much appreciated, Tito."

"Y'all lookin' for somewhere to kip for the night?" Before the girls could give an answer, the blond girl carries on. "Night at our Ritz will cost ya! Medicine or ammo. Either payment will suit us."

Naomi looks at Mary, and Mary nods back.

Mary: "How about some nice cold beer and some aspirin?"

Tito: "Wouldn't say no!"

Kelsey: "I can live with the offer."

Naomi: "Deal?"

Kelsey: "Uh-ha."

"Thanks," Naomi mutters, gritting her teeth together. "I believe we can sort payment out back at your encampment?" Her assured Texan accent shining through.

"Homegirl, huh?" Kelsey asks. "Where you from?"

"Texas," Naomi answers. "You?"

"Louisiana, just outside Baton Rouge," the girl replies.

"Go Pelican State."

"Union, justice, and confidence girl," Kelsey continues, referring to the State's motto. They share a laugh at being Stately neighbors. "Tito here…" and the blond girl beckons the Latino. "He's more of a southerner than both of us put together. He's a Puerto Rico homeboy. Ain't ya, Tito?"

A smile decorates his golden cheeks. "True, Kelsey, so true." Beneath his thick, coarse eyebrows, his eyes burned an emerald green. And beneath his thin line of a mustache, his white teeth gleamed against his skin.

"Looks like we've got ourselves some company for the night, Tito."

"Correct," he says, then turns to their guests. "Where's the rest of your group?"

Naomi's mouth opens—words tumble from her lips. "How—?" Before she sees the binoculars hanging around his thick neck.

The blond girl appears relaxed as if her friend's presence shifted the burden of responsibility from her shoulders to his.

"Been keeping an eye on you for the entire time since you came wandering into our house uninvited," he answers. "We didn't know if you were a threat… until now. Couldn't be sure. Still not sure."

Mary speaks; her voice lighthearted and juvenile, "We're not a threat!"

"Time will tell…" The Latino answers, and he goes back into the tall grass for a moment. Ten seconds later he reappears with a blue and white ice-chest. He grips the sturdy handle with ease.

Naomi: "What's in the cooler?"

"Dinner! Today we eat fish with our new acquaintances," he explains. "C'mon, will see if the rest of your friends are as friendly as you two girls."

Ten seconds later, Naomi and Mary found themselves escorted back to the encampment of vehicles by the blond girl and the Latino, ready to explain to the others that the camp wasn't exactly abandoned as they first thought it was.

52
CAMP OF BEWILDERMENT

"Oh sweet Jesus, I have just spilled sequins all over this luxurious home…" Carlos' voice filters through the Winnebago like he's standing inside a wind tunnel. "I've found a couple of bottles of tequila also, dawgs! Who's getting shitfaced tonight?"

"I guess it beats going to IKEA, buying chicken strips, meatballs, and ice cream!" Carl titters from the driver's seat. He'd been checking the ring of vehicles one-by-one to see if they still worked. No such luck. Each empty of gas.

Meanwhile, Jed and Deckard brought the supplies from the jeep to the center of the fortified camp as daylight was rescinding across the sky like bedcovers pulled close for the night. Jed was in the middle of starting a fire in the fire-pit with a small bottle of fuel he'd found. He squirts the liquid over some fresh wood; lights a match. *Vola!* The fire comes to life. Meanwhile, Deckard is back at the jeep bringing over a selection of canned food from their inventory in time for dinner.

Carl gets out from the driver's side of the Winnebago—levers from the seat and sees the reflections of the others returning in the side mirror. "Hey," he says, "I just thought, where you girls have gone to—" his words clipped short like his sideburns when he notices they are not alone.

Immediately he draws his gun, ready for action—

Jed seconds the action; he goes for his Bowie knife strapped to his leg; long blade glinting in flames, just as the firepit kicks with heat—

Carl turns to Jed. Jed to Naomi. Naomi to Mary. Mary to Carlos, who now stands at the top of the Winnebago steps; the Midwesterner holding two 750mL bottles of Margaritaville Silver Tequila in both hands.

"There's no way of quickly clearing this up!" he says, holding the two bottles of Mexican liquor up high (the label says 'Jimmy Buffet could have chosen a better tequila'), and Carlos knows for six bucks more, he could have gotten a far, decent hit of tequila. "Guess what? The only nice thing I can say about it is it's better than Landshark Beer," and titters to himself. (It's a drink that's good as it is but better when mixed with other flavors), but he doesn't care by the lack of choices on offer. "I'm gonna drink this shit down all by myself tonight, dawgs." That's when he catches a flicker of color out of the corner of his eye, a green Goose Down jacket wrapped tightly around a stick blond chick—

"If you put those bottles back where you found em' we'll share the good stuff with ya!" her soft voice interjects.

"Who are the fuck you?" Carlos misfires the sentence as his eyes lock onto another unknown face like a Japanese Zero fighter plane onto an opposing aircraft.

He sees a broad-shouldered Latino with a rifle marching closely behind Mary and Naomi across the campground. *Shit, they're prisoners!* He feels an uneasy sensation in the pit of his stomach. A jerking of anguish. A spasm of helplessness protruding like a blade stuck in his gut. He shouldn't feel this emotion as he sees Mary and the gun-toting stranger hovering behind her. (He imagines others with guns circling the fortified position), while at the same time, he stumbles for his weapon, and in the process fumbles both bottles of tequila like a clown juggling his batons for the adoring crowd.

Smash!

There's no applause.

***

Kelsey sidesteps the broken bottle that lands outside her front door; the shards of glass glisten with a wet, dreary *I told you, you should have drunk me the other night, Jimmy Buffet sure would have!* A frustrated moan escapes from her thin lips.

Meanwhile, Carlos catches the other bottle; bottom end in an open palm like an Outfielder at a World Series decider. Then he sees the blond; a sidearm attached to her thigh. A blue rucksack on her back. Refocuses back to the girls. *"Mary!"* he desperately hollers.

"It's okay," she replies, sticking up her hands to calm the Midwesterner before anything—he!—escalated the situation out of control. "They're cool. They mean us no harm." By the time Mary has finished her sentence, Carlos is standing by the doorway with his drawn barrel aiming at the slim blond.

She steps back, hands raised—

"Wow, wow, wow," her words clipped short.

At the same time, the Latino drops the blue and white ice-chest (inside, the catch of the day jumps in the plastic container as if they were still alive and swimming in the lake again). He raises the half-barrel rifle, points at the Midwesterner—

"I'm seeing a lot of angst directed my way."

"Uh-ha," the blond girl nods, hands still up. "That's Tito's favorite drink you just carelessly dropped."

Carlos holds the one remaining bottle in one hand while aiming the Glock with his other, eventually throws caution to the wind and quips, "Well… don't expect milk and cookies from *mwah*"—he smacks his lips tightly together—"anytime soon, babe!" and surveys the armed Latino and his sidekick, then Naomi and Mary.

Finally, Carlos sees Carl standing in the doorway of the front compartment—

"Totally!" Carl seconds the thought. Has his finger on the trigger of his own gun—ready to pull if necessary.

"Yeah, my bad, I get carried away when I'm rudely interrupted by uninvited gun-toting passersby holding my friends hostage!"

"Hostage?!" the blond says quizzically. "Y'all mistaken, fellas!" and a smile brightens her Southern face.

Carlos: "We are?"

Kelsey: "Uh-ha."

Mary: "Guys, we're in the wrong in this effed up situation. We were the ones helping ourselves to Kelsey and Tito's house."

Carlos: "Who the fuck is Tito?"

Tito: "I am. Who the fuck are you, Gringo?"

Carlos: "Well, fuck me, the racial slurs didn't take long to bubble to the surface."

That's when—

Deckard steps between the 60s-styled van and an RV and into the middle of the ring like a judge in a WWE match. He takes one look at his traveling companions; the boys first, their armory on display, followed by the two girls. Then he sees the two newbies. The wafer-thin blond standing next to the Winnebago's rear entrance. Then the Latino or—Hispanic—he's not quite sure with the fading daylight fast approaching. But Deckard sees the barrel of a rifle, half sawn away. He's inclined to join in but doesn't.

Instead, he says, "It looks like I've stumbled into a cluster-fuck of activity!" To Carl and Carlos, he says, "I bring this up in case you were wondering, but why in the holy hell has it only taken you kids a goddamn minute to find trouble?"

The Marine waits for an answer.

Everyone glances away.

***

It's left to Naomi to make the next move. She instantly moves between the newbies, Carl, Carlos, Jed, and the ex-Marine and starts talking very fast, telling the group that the camp belonged to Kelsey and Tito and they meant them no harm. They could stay for the night if they traded with them.

Several quiet seconds later—

With everyone standing in the circle of cars glaring at one another, the silence was eventually broken. "I love what you've done with the place!" Carlos quips for the second time without hesitation.

"What's your name?" Kelsey asks, her hands finally down by her side.

"Carlos. Carlos Haseltine. Why? You want my star sign as well?" and he lowers his Glock.

She dismisses his bullshit with a wave. "Whatever."

"He's got some issues," Naomi adds. "He'll also grow on you over time."

"Well… don't we all?" Kelsey manages a chuckle. "Now. No harm was done!" She raises a hand to her companion to lower his rifle. "It's okay, Tito. It's fine. Apparently, he'll grow on us over time!" and another chuckle ripens her lips, and the Latino lowers his weapon. "Anyway… It's good to see a new face around the place."

"Thanks."

"You're welcome, pardner."

"Don't judge us too harshly…" Mary says. "We try to do okay. And we're not all like that"—gesturing to Carlos with an outstretched hand—"Just the annoying amongst us."

"Then you shouldn't let the annoying speak!" the Latino replies harshly.

Mary figures that would be the answer, but trying to gag the Midwesterner's mouth was near enough impossible to do.

"What?" Carl prompts, lowering his pistol. "What comes next?"

Carlos shrugs—holding the remaining bottle of tequila out like a peace offering between squabbling friends.

Naomi lowers her hands to the rest of the group; tries to settle the unnecessary unease and lower the tension. "I guess supper?"

"Supper," Kelsey parrots. "That's a big leap from killing one another a few seconds ago. Nice touch, homegirl."

Naomi scratches an imaginary itch on her arm. "Uh-ha."

A platter of background conversations later and everyone starts afresh.

53
CAMP NIGHT AND WILDLY YARNS

The country night air hummed with a silence so silent all you could hear was the gentle *splish-splash* of the lake waters and far-away cricket *chirps*. Within the encampment of vehicles, golden flames danced to a serenade of chit-chat. Everyone relaxes, unwinds, and lets themselves fall into the rhythm of the evening while eating freshly caught fish and canned vegetables in a brothy stew. At the same time, the tequila, wine and—now—cool bespoke beers from Dolorosa Café flowed freely; the group's boisterous laughter filtered through the depths of the dark night. With their stomachs full at last, and the early unpleasantries extinguished, everyone started to enjoy each other's company as they perched on the two tables and a picnic rug.

"How did you two find each other?" Mary asks.

Kelsey 'Cindy' McAndrew. Born and raised in New Orleans. Her family has lived for 200 years in Louisiana; she has ancestors that were both slave owners and slaves, Cajuns and Creoles. She makes eye contact with her Puerto Rican companion. (Tito produces a smile back at her like a rose-tinted tropical sunset.) "You ever eat something, and while you're eating it, you keep thinking 'this is a bad idea' and sure enough, it's a bad idea?" she asks.

"Like magic mushrooms?" Carlos chips in.

The blond nods. "I made that mistake, y'all. I'd been on foot since escaping my apartment in New Orleans. Four months of running, hiding, evading the huge southern swarms of the dead. I hadn't eaten for over a week. I was foraging for anything, and I mean anything. Then I stumbled upon some mushrooms in the thick of some woods. I was always told by my Ma never to eat wild mushrooms as a young girl. Deep down in my subconscious, that same small Kelsey spoke to me again, *Don't you dare eat those mushrooms!* But… well, long story short, I ate 'em. Half a dozen to be precise. The next hour… I couldn't walk, I was doubled-up. Pit of my belly on fire and as far as I recall… barely conscious. A day later, maybe two, my head kept pounding like I had a whole African tribe inside my cranium banging ceremonial war drums. Then this Hispanic guy shows up out of nowhere to my rescue like a knight outta one of those old English fairytales. He kept my fever down for the next three days while single-handedly keeping the dead away from us too."

Kelsey snuggled up against her Latino lover, and her eyes sparkled with amusement as Tito de la Renta recounted their hairbreadth journey to their guests.

"You know, I honestly don't remember that much," he begins. "Probably just jacked-up on adrenaline back then. I'd only been back in America for a week when the first outbreaks occurred across the country. I tried to ignore the whole situation. Like many, just thought it was a hoax at first. You know, like charitable zombie fun runs! Then the real shit hit the fan, and those fun-runs turned out to be blood runs." Tito takes another shot of tequila and continues: "I was stumbling around, no idea where I was going myself. I had a plan in the beginning. Well, maybe a plan was being generous. Driving towards a long shot was more appropriate. Survival was my goal after I lost contact with my family back in Puerto Rico, and when the U.S. government stopped all flights from leaving the country, I finally realized there was no way back. Well… heck, I had a goal. Leave the crowded cities behind, and keep to the countryside. Live off the land. There was a time in my life that I would flounder around, doing odd jobs to make a living. But I was raised on a farm and knew how to hunt and to build. Those skills kept me alive when others around me would succumb to basic survival needs. That's when I stumbled upon…" He casts an endearing gaze at the Southerner, "my Kelsey in the woods"—Tito takes her hand in his—"I knew I couldn't leave her there, all alone, after I realized she wasn't infected. I saw a part of my former self in her laying there helplessly. For the first few days, Kelsey was sick. A fever had broken out, and it scared the shit outta me." Tito glances across at Kelsey again. "I wasn't the praying type, but I prayed that day to God, Allah, Buddha, or whoever was listening at that time."

"And all the while we were hunkered down in those woods for the next three days, Tito fought the dead away from me!" Kelsey chimes, her voice full of remembrance as she kicks a tuft of grass.

"Yeah. But eventually Kelsey's health returned, and she managed to keep down some food, and her strength came back. Not enough so she could walk."

"No, not quite," she says.

"So, I hoisted Kelsey onto my shoulders and fought a running battle against the living dead. We fought our way to be here; by ourselves. On the road, no one wanted to help us at first. I guess… they had other worries, friends, and family first. Strangers… come a distant third." Tito squeezes Kelsey's hand again, and she smiles back, and he turns to face the others around the flames. "Back then, I wish it were just a fun run. You know!"

Everyone gazes at the Latino around the fire—mouths wide open—marveling at how easy going his Caribbean coolness collides with the slick efficiency of retelling a story. A Hollywood blockbuster in the making.

Before anyone can react, Carlos says, "*Sonofabitch*, dawg. You're a fucking hero to the lady!" The Midwesterner sums the whole, heroic tale in congratulations-of-sorts in the best way he can.

And everyone takes a sip of drinks and salutes the Latino.

***

After a while, Deckard finally shows his face. The big man sits down on the end of the picnic bench (space had been saved for the ex-Marine), and Naomi pushes a bowl of food in front of the Okie. (He'd been keeping an eye on the perimeter for any undead drawn to the racket of the lively camp for a late-night human snack. But the night was uneventful, and he was grateful for not having to kill anything intent on killing them.)

"Appreciated, Naomi," he murmurs and tucks into the cooked food that the Southern lasses had prepared earlier.

Naomi takes another piece of fish from the large pot. (There was no running power to the camp, and everything was cooked over the fire pit in big black pans.) She eats. Consults with her digestive system. The fish is good. "Sure beats jerky again!" she jests.

A euphoria of agreement fills the evening.

Deckard spoons another frothy fish dish from his bowl. Slurps. The food is warming and fills a hole in his stomach. Eventually turns to their hosts. "How'd you find this place?"

"We found this site several months ago. Abandoned. It was just like a normal campsite back then. I guess that's why…" Kelsey's voice trickles away like a stream and a tight knot bulks in her throat.

Tito sees his companion and lover struggling with an explanation, and continues for her. "We buried the bodies of the resurrected and eh—unfortunately, not the dead." His eyes are downcast, and he grips Kelsey's hand tightly. She grips right back. "Only reason we're still stuck at this campsite. We used the last of the petrol to move the vehicles into position and then went to work building the barricades you see."

"Been living here ever since, y'all…" The blond's voice comes back stronger, filled with Southern strength and grandeur. "Nothin' like my pad back in New Orleans, but… we've made it our home over time."

The gang takes another swig of drinks; each depending on their poison of choice and reflects on the story for a while.

Until—

"Okay, I think we have established we have all led intense lives so far; can we please move the fuck on to another topic?" Carlos says.

"Cool," Naomi obliges. "Shout?"

A quiet period wraps around the campfire, and a gentle wind cuts across the ground.

54
WILD HOGS, WILD HOGS

"Naomi! Hey, Naomi!" Carlos says her name like a child wanting their mommy's attention at a sweet shop. He sits across from the Texan on the second bench next to Jed. "Were feral hogs really a problem in Texas?"

The Texan huffs a relentless breath and blows her dark hair from her face. They had had this conversation endlessly since they had first met, and it was not going to go away anytime soon. "I'm finally going to expel this myth from extinction, y'all," she hollers in her toughest Texan voice. "Uh-huh. It's true, Carlos. Those wild hogs numbered in the millions. They were shockingly destructive, and invasive and wreaked havoc across the southern states." Naomi moves her injured arm where she'd been shot; the pain still rampant in her muscles, and finds a better sitting position. "About 50 miles east of Waco, Texas; my Pa had a 200-acre farm cratered with holes up to five feet wide and three feet deep. On one such part, the roots below a row of huge oak trees shading a creek had been dug out and exposed. Where the grass had been stripped bare, saplings crowded out the pecan trees that provided food for our deer, and other wildlife that made the area their home. My Pa wanted to cut his hay but could barely run a tractor through there."

Carl sits opposite Naomi, between Jed and Carlos and asks, "Why?" He is intrigued to find out more about her former life (even if he's heard her tell the story a dozen times before), and can't get enough of her voice.

Naomi looks at Carl; eyes connecting over the edge of the flames, and she smiles as subtly and sweetly as maple over pancakes. "The whole damn field had gone to the hogs, Carl," she answers (no pun, intended). "In my spare time, over the weekends, I used to help my dad and uncle clear the land. In one weekend I trapped 75 of 'em. But another 100 or so still lay claim to the fields. At least we got some hay out of there that year. I remember, the first time in three years..." For a moment, Naomi gets lost in memories. Taken back to a time when she still had a family. Parents. A farm to run about on. A notable and upcoming career. A lovin' fiance, also. Before the outbreak of all outbreaks shattered that happy existence. She controls her breathing and hollers onwards regardless of those dreadful thoughts. "My Pa hoped to flatten the earth and crush the saplings with a bulldozer that year. Then maybe—maybe those damn hogs would have moved onto adjacent hunting grounds across yonder, and my Pa, well, he could once again use his land to full effect."

"Bullshit!" Carlos exclaims, rather loudly. (Naomi turns to the Midwesterner; a face like thunder.) "75? You sure you didn't kill seven one day and five the day after? And add 'em together to make your magical fucking number!"

"Eff you, Carlos," she retaliates. "I'd love to see you try and kill some fast, roving hogs! Those wild beasts are among the most destructive invasive species in the United States, wreaking havoc in at least 39 states! Half were in Texas, where they did untold damages annually. They tear up recreational areas. Terrorize tourists in national parks, and squeeze out other grazing wildlife from their natural habitats also."

"And now we have another destructive, invasive species in all 50 States of America, doing the same fucking thing!" Carlos sarcastically jibes.

For some reason, this was the moment the little flame of hope inside the campground blew out, and everything inside of everybody was oddly cold and dark and calm. (Wild hogs were the least of their problems.)

Carlos realizes he's pushed the conversation too far. "I don't like zombies."

"And I'm pretty sure they don't fucking like your face, either!" Naomi bites back.

Kelsey suddenly breaks out in a chorus of laughter on the picnic rug. "You drop f-bombs with such panache, girl!"

Everyone starts to laugh, even Carlos.

55
DRINKS, GIRLS, AND A LOVE LETTER OF POETIC JUSTICE

Above their heads, the moon was high—nearly on full show, except a small slither was still hiding. It's then that Jed takes the baton: "What do you miss from before the end of the world came around?" he asks, throwing the question out to the rest of the group.

"What is this?" Carlos asks. "Some interventional crap? You wanna be my therapist?"

The teen stutters for a response; the unusual word has no meaning to his young mind.

Deckard closes his eyes, blows a warm breath. "It's okay, kiddo. I'll go first." He pushes back on the table, bowl empty of food. "Liquor and a great bar with plenty of atmosphere. Patrons' stories and all that jazz... and the women too!" Then notices the look each of the girls gave him. Unapologetically he didn't care; he was from a different era. "I mean, when you're in a great atmosphere, you feel like the people around you would react badly if they knew what you really thought and believed. Places like those—you could pretend to be anyone, as long as you had a great tale to tell."

Jed shrugs as the ex-Marine finished—not really understanding anything coming from the older man's mouth. A moment later, he turns to Carl. "You're up next."

"Great food. Burgers and fries. Tacos, salsa..." (The teen nods along to the older boys suggestion, imagining a meat-pattie right about now would go down great. Everybody does.)

"Fucking A-Okay, dawg!" Carlos calls out, saluting Carl's suggestion.

Jed seems very content with the answers so far, and the teen glances over to where Naomi and Mary are sitting.

***

It takes a few moments, but Naomi starts: "Before the end, my fiance's family was going to pay for us to go to the *Camera Degli Sposi*. It was supposed to be a gift for our future together."

Carlos leans across the table. "Supposed to be some Italian restaurant in Texas?"

Naomi shakes her head at the remark. "Mantua, Italy—" she stalls mid-sentence, gathers her composure and continues passionately. "There may be more important works of art, like the 'David' or the 'Last Supper' or the 'Sistine Chapel.' But for sheer charm, there's nothing like the 15th-century frescoes by

'Mantegna.' You get to enjoy, to behold them and not in a mobbed museum full of tourists with selfie sticks. But in a small chamber in the ducal palace of Mantua. The brightly colored paintings literally shimmer with inlaid gold..."

Carl sits back, taking in the wealth of new knowledge from the pretty Asian lips. He never knew she was into art as much as he once was. "The paintings depict nobility, children, dwarves, passion…" He assertively says, remembering photos he'd once seen in some obscure library collection of famous Italian works of art. "All watched over not by a stern God but by an assortment of famously playful putti on the ceiling. The cherubs also seem to be looking down on some life-affirming activities…"

"W-which is why it's called… the Room of the Bride and Bridegroom," Naomi continues as she feels-a-flutter-of-love invade her heart, and a tear rolls down her cheek. Mary sticks an arm around her friend's shoulder and hugs her tight, kissing Naomi on her forehead.

Carl sits back; kicking himself for the reckless remark that makes the Texan relive her ex's death once again. *Great,* he thinks, *what a way to walk into a fucking brick wall, dude.* He looks back at the path that has brought them together and realizes Naomi still hurt deep within. Realizes she would forever hold a flame for her former fiance.

Nobody says a word for a short while after, just continues to drink.

***

Carlos stretches, moans. "*Ooooh.* Ouch." His ribs are still sore from the fall in Salt Lake City. He ventures next. "Sending a romantic confession voice message to any old crush. Done that. It wasn't pretty." He swigs back a beer. "I recommend writing and singing your own R&B love ballad—works every time."

"You did that?" Mary asks, a glimmer of amusement to her voice.

"Yip, Kansas. Some stunning rando, a waitress, working in a café in Brooklyn."

"How did it pan out?"

"Epic fail."

"I can imagine," she teases, "you big idiot."

And everyone laughs.

He goes on. "Actually, what really grinds my gears are… fuckin' spoilers about tv shows and films! I don't want to know 'who killed who' or 'who dies!' And that's the point. But some idiot blogger is mashing a 140-character fuck-fest torpedo with his or her pudgy digits and pointing it squarely at your Twitter feed. Fuckin' losers. On a personal note, I still hold it against the guy who told me how Game of Thrones ended."

And the laugh continues at the Midwesterner's expense.

"What about you, Mary?" Carlos asks Mary once the laughter dies down.

"Well, for starters, I don't miss social media!" she replies, matter-of-factly. "Instagram. Twitter, etc. was beyond my social boundaries. The whole outpouring of your heart's content for every loser in the entire cosmos to see.

Then for them to write an entire blog about you and your insecurities is way beyond my understanding! And all those 'postable' moments, and unnecessary amounts of time scrolling. Jesus! Cry me a river." (Everyone takes note of Mary's major dislike of Social Media and how it was ever-changing. And always a new crazy way people could document every aspect of their lives.) "Thankfully, I had an inner strength, and that was more powerful than the need to check my Facebook feed every ten minutes. Instead, I'd choose a good book."

Carlos deadpans the Yooper.

"What?"

The deadpan continues. "Just thought there'd be more of an answer from you, Kansas."

"No. Why would you think that?"

The Midwesterner shrugs. "No reason."

"Christ, you're infuriating!" A pause and the moment stretches.

And the Midwesterner salutes Mary.

***

"For me. It was to see that the Earth is round!" Kelsey says seriously, interrupting Mary and Carlos' banter.

Every single person gathered around the campfire gazes at the Southerner in a confused state.

"Bullshit!" Carlos exclaims, cutting through the girl's statement. "You some kind of 'Flat Earther member?' You believe the Earth is flat?" His tone is full of bewilderment. "The theory that the Earth is a disc with the Arctic Circle in the center and Antarctica, a 150-foot-tall wall of ice, around the rim. And if you climb over that wall, you will likely fall off the disc! It's total B.S. You realize the Earth is round?"

Kelsey titters at the statement. "I don't generally believe that the Earth is flat. No. But, the surest way is to set sail in one direction and not stop until you're home again." She laughs at her own words. "But for a cheaper, although not quite as direct method, journey north of the Arctic Circle, around the summer solstice and spend a night (ideally in a hot tub), watching the sun circle above the horizon."

"Cute," says Tito.

"I know," Kelsey replies, and the two cuddle up tighter together.

"Constant running power!" the Latino adds. "So I can join you in that hot tub, Kelsey."

Mary: "Get a room, you two!"

Within seconds, Carl and Carlos begin to wolf whistle at the couple and the boisterous atmosphere returns to the camp. That's when Jed knows his job is complete and he skedaddles from the group and settles in for the night in an empty RV.

56
A GUIDING VOICE

Kelsey stokes the fire; the tiny embers of yellows and oranges drifting up into the blackened sky. "So… why you folks on the road?"

Naomi regards her neighborly cousin's question for a few seconds. Contemplates various answers, but settles on: "A voice guided us on our travels."

Tito frowns. "Figuratively? Spiritually?" The Latino's tone is clipped and businesslike. "In the Old Testament way?"

"Sorry to spoil the illusion," Carlos utters. "Nope, not spiritually nor figuratively. Just literally. On the radio. A woman. Goes by the name of DJ Candice. She's directing us to Portland."

"Well, in that case, why so keen on Portland?" Tito was looking for holes in the story, weak points in the group's act. Still doesn't trust them (especially the cocky Midwesterner).

Carl: "Only place to go, Tito. Actual civilization. Fortified. Munitions, food. A growing society safe beyond tall walls where no undead can reach you."

"A safe zone?" Kelsey says, her voice inquisitive at the prospect of a better life away from the isolated camp.

Naomi reacts to the Louisianan's voice. "Uh-hu," she gestures with eyes wide. "Why we're traveling across the country in the first place, Kelsey. Cut through Utah from our old camp. Picked up Deckard on the way…" (At the mention of his name, the ex-Marine tips his fedora.) "And here we are now, chowing-down with you guys."

"First Class, all the damn way. Beats any Delta Airways flight," Carlos quips.

Kelsey pulls a warm blanket over her shoulders. "The voice on the radio!" she says more of a statement than a question.

Mary: "You've heard?"

"Uh-huh. We heard the transmissions a while back."

Naomi: "You have? So you realize the point of traveling on the road is goin' to somewhere better? A home. DJ Candice offers all of us a chance of a fresh start."

Tito: "Yeah. Yeah. Tempting."

"What do you mean by that?" Deckard ponders, gazing at the Latino's eye-rolling; his thick, black eyebrows rising in doubt.

Tito couldn't help a sporadic laugh. "I mean, I have heard that a hundred times before." (Those eyebrows move again like caterpillars across a leaf.) "Offering salvation. A chance amongst the living."

Carlos: "Way to trod on the celebrations Tito?"

Tito: "Blah, blah, blah, blah, man."

Carl: "It's hope."

Tito: "Whatever it is, it can't be better than what we have around us. Fresh fish, wild berries and veg. A defensible shelter. Hell, we've talked about goin' sometimes, but we have a sweet life by the lake."

"Wintertime?" Deckard asks.

Tito's glower flocks over a cheerful grin. "No doubt. It gets chilly, man."

Carl: "All good, dawg, until a huge herd decides to roll through your backyard. Trample your pink flamingos."

Tito shakes his head slowly. "Until then, man… not much will move us from our humble home." He casts an endearing glance at Kelsey.

Naomi: "Kelsey?"

The blond girl just shrugs her shoulders; unsure whether to give an opinion that differs from the Latino's. "I'm afraid you'll have to go by yourselves," she declares—blanket enclosing her shoulders.

Really, this seems all so strange! Carl wonders, but says, "Why not? We all could go. Together. We can make room in our jeep. Why don't you two think about—"

The Latino laughs again, cuts Carl off mid-sentence. "Why don't you guys just rest. Take a load off your feet and unwind for the night. It's safe here. Safe as houses."

"Except houses have four fucking walls and a roof," Carlos jests, and swigs the last of his drink. He moves forward and stares at the Latino.

Tito: "Point?"

"No point."

Tito seems pleased by the Midwesterner's answer. "Huh, cool, man. So you're all staying? The welcome mat is already unrolled for all yah."

Mary could see that Carlos wanted to add more to the equation like a back-row country at a U.N Conference. She gets there before he does. "Sounds fantastic," Mary chimes.

Naomi nods approvingly at the plan, noticing Carlos staring at Mary. Mary at Carlos. The silence stretching.

"Tomorrow, we'll refresh, unwind, and talk more about the future!" Tito says, concluding the conversation.

"Uh-huh," replies Kelsey. "It's getting late." And she lets out a deep, southern yawn, gets up with the warm blanket draping her shoulders and takes her lover's hand. "We'll see y'all tomorrow morning. You'll have to share the RV's. Spare blankets and pillows in each."

Carl gets up from the picnic table and shakes Kelsey's hand. "Thanks for the hospitality, guys. We appreciate the kindness." He throws a glare at the Latino and shakes his hand slowly. "Keep in mind what we said to you guys regarding Portland. There are better odds if we all go together."

"Thanks for the offer," Tito answers, taking back his hand. "We'll talk 'bout it 'morrow." He grabs Kelsey by the hand and tugs the slim blond to the Winnebago. The Louisianan waves goodnight to everyone.

***

Moments later after the Winnebago's door closes, Carlos stands, stretches and says to the others, "I'm going to sleep. Leave a post-it if any end of the world stuff comes along, and I'll read it when I wake!" and he too makes his way to the confines of a vehicle.

The others follow the Midwesterner's decision to 'hit the hay' one-by-one. Mary and Naomi take one RV, while the boys take the other.

An hour goes by and Deckard is the last to sleep. Kicking out the fire he grabs the sleeping bag and spare blankets Mary has laid out for him on the picnic table. It's cool, but not too cold a night, and he falls asleep underneath the stars.

57
TRANSMISSIONS FOR BREAKFAST

The morning sun cuts through the cloudless sky with the thump of Thor's hammer; the Norse God himself delivering the required effect from the heaven's above. Below, the encampment basks in warmth. The Winnebago's door bangs open behind Kelsey. Tito walks out into the middle of the campground; shirtless, body gleaming like a God. A second later, he throws a shirt on. Naomi comes from the RV to the right waving a 'good morning' to their hosts. While Mary brings over a tray of hot, instant black coffee to the two picnic tables where Carl and Carlos are distributing breakfast (cooking in turns was always how they'd kept normality).

Meanwhile, the teen sits at the edge of the other bench—oblivious to the world, unaware of a figure creeping up from behind. A hand; a touch on his shoulder makes him jump. He spins, reaches for the handle of the Bowie-knife, and sees that it's Naomi standing behind.

"*Wooooooo!* Soz, Jed," she apologizes, hands up in defense. "My bad. Didn't mean to freak you out."

"It's okay," he replies; knife sheathed.

"What's that? Some kind of radio?" she asks, looking over the teen's shoulder.

In his hands, he holds a radio. It's almost like a car stereo, but this is a CB radio with a hand-held receiver attached to it. An antenna sticks out from the top, and the front side has a small dial and a few switches. Red and black wires stick from one side and feed into a curious black device. A portable battery pack straddles the lower bench of the table.

"Just a little toy I've been working on, Naomi," he declares.

"You did all this, this morning?" Mary ponders as she puts down the tray of drinks by his side. Carl and Carlos go to grab one each, and so does Kelsey; the blond joins them around the table for morning breakfast.

"Yip," he answers, all bright-eyed and matter-of-fact and begins to wire both components together using both wires. "I took the CB radio and handheld receiver from the house in Salt Lake City. Hopefully the powerpack I brought from our old camp will boost the range of the CB radio's signal so that we can communicate with our radio host." He clicks on the power switch and begins to turn the frequency adjustment dial. "Hey presto!" he says with an acne covered smile. "When we draw close to DJ Candice's position, we'll be able to communicate with her for real!" Jed shrugs. "Well, once I can get the receiver working properly. And… only if she wants to communicate back."

"Smart, Jed. Really smart," Mary says, impressed with the youth.

"Uh-ha," Naomi agrees as she starts to chow down on some peaches.

That's when Mary notices a sleeping bag by the far table.

"The kid's got brains!" a voice says from within the comfy confines of the sleeping bag. Deckard rises to the smell of a hot 'Cuppa Joe.' Stretches his joints like a Sasquatch in the morning sun. Sits. Sips the black coffee. "Go ahead, kid, See if your side project works."

A smile forms across his adolescent face, and Jed tests his 'project' by turning the switches and dials, looks for the frequency and eventually finds it. But the DJ's voice isn't on the airwaves. "Come in, Miss… eh, DJ Candice! Over." He says through the hand-held receiver.

(Static.)

"Suave, Jed. You're such a ladies' man!" Carlos chips in. The Midwesterner comes up from behind, a plate of beans and corn in hand.

Jed ignores his comments and says in a maturer voice, "Can you hear me, DJ Candice? We are survivors on our way to Portland. We heard your radio broadcasts and have been on the road looking for your location! Is anyone there? Over."

(More *crackles* on the airwaves), and Jed begins to switch between the static to the accompaniment of a pronounced dial *'click'* as an indistinct voice fades in and out of focus. "My friends and I have come a long way!" Jed says again into the small transmitter. "DJ Candice—we need to know if what you are saying is true. Are you in the Portland region? Over."

***

Eyes opened expectantly as a voice filtered through the small speaker. Reality trickled into the group as the radio voice became stronger: "Welcome, Friends of the Inner Sanctum, this is your host DJ Candice, welcoming you once more through the squeaking door of my humble home. C'mon in, why don't you, and make yourself comfortable in the safe zone."

"The chick's got style… bet she's got 'filth' written all over her…" Carlos murmurs beneath his breath, and the comment draws an unwelcome glance from all the girls. No matter how stubbornly he tries to flush their stare away, it bobs around like an annoying turd in the bottom of a stink-hole. He lets out a groan. "Okay"—hands up in defeat—"Worst choice of words. Soz, girls."

He does enough to appease them, and they all listen willingly to the DJ's voice.

"Hello again, friends, this is your host, DJ Candice. Listen. The outside's awful, isn't it? It is true. The dead have conquered our streets. Stolen our family and friends. But I can offer all survivors the whereabouts to salvation…"

(More static.)

"Whereabouts are you broadcasting? Over," Jed asks, but there is no reply, just white noise. "Come in. Are you there?" (Static continues.) Jed turns to the others. "She's off the air, guys!"

Carlos: "No, shit, Jed."

Deckard sighs, ignoring the Midwesterner's tone. Turns to Jed. "She can't hear you."

"Maybe I just need to keep on working on the receiver?"

"No, kiddo. We can hear the DJ. She can't hear us. Probable cause—transmitter's too weak."

"Maybe if we can boost the signal. Maybe… triangulate her position."

(An even louder static sound comes over the airwaves.)

"That's a helluva lot of maybe's!" Carl says, sipping coffee.

The radio is silent for several seconds longer as the gang perch nervously around the makeshift CB radio, before crackling to life with the soothing sounds of 'Karma Police' by *Radiohead.*

"This chick really knows her playlist." Carlos is impressed by her musical selection.

Carl: "Yeah. A song for the end of the world."

Carlos: "I wonder what she looks like. Blond? Brunette or—"

"Will you give it a rest, Carlos," Mary utters, thoroughly annoyed. "You're like a goddamn hormonal teen…"

"Or an over-excited-dog-pining-to-hump-its-owner's leg!" Naomi adds by her friend's side and shudders at the thought. Yet, she can see how utterly unimpressed Mary is by the dumb Midwesterner's constant quips regarding the mysterious voice.

Deckard says to Jed: "Keep at it, kiddo. You'll get there in the end."

Jed half smiles at the ex-Marine. "I don't know," he says half-heartedly, but goes back to working on fixing the radio, while the others go back to the early morning rituals of enjoying life and freshening up for the coming day.

58
CHOICES ARE MADE AS ONE, TOGETHER, WILL BE BETTER

As the morning drifts into noon, Naomi comes and sits by Kelsey's side. Both swing their legs over the side of the dock jutting out into McKay's reservoir like two youngsters on a quiet Spring Break. "'Bout last night."

"Mm. What's your point?"

"We didn't mean to press the idea of you guys leaving your home behind," Naomi says. "Hell, nowadays, it's hard enough to find a place to call home. It's just… you seem like nice people, and we want to bring you guys along on our trip."

Kelsey rubs her eyes from the strong sunlight bouncing off the surface of the water. She considers for a moment. Taps a mossy, wooden plank beneath her forefinger. *Tap, tap, tap.* "Thanks. Will consider it during the day. I'm all for goin'…" Her words drifting away as she glances across at Naomi.

"Tito?"

"Uh-huh. How'd you'd guess, girl?"

"He didn't quite keep his emotions in check when we had the discussion last night."

"He's… I mean"—she taps that same plank again. *Tap, tap*—"Tito has a purpose. It's keeping me safe from the world, Naomi."

Naomi knows how the Louisianan feels; remembers her ex-fiance, how he took care of her. "That's a noble cause," she ends up saying. "But someday you have to let go and rejoin society. Civilization needs all of us to pull together for the greater outcome."

"Uh-huh," the blond girl nods again.

"Can't you…" Naomi thinks. "Can't you appeal to his gentler side?"

Kelsey laughs at the comment. "He's all gentle. Squishy on the inside like a sponge. Crumbly like a fancy cupcake. I'll speak with Tito later. 'Kay?" and the Louisianan gets up and leaves the native Texan alone on the dock.

Naomi splashes cool water with her feet; lies back and watches the cotton clouds go by.

***

As the day stretches onwards, everyone catches a breath of fresh air, relaxes, rewinds and chills out by the lake. Even Deckard could afford to have a day off from the rigors of Military Life, and finds the time to enjoy a swim in a safe area where their hosts had strung up a huge fishing net across an area of the water—it was a safe area where they'd been able to fish and be able to bathe. The water was cold, but at the same time refreshing and offered the chance for everyone to cleanse their skin and clean their injuries.

***

The day shifted into night once again, and grilled fish was back on the menu. Beers and the last of the tequila gone, everyone played a couple of card games. Blackjack and King of Assholes were the popular winners in a night of entertainment.

A short time later—

"You know what this place reminds me of?" Mary whispers as she lays on a blanket looking up at the stars; above, a magnitude of a thousand tiny lights sparkle in the sky.

"Go on?"

"Camp. Brownies. Girl Guides."

"Oh—*right*."

"Aaa… you never went?" she says, shaking her head. Faces Naomi as the fire-pit gently roars by their side. The heat was nice and comfortable, warm, and enticing.

Naomi continues, "It's not that I never had a chance to go. I was always needed on my father's farm when I was younger. His ranch later as I grew older and skilled at cattle drives." She felt warmed by the memory of her father like the roaring fire igniting in the pit of her soul. The process of moving a herd of cattle from one place to another across vast swathes of land. The open wilderness, sleeping under the stars like cowboys, but she never experienced the sensation of camping with kids her own age. She eventually shrugs. "Never had the opportunity to enjoy those moments with friends. I missed out."

Mary breaks the tension. "You didn't miss out on anything. You would have absolutely hated it, Texas girl."

"How come?"

"No cowboys to keep you company! Just a gaggle of girls bitch-slapping about you at every opportunity they got."

And they share a giggle of amusement.

Mary tries to maintain calm in her voice. "True."

"Sure Mary."

And the laugh resonates through the night.

59
PERSUASION

Kelsey rolls over in the bed. “What choice do we have, Tito? They’re offering us a golden ticket away from this place! We can’t just throw it away.” The inside of the Winnebago is large, with its light and airy crèmey biscuit interior. The bed is comfy and deluxe. Assorted bedsheets and linen keep their naked bodies nice and comfy, but the atmosphere is far from appealing.

“I could think of a few, Kelsey.”

“Well, yeah… I’m listening.”

The Latino sits there quietly.

“I’m waiting, Tito!”

“I’m thinking.”

60
THE NEXT MORNING

Carlos wanders back to the perimeter of the camp. "I hate to cut this love-romance short," he says, stubbing the grassy ground with the sole of his trainer. "We should've left hours ago, but we're waiting on the two love birds to return."

"I know, Carlos But they showed gratitude to us," Naomi replies; she's standing on the roof of the Winnebago beneath the umbrella scanning the horizon for Tito and Kelsey. "The least we can do is say farewell to 'em."

"It was perfectly clear they weren't gonna leave with us!" he replies. A moment later, adds unashamedly, "We hardly know them. They're not officially our friends. Just acquaintances on the road."

Naomi doesn't even bother to make eye contact with the Midwesterner.

"Do you have any idea where they are?" Jed calls.

"Naomi, we've gotta get movin' while we have a full day of sun," Carl says by the teen's side. "Portland won't wait for any stragglers. You coming?"

"Hey, what are you staring at?" Mary hollers, walking towards them at the group from where 'Priscilla' has been parked for the last day or so.

"I… I thought they would come, Mary."

"Kelsey and Tito?"

"Hu-huh." Naomi nods to Mary's question. "I thought I reasoned with her. Persuaded it was in their best interests to join our road trip to Portland's safe zone."

Carlos: "You thought wrong, Naomi."

She looks back down as the others wait impatiently. She's about to say something else. Then she hears it; noise in the distance. A car.

The others hear it too—

"Anybody got eyes?" Carl says as he starts to climb onto the bonnet.

"Over there!" Naomi says, pointing over the roof of the Winnebago toward the distant treeline. "Vehicle comin' up fast along the road."

Sure enough, a fast approaching car was speeding towards them. It took another three minutes of nervous anticipation to realize Tito was behind the wheel; Kelsey riding shotgun next to her Latino lover.

***

After hearing the voice over the airwaves the previous morning, the day had flown by in a rush. Tito and Kelsey were reluctant to leave their encampment. Being on the road meant being out in the open and who knows what dangers were out there. But the human contact had ultimately persuaded Kelsey that leaving the camp in favor of seeking a better life was the right thing to do. She had pestered Tito all through the day. Finally, the Latino gave in to defeat late during the night and agreed to go with the others. It was a hard decision to make, but he felt obliged to go considering Kelsey's persuasive nature.

By the time the gang had eaten breakfast and packed away and were ready to leave the camp without saying goodbye to their hosts, Tito had rolled up in a Ford Ranger. The vehicle had been secured and hidden away under some thick bush several hundred yards away. It was the lovers' bugout vehicle, in case the camp became overrun with the undead at any given time.

No one was surprised that the newbies had lied about running out of fuel, or having an escape vehicle, either. Everyone was just happy that the couple had decided to come along for the journey.

"You ready?" Tito says as he gets into the front seat.

Kelsey nods, taking one last look at their former home.

Tito takes a deep breath. Kelsey can see that's he's scared of leaving. Which is the right amount of sense—because she is too. Ultimately, deep down, she knows the choice is correct. They have to go. She squeezes his hand one final time, and Tito starts the engine and follows the others.

61
ON THE ROAD

They couldn't initially take Interstate 84 because the road was clogged with abandoned vehicles, so they passed through Pendleton. A small city that used to hold 18,000 humans, in Umatilla County, looking for a viable route. The city had developed both sides of the Umatilla River, and some of the former residents came out to meet them—investigating the noise as the convoy rumbled through the streets. They passed a grocery market (whereas in a previous life you could buy cheap vegetables), and fast food chains, selling burgers through to pizzas and tacos. All these buildings were now void of life, except for packs of wild dogs sniffing for snippets of rotten food, and walking corpses in search of fresh meat (that was not available on the grocery shelves at the market anymore).

"Which way, kid?" Deckard asks, as he drives the jeep through the tree-lined streets, past an intersection; the lights not operational.

Carl begins to get his map out just as they pass a block-long complex. A Creep lurches at the passing jeep—from the forecourt of a tire center. It still wore its dirty, gray overalls and had a wrench clutched in its hand. The Z moves fast, and was looking to take a bite out of the cold steel of the vehicle, and more importantly, the human contents. But Deckard veers into the Z as its mouth tears apart; the sharp-teeth making a frightening appearance. The ex-Marine knocks the former mechanic over onto the sidewalk; cracking its skull on the ground. The wrench escapes its hand and clatters across the sidewalk. Deckard drives calmly away from the tire center with its broken windows and empty forecourt. Turns down a residential street.

Tito follows close by—running over the Z's skull first; it goes crack beneath the mighty tire of the Ranger's tire, and the Latino drives onwards, following the others with a satisfied smirk.

Carl unfolds the Oregon map which he had planned their route on. Using what his parents had taught him about reading maps when he was much younger. He figures they would get the majority of the Interstate driving done by the afternoon, hoping that the roads were clear and that no unforeseen problems would lurch their way, and hopefully land on Portland's outskirts before darkness descends.

Gas was precious, now that they had two vehicles on the road, so they couldn't speed excessively, and Deckard and Tito kept the jeep and Ranger odometers to fifty miles per hour. (But luckily, the Latino had kept a few cans of petrol safe and secure with his vehicle. The gas was still good, and hopefully the supplies would stretch to both cars.)

Back at the camp at McKay's reservoir, Jed and Deckard had circled an area on the laminated map where they guessed the voice on the radio was broadcasting from. But being unable to communicate with the DJ, finding her exact whereabouts would be hard to pinpoint, and Jed kept working on the CB radio receiver in the back of 'Priscilla.'

Eventually, they bypassed rows of abandoned vehicles and re-joined Interstate 84, leaving Pendleton behind to the city's few former residents.

***

They drove by rolling fields of green grass along the Vietnam Veterans Memorial Highway and passed a sign that directed them to: Umatilla Chemical Depot, (UMCD) based in Umatilla.

"It's an old U.S. Army installation that stored chemical weapons," Deckard explains as he drives. "The chemical weapons originally stored at the depot consisted of various containers containing GB and VX nerve agents. All munitions had been safely destroyed by 2011." He tells them as if it was an everyday fact. "Base closure on operations was completed by 2015."

Burnt out civilian vehicles stretched along an unnamed road leading to the former outpost. The gang guessed the civilians were looking for protection from the base military personnel—but found only abandoned buildings and unused land. It was a shitty end to all those families' hopes of survival.

They continued traveling along the Vietnam Veterans Memorial Highway and eventually passed through the scorched city of Boardman, 164 miles east of Portland. All the previous buildings were now heaps of rubble, and the scene reminded everyone of old black and white photographs in history books about the Blitz of World War 1. The devastation caused on London and other cities across the UK by the Germans was catastrophic. The only structure that still stood was an old water tower which was surrounded by circles of tall grass. But with the emptiness of the town buildings, it afforded them a beautiful panoramic view of Columbia.

Deckard and Tito drove through the old, demolished town and kept close by the river's edge.

***

An hour later, the highway was barren, void of life. Any vehicles along the stretch of road were unmoving and long abandoned. There were a few infected that moved slowly by the highway, but the group easily avoided them. The constant companionship of the Columbia kept by their side. Eventually, they passed the John Day Dam that spanned the river. (The mammoth structure stretched across the flowing water, and on either side, huge metal fish ladders that enabled fish to pass around the barriers by swimming and leaping up a series of relatively low steps still functioned.) It was then that the highway started to become congested and Deckard had to maneuver around parked vehicles as they passed The Dallas—the largest city in Wasco County, Oregon.

Six miles west of Hood River on Interstate 84 led past the Wygant State Natural Area. The park adjoined two other state parks nearby—creating an endless canopy of greenery that endlessly stretched forever, enforced by the blue river that continuously flowed opposite.

Naomi gazes through the window at a dense, forest area. Where hiking trails existed through the hilly wilderness and (once, also an ideal spot for backpackers who were looking for a little solitude in the weary world).

"Ohh," Mary squeaks, feeling like the kid with a sparkler on the 4th of July, and tugged at Naomi's elbow. "Look!" Both girls gazed through the glass and saw wildlife that was becoming braver by the day. A few Whitetail deer watched them as they drove by. Others were grazing in a nearby ditch, not too far away from the highway.

"Maybe that radio chick is right. Maybe there is a safe haven," Naomi concludes, looking at another deer grazing on the grass—not even glancing up as the two-vehicle convoy passed by.

"I hope so," Mary replies, squeezing Naomi's arm.

The Texan nods back. One final time, looks towards the deer, feeling as if she has just witnessed a Dreamscape Display of Magical Unicorns, and it brought back childhood memories of deer on her father's farm.

PART SIX

PORTLAND

62
EYES FRONT AND LEFT, AND A GOOD OLE' MORNING PISS

An old man stands on the metallic ledge looking out over the clear blue waters below. A scraggly gray beard on a gaunt face, not much hair up top, except with any gush of wind his remaining strands will take off like sails on the high seas. Tall and slim too, 160 lbs of wrinkly bones. Still sprightly for his age, an almost hippish swagger as he lets out a long, diluted yawn, like a bear cub waking upon a crisp, spring day. Hands stretched up to the sky like a Mayan civilian worshipping a Sun God. A red gown flutters in a light breeze. A wrinkly penis wedged in a thick, gray pubic bush keeps his 'little fella,' all nice and snug like a camper in a sleeping bag. A soldier in a fox-hole. His apartment; house, and home sits on the river's edge. The tower, steel, and faded wood stand in the middle of the fenced property. Old keelers and dingies stand next to one another—on the dry land—like boats in a dockyard or a dry dock. More precisely, this was once a marina; populated with abandoned, pre-owned and all sorts of sea-faring vessels once-upon-a-time. The rich and not-so-rich having a piece of the 'beautiful life,' a slice of the American Dream at the roaring river's edge.

But now, all that remains of the former marina are just a few shallow sea-worthy vessels attached to the jutting wooden docks that poke out into the water. Not much at all in options. A 2016 blue and white Bayliner berthed at the end of one of the long docks. A white, slightly garish, Boston Whaler 130 Super Sport sits by its side. And a Boston 6-person Whaler 150 Montauk. The boat is incredibly easy to operate, easy to clean and is perfect for river fishing. Currently, the yellow fibreglass hull is green with slimy algae and has seen better years.

Oh, and the old man's tower, that stands tall amongst the derelict outbuildings of the disused property. It was once going to be a plush apartment block (a real estate idea to entice more wealthy clients to the outskirts of Portland. And what better idea to sell a new location than the stunning view of the Columbia. Unfortunately, the realtors never expected the Z-Apocalypse to collapse the housing market like a stack of cards, and the solo tower stood solemn amongst the former marina until the old man took up residence in the uppermost, and only finished apartment over a year ago).

He arches his back—not in pain in the kidney section—but from wear and tear and goddamn old age. He's fit, though, but his bones feel his age. An age that he was 'bopping' to *The Beatles* Classics once as a youthful sprog. The influential electric guitarist's rhythms of *Jimmy Hendrix* a few years on, and *Bob Marley*-infused Rastafarian Reggae a decade or so later. He's old, but at the same time, he's still alive (not so, some of his favorite musical heroes, all succumbed to death one way or the other, but, thank god none by a goddamn zombie bite). And then… he pisses a golden arch of urine over the edge of the balcony that circles the high-rise apartment and offers a complete 360-degree view of the urban sprawl. A golden spray of morning glory and last nights, Tennessee bourbon. A salute to another glorious day of being alive and free from a normal day job. Thirty long seconds later, and he finally halts. Gives his 'little man,' a well-deserved shake. The old man looks down at his paunch, a small round belly with a white-snail-trail-of-curling hair leading up to a slim white-as-snow, covered chest. A dribble and a wiggle later, he goes back inside the sliding doors. A few seconds later he emerges with a pair of binoculars in one hand and a cookie in the other. (Not hot, not stale, recently cooked but satisfying nevertheless.)

It was his job to be the lookout.

The 'Watchman' along the Columbia River, surveying for signs of Zs and more importantly, 'fucking clowns.' Survivalists and asshats who'd taken it upon themselves to steal, kill, terrorize and take what is not theirs from the survivors of Portland. Anyway, he likes the isolation, the loneliness, and kept away from New Portland's only human population center—smack-bang in the middle of Government Island. Sometimes he'd had to venture back to the encampment but tried to keep to himself as much as possible.

He pulls the binoculars close and peers through the lenses; west to the base of operations. Three black steel curved buildings were built just before the beginning-of-the-end-of-the downfall of the once eco-friendly-city filled with microbreweries and coffeehouses. The buildings are well-fortified and surrounded by dense trees and protected on all sides by the roaring Columbia River. (There is only one way to get onto the isolated island even though the Interstate 205 bridge runs north and south over the island, only using it as an anchor spot between Washington and Oregon. A small jetty guarded at all times by the local military. No, not your Government-affiliated-soldier-army, they were long gone from the area, but a small, determined defense force that had acquired the island once Portland and the outer regions were compromised by the dead.)

The old man smiles as he notices five whitetail deer frolicking at the water's edge. A few civilians fishing too. Then he scans across the glistening waters, past another small uninhabited island to the other side of Columbia River, where the Washington and Oregon divide comes into play. Where the Lewis and Clark Highway ran. Past that point was no man's land; territory only belonging to the millions of undead that now resided across the water. Nowadays, there wasn't much activity from the graveyard yonder; just a few stragglers of bones and rotting corpses kept at bay by the thundering river. Then he scans across—showcasing a panoramic view—as if he was a cameraman for a 'Green Planet Documentary.'

To his right—was another story altogether.

He zooms in—

Past the FedEx Ground on Sundial Road; the facility, once where workers would go state-to-state to drop off parcels now sits in ruins. Everything is broken windows and very long shadows. A few abandoned trucks sits idly on the sprawling property.

Closer—

Closer—

Past the abandoned airport.

And he sees it—

Approximately 14 miles east of Portland central, and several miles from his plum eye-in-the-sky lookout, two vehicles maneuvering across the only remaining bridge coming into the barly recognizable municipal spread of Troutdale from the Vietnam Veterans Memorial Highway, Route 84. (The former small city served as the western gateway to the Historic Columbia River Highway, the Mount Hood Scenic Byway, and the Columbia River Gorge.) The area now sits as a smoking-mess-of-former homes and wind-swept streets of rubbish and bricks. Both vehicles slowly maneuver across the bridge over Sandy River.

Sightseers, a mix of girls and boys by the looks of it, and an older gentleman too, built like a boxer (*maybe military?* he thinks), and all mixtures of States and colors. It's been a long time since he's seen a group of survivors this large. *Friendlies,* he hopes. "Please let 'em be friendlies!" he says to himself, just before he spies movement through a thick thicket of trees on the eastern side of the airport. "Fucking asshats, clowns!" His moans of clarification become louder.

For all his old world charm; the old man knows the group of good-hearted survivors (he hopes that they are!) will need a little guidance. Will need his help to get to the safe zone, to Government Island.

Then he acts, chomps down on the remaining cookie, turns quickly, rushing back into his plush apartment—dick swinging left and right—red gown flapping behind his hairy ass cheeks like a cape. *Where the fuck did I put my clothes?* he hastily wonders, more importantly, *where's my truck and fucking C4!*

63
A BROKEN BRIDGE WILL LEAVE YOU HIGH AND DRY

Priscilla came to a screaming stop, and mixed obscenities filled Deckard's ears. It took a moment for everyone to realize why the ex-Marine had slammed the brakes. A line of vehicles stretched across the bridge nose to tail, like clothes on a washing line.

Deckard leans back in the driver's seat, studying the metallic blockade obstructing the route. Drums prodigious fingers on the steering wheel. "Hey, kids. Ride's up. Time to scan the area like happy troopers," he suggests and cuts the engine.

Jed scoots up from the back compartment. The teen has been asleep for some while. "Are we there yet?" he asks while rubbing eye-boogers from the corners of his eyes, oblivious to the problem.

Carlos flicks his ear. "Fat chance, Jed. Look! Someone's put up a fuckin' blockade just as our ancestors did with that 75-ton chain stretching across the Hudson River to stop the British in the American Revolutionary War."

The teen rubs his ear; remembers the fact from an old history lesson which was led by an equally old history teacher. "Just asking," he replies and returns the gesture.

Carlos winces from the unnecessary flick of the teen's little finger—brings a hand up and swats Jed away like an annoying buzzing bee before rubbing his sore earlobe.

"Shhh!" Mary says, shaking her head. "I will hit both of you boys if you don't play nice with one another." Her warning comes thick and fast like she's a mother of two unruly teenagers.

Carlos grins a devilish grin. "Yeah, uh… I'm good, thanks. Maybe some other time, Kansas."

Deckard ignores the juvenile activities of the kids. He says nothing. Hands at 10 and 2 on the wheel. He focuses on the blockade blocking their route. "You're right, Carlos. It's a neat trick. Either in defense or…" He doesn't finish his sentences, and after several seconds of deliberation leaves the jeep—revolver in hand and gazes at the barrage of cars.

He is followed by everyone else; a pitter-patter of nervous feet; gun hands ready and everybody starts to survey the area for a trap. (Each had occasionally crossed paths with various groups since Good Ol' America fell to the undead; marauders, thieves or gangs of punks trying to be the next Big Bad in the Mad-Max styled World of Survival.

"You okay, Deckard?" Carl asks.

He grumbles. "Hmm. I can't help feeling this is a big mistake."

"Something doesn't sit right?"

"Yip, kid. Something sure doesn't connect," he utters. "Let's move in easy. Check it's all clear. Then we'll deal with any problems that arise. Clear?"

A murmur of agreement.

"Cover me."

Deckard and Carl approach while Carlos and Mary cover their advance. The first vehicle is a lime people carrier. No signs of movement. Moves onto the others, one-at-a-time. No signs of life.

"I don't mean to be a buzzkill or anything, do you think it's odd, the bridge blocked off?" Jed asks.

Carlos doesn't even bother to turn around to answer the teen's dozy question. "Do you know what's odd, everything that's happened to us since the world went Z-crazy. That's what's fuckin' weird, Jed." No response comes back from the teen. The Midwesterner steps closer—Glock drawn. "Do you see anything, Deckard? Any signs of the dead?"

Deckard listens to the quietness of the surrounding area; the birds in the nearby trees, the sound of the river flowing beneath the bridge.

"Cars clear, kid. No one's about. Dead or alive."

"Whatcha, think?" Tito hollers from his own transport a second later. The Latino's head pokes from the Ranger's window like a dog on vacation; the engine running in the background. "A trap, man?" He echoes Carl's nervous question.

Deckard rubs his gruff chin; his stubble itches his sweaty palm. Worry bleeds in his gut. This all seems suddenly familiar. He's been here before; has done the same thing on a foreign battlefield. He knows the barrage of vehicles would make an excellent trap for any unsuspecting incoming vehicles of out-of-towners making their way into unknown territory. But he sees no movement of any kind—dead or alive from in front or behind—and after a few seconds, he states: "Looks clear. No sign of movement."

Tito hollers, "You vouch?"

"I vouch."

"What next, man?"

Again, Deckard rubs his chin but doesn't worry about the concern swishing about in his gut. He focuses on Carl and the others. "I guess we'll try to move these vehicles outta the way…"

Carlos: "Cool, dawg, I'll just pop my Superman pill, shall I?"

Mary: "Huh?"

Carlos looks at her. "Man of Steel. He's a damn superhero. Super strength and all dat shit." The Midwesterner flexes his muscles, kisses his guns in front of the Yooper. Then realizes he's got a broken rib and winces in pain; a stab of burning punctuates his lower abdomen.

Mary: "Ohhhh, *okkaaayyyy!* Totally cool. Let's just keep you wrapped in cotton wool for now."

"No, dipshit…" Deckard bemoans and points with a firm stab of a decisive finger. "We'll hook the backends up with the tow chain from Tito's ride and hoist these vehicles outta the damn way. After, we'll carry onwards into Portland, hoping to find this salvation of yours."

Carlos smiles an oh so stupid smile and grins shyly. “Yeah, yeah, yeah, I was getting to that point soon enough, Marion.”

Everyone looks at him in a *sure you were, kinda way.*

“Cool. I’ll bring the Ranger over in a moment, man,” the Latino hollers from behind, breaking the uncool moment (head submerges back into the Ranger), and he converges with Kelsey; the Louisianan waits for the details to be told.

Back outside, next to the blockade, Carl agrees. “Good idea, Deckard.”

“Sure is, kid.”

***

With the surrounding area clear of traps, the three girls stroll to the side of the bridge and gaze at the rushing river flowing beneath them. Jed follows.

“Seems a nice place,” Naomi states.

“True,” Mary obliges with a fair assumption of the refreshing water beneath. “I always loved rivers. How they cut through whole swathes of land; the way they feed into the oceans.”

“I remember when Hurricane Katrina made landfall off the coast of Louisiana in 2005,” Kelsey says, interrupting the peaceful moment between the two friends. “I was four at the time. My parents decided to stay in the city, never expecting the hurricane to make much of an impact. Jeez, the lack of preparedness for the storm astounded everyone affected, particularly in the poorer communities. And concerning the city’s aging series of levees—50 of which failed during the storm—flooding the low-lying suburbs. I remember seeing the waters rise from our hotel room. Knew how scary rivers could actually become once they ran free and wild with nothing to keep ‘em in check.” She grips onto the guardrail, and peers off into the distance, the memories literally, flooding back to her.

Several seconds of quietness follow.

Naomi finally breaks the silence.

“No fret, Kelsey,” she says and throws a supportive arm over the girl’s slender Louisianan shoulders. “We’re way above the river line. We’re safe.” The words feel refreshing, calming, and the Southerner smiles in gratitude.

“Uh-ha.”

***

Meanwhile, Deckard paces to the forefront of the nearest vehicle—the girls’ conversation fading into the background noise of the thundering river—and he clambers on top of the hood of an old emerald green pick-up. A sign on the side door reads: Eddie’s tow and pay. *‘You’ll pay for making me take it away!!!’*

It brings amusement to his face, before he raises the binoculars high; he scans the vicinity for movement. Further afield, a sprawling complex rises to the left of the bridge. A huge sign advertising anything from everything, offering brand-name clothing stores & specialty retailers with reduced prices: Tommy

Hilfiger, Levi's, Van Heusen, and the list of top quality products endlessly went on. On his right, Troutdale Airport stands motionless; the runways empty of planes. An air control tower standing tall, as overgrown vegetation starts to take back the tall building. Deckard navigates the military-binoculars further afield. He knows the region has been burnt a long time ago and sees the remains of blackened, empty silhouettes of former homes. Long stretches of shadows converging over whole neighborhoods. But beyond, he sees Portland in the distance (23 kilometers) 14 miles from where he stands, or a touch nearer. He's undecided. Finally satisfied the area is all clear, he throws a gaze at the millennials and clambers down from the truck.

64
FUCKING CLOWNS

Deckard doesn't see the eyes prying on him from the side of the road. A bank of fallen trees obstructs the visibility of several quietly approaching armed figures.

Then it happens—

He doesn't see anything, yet he hears it instead. And a shudder runs up his arms, leaving the flesh all prickly like a porcupine. Shapes move to the side of his vision. Four from the embankment of trees, semi-automatics *clicking* into action. He's a fool for not trusting his instincts earlier. There was a time when he was prepared for such a situation. He was built for them, trained for them, but time has taken a toll on his body, his senses, and his addiction to a good ole' drink hasn't helped, either. Marion Deckard reaches for his sidearm—knows it's already too late to act.

***

At that exact moment, Carl has his maps out on the bonnet of 'Priscilla' trying to find the correct street map for Portland. "Shit!" he hisses. "I can't find the right one." Ruffles through another couple of A4 map systems. "C'mon, where are you?" he asks himself, more so than actually Carlos who stands by his side. The Midwesterner looks on with a sly grin etched across his lips.

"Put 'em in fucking order, dawg!" he suggests.

"I have, uh, I did, Carlos. I'm not an idiot."

Carlos leans in close. "Well… just saying. It makes sense to keep 'em in chronological order, dawg. P should be behind O!"

Carl flashes a look of annoyance over his shoulder. "Pointing out the obvious doesn't make it any less frustrating."

Another demon smile from Carlos.

Then they hear a familiar sound; an engine in the distance.

Both turn, thinking Tito is moving the Ranger into position—

They are mistaken—

An SUV that is blacker than night approaches. It stops about ten yards away from the Ranger. Dust on the tinted windscreens. A low beam of light from the headlights hits their pants.

Carl and Carlos turn to one another. This all seems suddenly dangerous and predictable.

The passenger door opens, and black boots touch the hot asphalt of the bridge, beige cargo pants, and a heavy-set individual follows.

Carlos says, "A fucking clown?" It's not meant to be a question but escapes his lips as one. The heavy-set figure wears a mask (of all fucking things, it had to be a clown's mask. Nonetheless, the perpetrator is capitalizing on the Midwesterner's longstanding love-hate relationship with clowns, tapping into his primal dread that he, and so many children and more than a few adults, experience in their presence). "It's no wonder so many people hated Ronald McDonald!" he adds, reaching for his Glock, but it's already too late.

***

Mary, Naomi, Kelsey, and Jed stand at the edge of the bridge, intent on seeing who's driving the SUV. Together, moving forward, one-step-at-a-time as if they are participating in a cowboy-line-dance-of-sorts-at-a-county-fate rodeo.

A flat-footed glide with some heel and toe touches later—

That's when—

They turn and see figures materializing behind Deckard. Maneuvering over the blockade of vehicles; heavy black boots and semi-automatic tactical rifles in hands. Three bogies. Another one makes four, and they're all wearing masks too.

***

Tito has the driver's door open on his Ford Ranger, head stuck inside, unaware of the masked villains descending on the group's position from every possible direction with all the planning of a Black Hawk Down mission. But he hears the unmistakable tire squeaks of a nearby vehicle pulling to a stop behind his transport.

A door opening behind—

That's when—

"Hey, man, hands where I can see 'em and kiss the ground, A-hole!" a stern voice commands from behind.

"Who-whatcha?" his words come out awkwardly like he's chewing on a caramel fudge, spinning around to an advancing boot-heavy figure in a mask. Tito shudders back from the driver's side; with a deep fear rising through his muscular body at the unknown voice—his shortened rifle lays just out of reach on the front seat.

A big black dude comes at him—with a shotgun. The guy's large, bigger than Tito. His face obscured by a rubber clown mask. Tito's fast, but at the same time clumsy—as his reaction is delayed by the look of fear for Kelsey's safety first plowing through his mind. The quick glance costs him. He's too late to reach his weapon, and the butt of the unknown man's shotgun comes down—hard—across the Latino's jaw, and he face-plants the ground. Blood immediately soaks the asphalt like a piping-hot sponge cake from the belly of an oven absorbing a layer of strawberry jam.

Blood bleeds into the surface.

Kelsey screams a hoarse scream as she witnesses her lover hitting the ground in a splatter of blood and snot.

65
CHAOS DESCENDS

"Uh, hold on partner, hands up high!" a Dallas voice warns.

Deckard's eyes flicker left first, right second. His hands go up; revolver left in its protective holder—sleeping snug like a bug in a rug. *Be smart,* a little voice serenades from the back of the Marine's brain. *Wait, judge the situation first and foremost.* Pushes the immediate danger to the forefront of his mind. *Plans! Actions?* He counts four dudes—thinks they're men, but could be mistaken—each wearing a clown mask, heavy tactical firepower directly pointed at him, and at the girls, Jed and everyone else who wasn't already in on the heist.

Another voice: "Don't make a fucking move, losers!"

A third voice: "We'll put so many holes through your body, you won't know which one to piss outta of!"

The enemy shows no respect regarding Deckard's fellowship.

Carlos is about to say something, but Deckard steps in. "Stop!" he demands, not to the turds in the masks, but to the Midwesterner, and everyone else nearby about to raise weapons in retaliation. He doesn't want a bloodbath on his hands, so close to 'The Promised Land of Zombie-Free Civilization.'

He still hears the Louisianan's screams for her lover—

Out of the corner of his eye, he sees the Latino struggling on the ground—

The blood soaking into the ground beneath Tito's body—

Knows Carl and Carlos are itching for a fight, especially the Midwesterner—

Deckard understands the situation; know they're all in danger. From who; he has no fucking idea. No idea what these clowns want, either. But he knows when to be quiet. Not to make any sudden movements. Entice the enemy to put a hole into his body. It would be a shitty ending to the road trip, especially when they're all so close to a sliver of hope. Salvation within their grasp.

He shoots a look over to Carlos—hopes, no prays—the Midwesterner can keep his mouth shut. It is a big ask; a bona-fida leap-of-faith. Or a deluded wish.

But both kids listen, respecting the ex-Marine's authority, which Deckard is grateful for. And he draws a sigh of relief, understands Emperor Death waits on the sidelines 'with all his Divine Glory' teasing them all for that elusive stupid mistake that'll get them all killed—

***

The others are marched over one-by-one to where Deckard waits—all except Tito, the Latino still kisses the ground in the shade of the heavyset black dude wearing a 'Papa Roach' mask and brandishing a shotgun.

"On your knees," Dallas says.

"We'll co-operate," Deckard gestures to the others, nodding his head. "Besides, we don't want any trouble!"

"Then you all pulled up at the wrong fucking rest stop, folks. Now move."

It's a slow, painful process, especially for Kelsey (she keeps flashing a nervous look over her shoulder to where Tito lays injured), but the gang has no choice and follows orders.

The one who's in charge, a tall, thin beanpole moves forward, growls in a throaty *Christian*—Batman—*Bale's* voice. "Who's in charge?" He wears a *Herschel Shmoikel Pinchas Yerucham Krustofsky* mask, better known as 'Krusty the Clown from The Simpsons.' He taps an unnecessarily distracting foot on the floor. "Time's a-tickin', folks!"

Deckard realizes he has a choice to make: he has to choose between thinking of himself and saving everyone else. Because he chooses not to be weak, and it's what he does next, that separates him from the rest of the asses, dicks and self-loving losers of this fucked-up world.

"Affirmative."

The answer seems to please the head clown.

"This your family?"

"Family?" *Yeah, kinda,* he thinks, but actually says, "Different family." It's an honest answer. A truthful reply to an awkward question.

"Brothers? Sisters? Kids?" Krusty looks down through pitted holes for eyeslits. "You the mother-fuckin' hen goose? All these folks… your chicks?"

Deckard shakes his head at the question.

Then it happens—

***

"Does it look like we're blood? Dipshits!"

The insult pulls the leader over; hand held tightly around the semiautomatic's grip. Krusty's head arches at a peculiar angle over Carlos' body. "Jeez, you must be the mother-fuckin' ugly duckling of the family?" It draws a laugh from the two nearest clowns by Krusty's side.

It also draws for another confrontation, and more importantly another comeback from the Midwesterner's mouth.

"Fuck yeah, turd-burger. What's your game here? You gonna perform some tricks for your adoring crowd? Or drop your balls, while in the middle of this macho-fuckin'act?"

The lead clown says, "Wanna be funny? I'll show you somethin' to laugh about!"

"Try taking your mask off for starters!"

The insult brings a slap across Carlos' face and brings a laugh from Krusty's right. (A red-eyed Charles Lee 'Chucky' Ray from the Child's Play slasher film series sniggers away like a tenth grader.) The snigger brings an annoying glare from Krusty.

"Sorry, Clayton—I mean, Boss. The fucker's fun—"

"What the hell! We said no names, Barry." A second goes by, and Krusty realizes his mistake. "Fuck, shit, fuck you, Barry." (And Barry—no, Chucky from Child's Play—sniggers again.)

“Fuck me, great introduction shitbrains, you clowns come from a convention, or an after work bash?”

Krusty shakes his head. “I feel like you’re not listening to me, asswipe.”

“Are you calling me a bad listener?”

“Yeah I am, asswipe. I’m just saying that you’re not hearing me correctly.”

“Oh. So now you’re saying I’m stupid!”

Krusty leans closer. “What the fuck is your problem, asswipe?”

It takes several seconds for Carlos to form an adequate response to Krusty—no, Clayton, the fucking moronic chief clown’s question, and his band of Grade-C clown highwayman. Carlos can’t help himself, he should have shut his mouth. Locked it with a key, and then thrown that key into a deep, deep lake. “Fucking scum like you for starters! Everyone who pisses on my parade when I’m least expecting it.”

Krusty launches another slap across the Midwesterner’s face—

Carlos spits blood from a split lip—

“Shut up!” Mary says from his left. “*Jesus!* Just keep your trap bolted! If someone asked me, ‘what’s my problem?’ I would say ‘nothing’ and keep quiet. The worst thing you can do is talk back.”

The leader of the clowns applauds Mary’s wise words. “Be smart, listen to your woman, asswipe!” he assertively says to Carlos before turning back to Deckard. “Take control of your group, or I’ll start popping you one at a time.”

***

Deckard clears his throat. “We’re listening. What’s on offer?”

Krusty wanders back to the ex-Marine, straddling the ground. “Supplies, Army Man.”

“I’m a Marine.”

“I don’t give a fuck what you are!” Krusty responds harshly. “I expect all of you to be giving up your valuables. Guns. Ammo. Munitions. And after… you’re free to leave. Make your way to Portland’s loving shelter for the poor and needy.”

The remark brings a look to the groups’ faces—a telepathic link shared between everyone; *Portland’s safe haven is goddamn real?*

“Okay. Okay, we can handle that arrangement,” Deckard grudgingly replies, but at the same time looks for a way out of this unholy predicament. A long shot to freedom. Just a fucking break of good luck. Deckard thinks he can take him. Disarm the lead clown. Or point the gun elsewhere. He just needs opportunity. But when?

“That’s all cool…” Carl says from the former Marine’s right, hands up in surrender. “Guys! Give ‘em… what they desire,” he says to the rest of the group in a commanding, yet at the same time, dry, uneven voice. “We can be on our way to Portland. No need to entice ‘em further.”

“Except the woman. Huh, Boss?” The whispered question comes from Barry behind his Chucky mask. He stands close behind the leader.

The Dallas' voice declares, "Yeah, the woman!" The third clown wears an iconic Stephen King creation. Pennywise the Clown, stands behind Krusty the Clown on the bonnet of the pick-up truck.

Another clown, one you'd find entertaining at a kids 8th birthday stands next to Pennywise; he laughs, and gold teeth sparkle with the rays of the sun.

66
OBJECTIONS

Carlos draws a sharp breath. “What did you say?” looking up at the lead clown.

“I’m sure you heard my friend, asswipe.”

Carlos feels a stab of anger. “I’m warning you… if you hurt those girls in any—”

“It’s far too late to be a hero,” Krusty says in an amused tone. “If you wanna live, I suggest you play nicely.”

Krusty and his band of clown highwaymen stand there with guns, and big-dick-swinging egos on show. He hopes his—captive—audience is enjoying the show. He can feel that he has won in his mind.

That’s until—

“No, man…” Tito wheezes. “That ain’t cool!” The Latino lifts himself up from the hot asphalt slowly, like the dead rising from a graveyard as an extra from an ‘MJ video.’ A split lip, a saw jaw; crimson runs down his golden chin like a blood-suckin’ vamp, soaks into the v of his pale blue tee.

“Who was that?” Krusty demands—eyes searching beneath his mask.

“Me…”

Krusty tilts his head; another peculiar angle and glares at Tito—now—sitting against the Ford Ranger’s passenger door. “Sorry to hear you disagree with our plans, A-Hole. But I have the firepower to do pretty much whatever I want. And that’s what’s gonna happen.” His words are sharper than blades. “All those bitches are coming with us.”

It only takes three seconds for retaliation—

Naomi: “Fuck y’all!”

Mary: “You have the intelligence of a pea lid, assholes!”

Kelsey: “What the f-you call us?”

“Boss called you all ‘bitches’ bitches!” a voice interjects. It’s the large black guy covering Tito with a shotgun. It’s then that Kelsey can’t stand it any more. She gets up, begins marching over to the big guy standing guard over her fella.

But she doesn’t get that far—

A backhand comes from nowhere and connects with her side. She falls, whines in agony and drops to her knees. A second later—holds a hand to her tender split lip.

“A tough guy, huh?” Tito swallows a hard knot. Finds his love with hollow eyes. *Be okay, Kelsey.* “C’mon chickenshit, if you’re man enough to slap a lady, you should be man enough to have a one-on-one with me.”

“*Wowwwwww,* chill out!” Krusty hollers, hands parading in a fancy flutter, while the other clowns cheer at their boss’s comical antics. The leader of the clowns lends his apparent turn of charm a loony sort of Willy Wonka menace. “Think I will. Thanks.” And he marches over towards Tito. “Some 250 years ago,

America was a wilderness full of frightened, violent lunatics intent on conquering all before," he says, rather happily.

Tito laughs; he can't help himself.

"Your point?"

Krusty lowers his assault rifle; *blam* and a single bullet enter Tito's cranium. The Latino slumps back; skull open to the warm elements of the sun with his blood splatter across the side of the yellow Ranger. "I guess we haven't progressed one iota."

And death strikes, taking the Latino's soul.

67
A LUCKY INTERLUDE

Deckard kneels there. He knows he should help, move, attack and conquer the enemy. Should reach out and help the Latino. *Should've done more!* But knows what would have followed. A bullet to the head too. Another pointless death so close to salvation. He wasn't ready to die; to be a martyr. Not yet. Not here, like this, on his knees.

He hears Kelsey's uncontrollable sobs of dismay. The other two girls' bewildered looks of horror. Jed, Carl and Carlos's gazes of uncertainty that their time on this fucked up world is coming to an end, sooner rather than later. Their fantasy dipped reality covered in glitter and rainbow sprinkles was now about to abruptly end. (Lady Luck had deserted them. Skipped town and was now heading outta state.)

After several delayed seconds, Jed eventually says: "Tito could be okay! Well—not okay."

"Nobody's okay after getting shot in the head," Carl bemoans.

"But some people survive it, right?"

"Fuck no, Jed." Carlos answers.

Carl's head spins. His entire reality falls off a high cliff, like Lemmings plunging over the edge. This wasn't part of the plan. For someone to die so close to safety. "Is this real? Is this a real thing? Did we just witness…"

"Tito's brain candy displayed over his ride?" Carlos says. "Yeah. Sure did, dawg."

***

But then whatever Tito thought he could have achieved by antagonizing the leader no longer matters as a small RC truck whizzes past Deckard's aching knees. The small child's toy is black and blue. Racing stripes across the small bonnet. It's fast and whizzes in and out of the gun-wielding posse of clowns' legs. Its toy engine goes *vvvvzzzz* as it completes a perfect doughnut in front of its bemused audience. Then it stops just in front of the barrage of vehicles on the far side of the bridge.

Pennywise, who stands on the bonnet of the pickup, captivated by the remote control toy, jumps down to inspect the peculiar sight. He had a similar one once when he was younger. Loved to build them from scratch with his old man. The other two clowns clamor around to see the toy as well.

Pennywise, the Party Clown and Chucky from Child's Play looks at the remote control truck. A fond expressionless glare then filters behind each mask in turn—

Who's controlling the toy?

Krusty holds out a hand. Points to the truck with his semi-automatic rifle as it revs and shouts, *"Get the fuck away from that toy truck!"* He backtracks past

Tito's lifeless corpse, the Ranger and runs towards the black SUV. His accomplice who's holding the shotgun retreats to the driver's side and starts the engine, and within seconds, the vehicle reverses away with speed.

With a willfully quirky wisp of sheer luck, Deckard knows what he sees. *A ticking, fucking timebomb.* C4 strapped to the side of the toy truck. All he can say is: "Fucking move, move, move, kids. It's gonna blow!"

Just in time, the gang are up and running—catapulting behind 'Priscilla' as she offers the closest barrier of protection against the oncoming—

Kaboommmm!

68
LIFE LESSONS

It takes several seconds for the sounds of the explosion to clear, the shrapnel of the pick-up truck scattered across the westbound bridge in every direction. Now, the vehicle is just a metallic mess of metal upon metal. A thundering black cloud of smoke billowing upwards from the wreckage resembles Native Americans using smoke signals to communicate messages across vast stretches of land.

Pennywise, the Party Clown and Chucky are no longer around to entertain the masses and have joined Tito in the afterlife. Just body parts and rubber masks decorate the smokin' asphalt. The other vehicles which formed the barrier across the exit ramp of the bridge are in disarray too, smashed windows, blown apart headlights, disintegrated bumpers.

Meanwhile, Krusty, the leader of the Clown Highwaymen and his sidekick have fled. The black SUV maneuvering backward across the bridge at a deadly pace. The car does a 180-degree turn, tires *screeching* like a Nascar on a Daytona speedway, rubber burning and kicks into third as it reaches the end, and it's gone—just a black blob dissolving into the horizon back along the Memorial Highway.

'Priscilla' miraculously sits with barely a scratch upon her body. A few scrapes and dents where the blast and pummeled her side. A cracked side-mirror too. Behind the jeep, it takes a few moments for the others to clarify what the fuck just happened. More importantly, they're no longer on the verge of being killed by the gang of Highway Clowns.

***

Deckard is up, dusting himself down; sees the remnants of bodies and vehicles scattered across the bridge; he doesn't know what the holy hell has just happened (but believes Lady Luck has returned from her voyage just in time and spared all of their—sorry asses—from the clutches of Death). His first port of call: the bastards dressed as clowns, and where were they? Takes a peek up the stretch of bridge. Nothing. Na-da. Zero. The bridge is clear; the SUV gone. No need to raise his weapon. But the second thought now comes into play: who the holy-hell strapped some C4 explosives to a kid's RC truck? And where were they now hiding?

Together, Carl and Carlos stand like conjoined twins; looking at the girls, at Jed still kneeling beyond 'Priscilla's' impregnable defense. At the same time, both share doubts with Deckard, and at this particular moment in time is that on the one hand, 'what the fuck just happened' and on the other hand, 'no seriously, what the actual fuck?'

The ex-Marine stares back, mouth slack—

Together, all stand nervously in an *I didn't see that coming moment!*

***

Then a figure emerges behind the dust cloud of smokey vehicles—

"Is everyone, okay?" a ragged voice says. "Hey, folks, are you all breathing, beyond 'em flames?"

Carl, Carlos, and Deckard squint through the dissipating smoke and see a gangly figure approaching. He's an unmade bed of a man; lean with a full gray beard and straggly head hair the same color as his whiskers. He wears mustard colored corduroys, boots, a gun belt, and a red robe—half undone, exposing his old man's silvery chest—that flaps behind like Superman's cape.

Deckard's instincts sense nothing that cause him fear. *Pity, they let me down before*, he winces at the thought of Tito's brains pebble-dashed across the side of the Ranger a few minutes prior—but he can't let those thoughts distract him now. Not with this new face entering the game at such a late stage. "Who are you?" he asks, unsure what answer he'll receive.

Then Deckard sees: the man holds a small revolver in one hand, and a small plastic black box with a pair of antennas sticking from the top and two red control sticks. A remote control. Deckard already likes this Old-timer. Human instinct was his own first line of defense against trouble-makers. It was proven that human intuition was a more accurate detector of danger than all the electronic gear in the entire world—more so now, considering all those devices were relics of the past.

"You did this?" Carl cuts in stepping from behind the jeep.

The old man smiles a dentures grin back. A smile made all the bigger by the fact he'd gotten the correct amount of explosives right this time around.

"Who the fuck are you, old man?" Carlos says. He tries to yell the words, but they come out as heavy wheezes.

"The cat who's gonna save all your nine lives. Now come. We have to move."

"What about our supplies?" Carlos thinks he says the words as quietly as he can but is, in fact shouting into the old man's face because his ears are still ringing from the blast like the opening credits of a vintage film (when there's a guy banging a great, golden drum to signal the beginning of the movie).

"We can take our ride. Pile straight through the gap that's been created by that explosion!" Carl replies, pointing to the debris of the ex-pick-up truck scattered across the bridge.

"No good, boy," the old man chucks the idea straight from the Window of Hope. "Road's busted up good and proper beyond this point. No way into Portland by car. You'll all be on foot after a few miles past this point. So much of the city is in a state. Run-down areas. Whole areas flooded. And then… it's just trekking through beat-up streets like finding your way through a maze with no exit in sight."

"Unacceptable," Carl replies, not believing a word from the old man's mouth.

"It is how it is, lad."

"Plans, old-timer?" Deckard says.

The old man doesn't wait and dives straight into an answer. "I'm going to keep you alive. Show you a rcute to safety. C'mon, folks. Grab what you can from your transport, Chief, and be ready to move in five!"

Carlos turns. "This shit really happening?"

Carl echoes his friend's question. "Yeah, I assume so. What choice do we have, man?"

Carlos starts to laugh at the crazy situation, it's the only thing he could do.

It's enough of a plan from the old man that Deckard just hrmms a tired moan. "Time to move, kids," he puckers up, breaking up the convo between the two boys, just as Mary, Naomi, and Jed rise from behind the safety of the jeep to see an old man wearing a red dressing gown. "Grab what you can carry from the vehicles, kids. Leave the heavy stuff behind, and get ready to move ASAFP."

***

The background is filled with sobs. Tears, tears and more tears; enough to fill the river beneath; ready to burst its banks and flood the smoking ruins of Troutdale. Kelsey stands over Tito's body looking down at the dead Latino.

"Tito!" she whispers his name—hoping he'll wake. *"Tito!"*

From behind, the old man stands a yard or two away from the blonde. "I feel for the poor lass, Chief," he says to Deckard. "But… we gotta be smart and move. We can mourn for our lost ones another time. Hell, we've all lost people."

"Just give her a sec, Old-timer."

Deckard looks at the blond Louisianan standing over her dead lover; tears, tears, and tears cascading from her eyes like twin waterfalls; flooding the land beneath her feet with grief. He'd never lost loved ones, except his parents of course. But that was a different situation, a different time. They had died in a car collision when he was far to young to remember. Yet, he wonders if his brother is still alive, somewhere, out there in the world. He forces himself to look at the Latino's body. The bullet in Tito's head. The blood splatter on his vehicle. But—*warfare* was different. You'd expect to lose your mates in those conflicts. Hell, he'd lost companions before on tours of duty. Remembers those haunting faces. The fear, being injured, losing a comrade. This was just cold-blooded murder. An intimidation experiment from some fucked-up individuals—*society* already collapsed. The End of the World and all of Hell's puppets now running the show—and this, Deckard thinks, *is what it must be like to lose someone you really love.*

"We can't carry dead weight. No pun intended, Chief!" The old man moves next to the ex-Marine. They stand at near enough equal height, considering the mighty age gap. But where the old man is thin and boney, Deckard has military muscle. The old man knows Deckard is ex-military. Army, he thinks. Marine, he suspects. Seen enough of 'em in his lifetime to know a guy from the forces. He asks, "Chief? You listening!"

"I am, Old-timer," Deckard counters, then says to Naomi. "Pick Kelsey up." It was an order.

The Texan looks at him for a second, caught off guard—which feels like a lifetime and gives a yes just as automatic and hollow as such a question demands, and goes to the Southerner's rescue.

***

Naomi squats beside Kelsey. The sight of Tito's brainless cranium splashed across the Ranger's red exterior makes her want to vomit her breakfast. But she resists and focuses. "Okay. Can you walk?" Naomi says, laying a comforting hand on her stately cousin's shoulder.

"I... I..." Voice trembling. Sobs and tears. "I can try." But she finds herself frozen at the scene of her ex-lover dead in front of her own eyes in a childish nightmare that has become all the more real. "Hu-huh."

Kelsey stares like a frightened five-year-old at the blood splatter and the side order of brains on the red Ranger. Both reds blend into one another, and it was hard to know what was blood and what was paint.

"Good. Now we..." (Naomi thinks to herself, *What the hell are we supposed to do? Follow this half-naked old man into the trees? It's a fucking ridiculous idea!* But doesn't say it aloud.) Instead, she says, "We have to move. C'mon, Kelsey."

"We can't leave Tito!" She manages to push a response from her mouth. Each word is hard to swallow; full of sorrow and love, and hatred, and dread. *"Tito!"* She calls in the hope that the Latino will get up and follow her voice, but deep down, she understands he's dead. Gone. Never to return to the world of the living.

"He's gone, Kelsey."

"He's..."

Mary hunkers down beside her. She tries not to look at the devastating scene, and manages to hold bitter boil in her mouth. "He'll want you to live, girl. So get up and move your ass so he won't be disappointed."

"I made him—He n-never—*Tito never*—wanted to go—" Her words are rambles of words.

"C'mon," Naomi agrees with Mary and hooks her arm beneath Kelsey's skinny shoulders, and together they lift the girl from her knees, from her dead lover's motionless body. Kelsey's galloping pulse is on the verge of exploding from her wrists like horses beginning a race. Her heartbeat quickens, and then she just stops crying, stops talking, and goes with them.

Two minutes later, Mary has her yellow rucksack shouldered; a hunting rifle slung over her arm. Jed carries one of the red rucksacks they'd found within Salt Lake City—full with supplies. And his makeshift CB radio. Carl and Carlos do the same, rifling through the jeep and Tito's transport, grabbing supplies, munitions and anything else that can be taken along in two other rucksacks. Carlos grabs Tito's shortened shotgun.

"You seriously taking that!"

"Yeah, yeah, I am, dawg." Carlos gives Carl an iffy *why the fuck shouldn't I take a perfectly good gun? It's not like Tito will have any objections.* "Tito doesn't have any use for it no more, and I'm not gonna leave it here like a present for when those fuckin' clowns come back," he says, with as much pride as any person who doesn't give a damn shit could convey through those words. "Here, take these rounds too, dawg," And the Midwesterner throws a white box of ammo from the glove compartment.

Carl steps back to catch in midair the box of ammo; a one-handed catch, inadvertently kicking the vehicle. They hear a slump; a cold dead body hits the ground. A few seconds later, both shoulder a glance along the parked vehicle's side; and sees the Latino's body keeled over on the asphalt—the hole in the back of his head was unsettling.

Each gulp back the reality that they are lucky sonsofbitches and have not ended up in the same position as the Latino. In front, Mary looks back at the boys. She can feel queasiness growing in her stomach, and shoulders a gaze to Kelsey, luckily the girl hasn't seen her ex-lover splatter to the ground like a sack of potatoes. Naomi shelters Kelsey's body; cuddles the skinny blond's body close to hers. Both are tracking over the remnants of the barricade. She has a hunting rifle slung across her chest.

Reality feels like it flipped upside-down.

"Sorry, girl," Carlos says, patting Priscilla's hood. "Been through a lot babe. Another time. Another place. Another life, we would have lasted forever."

"Okay, man?" Carl asks, hand on the Midwesterner's shoulder.

"Yeah, dawg," he replies, "all good things must come to an end sometime."

There was silence until there wasn't.

"Ready to move!" Deckard hollers, breaking up the emotional moment between friends and vehicle. He shoulders his military backpack like a pro; easy and without hassle. "Let's go."

"Thought you'd never leave, Chief," the old man hollers to Deckard as he helps Naomi and Kelsey across the barrier, smiles a bushy grin. "Follow me, lassies."

"Where we goin'?" Naomi asks.

"Safety, lassie. Safety."

69
BERT ERNIE, 'THE WATCHMAN'

The old man's escape vessel is moored by a sandy, shaded bay five minutes away. They board a small yellow boat, heaving their gear on board one-at-at-time. (Incredibly easy to operate, the 150 Montauk once exceeded for fishing and watersports.) Now, just an escape ship like the small boats rescuing the soldiers on the beaches of Normandy. A spacious center console layout maximizes every inch of its nimble size, while the precision-engineered hull ensures a soft, smooth ride. But the combined weight of bodies and equipment was putting a strain on the fibreglass body of the small boat, and it lowers absurdly low into the meandering river like a fat man floating on an inflatable in a pool but manages to keep afloat.

The old man starts the engine. *Click, click*, it turns over, and he throws it forward, and they're off—leaving the remnants of the smoky bridge and the dead bodies, leaving the outskirts of Troutdale behind, and leaving their fallen companion to the nearby birds.

"Optional teak port and starboard mid-ship boarding steps for easier access than ever. The optional fishing package adds a 36-quart cooler seat, console-mounted rod holders and tackle drawers," the old man says as if he's trying to offload the boat to a prospective buyer.

Deckard stands next to their gray-beared savior behind the stylish helm. He wears a red dressing-gown. The Old-timer looks like Santa on a day off. The girls and Carl are up front, holding onto the chrome railings—resting in the blue interior of comfy seats. While behind, Jed and Carlos sit at the back of the small boat; two-rod holders with long fishing poles attached to the rear.

"Thanks for the save, Old Timer," Deckard gestures with an outstretched hand.

The old man shakes it. "No worries, Chief. Glad I could be of service."

Deckard gets a whiff of grandpa's former career. "Navy?" he suggests.

"Shucks, no, Chief." He lets out a tittle of a raspy laugh. "Close, though. Army once before peacetime. After my enlistment… Coast Guard for thirty long years. USCG 'Cutter Tantillo' in Hawaii. Boatswain's Mate (BM) for short. Jack-of-all-trades job. Heck, the Navy describes boatswain's mates as the 'backbone of every ship's crew.' We trained, directed and supervised all ship's personnel," he says with pride and fond memories. A blast from the past. "Originally from Florida, though." He asks: "You army?"

"Marines," Deckard answers as the man steers the boat along the bends of Sandy River. Sticks out a welcoming hand. "Deckard." The old man shakes it. "What's your name, Old Timer?"

"Bert. Bert Ernie," he says in formal recognition.

"Fuckin' kiddin' me!" The words burst from Carlos' mouth like a shotgun emptying its chamber. "Like a muppet?"

He chuckles—throws a contemptuous stare at the Midwesterner. "Nice. Call an old man a muppet. Expect him to keep giving you a lift, sonny-Jim? I should throw you overboard and leave you to the fish."

Carlos raises his hands at the old man behind the wheel. "No. No, I mean…" trying to backtrack. Eventually he gets there. "You're named after characters from Sesame Street!"

Bert Ernie laughs harder. "Now you say it! It does sound that way!"

"No shit, Bert Ernie."

"No, shit, sonny-Jim."

And they both share a laugh.

Bert Ernie leans back, hands on the wheel; a small silver compass sits above, while all-sorts of goodies cram the helm. Cup holders. Circuit breakers and a fusion stereo. Once a working GPS navigation screen and radio. Mercury engine control and a goddamn extra beverage holder. And the craft cruises the river at speed, clocking up those knots.

"Who the fuck were those guys?" Carlos expels in a mighty huff. He glares back over his shoulder—hand on his Glock, ready, expecting a fleet of warships to be following close behind with a fucking red nose attached to the bow and large clown cannons to the amidship.

"Clowns…" Bert Ernie reluctantly replies.

"No, shit, old man. We could see they were clowns. Who were the dickheads behind the masks?"

"You ever hear of Robin Hood?"

"Of course. Which one. Connery, Costner or Elwes," he reels a list of famous actors who have portrayed the Robin Hood-like role. Connery was way before his time while Costner put in a great Hollywood performance, but Cary Elwes was his favorite actor and was the best part of Men in Tights; the Princess Bride actor's sly charm and, yes, even the English accent would make him a good Robin even in a movie that takes the hero seriously.

"You're a smart ass fucker, ain't' you, kid."

"Carlos," Carlos says by way of introduction. "My name's Carlos Haseltine."

Bert Ernie laughs. "You're a smart ass fucker, ain't you, Carlos Haseltine."

"What gave it away?" Mary hollers from the bow as she listens to the conversation growing, as does everyone else. And the Yooper introduces everyone to the captain of the small boat. Carl nods. Jed smiles. Naomi waves to the old man with her good arm, while Kelsey just stares.

Carlos raises his eyebrows. "So what, Bert Ernie? Robin Hood supposed to be stealing from the rich and giving to the poor."

"Not anymore—just ex-corporate punks dressed as scary clowns. A whole gang of 'em terrorizing this area for the past few months…"

***

Deckard listens to the story spilling from the grandpa's whiskery lips like water from a bucket. (Well, the Marine bops up and down as though he's on a kiddies rollercoaster. Up and down, up and down—gently does it.) He's trying to figure out how old the Old Timer is. Older than him for sure. Late 60s? Early 70s? Older still? The bearded face offers no hints, truths of his real age, just his liver-spotted hands, and a grey-curly-chest-of-hair. The old man has his own gentle swaying, like a cruise liner on an ocean, but more accurate, a small boat on a river. Deckard is relieved—happy this Old Timer has come to their rescue. Not just for rescuing them from the bad situation on the bridge with the fucking clowns, but saving the ladies from a certain rape scenario.

"How'd you find us?"

"Saw you from my pad in the sky, Chief," Bert Ernie says. "And part o' my job, of course." A big smile slides across his face.

"Is that a 9-5 job? Or a 7-11 career?" Carlos quips.

Deckard ignores the Midwesterner. "Job?" he asks instead and looks at the old man as if to say 'please explain more.'

Bert Ernie duly obliges. "I help unfortunate souls like yourselves navigate safely towards Government Island. Safety of Portland—"

"Government Island?" Carl says.

"So it is true?" Mary interrupts. "A secure base for survivors?"

"A colony?" Naomi says.

"People too?" Jed adds.

Carlos jeers. "Hu-hu. Populated by the U.S. Government, no doubt?"

The old man titters to no one but himself. "No. Just civilians. A few—Regular Joe—scientists striving to create a community for the living," he answers Carlos. Smiles at Mary. "Animals also, lassies. Fresh milk and eggs. Hot showers. Water pressure isn't so hot on some days—"

"You have chickens and cows?" Naomi hollers.

"Yeah, lassie. The whole kaboodle. Chickens for the eggs. No cows. Goats for the milk."

Mary nudges her friend. "Makes you feel at home, huh, Naomi?"

"Sure does," the Texan replies to Mary, fond memories of her families farm coming back to her, before throwing a reassuring arm around Kelsey. "You hear that girl!" she says, an eager-beaver to her voice. "We're goin' to make it." But Kelsey remains quiet; staring off into the distance. And Naomi cradles the blond Louisianan harder like a mother caring for a sick child.

"I'm guessing, from the looks on all your faces, it's what you've been searching for?"

The chance for a better life? A safe haven? Deckard lays a hand on the Old Timer's shoulder. "It's the dream."

"Then you're all in the right boat."

"And it's all safely secured?" Deckard asks, intrigue piquing. "This Government Island?"

"Sure is, Chief. Don't fret. Government Island is just the name of our secure haven. No U.S officials here dictating law and order. Plenty o' Republicans and

Democrats, and a few Liberals. But we all get on well enough, now there ain't no proper functioning Government dictating its citizens' lives. No taxes, nor healthcare either." Bert Ernie coughs an ex-smokers cough. "But we have our own rules. Rules you have to abide by—to *stay*. Need to contribute to the new society!"

Mary grips Naomi's hand. "We can do that."

Both girls stare at the old man standing in the small bridge of the Boston Whaler.

Carl: "We'll do whatever it takes."

Bert Ernie looks back. "I expect you will." Then he goes back to steering the boat up the river.

***

A short time later, the mouth of Sandy River eventually connects back to the Columbia River, and the roaring waters help the Boston Montauk along at a steady pace.

They pass abandoned marinas—floating communities that consisted of floating homes for year round living and boat slips for seasonal leasing. A giant billboard welcomes them: 'Welcome to Big Eddy's Marina.' *We love the ease and carefree living of marina life! Far from the challenges and noise of urban living!*

"Didn't know you could live so close to them—I *mean* on them, though?" Jed says. The teen was taking in the surprising sight of the houses above the roaring river.

"It's surprising where humans will build their homes, Jed," Carlos says. "We'll thrive just about anywhere we can. We have to."

The teen looks back at all those houses—contemplating the Midwesterner's words.

***

Several seconds later, Bert Ernie asks: "Chief, do me a favor. Open my tackle box and retrieve my Lucy in the sky."

"Lucy?" Deckard questions with raised brows. Wondering why the Old Timer was referencing *The Beatles* 'Lucy in the Sky with Diamonds' song from their 1967 album Sgt. Pepper's Lonely Hearts Club Band. He was picturing himself on the river, but there was no tangerine trees or marmalade skies.

"Yeah, Chief. Lucy."

Okay, Deckard wonders what the Old Timer's actually after. He bends down. Next to his legs is an old fisherman's box; bright red like a postman's letterbox. Inside, he finds hooks, fishing tackle; a small Tupperware box of worms, and everything else you'd expect to find in a fisherman's box-of-delights.

Then he notices it—an orange flare gun staring at him like a dame with garish lipstick color. "Here," he says, handing over the pistol.

The Old Timer takes it. Makes sure Lucy is loaded and fires it up into the sky. The flare shoots upwards, rising and blazing to the heavens above. A calling card to the Unknown Gods. A colorful explosion and the flare slowly descends in the gentle breeze. Within a minute, another identical flare, some way off in the distance joins it. Both signal flares burning bright red.

"Thank heavens for flares," Bert Ernie's eyes catch the show above. "Saved countless lives at sea." And shows Deckard the gun. The model is newish: *Harrington & Richardson Company* decorates the pistol's side. "Fun fact; the original was invented in 1942 by John R.Smith."

Facts are good, Deckard muses but is more interested in why the Old Timer has just fired the flare. More interested in 'who' returned the curtsey?

Recognizing the Marine's concern growing, Bert Ernie says, "No worries, Chief. Just friendlies on Government Island. I fire my 'Lucy' off if I require assistance. Found you guys and girls in need of help. A few injuries too looking at the state of you. So that's why my 'Lucy' comes in handy."

Deckard just hrmms and waits.

70
GOVERNMENT ISLAND

At the front of the small Montauk, Mary comforts Kelsey. The Louisianan is still quiet—dead silent since she'd left her lover on the bridge with a wide-open hole in his cranium. Mary tries to bring her around but with no luck. Instead, the two girls stare off into the distance. Behind them sits Naomi and Carl.

"I'm still wondering if it was worth it!"

"Worth what?"

"Us… coming all this way!" Naomi says, her voice shuddering from the spray of the river hitting her cheek. "Kelsey, she's… just lost Tito."

"We've all lost someone we love," Carl replies. The realization takes a moment to sink in, and he realizes the casualness of the words. "I didn't—"

Naomi steps in just in time, in full eye-contact mode. "Okay, Carl. I know you didn't mean to offend me. It was a long time ago what happened to my fiance. I understand everyone's loved and lost in this world."

He registers her words, swallowing back the slight guilt growing in the back of his throat, and nods back. "We have to keep faith amid this Apocalyptic shitstorm, Naomi."

"Uh-huh," she puts forward. "But really, is it really worth it?" Naomi was wearing her most transparent, honest, and somewhat flimsy unconceding face like a semi-nude model on the front of a Hustler issue.

"Yes."

She gives that some thought. Her control isn't a one-way street. They had shared responsibilities on the trip. With all that had happened to them on the road: Leaving their encampment behind. The fuck-up at the silo. Finding Deckard. Salt Lake City. Meeting Kelsey and Tito at the lake. She finally concludes Carl is correct. But her face saddens a bit.

He sees it, her feelings masquerading behind her face like a 17th century Royalist Ball.

"Naomi, I may not be able to fix everything that has happened to us. On our trip, our journey here, but I promised we'd arrive at Portland. All together." He gulps back phlegm; a little doubt also. "We succeeded in doing just that."

Naomi nods. "Uh-huh. You did us all proud."

Suddenly they didn't speak no more, only the growl of the small boats engine and the thump of the water on the fibreglass hull are the only sounds.

Another mile and Bert Ernie steadies the small boat, he concentrates his attention on a particular stretch of shoreline in the distant waters. A dark forest rises at the tip. In the background, the blurry shape of a bridge crosses the width of the water. "Only one way onto Government Island by boat," he says, using his memory as a map to navigate around the shore. Off the upstream tip of the large Island, towards the left bank of the Columbia, is McGuire Island and a smaller unnamed island also. He looks at the stretch of water in front of the boat. Math and science blur together as he figures the best path to travel. Searching for the snags, eddies, slack currents, straightest paths, and shallowest waters.

But the old man's words come under close scrutiny from his cargo's watch.

The island grew in the small windshield before them. Above, the clouds were shifting and the afternoon heat was cooling while the evening was slowly creaking in. The boat lifts over the shallow waters but the river remains calm, and towards the right bank of the Columbia is a one-mile-long island listed as Ackerman Island. Further along on the Washington divide, a lumber yard and residential houses sits on the rivers edge. The boat thumped along gently, as Deckard keeps on red alert, while the others whispers in small groups.

Five minutes later, assembled by a dock yonder, the old man points to where an L-shaped white pier juts from the craggy shore. Another similar boat bobbles up and down close by. Behind is a small boathouse, shallow rocks rise from the edges of the island. Several hundred yards where another forest stretched; a glimmer of fortifications rise behind the tree-line, and remind them of a castle ramparts from a Grimm Fairytale.

Carl's eyes were drawn by sudden movement. Several figures; each in coats of black had run out to the end of the pier. They were still too far away to see details but could hear the distant calls of friendly voices. He reaches out and gently takes Naomi's hand. She doesn't resist.

"We made it."

"We did," he replies.

They had survived.

Salvation was real.

THE END

CHECK OUT OTHER GREAT ZOMBIE NOVELS

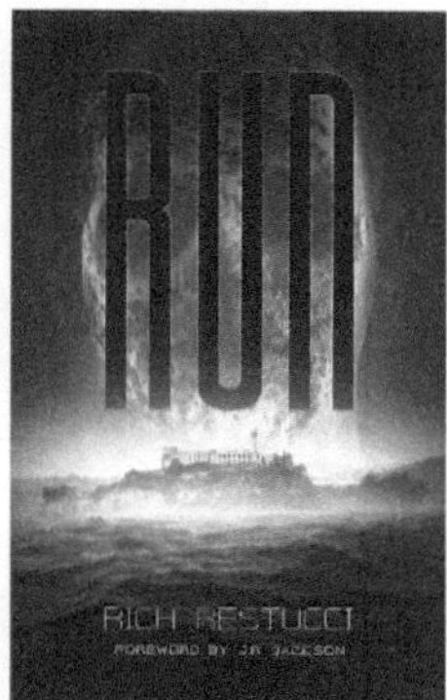

RUN
by Rich Restucci

The dead have risen, and they are hungry.

Slow and plodding, they are Legion. The undead hunt the living. Stop and they will catch you. Hide and they will find you. If you have a heartbeat you do the only thing you can: You run.

Survivors escape to an island stronghold: A cop and his daughter, a computer nerd, a garbage man with a piece of rebar, and an escapee from a mental hospital with a life-saving secret. After reaching Alcatraz, the ever expanding group of survivors realize that the infected are not the only threat.

Caught between the viciousness of the undead, and the heartlessness of the living, what choice is there? Run.

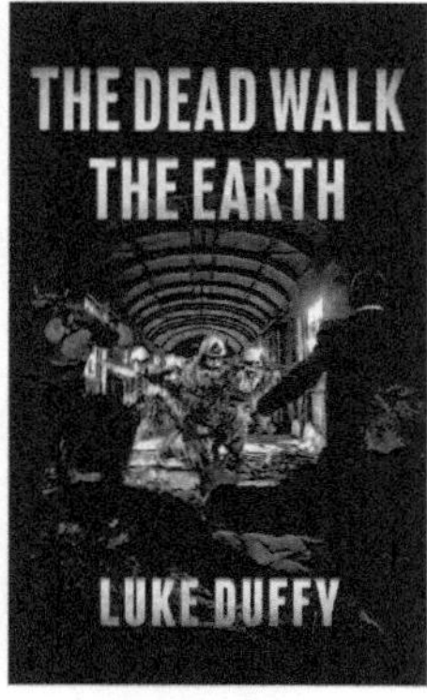

THE DEAD WALK THE EARTH
by Luke Duffy

As the flames of war threaten to engulf the globe, a new threat emerges.

A 'deadly flu', the like of which no one has ever seen or imagined, relentlessly spreads, gripping the world by the throat and slowly squeezing the life from humanity.

Eight soldiers, accustomed to operating below the radar, carrying out the dirty work of a modern democracy, become trapped within the carnage of a new and terrifying world.

Deniable and completely expendable. That is how their government considers them, and as the dead begin to walk, Stan and his men must fight to survive.

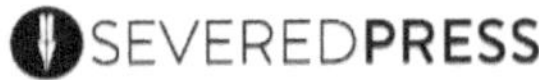

CHECK OUT OTHER GREAT ZOMBIE NOVELS

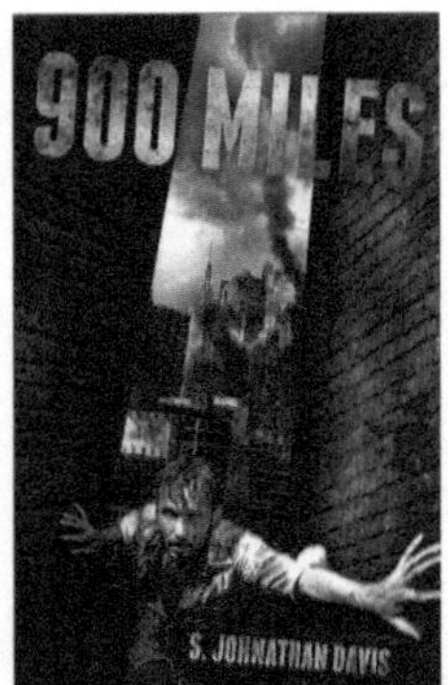

900 MILES
by S. Johnathan Davis

John is a killer, but that wasn't his day job before the Apocalypse.
In a harrowing 900 mile race against time to get to his wife just as the dead begin to rise, John, a business man trapped in New York, soon learns that the zombies are the least of his worries, as he sees first-hand the horror of what man is capable of with no rules, no consequences and death at every turn.
Teaming up with an ex-army pilot named Kyle, they escape New York only to stumble across a man who says that he has the key to a rumored underground stronghold called Avalon..... Will they find safety? Will they make it to Johns wife before it's too late?
Get ready to follow John and Kyle in this fast paced thriller that mixes zombie horror with gladiator style arena action!

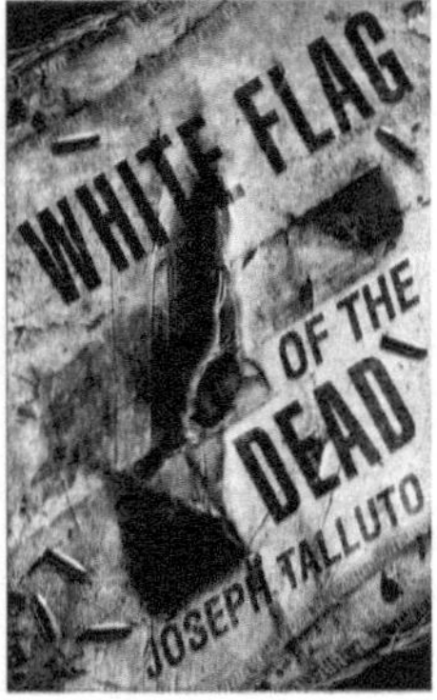

WHITE FLAG OF THE DEAD
by Joseph Talluto

Millions died when the Enillo Virus swept the earth. Millions more were lost when the victims of the plague refused to stay dead, instead rising to slaughter and feed on those left alive. For survivors like John Talon and his son Jake, they are faced with a choice: Do they submit to the dead, raising the white flag of surrender? Or do they find the will to fight, to try and hang on to the last shreds or humanity?

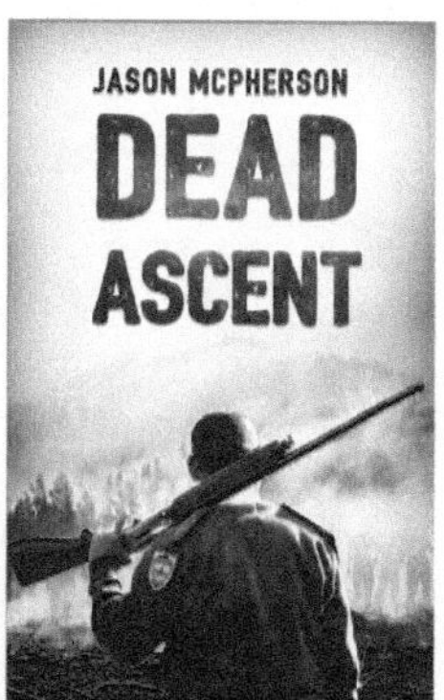

DEAD ASCENT
by Jason McPhearson

The dead have risen and they are hungry...

Grizzled war veteran turned game warden, Brayden James and a small group of survivors, fight their way through the rugged wilderness of southern Appalachia to an isolated cabin in the hope of finding sanctuary. Every terrifying step they make they are stalked by a growing mass of staggering corpses, and a raging forest fire, set by the government in hopes of containing the virus.

As all logical routes off the mountain are cut off from them, they seek the higher ground, but they soon realize there is little hope of escape when the dead walk and the world burns.

CHAOS THEORY
by Rich Restucci

The world has fallen to a relentless enemy beyond reason or mercy. With no remorse they rend the planet with tooth and nail.

One man stands against the scourge of death that consumes all.

Teamed with a genius survivalist and a teenage girl, he must flee the teeming dead, the evils of humans left unchecked, and those that would seek to use him. His best weapon to stave off the horrors of this new world? His wit.

www.ingramcontent.com/pod-product-compliance
Lightning Source LLC
Chambersburg PA
CBHW020107180626
46812CB00006B/2506

9781925840933